PRAISE FOR
ALLEY POND PARK

"*Alley Pond Park*'s brilliance lies in its poignant portrayal of a tortured Seth Matthews, haunted by perceived wrong-doings and aching for love, desperately trying to navigate his nascent adulthood amidst a world undergoing unprecedented social and political upheaval. By turns heartbreaking, funny, painful, maddening, and utterly engrossing, the novel unsparingly, but compassionately, explores the heart, mind and soul of a troubled, yet fascinating, young man and the essence of the times."

—**Nancy Johnson**, author, *Redefining Success: Women's Unique Paths*

"*Alley Pond Park* is a captivating coming-of-age story that follows Seth Matthews from his socially awkward arrival at Wisconsin's Beloit College in 1969, where he aspires to be a 'Woodstock man,' to his drug-fueled odyssey through Mexico and his ascendance during the 1980's avarice of Wall Street, where he single-mindedly focuses on becoming a Lehman Brothers partner. This yearning and striving, and the story's momentum, is driven by Seth's insecurity, unresolved family secrets, and his aching search for his identity. Readers may find themselves hating the lead character's blatant narcissism one moment, then rooting for his very survival the next. This is an epic tale of a flawed, loving, confused man who persists in finding his way in a very difficult world, and ultimately a universal story of finding oneself despite the lies and secrets buried within a family. The ending is breathtaking."

—**Susan Kasten**, Editor Emerita, *Beloit College Magazine*

"Zachary Todd Gordon's ambitious debut novel explores the complexity of family and identity, love and belonging, with humor and care. *Alley Pond Park* is bighearted and compelling—enjoy the journey."

—**Michelle Gutman**, owner, Up Up Books

"Gordon's singular and captivating story of love and heartbreak, by turns hilarious and haunting, manages to capture the vast madness of the late 20th century. A resounding paean to the redemptive power of love, this deeply felt debut novel is perfect for fans of Jonathan Franzen and Scott Spencer. It will stay with you long past reading. I couldn't put it down."

—**Rhianna Walton**, former Managing Editor, Powell's Books

ALLEY POND PARK

Zachary Todd Gordon

ALLEY POND PARK

A NOVEL

This is a work of fiction. Names, characters, places and incidents are the product of the author's imagination or are used fictitiously. Any resemblance to actual persons, living or dead, events or locales is entirely coincidental.

Copyright © 2024 Zachary Todd Gordon

All rights reserved. No part of this publication may be reproduced, distributed, or transmitted in any form or by any means, including photocopying, recording, or other electronic or mechanical methods, without the prior written permission of the publisher, except in the case of brief quotations embodied in critical reviews and certain other non-commercial uses permitted by copyright law. For permission requests, contact the publisher at the address below.

shepherdess books
shepherdessbooks@gmail.com

You Keep Me Hangin' On
Words and music by Edward Holland Jr., Lamont Dozier and Brian Holland
Copyright 1966 Jobete Music Co., Inc.
Copyright Renewed
All Rights Administered by Sony Music Publishing (US) LLC on behalf of
Stone Agate Music (A division of Jobete Music Co., Inc.),
424 Church Street, Suite 1200, Nashville, TN 37219
International Copyright Secured All Rights Reserved
Reprinted by Permission of Hal Leonard LLC

Printed in the United States of America
First Printing, 2024

ISBN 978-0-9970780-3-9

Library of Congress Control Number: 202490048

FRONTISPIECE IMAGES:
young man © bowie15 | 123rf
trees reflected in water © Lolame | Pixabay
branches © ananaline | iStock

Copyediting by Wendy Avra Gordon
Book design by K. M. Weber, ilibribookdesign.com

In loving memory of Olivia Terry Feir and
Andrea Helaine Kaplan, who left us too soon

"He who fights with monsters might take care lest he thereby become a monster. And if you gaze for long into an abyss, the abyss also gazes into you."

—NIETZSCHE, *BEYOND GOOD AND EVIL*, 1886

HISTORICAL NOTE

ON FRIDAY, FEBRUARY 26th, 1993, a small band of Islamic terrorists drove a rented van containing a fifteen-hundred-pound bomb and several tanks of hydrogen gas into the underground garage below the North Tower of the World Trade Center in New York City. At approximately 12:17 p.m. the vehicle detonated on Parking Level B2, opening a blast crater six stories deep and two hundred feet wide in the deadliest act of terrorism ever perpetrated on US soil up to that time, killing six people and injuring over one thousand others, several critically.

PROLOGUE

JAKE'S SECRETARY CALLED. Her brusque "Twelve o'clock sharp" unnerved me, more command than invitation to lunch in the partner's dining room.

I twiddled with my wedding band. Why now? My division topped the broker rankings; we were the lead underwriter in the country, our investment banking business burgeoning. Despite management responsibilities, I still outperformed the entire sales staff. What more could they want? Sure, I'd eased back a bit on the throttle, tried to make it home for dinner occasionally, spend more time with Erin and the kids on weekends, but heck, I still worked fifteen-hour days. Had my brokers rebelled, accused me of placing my own interests above theirs? Was I embroiled in a power play with research and trading? I'd no doubt made enemies throughout the division, having dominated the three departments.

I put on my suit jacket and straightened my tie, ran a hand through unruly hair noting the encroachment of grey, wishing I'd time for a quick trim before going upstairs. It was February 25th, 1993. I was forty-one years old, with Lehman Brothers for almost 20 years, one helluva run for an actor; only the *The Fantasticks* at the Sullivan Street Playhouse in the Village had a longer gig. Exiting the elevator, I took a deep breath and put on a happy face. If the curtain was coming down, so be it.

Jake greeted me at the door. Clapped his still rock-solid arm around my shoulder. I glanced about the room, a bastion of testosterone. Times were changing elsewhere, certainly in my own household, but not here, not yet. "It's my retirement party; sixty-five, can you believe it? I'm handing the ball off to you, Seth. The partners have named you the new Head of Equities, and I don't think they could have made a better choice."

Echoes of "Hear, hear" resounded around the room as these men, the elite of the elite, masters of Lehman's universe, accepted me into their exclusive club with handshakes and back slaps, but even swathed in effusive self-congratulatory fraternal bonhomie my stomach churned with naked foreboding. I didn't belong here; I was nobody without the numbers I put up on the scoreboard every day. What was going to happen with my accounts?

CEO Pete Masters grasped my hand and shook it aggressively. "Enough salesman talk. You're now responsible for every aspect of the firm's equity division. Think collective accomplishments. We'll talk specifics tomorrow morning at breakfast, but I've no doubt you'll be pleased with your new package."

Chris Harrington, chairman of the board, took me aside. "Tell him you expect to be making one hundred thousand dollars in three years...per month."

The festivities extended late into the afternoon. I sat dazed throughout, without appetite, smiled and nodded when spoken to, laughed when appropriate. I'd worked so hard and sacrificed so much for this brass ring on the merry-go-round, never anticipating what would happen should I grasp it.

PART ONE
THE WONDER BOY

CHAPTER 1

JERRY'S CANARY-YELLOW Sedan De Ville glided down College Street amid a sea of sleek foreign cars. I leaned against the cold glass of the rear passenger window gazing at my new home, the self-proclaimed Yale of the Midwest, but the only thing ivy I could detect were vines crawling up the old stone and brick buildings. I ground my teeth, frigid air blasting from the AC, nervously twirling Jonah's ring while glaring into the back of Mitzie's head, about to scream get me the hell out of here as Jerry pulled into an open parking space in front of a dormitory. He glanced at the odometer and grimaced. "Eight hundred and eighty fucking miles from Huntington."

Hot, humid, foul-smelling air enveloped me as I popped the trunk, grabbed my heavy duffel and Super Macy's portable stereo system and maneuvered my way through a swarm of hippie kids forming a new colony, Jerry right behind with a crate of LPs. Mitzie's high heels clicked on the pavement as she followed with my new electric Smith Corona typewriter.

An old man in bell bottoms, khaki jacket with epaulets and a gold peace symbol chain stood in the doorway to Suite 201, collar length hair carefully combed over to disguise a shiny bald spot. "You must be Bart's roommate Seth." He clasped my hand in a power handshake while informing me he and Bart had just been to Woodstock. "A really groovy scene," like that was going to impress me.

Bart appeared and we shook hands. "Hey Seth! Great to meet you, man. These your parents?" He grabbed the crate from Jerry and asked if there was anything else.

"Yeah. We're parked on College Street. Got a couple of crates of LPs and books in the trunk."

As we bounded downstairs his long straight hair flopped against his back and cute girls smiled at him. Tall and lanky, with a full beard, he was the essence of cool. Everything I wasn't.

MITZIE HAD ALREADY unpacked half my clothes when we returned, her neat color-coordinated piles arrayed on my bed alongside a several months supply of Ritalin. I wrenched the duffel from her hands and suggested we tour the campus, but Jerry, impatient to leave, pissed off I'd chosen Beloit over Cornell University, theatre over pre-law, was pulling her toward the exit as she ran through her motherly check list: call every Sunday; take my meds; watch my weight. Mr. Feldman also departed, but only after a bro-hug. Bart scoffed. "Parents! Can't live with 'em. Can't wait to live without 'em."

I tossed my meds in the garbage pail. Good riddance.

SUITE 201 HAD two rooms, a bunk bed and two dressers in one, two desks and bookcases in the other. Outside our window a chimney effused a brownish grey particulate in the hot, dank air, the obvious source of the malodor. A cheese factory. Wisconsin, America's Dairyland. Not the pastoral scene I'd imagined.

Bart placed his state-of-the-art component system in our living room (consigning my cheapo record player to the closet) while I positioned the wood and metal dressers on both sides of the bunk bed. I nudged them a tad until they were equidistant, then centered Jimi Hendrix Experience and Cream posters over each dresser. The Cream poster was off center. I repositioned it.

The silence in the room felt awkward, almost oppressive. I wanted Bart to like me, think me cool, and wracked my brain for something pithy to say to break the ice, but merely asked what he planned to major in, the kind of bullshit question adults always asked. Pathetic.

"Psychology. The department's really good. You?"

I nudged the Cream poster an inch to the left. "Theatre. The whole world's my stage."

I STOWED MY treasure trove of books plus the required summer reading list of Dostoyevsky, Tolstoy, Fitzgerald, Steinbeck, and Malcom X into my allotted bookcase. Bart offered his for the overflow. I held out my dog-eared copy of *The Sun Also Rises*. "They should've included Hemingway on the list. This ranks with Dostoyevsky's *Crime and Punishment*."

"Only if you're into manly men and cardboard women. Dostoyevsky's characters are nuanced. I could feel Raskolnikov's guilt-ridden anguish and spiritual torment. Hemingway would've said 'Suck it up, Rodya'. But your comparison is interesting." He perused my library, extracted my copy of the Torah.

Oh geez, he was going to think me some kind of religious zealot like the Hasidic Jews from Brooklyn who taught at my Hebrew school. "I've also got Homer's *Odyssey* and *Iliad*, the Bhagavad Gita, the Book of Mormon, the Holy

Quran, even the New Testament. Religious mythology's kinda like cookbooks, same ingredients, different recipes..."

"Cookbooks, huh? Interesting analogy. Ever read Damon Knight's short story 'To Serve Man?'"

The Twilight Zone, Episode 89. I was such a geek. "Mr. Chambers, Mr. Chambers, don't get on that ship... It's a cookbook," I shrilled, and Bart hooted. Fat boys were supposed to make people laugh.

The Torah flipped opened to Genesis 2:3. My well-worn Haftorah portion, the story of Adam and Eve and their expulsion from Eden. The original warning: God was vengeful. Watching. Judging. There would be no forgiveness or second chances for me. "Funny, last thing I would've pegged you for was Jewish with that red hair and blue eyes. You look Irish, totally different than your parents."

"I was adopted. I identify as Jewish for the sense of connection. Who my birthparents were, where they came from, or if they were even Jewish, I've no idea, but we all need roots, right? Without structure my whole life would be improvisational theatre."

"Hence the theatre major. That's very interesting." He pointed to the Sabbath candle sticks I'd extracted from the bottom of my duffel. "That why you have these?"

"Yeah. They belonged to Grandma Matthews, given to her by her mother when she left for America, part of a continuum, you know? I really loved her." Mitzie would have a cow when she noticed them missing but fuck her. She didn't deserve them. I nervously twirled the ring on my finger.

Bart could only trace his heritage back to his grandparents, but it was pretty obvious where he came from. The spitting image of his dad, only younger and hirsute. Just like Jonah and Jerry. Big Jerry and Little Jerry. The same stride, same mannerisms and physiques, a source of family humor every summer when the Matthews clan gathered at Rockaway Beach to swim and bake in the sun. I stood out in that olive-skinned crowd, the sole paleface.

Bart closed the Torah, started to put it back in the bookcase, and paused. "All alphabetical. Hmm." He placed it with the *T*'s and pulled out *The Lord of the Rings*. "My mom read me this at bedtime."

Probably along with a good night hug and kiss. Mitzie merely switched off my room light and shut the door, enveloping me in terrifying darkness. Every sound, every creak, a bad person coming to kidnap me, or worse, the Cyclops from *The Seventh Voyage of Sinbad* just outside my window. "So, you were at Woodstock with your father? Must've been dynamite."

"The Chrome Dome talks like he was there. Thinks he's groovy because he smokes pot, bogarts my LPs and tries to relate to my friends! He's a friggin' dentist, man! He and mom spent the weekend in a hotel in Woodstock. I went with my girlfriend Debbie. But it was mind-blowing, man, hundreds of thousands, a sea of humanity. Even when it started pouring people hugged each other, shared food, drugs, the whole brotherhood of man thing. Everything felt possible, like we really could change the world. And Debbie and I finally did it. Fuckin' awesome!" I'd spent that weekend imagining I was there making love to hippie goddesses traipsing about in diaphanous gowns with garlands of flowers entwined in their long golden tresses. The floor by my bed littered with wadded up Kleenex. "We broke up when we got back home. Didn't make sense to stay together. Going to different schools, so far apart, and it's a big world out there, right? New people, new experiences. Free love, right?" I nodded as he picked up the framed senior class photo of Abby from my bureau. "So, did you and your girlfriend . . . ?"

"Abby and I are just pals." Maybe if I'd gone to Cornell with her things would be different.

"So, ah, you still haven't done it?"

A black spider crawled across the industrial tile floor. I stamped on it. I'd yet to get to first base.

CHAPTER 2

AFTER DINING IN Commons on mystery meat that rivaled Mitzie's cooking, a few of us congregated in John and Max's adjacent suite to chill, listen to tunes and get to know each other. I was nervous, eager to make the right impression, not be labeled a loser like in sixth grade when I showed up at my new elementary school so sunburned kids called me "Pinky," a nickname that stuck through high school.

John was a buff surfer dude from California, like the guys in *Hawaii Five-O*. Golden tan, straight sun-bleached blond hair. A surfboard medallion necklace. He spoke softly, his words floating through the room, unlike his hyperkinetic roomie Max, with his thick BAAhstan accent, halo of frizzy black hair, Fu Manchu moustache and five o'clock shadow. Like one of those early puberty guys who teased me in the shower after middle school gym class, me being hairless as a mole rat. Even now, having zealously shaved for two years to stimulate the growth of hair follicles, I'd only patches of fuzzy red down on my cheeks. Tim, from Albuquerque, and his roommate Harry, from Austin, self-described freaks in tie dye, rounded out our group. They smelled like wet socks; bonded in a mutual passion for reefer and disdain of bathing. Mex and Tex.

John lit a bodacious joint, took a few tokes and passed it to me. I'd never smoked. The smell awakened bad memories, and I worried I'd become paranoid and mush-mouthed, sound stupid, but they were all looking at me, so I took a convincing fake toke and pronounced the weed "Dynamite." Even started to feel the groove until Max asked, "Who's gotten laid?" Eyes darted about like Clint Eastwood, Eli Wallach and Lee Van Cleef in the gunfight scene in *The Good, the Bad, and the Ugly*. Max drew first, followed by the others. I almost blurted out I'd been going at it from age thirteen with this older hippie chick who lived next door and looked just like Peggy Lipton from *The Mod Squad*, almost true, at least in my dreams, but Bart came to the rescue, turning the discussion to my awesome LP collection. "No big thing," I huffed. "Just stuff I picked up in The Village on weekends. Great scene, you know? Hung out in Washington Square

Park, in the Peace Eye Book Store with Tuli and Ed and the rest of The Fugs, saw dynamite acts at the Fillmore. The Joshua Light Show was outta sight!" Everyone seemed impressed.

All afternoon Bart had left his bed unmade, which really grated, so I made it for him. What the hell. He'd had my back in John's room. I winced when he flopped down on it, messing the perfect hospital corners. "You should've seen your cheeks all puffed up, holdin' in all that smoke. You looked like a chipmunk!" I groaned. "No big, they were all blotto, but roomies look out for each other, right, so let's get totally real, and I'll start. Breaking up with Debbie wasn't my idea. She didn't want a long-distance relationship; wanted to be open to new experiences, new people. It hurt... still does. Guess I still love her." He frowned, pulled a framed photo from his desk drawer and handed it to me. "Her senior class photo. Not sure why I brought it. Now it's your turn. Did you really hang out with The Fugs?"

"We were in the store at the same time. That's kinda like hanging out."

"Dude, you're a natural born storyteller. Gonna be hard to know what's really you." He stretched and yawned. "It's friggin' late. My brain's like totally fried. Let's finish setting up tomorrow." He was asleep in seconds. I lay awake listening to the rhythmic pattern of his snores. Pulled the blanket over my head.

Jonah and I are in our space ship exploring unchartered reaches of outer space, powering past planets and comets when suddenly a huge meteor heads directly toward us, and we veer our craft to the left, then right, trying to avoid an imminent collision but it's too late, we go careening off course, heading for a black hole, and I reach out to Jonah but he's a jack-in-the-box, grinning and boinging up and down singing "All around the mulberry bush the monkey chased the weasel. The monkey thought 'twas all in fun. Pop! Goes the weasel" and our escape hatch opens, sucking all the air, and me, from our ship, and I tumble alone and powerless into the vast black vacuum of space and I'm so scared, so scared, so scared.

Gasping for breath I bolted upright, heart thumping, disoriented. Sheets damp with night sweat. I tentatively shifted one leg off the bed. Felt for solid ground. Jimi Hendrix' demonic eyes blazed with light emanating from the parking lot. I squeezed mine shut. It's good. It's all good. Think happy thoughts. You're not alone. You're in a forest with the girl next door entwined under a canopy of evergreens and white birch making endless love, dappled sunlight dancing over your glistening bodies, and suddenly Bart's shaking me. "Wake up, Seth. Freshman orientation is in fifteen minutes."

CHAPTER 3

BART PICKED UP the framed photo of Jonah carrying me home from Alley Pond Park, chubby three-year-old astride eight-year-old shoulders, my first, most cherished, memory. I nervously twiddled with my ring. "Your brother looks like your dad."

"I haven't seen him in a while. You have siblings?"

"Yeah, a little brother, Aaron. Stayed home with mom; didn't want to miss a United Synagogue Youth dance. Wish he'd come along, you know, a buffer between me and the Dome! But about your brother . . . ?"

"I wondered if your parents were divorced."

"Nah. Mom had a tennis tournament at the Scarsdale Club. That's her thing."

I rummaged through my albums and pulled out an LP. "You ever listen to the Incredible String Band? This album is awesome. Called *The Hangman's Beautiful Daughter*."

"New to me, but wait, what happened with your brother?"

I unfolded the poster that came with the album. "I'm thinking 'bout tacking it up in our living room. Everyone in high school thought my taste in music iconoclastic, except Abby. We saw them last year at the Fillmore East. Amazing concert."

"Cool. But about your brother?"

Geez, he was relentless! "Jonah had a big blowout with his dad over Viet Nam after graduating from college. Man, they really went at it. Jonah said he'd leave the country before fighting an illegal and immoral war and Jerry called him a draft dodger, threatened to disown him. Jonah told him to shove it. Stormed out of the house." I held out my hand. "But he gave me his prized possession before he left. This gold signet ring from his grandfather. Asked me to keep it for him. Then he jumped on his motorcycle and roared out of there, me chasing after, screaming 'Don't leave me.' But he did." Everyone did. The ring chafed.

"I'm sure your parents..."

"I already told you, those two clowns aren't my parents." I recalled Mitzie's lovey-dovey act when I was admitted to Cornell. She'd already bragged to her friends in the Temple Sisterhood, embarrassed when I told her I was going to Beloit instead. I relished that moment. Bart hugged me, said if I ever wanted to talk about it, and I immediately pressed the album, a rare UK pressing, into his hands. "They're Paul McCartney's favorite Scottish band. It's a present... for you."

"Seriously? So righteous!" He extracted another joint from his shirt pocket. "Check this out. Way better than John's stash, only no fake toking this time!"

I passed, told him to go ahead, and as he lit up, Jonah and his friends materialized in my mind, sharing a cigarette behind our garage. My perfect big brother doing something so bad. He laughed at me in front of his friends when I threatened to tell our parents. Told me to go away, play with my baby toys. Mortified, I ran inside and sat on the window seat in my bedroom watching a black spider scuttle across the window. A fly had become trapped in its intricate web, and I was about to free it when Jonah barged in and told me it was marijuana. Marijuana! I'd seen the drug movie. Kids walking into oncoming highway traffic, in front of trucks, diving off buildings like they could fly. I had to protect Jonah. Told him I'd say nothing to our parents if he promised to stop smoking it, but he merely sneered at me. "You mean my parents. You were adopted!"

Bart's joint went out. He relit it, held it out again, but I waved him off. The smell was nauseating.

Jonah's words. Pain so visceral. A shiv plunged and twisted in my gut. Not my parents' child. Not his real brother. My red hair and blue eyes, pale skin and freckles; wasn't it obvious? Hadn't it always been obvious? His mother never loved me, never hugged or kissed me. His father worked late nights to avoid me. I was nothing to them. Only he loved me. I glanced at the window. The black spider had devoured its prey.

Bart's joint burned down to a roach, wasted now, his mission to get me high forgotten. He abstractedly flipped through my LPs and pulled out Led Zeppelin. "This album rocked me all night long!"

"Abby bought me that as a consolation prize for wasting an entire afternoon at the mall while she and her stoner girlfriends tried on paisley mini-dresses and Go-Go boots, applied makeup on each other, ridiculous shades of lipstick and eye shadow that made them look like creatures out of a cheap horror flick. It wasn't like they were actually going to buy anything. You should have seen them." Eyes wide and vacant, I lurched across our room like a zombie droning "Must shop, must shop" and Bart cackled. Stoners, such good audiences. I made Abby laugh all the time. "They even asked my opinion on stuff, like I gave a shit. I just wanted to get to Sam Goody's before it closed to buy the album, but too late. I was bummed. Next day she gave it to me."

Bart lit another joint. "I understand doing that kind of stuff for only one reason, man. Sex. Think maybe she wanted to be more than just friends?"

The times she'd leaned into me, put her head on my shoulder or placed her arm through mine. Had I missed something? Been afraid of misreading signals, destroying the only real friendship I had? Besides, she was taller than me. "When I got home, I played it full blast on Jerry's stereo console. He told me to take my shit down to the basement."

"At least he didn't borrow it like my dad!" He started to return the LP to the crate with the *Z*'s, but I grabbed it from him and placed it with the *L*'s. "Did you know rigid control is a classic sign of deep-rooted fears or insecurities?"

"Dude, you definitely picked the right major! You gonna psychoanalyze everything I say and do?"

"Only the interesting stuff which so far is just about everything." He chortled. Gave me a friendly shove. Only kidding, but he wasn't. I was a good actor trying to cover up the fact I was a pathetic loser.

He took another hit, suggested we order a pizza, then promptly fell asleep. But I couldn't. I saw myself sitting atop my special rock at Winona Beach crying, processing Jonah's revelation. If I wasn't me, who was I? I'd stealthily rifled through family albums for contrary evidence, for proof I was my parents' son, but found only baby photos of Grandma Matthews feeding or snuggling me, even guiding my first tentative steps. Nothing with Mitzie. I knew he was right. I think I'd always known it. I never called Mitzie and Jerry Mommy and Daddy ever again. They only loved him, and only he loved me, so I kept all his secrets until the day I didn't.

CHAPTER 4

OVER ENSUING WEEKS Bart kept badgering me to get high with him, and one night, after dragging him to the Student Union to see *Lonely Are the Brave*, I finally caved. I wanted to be cool. Smoking pot separated the straights from the heads.

Bart rolled a jay, slid his tongue across the edge of the paper and twisted the ends. He thought the film a total bummer, two hours wasted watching a man make an almost impossible summit up a mountain with his horse only to get wiped out by a semi. "I mean, I was rooting for the guy, and the whole thing turned out to be pointless." He lit up, took a big hit, and exhaled. "I question your idea of a good time."

But he'd missed the whole point. It didn't matter if the guy overcame unbelievable adversity. When your time's up, it's up. "It was his karma to collide with that truck, his fate."

"I think he just had plain bad luck." He took another hit and held it out me expectantly. "He and the truck happened to arrive at the same place at the same time, but he purposely got into that bar fight so he'd be thrown in jail and could help his friend escape, so if you're gonna insist on analyzing the movie to death I'd say it's all about bad choices, individual freedom, not fate. You gonna take a toke or what?"

I ignored the skunky odor and inhaled smoke and heat, Bart monitoring me all the while. I exhaled and shrugged. No revelation; just a sore throat. "The only free will we have is knowing we have none. Every action the cowboy took led inevitably to his intersecting with the truck driver. That's called fate."

"You must be stoned because that makes no sense."

I shook my head.

"Man, I've got the munchies." He devoured a bag of potato chips. Spread canned tuna on Saltines with his fingers, stuffed one in his mouth and held another out to me. "Wha whon?" Tuna. Mitzie put it my school lunch box with a scoop of cottage cheese and carrot sticks. Jonah got peanut butter and jelly sandwiches and a dime for an ice cream sandwich. Bart licked slimy fingers. "Okay, I'm not giving up. Let's roll another one. You're fated to get high."

"I'm just saying everything that happened was meant to be. You ever read Spinoza?"

"Yeah. It was preordained I'd room with an obsessive neat freak who can't even get high." He fumbled with the rolling paper, scattering little clusters of marijuana leaf I immediately swept up, crooning, *"Don't bogart that joint, my friend, pass it over to me."*

"Hey stop that. This isn't easy."

"Christ you know it ain't easy. You know how hard it can be . . ."

"Stop turning everything into song lyrics. Jesus Christ! How can you not be stoned? I'm obliterated! Come on Seth, take bigger tokes this time and hold it in longer." I grabbed a rolling paper and mimicked his motions. I licked the edge and twisted the ends. Picture perfect. Maybe I couldn't get high, but I could roll them.

I'd gotten big news earlier in the day. I'd been cast in the senior production of *You Can't Take It with You* playing a madcap character called Mr. DePinna. Freshmen rarely got juicy roles, and I was excited, though somewhat ambivalent. The DePinna character was balding and fat. Played for laughs. Not leading man material. Surprise, surprise. Even so, I wasn't sure that was the real reason I'd been cast. "If I tell you something, you gotta promise not to tell anyone. I'm serious. You gotta promise." I took a deep breath. "You promise, right?" He nodded. "The theatre department's a little weird."

"Like that's news? You define weird."

I handed the jay to Bart, describing how the department head sashayed around the theatre in a powder blue jump suit and pink chiffon scarf he'd toss over his shoulder with insouciance, uttering "Well, ladies" before every comment. Bart took a huge hit, must've held it in for a minute before exhaling a cloud of yucky smoke. "Get the idea? During the tryouts he kept touching me, massaging my back, even squeezed my butt. Invited me to his house to practice my lines. This other freshman guy said I got that part because I was his new sex toy."

"A pink chiffon scarf? Really?" He handed me the joint. "Did that other guy get a role? Sounds like sour grapes to me." Maybe. But I had to wonder if I was giving off some kind of signal. When I was twelve a middle school friend and I rubbed our penises against each other to see what would happen. It worried me that it felt so good. "Jesus Christ, Seth, are you actually not stoned yet?"

CHAPTER 5

SEVERAL OF MY DORM mates gathered in Haven Hall's dingy, dark, overheated basement to watch the New York Mets and Baltimore Orioles in the '69 World Series on the one TV. A musty odor permeated the hot house air. Mangy couches smelled of body odor and cat piss, plumes of dust mites exploding as guys plopped down on them. A landfill of empty soda and beer cans, overflowing ashtrays, empty cardboard pizza boxes and fast-food containers. They seemed oblivious to the mess. I resisted the urge to start cleaning.

Max knelt as he repositioned the rabbit ears atop the small box, butt crack exposed as he vainly attempted to enhance the static-distorted image on the small screen. One of the guys stealthily stuck a lit joint in it. Hilarity ensued. Cursing, Max gave the TV a swift kick, actually improving the image, and took a big hit off the joint. Gross. Then announced he had the munchies. John proposed fries from the local A&W. Bart donuts from George Webb's. Some guy from down the hall burgers from Geri's. But none of them budged, the lights of Shea Stadium reflected in their glazed, wasted eyes.

Bored, I rifled through old, mildewy Beloit College yearbooks lying about. Blew dust off one cover, almost gagging. *1959*. I opened to a photo essay of a panty raid, black and whites of fraternity dudes with crewcuts running around Commons with girls' panties over their arms, legs and heads. I looked about the room at all the long-haired hippies. The times' they were a-changin.' Maybe too fast for me. "Hey guys, you're not going to believe this! They had panty raids on Beloit's campus ten years ago!"

Bart glanced at the photos. Couldn't imagine girls giving up their panties in the Fifties. Thought they were all uptight virgins. "Can you imagine anyone organizing a panty raid now?"

It would be audacious. Something memorable. Give me a chance to show my hipness. "Why not? We threw Fifties parties in high school. Let's throw one here." I pushed the guys out the door. Told them to drum up interest in the male dorms. Only Max wouldn't budge. Suggested a pizza run instead.

I cruised College Street rallying the Neanderthal frat guys. I was so pumped. Had a hundred guys behind me as we headed toward Commons and the girls' dorms. I'd set all this in motion. I was a man in control when I entered Blaisdell Hall shouting "PANTY RAID, PANTY RAID."

Girls were lounging about the comfortable looking parlor, a far cry from Haven's Salvation Army décor. They were studying, reading, talking quietly amongst themselves on nice sofas and chairs upholstered in chintz and velvet. Heck, the lamps even had shades, coffee tables covered with lace doilies like the ones Grandma Matthews made. But for our common humanity, girls were a separate species. One asked what I was doing and I politely asked for her panties. "You're like kidding, right?" she said, while others giggled, rolled their eyes and made supercilious comments about freshmen, but she shimmied out of her panties and tossed them to me. "Oh, come on, girls. They're so cute. Like puppies."

Several chattered amongst themselves for a moment, lay aside their books, wiggled out of their panties and threw them at me. "Enjoy sniffing them, cutie. They're as close as you'll get to the real thing." They exchanged high fives.

I excitedly ran down the first-floor hallway with several pair dangling from my arms. Oh my God, oh my God, oh my God. This is so dynamite! Shouting "PANTY RAID, PANTY RAID," I knocked on doors, told to scram or go fuck myself until one girl in a T-shirt and panties opened hers wide and I could see naked photos of her tacked to every wall. My mouth hung open. My throat went dry. I gulped. Act natural. Don't stare. Retreat. "Uh . . . I'm . . . ah . . . sorry for bothering you."

"Hey, what's your hurry. Come in . . . you want my panties, right?" She pulled me in, slammed the door, jumped on her bed and pulled off her panties while I stood frozen, staring at stuff I'd only seen in the *Playboy* and *Penthouse* magazines I'd secretly stashed under my mattress. Those magazines had been fantasy, but this, this was real. Her legs yawned wide. "Come and get them."

I back peddled toward the door. "Uh, that's . . . uh okay. It's like, you know, only a panty raid."

Hopping off her bed, she grabbed my arm and literally flung me onto her mattress. Then straddling me, she crossed her arms in front of her, pulled off her T-shirt and oh my God, rose-hued nipples the size of Kennedy half dollars grazed my face as she unzipped my jeans, reached inside and grabbed me. My body quaked and I groaned, just like that day in middle school but totally different. I couldn't tell if her expression was utter disgust or disappointment, but it was pretty damn clear I hadn't met anyone's expectations. She withdrew her hand covered with gooey me and wiped it on my chest. I was such a loser. Everything was wrong. Out of kilter. I was the guy. I was supposed to be the one in control, the one making the moves, just like I'd read in all the magazines. Where was the foreplay? The kissing, groping, bra removal, all the things I'd carefully planned out in my dreams. Hell, she wasn't even wearing a bra! My first time and I'd blown my wad before doing anything! I jumped off her bed and stumbled out of her room, my jeans and undies at my ankles. I'd never be a Woodstock man!

I adjusted my clothes and exited the dorm. Immediately, some guy aimed a camera at me. The editor of the school newspaper, *The Roundtable*, demanding my name, was I a freshman, what dorm did I live in, stuff like that. Light bulbs flashed in my face. I was shellshocked, a deer caught in headlights. He threatened to label me "Panty Boy" if I didn't answer his questions. Oh God, another "P" like Pinky. "Why me?" I asked as he scribbled my details on a pad. Guys were all around me, whooping it up, running from dorm to dorm, covered in panties.

"Everyone says you started this; that makes you the ring master."

"A bunch of us got together . . . it . . . it just, you know, was supposed to be for laughs."

"Yeah, well, maybe in the Fifties, but this is 1969." He snapped another photo and walked away.

I wanted attention. I got it. Me on the cover of the next issue, short, fat, pink-faced, freckled. A seventeen-year-old virgin covered with girls' panties. Thank God the photo was too grainy to pick up the goo smeared across my shirtfront. The headline story: "*ICONIC CLASH OF GENERATIONS. Panty Boy Seth Matthews, a Fifties throwback, leads raid insulting every woman on campus.*" Sonuvabitch still called me Panty Boy, and when I entered classrooms, girls shot me withering looks. Professors affected expressions of exaggerated seriousness to keep from laughing. Even guys who'd participated passed judgment, like I'd perpetrated an offense against our generation. But the fraternities loved me and I was rushed hard.

CHAPTER 6

I JUMPED ONTO the back of a rusty old Ford pickup blanketed with straw along with Bart and other freshmen, headed to a Homecoming rush party sponsored by one of the fraternities. Our bodies bounced about like Mexican jumping beans as we rattled down the hill toward downtown, the ivy-covered campus disappearing in a haze of blackish smoke belching from smokestacks of large industrial plants dotting the banks of the Rock River. Electric beer signs flashed "Blitz," "Leinenkugel," "Hamm's," "Huber" in front windows of numerous taverns that lined downtown streets, but beyond lay vast stretches of bucolic farmland, a patchwork quilt of multi-shaded greens transected with meandering rivers and clear blue lakes. This was God's country. What I'd imagined when I came here. Happy farmers tilling the soil, calling in the cows, beautiful old Victorian houses with front porches and swings. Big red barns. A simple back to the land life impervious to the vagaries of city life and industrialization. And I wasn't disappointed when we arrived at Farmer John's farm, the party held in a large two-story red barn, bales of hay stacked to the loft space. Shafts of light beamed through an open trap door illuminated a flotilla of straw particles rising like little ships in turbulent air, kids gyrating free and easy on the straw matted dance floor stimulated by copious amounts of weed. These frat guys knew how to throw a party, the barn abounding with cute freshman girls hand selected from the new student directory known colloquially as the Pig Book. After filling a plastic cup with purple liquid from a large garbage can, I leaned against the barn door and listened to the rock band cover the Rolling Stones hit song "I Can't Get No Satisfaction" eyeing the prettiest girl on the dance floor. I took a sip and turned to the guy standing next to me. "This tastes like Kool-Aid."

He grinned, held his hand out. "It's Purple Passion. I'm Jack, one of the Phi Psi's. Seth, right? Loved your panty raid, dude. Sometimes it's good to shake things up a bit. Remind people not to take everything so goddam seriously." He winked and lightly smacked me on the shoulder. "You're the new blood the Phi Psi's need, bro." We shook hands and he hoisted his cup in salute. "Bottoms up."

I drained mine and refilled it, still captivated by that girl swaying to the music, as light on her feet as a ballerina, her gauzy Indian print dress billowing every time she twirled, exposing panties I wished I'd collected. A vision. "Nice, huh?" Jack said. "Name's Ashley. Freshman. Lives in Blaisdell. Who knows, maybe you grabbed her panties." He gave me a shove. "Go on, get out there and dance with her."

I sidled over to her, heart in my throat, re-experiencing the anxiety of approaching my unrequited heart-throb Callie Winslet from across the Simpson Junior High School gymnasium floor. Thank God it was a fast dance. I swallowed hard.... *he's telling me more and more about some useless information, supposed to fire my imagination* ... "WOULD YOU LIKE TO DANCE?"

"WAH' Y'ALL THINK I'M DOIN', PANTY BOY?" Her voice like maple syrup.

Cringing, about to skulk off, she grabbed my hand just as the band started playing "A Salty Dog," my favorite Procol Harum song, but a slow one. I tentatively placed one arm around her waist like I'd learned in dance class, but she pulled me toward her, my cheek brushing against her silky-soft skin. Hard nipples pressed into my chest. She smelled nice. Like baby roses. Her body warm. Eyes as blue as the clear sky. Long straight straw-colored hair parted in the middle, accentuating a heart-shaped face. I was in love. Beads of sweat tickled as they trickled down my back. "I'm Seth," I whispered.

"Ah know. You looked so funny in that photo. Ah almost peed my pants."

"I wasn't expecting to be photographed. Bastard made me look like a bozo. Where are you from?"

"Lil' town in Loosiana." Louisiana! Visions of *Gone with the Wind*. Pristine southern belles.

"Did you grow up near New Orleans?"

"It's pronounced Norleans, honey. Ah was "Born on the Bayou," jes' like the Credence Clearwater song. You gave that reporter ample material to work with." I blushed, eyed my feet, but she lifted my chin and looked at me with curious amusement. "Are you a bozo?"

"I'm just me." Her eyes bore into mine; I felt naked.

"Hmm, that a fact. You gotta have a thick skin if you're gonna insult all womankind. Ah thought you looked kinda cute, like a kid in a candy store, and you have the mos' beautiful blue eyes."

She liked my eyes! Oh, the rapture! We danced, chatted about school, things we were interested in. So easy to talk to, like Abby. We drank more of the sweet purple stuff and as the afternoon progressed danced closer and tighter, our bodies separated by a thin film of damp clothes. I couldn't believe this was happening to me. She was so exotic, so beautiful. "You're a great dancer; like a ballerina."

"An' Ah've the gnarly feet to prove it. You're pretty good yourself."

"You really think so? I love to dance. I've been in a bunch of musicals, and . . ." I leaned in close so no one would overhear me, "I know this is going to sound silly . . ."

"Sillier than bein' the Panty Boy?"

". . . when I'm alone, I do ballet moves around the room."

"Why didn't you take ballet lessons?"

"Everyone knows about guys who take ballet . . ."

"Not all of 'em, sugar. Trust me on that."

WE RETURNED TO campus in the open back of a farm truck, lots of drunk kids sitting on bales of hay, bouncing along the dirt roads singing songs from the new Crosby Stills and Nash album dominating the FM airwaves, about to hit the stores. I sang *Helplessly hoping her harlequin hovers nearby, awaiting a word . . . ,* hoping to impress her, and she told me I sounded like David Crosby! And then she kissed me, my first real kiss, and all my worries vanished in a haze. Love was in the air. Love was everywhere. Everything was perfect, a scene out of an idyllic Norman Rockwell painting. Beloit College had been the right choice. It was fate.

CHAPTER 7

WE TOOK ADVANTAGE of the crisp fall air, rode bicycles out to Big Hills Park and lay in the tall grasses on the bank of the Rock River. I sang lyrics I'd penned for her: *Cajun lady, look into my eyes of blue, they're the same bright color as the Big Hills sky and the ocean too, and I found myself in you, Cajun Lady.* She said it was the most romantic thing. I closed my eyes, leaned in for my first French-kiss and banged into her teeth. She giggled when I blushed. "Be gentler. Let our tongues do a pas de deux, like this."

A rabid football fan, she insisted we attend all of Beloit's varsity games, knew every player's stats, their strengths, weaknesses, and wasn't shy about heckling the coach from the stands. She loved Jack Kerouac, Beat poetry and Khalil Gibran, liked to hang out at the campus coffee house. A multi-faceted diamond who defied classification, with me, a guy who categorized everything.

Breaking away to study after evenings spent with Ashley took an act of will. I studied late into the night pecking away at my new typewriter, exploring ideas and concepts in History and Economics, Philosophy and Sociology, and memorizing lines for the school play, time pressure so intense I became increasingly anxious. I wasn't naturally brilliant like Jonah. Throughout high school I struggled for the *A*'s that came so easy to him, desperate for the praise that rained down on him. But now, I was having trouble concentrating; couldn't sit still. Felt like a volcano about to explode. Maybe I shouldn't have thrown my meds away. I asked Max how he maintained focus despite appearing blotto most of the time. He grinned and handed me a bottle of White Cross. "Mother's little helper. Keep it," he said. "It's easy to score."

It was revelatory. Invigorating. Made everything crystal clear. Imbued me with a can-do attitude, swept away troubling thoughts or memories, cobwebs of fear and obsession, way better than the prescription medication Mitzie had foisted on me. I could study all night. Think brilliant, profound thoughts while the rest of the world slept, but Bart grumbled my night owl schedule and Ashley's constant presence made it impossible to study, the endless refrain of "My Lady of the Island" driving him nuts. He felt the odd man out in the suite we shared. I suggested splitting the rooms, affording us each space and privacy, and he agreed with one caveat: his stereo stayed on his side. "You and Miss Loosiana can screw to the sounds of your crappy one."

We hadn't actually done it yet, not that I wasn't ready, willing and able. I was the one in control this time. Taking it slow for Ashley's sake. So sweet and innocent, not one of those free-love girls like Ms. Panty Raid. I wanted our first time to be perfect.

CHAPTER 8

A FERVENT ANTI-WAR activist, Ashley demanded I bring my voice and passion to something more important than panty raids, and if the key to her heart and body was joining the Movement, I'd play that role. She wanted to picket Beloit Corporation, the defense contractor that employed most people in this Company town, even barricade the entrances to the factories, strident ideas akin to Jonah's, a member of Columbia University's radical Students for a Democratic Society organization, but inconsistent with my image of southern belle gentility. I explained Beloit's entire economy had depended on war efforts since the Civil War and ritual bloodlettings dated back to the dawn of mankind. "People are mindless sheep who prefer authoritarian rule to thinking on their own. Look at the Nazis and Japs. We killed millions fighting totalitarianism and now they're our best economic buddies. It's all pointless bullshit!"

"A whole lotta bullshit excuses, you mean, but body counts are real. Think the kids in your high school who didn't have rich parents, tutors, SAT review courses. Where are they now? I'm not one of your east coast elites. Lots of good ole' boys I knew in school are overseas now, risking their lives . . . and for nothin'." I hated being guilt tripped. I just wanted to enjoy being in love, but she was right. They didn't want to go to 'Nam any more than me, facing death while my paramount concern was when we'd finally do it.

Beloit's chapter of Student Mobilization Against the War assigned us a section of the city to canvass. Talking points would've helped, maybe a script, but we were told to improvise and heck, I'd been doing that my entire life. What a sight we must've been. A pretty girl in an Indian print mini-dress that barely covered her panties. Me in scruffy patched jeans, a chambray work shirt, moth ridden Goodwill herringbone tweed coat, and shoulder length strawberry blond curls. House after house people either didn't answer or opened the door a crack, took one look and slammed it shut. Occasionally someone listened to Ashley's bellicose admonitions for a few seconds before becoming apoplectic. It wasn't working. We needed to win their hearts and hope their minds followed.

A middle-aged man in a sleeveless white T-shirt answered at one door, his gut overflowing his sweatpants, a copy of the *Beloit Times* in one hand, smoldering cigarette in the other. "Whataya want?" His gravelly voice and stained yellow fingers eerily reminiscent of Mr. Finway, my chain-smoking high school chemistry teacher who lit cigarette after cigarette off the gas burners in the lab room, scaring the shit out of me but always engaging my attention.

"We've got to end the Vietnam war an' bring our troops home now," Ashley declared.

"You goddam Beloit College kids," he grumbled, "up there in your ivory tower. Come on in. I'll show you something real."

Ashley followed him, me reluctantly after. His living room was unkempt, the stale stench of cigarettes pervasive, the white ceiling above a threadbare recliner a discolored sphere of brownish yellow, overflowing ashtray on a side table. Incongruously, imitation Victorian couches were encased in plastic and cutesy ceramic tchotchke's populated built-in shelves, ceramic angels and whatnot. Even a throw pillow embroidered God Bless This Home. A home no one had blessed in a very long time.

He drew us to a table laden with framed photos of a young man at various stages of life up to maybe twenty and picked up a high school graduation photo. "This was my son, Fred Junior." Was. My heart raced. A shrine. Jonah. I started to back-pedal, but Ashley grabbed my hand and pulled me toward her. "When he graduated from Beloit High he joined the Army, not out of patriotism; he thought the war was stupid but his ticket out of this shithole town. Figured he'd do his tour, go to college under the GI Bill. I pushed him to go; thought it the right thing, but he never returned. Killed in that godforsaken swamp for nothing, and now you come here and act like you're telling me something I don't already know?" Tears cascaded down his cheeks. "This fucking war cost me my son ... and my marriage. Now I've got nothing."

I felt so guilty, his son sacrificing himself for things I took for granted. I tried to tug Ashley toward the front door, even as she yammered away, suggesting he help his neighbors not make the same mistake, suffer the same loss and grief, and once outside she wiped her eyes and nose with the back of her hand and took mine. "That's why we have to do this, Seth, why you have to. No one should die for nothing, right?"

We needed to try a different, more relatable approach, and I suggested Ashley let me do the talking at the next house. I understood loss and grief, the too familiar ache in the pit of my stomach. It was simply a matter of making it work for me, finding the character, projecting the empathy, offering personal testimony. "Hi, I'm Seth and this is Ashley. We're your neighbors from Beloit College. We were just talkin' to your neighbor Fred. Hearin' about Fred Junior really hit me hard. I lost my brother, and it devastated my family. We're as concerned as you with what's happenin' in our country, how it's rippin' us apart at home. We know you've got families to feed and kids to raise, and someday Ashley and me are gonna be parents just like you. We know how critically important good jobs are here in Beloit, but maybe you and your co-workers and friends could plant seeds with management, better ways to do things, better products to make, still providin' for your families and givin' your employer the chance to be a better corporate citizen." It was a good monologue. Tonality just right. The touch of anguish. Droppin' the *G*'s dead on. I repeated it at every house and more people listened, even if they didn't agree.

Walking back up the hill to campus Ashley stopped and turned to me. "You never told me 'bout your brother. Ah'm so sorry. Mus' be awful for you and your folks."

"Well, I don't know if he's actually dead. He dodged the draft and left the country, probably went to Mexico. I figured that was close enough."

"Ah totally believed you."

"You were supposed to. I'm a good actor."

CHAPTER 9

I'D NEVER EXPERIENCED anything like the late-October weather in Wisconsin. The Beloit College brochure illustrated happy kids in summer apparel or light sweaters sitting on Indian Mounds in front of Middle College blanketed with multi-colored leaves, not the invasion of Eskimos in furry hooded parkas, wool scarves, mittens and winter boots scurrying about. The winds attacked from every direction, serrating exposed skin like straightedge razors. Discerning the identity of anyone under all the layers almost impossible, including the bulky form trudging toward me shouting my name. It wasn't until he was within spitting distance that I recognized six foot four, 245-pound Lawrence Brown, starting Buccaneer linebacker hailing from Notre Dame Academy in Green Bay, Wisconsin, stats Ashley had shared during one of Beloit's pathetic football games. He loomed over me. "I must be nuts. I could've gotten a scholarship to play for Chapman U. in Southern California."

"Why didn't you? Better weather. Maybe they even win occasionally."

"You still hanging with that cute southern chick?" I prickled like a porcupine. "I wanna hook up with her if I'm not stepping on someone else's turf. That accent's enough to give you a hard-on and the guys on the team say she fucks like a bunny; hops from garden to garden. Nice metaphor, huh? Or is that a simile? I can never keep them straight." He laughed. "Whatever! My high school teammates wouldn't know either if they tackled it."

Only Beloit College would have literate football players. No wonder they sucked. And I hated rumormongering. Abby had been labeled "The community chest" in eighth grade for supposedly allowing school bully Brad Taylor to feel her up, a bullshit story he embellished with each retelling. Poor Abby. She hadn't known what hit her. Sweet and smart, a gawky string bean of a girl with a mouth full of metal and a totally flat chest. We walked home together. Shared a passion for music. Tuned into Scott Muni at WNEW FM radio before anyone else. I'd go to her piano recitals, she to my theatre performances. We saw our very first rock show together, Paul Revere and the Raiders. I always felt comfortable around her, except when she hung out with her stoner friends. I could tell her almost anything, even stuff about Jonah. One afternoon after school, Brad and his goon squad accosted me. "Hey Pinky, even tramps have standards. You won't get to first base." I hadn't tried. We were pals!

"You always believe everything you hear, Larry?"

"Come on, dude. Don't get your panties in a wad. Just between us guys, does she fuck as good as she looks?"

His words "Hops from garden to garden," a stake through my heart. I thought my head would explode. Black spiders scampered up my spine, over my neck and face. My vision blurred. He was a liar. A liar. She wasn't like that. Couldn't be, not my sweet, innocent Ashley whose voice was honey on a warm buttery biscuit. I began to quake with uncontrollable rage. Suddenly the lights went out and Larry's standing there cupping a bloody nose. "Stupid pipsqueak. You could've told me you still loved her. You breathe a word of this to anyone I'll kill you, understand?" Oh my God. I'd punched him. A guy twice my size! The spiders were gone.

CHAPTER 10

LARRY'S WORDS RICOCHETED inside my cranium like pinballs and I tried to repress them by staying busy. Even joined Ashley and a group of kids involved with Student Mobilization for a folk dancing anti-war rally at the Civic Center Plaza in Chicago, though folk dancing wasn't my thing. I'd watched the 1968 Democratic Convention in Chicago. Still recoiled at the TV images of havoc, of Richard Daley's Nazi-like pigs bashing in kids' heads and dragging them unconscious to paddy wagons, coming face to face with the realization there were two Americas, two deadly war zones and no one was truly safe.

Ashley, fierce determined Ashley, a girl on fire, ignited sparks in everyone around her. "Come on, y'all, join hands in a big circle, that's right, around the Picasso statue." Her enthusiasm drew bystanders like bees to honey. "Make the circle bigger, BIGGER! Dance for peace!"

Our small raggedy group of twenty soon burgeoned to a hundred, mostly well-groomed adults in business attire, but she also drew Daley's storm troopers, cops in riot gear, anonymous in their football-like helmets and goggles, wood batons and guns in hip holsters, the haunting image from the TV screen. At first just a few on the periphery, but soon more, like wasps to a hive, ready to sting; I could hear the smack of their thick wood batons against their palms. I squeezed Ashley's hand and jerked my head toward them in warning, but she just shouted "Look, y'all. Even the police are joining us. Make room for them."

Unamused, they cut through the crowd shouting "Move along. You're disturbing the peace." But when Ashley responded we were dancing for peace and tried to take an officer's hand, he roughly pushed her, stating "We don't need a bunch of dirty hippies here." I stepped between them. We weren't disturbing anyone. We were just dancing.

"Really?" I made a grand sweeping gesture. "Look around. There must be a hundred people here. Your fellow citizens, dancing for peace."

A rising chorus of "PIGS, PIGS, PIGS" echoed off the Civic Center walls and through the concrete and steel canyon. Another officer butted me in the stomach with his baton. I doubled over, gasping, as Ashley was dragged off by two other cops and flung against the glass wall of the building, her head connecting with a loud thunk. Dazed, she dropped to the ground and I ran over to protect her with my body, trying to quell my own fear, sound calm and rational. "Officers, we're not here to cause trouble. We don't want violence. Just the opposite." One of the cops kicked me hard in the shin, dropping me to my knees, and all hell broke loose. More cops arrived, reinforcements to quell the riot of dancing. They were all over us, pushing and shoving. One trampled the tape recorder under his heavy boot, smashing it to smithereens.

A well-dressed man in a three-piece business suit approached the officers, his red hair, so like mine, aflame in the sunlight. "LEAVE THOSE KIDS ALONE!" He carried a briefcase. Probably a lawyer. "They're just dancing. Not bothering anybody. You're violating their Constitutional rights."

A cop caught the light of a flash camera as he swung his baton and smacked the man upside the head. The crack of wood on bone. The splatter of blood as he crumbled to the pavement. "That's what I think about your fuckin' rights," he grunted, about to hit the fallen man again when another cop interceded, grabbed his baton and told him there would be hell to pay for this. The fallen man was Sean McGuire, the district attorney.

Several people rushed over to help him. One middle-aged woman, around Mitzie's age, pressed a white handkerchief against his head and screamed for a doctor. It turned crimson red. Newspaper reporters and photographers appeared out of nowhere and snapped photos, the cops now getting nervous. I needed to control the situation. "Come on guys," I said, helping Ashley up, "this is supposed to be about peace. right? Let's show 'em we're better than the cops." But no one listened, too caught up in the frenzy.

A WLS-TV van arrived, a cameraman about to capture the scene. I looked at the man bleeding on the ground; looked toward the camera. Improvise, Seth. You can do this. "You see, this is what happens when we stop talking to each other." I turned to the intervening officer. "You probably have friends or family fighting in Vietnam, right? So do we. You want them to come home safe, right? So do we. We're not your enemies. We want the same things. We're just starting from a different point of view."

The officer went over to the man on the ground, a nimbus of blood encircling his head. "Don't try to move, Mr. McGuire. I've sent for a medic." Then he turned, glared at his cohort, and started toward me. I reflexively put my hands up to shield myself, but he patted the air with both hands. "It's okay. This is over. You kids should leave now." Driving back up to Beloit, Ashley gazed at me with approving eyes.

CHAPTER 11

THAT EVENING WE danced to the Siegel Schwall Blues Band at the Student Union, then returned to my room all hot, sweaty and horny. I knew this was going to be the night. I cued CSN's "My Lady of the Island" on my little portable system, lyrics so right, so real, written just for us, and as I held her close, I could feel the pressure in my chest as she breathed in my ear, and I gazed into her eyes, gently cupping a firm, flattish breast, her nipple stiffening under my palm while my free hand wandered where the sun refused to go and she placed hers over mine and pressed my fingers inside her lushness, third base at last. She stroked me, both of us now panting, and purred "Come inside me."

Home run! I mounted her, ready to be drowned in her body, assuring her I'd be gentle, wouldn't hurt her because I'd heard it could hurt the first time, and she looked up at me with an expression so sad and confused, her thighs slamming shut like crashing cymbals. "Seth, Ah'm not a virgin."

But I wasn't listening; I didn't care. My balls ached; my penis so engorged it was ready to lift off like a rocket. I needed to get inside her, nothing else mattered. I tried to gently pry her legs apart. "Please Ashley, please . . ." a supplicant at the foot of her altar.

"No Seth, don't. What made you think Ah was a virgin?" If she wasn't, what the fuck had we been waiting for? "All this time I thought you were seeing all of me, not just my body. It was so special, so different from other guys . . ." Hopping from bed to bed, he'd said. And I'd punched him in the nose. I didn't want to be different. Jonah was different. I attempted to remount her, but she pushed me away, gently but firmly. "Don't you understand? Ah thought you saw me and loved me for myself . . ."

"I do love you, Ashley, I do. Forget what I said. I want you. I need you."

"No, you're in love with an image of someone else, someone Ah'm not. We're not comin' from the same place."

"This is our moment!" But she'd already had too many moments. Insisted

I'd just end up hating her. A bogus excuse. She was rejecting me. Didn't find me attractive. Not man enough. Too fat. "I'll lose weight. I'll work out. I promise."

"This isn't about you. It's about me. Ah want someone to love me for who Ah am, not some fantasy of a perfect girl. Ah can't be that for you. Ah wish it were otherwise." I turned away from her, my heart breaking. No one wanted me, not my real mother, not Mitzie, and not Ashley. I'd always be alone. She put her arms around me as I lay there, my body racked with sobs. "Seth, Ah do care for you. Ah think you're funny and smart and sensitive and Ah want us to be good friends, but Ah'm not the girl who can make everything right for you. Ah can't even do that for myself."

We lay side by side in profound silence. My balls ached. If only she would touch me. Just touch me. But I could feel her body relax and soon heard the sound of her gentle rhythmic breathing. She'd fallen asleep. The first night a girl ever spent with me. A night that should've changed everything. I was being punished for what I'd done to my brother.

CHAPTER 12

IT HAD JUST started to flurry when Bart and I hurriedly dashed to Morse Hall for Professor Sumner's thrice weekly eight a.m. Underclass Common Course, or UCC, Bart in a down parka over flannel pajamas. I was still brooding over Ashley's rejection, feeling increasingly disconnected, and had started ingesting White Cross just to help me get through the day. How could everything feel so right and go so wrong?

Today's discussion focused on Betty Friedan's *The Feminine Mystique*, a book I'd found intellectually stimulating. I truly believed men failed to grasp the preeminent role women played in human society and stated so, confident my female classmates would appreciate my sensitivity, totally unprepared for the maelstrom that followed. "Absurdly simplistic," one girl chided. I recognized her from the theatre department. Another Peggy Lipton lookalike, like the fantasy girl next door. "My anatomy doesn't determine my destiny! The mystique of the happy housewife is a post-WWII fiction foisted on us by male-dominated advertising to keep us in our place and sell us goods and services, as if being a good housewife was supposed to fulfill us."

Another agreed. "Yeah, I must be better than those other wives because I can get hubby's shirts so white with no ring around the collar!"

Surprised by their vociferousness, I countered everyone was subject to advertising in a capitalist society, but that only made Peggy's doppelganger angrier. "Well, won't you look sexy in an apron and duster. I expect the house to be spotless and dinner on the table when I get home from work, and I'd better see my reflection in the dinner plates 'cause that's a reflection on you! And be looking fresh as a daisy because after all, all you've done all day is watch soaps and eat Bon Bons!" All the girls giggled.

I didn't appreciate being the butt of her humor. "Oh yeah? That why you bleach your hair blonde? 'Cause everyone knows blondes have more fun?"

Professor Sumner stepped in. "Okay, Lucy, Seth, this is all very spirited, but a bit off topic." Ah, Lucy.

"It's exactly on topic, Professor Sumner," Lucy continued. "How many of your tenured colleagues at Beloit are women?" He looked flustered. "We do comprise fifty percent of the population, right? Why isn't a woman professor teaching this course?" She was on a roll, encouraged by other girls in the room. "And maybe we should discuss how all you men treat us like sex objects and fetishize us."

I looked about me. The guys sat there like lumps. I'd read Erich Fromm's *The Art of Loving*. I knew what I was talking about, well, theoretically. "It's just human biology. Its natural girls dominate our thoughts, right guys?" I looked around for support. Bart, sitting next to me, covered his face with his hands.

"Just the sort of misogynistic attitude I'm talking about, and by the way Panty Boy, I'm a natural blond." My God, she was lovely. "Just because some asshole gets aroused by me doesn't mean I magically control him or should be required to cover up my body."

"Well maybe you should read the Old Testament. It's Eve who caused Adam to eat from the Tree of Knowledge, an obvious metaphor. Doesn't that speak to power and control?"

"Of course, how stupid of me." She shook her mane of long, flaxen hair. "There's Adam, looking up at God, pointing an accusing finger at Eve. 'It's her fault! She's so hot, I couldn't control myself.'" Most of the women in class clapped and cheered, "You tell 'em, Lucy."

Professor Sumner leaned against the front of his desk. "Interesting, but let's hold that for next week when we discuss Spinoza's philosophy of Determinism versus Free Will and its religious implications; for now, let's stick to this week's discussion of Feminism."

"Well, to that point, guys never take responsibility for anything, particularly involving sex. So much easier to shift it to women." Lucy looked directly at me. "Of course, I should consider the source, Panty Boy."

"Whoa, whoa, whoa." Professor Sumner separating two prizefighters in a verbal clutch. "Discourse is good, Lucy, name calling is not. Let's keep this at a Socratic level, okay?"

"My heartfelt apologies. I'm sure every woman in this room will agree guys are perfectly capable of exercising self-control . . . they simply don't try."

Christ almighty, I was always respectful, opened doors, stood until they sat down. Even walked curbside so they wouldn't get splashed by passing cars, but so what, right? Chivalrous Sir Walter Raleigh placed his cloak over a puddle to keep Queen Elizabeth's feet dry and she still lopped off his head. My own beheading figurative but bruising. "That's unfair. If a girl says no, it means no."

"Like what planet are you living on, Seth? Guys never take no for an answer." I did, but I wasn't like other guys. "You even have your own little codes; first base, second base, third, et cetera, like we're objects to be explored and exploited. You try to control us, reduce us to body parts, turn us into sex toys, but if we exercise the same rights we're labeled bad girls, whores, outside male-defined societal norms. It's pure sexism!"

Rendered speechless. Guilty as charged. I would have crawled under my desk had another girl not intervened on my behalf. "Stop haranguing him. He's just saying the roles men and woman play in society have to be different. It's a biological fact. We're the ones who bear children." I turned to see who she was. Chubby, like me. Figures.

"Not to mention being totally incapacitated one week out of every month." Finally, a male voice, but unfortunately Josh's, the only guy on campus wearing a *Nixon for President* button. The girls were appalled. Did he actually think having a period justified treating them like second class citizens? "Well, it's pretty clear, isn't it? If you read scripture, it says God created man, Adam, in His image, and then fashioned Eve from Adam's rib. Creating man the dominant act, woman secondary. Men are meant to be in control!" He looked to me for affirmation. The end of period bell chimed. Saved.

Professor Sumner chuckled as he gathered his papers and placed them in his briefcase. "Well, this has certainly been interesting. We'll continue this discussion on Wednesday along with Germaine Greer's *The Female Eunuch*. I'll be particularly interested in your thoughts on whether the traditional nuclear family amounts to sexual repression, and for next week be prepared to discuss Fullerton's translation of *The Philosophy of Spinoza* and John Locke's *An Essay Concerning Human Understanding*. They're both relatively short works and while reading ponder the difference between determinism, fatalism and the exercise of free will."

"Excuse me, Professor Sumner, I've one more thing to say to Seth." God help me, the golden goddess again. "How many women do you think were involved in writing the Bible? Throughout human history men have viewed us as extensions of themselves, of their own desires, not as equal and separate human beings." She turned and glared at me. "Maybe you should spend some time thinking about that, Panty Boy!"

Several inches of fresh snow blanketed the campus. Thick flakes still falling, all of it sticking. Kids were whooping it up in front of Commons. Several snowmen under construction. Perfect for snowballs. I packed one tight with bare hands and aimed it Bart's head, but he ducked in the nick of time. "Thanks a lot, dude. I really appreciated your support in class."

"No way I was getting involved in that cat fight. Plus, you had Josh on your side."

My hands were freezing. Turning numb; I placed them under my armpits. No gloves. How stupid of me. Larry was right. To hell with Cornell in upstate New York. Southern California was the place to be. "It's supposed to be an open exchange. Isn't that the whole idea behind the Socratic Method? You had my back when it was just the guys. Guess everything changes when girls are involved."

"Saying women are in control? Leading us poor guys into temptation. Holy shit, dude, I thought you were going to be lynched in there . . . and me by association!"

"But they do, Bart. Remember what you told me about Debbie?"

"Did it occur to you some opinions are not meant for public consumption?"

"And you heard that girl agreeing with me. Women perform the single most important human function; they give birth . . ."

"We're involved in that process as well, you know. There would've been no Jesus without Joseph; it doesn't happen through immaculate conception. Speaking of whom . . ."

I turned in the direction he was looking. My defender waddled toward us, huffing and puffing balloons of steamy air like a locomotive on an incline, a camera on a shoulder strap bouncing against her side. "Wait up, Seth." She looked from me to Bart and back again, stomping her feet. "Ah, am I interrupting something?"

"Sinead, right? Seth was about to enlighten me on immaculate conception . . ."

I sighed. "That's a misnomer, Bart. Immaculate Conception refers to Mary's birth, not Jesus'. You're referring to the Doctrine of Incarnation . . ."

"Really? And who exactly were Mary's parents?" Flummoxed, I'd no idea. Bart turned to Sinead. "Can you believe this shit?"

She pointed her camera at me and clicked. Nothing happened. "Shoot! Damn thing's frozen." She gave me an encouraging smile. "I think it's really interesting."

"Me, too. I've always been interested in religion, and just so you know, Bart, it wasn't until the first two ecumenical councils, Nicaea in 325AD and Constantinople in 381, that Jesus' duality was even affirmed by the Church, along with the virgin birth."

"Wow, as super impressed as I am with your extensive knowledge on the subject of virginity, you have me confused with someone who gives a shit!"

I told him men had attempted to subjugate women through the ages because they knew women have more power, probably starting with the Church's treatment of Mary Magdalene, and Sinead, watching our exchange like a spectator at a verbal ping pong match, agreed. Smirking, Bart looked from me to Sinead and flicked his forefinger like Patrick McGoohan from *The Prisoner*. "Be seeing you," he said, walking away. I packed one more snowball and threw it at him. Splat. Square in the back. That felt good.

"Those girls were so rude to you, especially that Lucy, Ms. Perfect hippie . . . everything. Think they're feminists because they're on The Pill, like they're no different than guys now, which is like biologically absurd. Lots of us are uncomfortable with some of the attitudes prevalent now. You've a right to your opinions, even if they're not cool."

"I was just playing devil's advocate, stimulating discussion."

"Well, that's certainly not the way it came across . . . So, anyway, I'm head of the campus Christian Fellowship Group and we have Chapel dinners Sunday nights and I thought maybe you'd like to join us?" The corners of her mouth turned up. Shirley Temple dimples. She was pretty. If only she wasn't so chubby.

"Who said I was Christian?" That jet black hair really made her bright blue eyes pop. "I'm Jewish."

She shivered, stomped her feet. "You sure don't look Jewish."

"Gotcha. I'm supposed to look like Fagin in *Oliver Twist*."

Her cheeks reddened. "No silly. It's just, you know, with that red hair and freckly pale skin and those bright blue eyes, I assumed your family was Irish or Scottish, something like that."

"I don't know anything about my family background."

"That's a shame. My great grandparents were Wisconsin pioneers, but I can trace my family's heritage back even further. Anyway, I'd love it if you maybe joined us? I'll make sure no *Roundtable* photographers are around. Personally, I thought you looked . . . well anyway, just let me know, okay?"

She turned to walk away, but I called after her. "Hey Sinead, I was just wondering. Those girls came down on me pretty hard. Am I a male chauvinist pig?"

"Seth, I've a father and brothers. I've yet to meet the boy who wasn't. It's just kinda the way it is. A lot of guys today talk a big game about equal rights for women until it's time to do the dishes or laundry or take precautions . . . or so I've heard anyway." Wish she wasn't so chubby.

"Mind if I ask you something personal?" She blushed. Her body tensed.

"Depends."

"Do you really believe Jesus died for your sins?"

She relaxed. "Oh, I wasn't expecting that. Maybe we should save that heady topic for Sunday."

"What I mean is, did he die for your sins, or mankind's sins?"

"I don't think he's looking down at me personally and watching everything I do. Believing doesn't give me carte blanche to commit sins, but I won't carry the burden; it's too heavy a load. We all sin, right?" She stomped her feet again. "Geez, it's cold. Do you imagine God as an old man with a long flowing white beard looking down at you from a cloud, watching every step you take? Isn't that kind of ridiculous?" A girl who worshipped a white-skinned, blue eyed Middle Eastern hippie who lived and died and lived again two thousand years ago would know ridiculous. "Without hope of redemption there'd be no reason to live!"

"Remember Marley in Dicken's *A Christmas Carol*? He bore the chains he forged in life, forever doomed . . . like me."

"But Scrooge was given an opportunity to repent and make amends, remember?" She gazed at me with genuine concern. "How can you be so fatalistic?"

The strange-looking men who schlepped from Brooklyn out to the Huntington Jewish Center thrice weekly in their long wool coats, felt hats, fringed shawls and funny looking side-locks to teach Hebrew school had warned us to atone for our sins before the last sound of the shofar on Yom Kippur or suffer God's certain punishment; He heard every word! We were inherently evil. Every bad thing that happened to us deserved, even the horrible Holocaust! Redemption nothing more than a pretty dream. "My life is set in stone."

"That's bullshit. You can always change. Maybe accepting Jesus in your heart would be a good start. You're not alone. It's a struggle for all of us, for me, too."

"It's too late for me." My sin was unforgivable.

"Well, you can look at the glass as half empty or half full. Should make next week's UCC class discussions of determinism, fatalism and free will lively. I'm sure Ms. Perfect will have thoughts are on those topics, too. Better come armored."

I thanked her; told her I'd think about Sunday night. Watched her trod through the accumulating snow toward Commons until she disappeared in the whiteout. I kind of liked her. She was really nice, but what would people think? Two chubby losers. Not Woodstock cool. Not like Lucy.

CHAPTER 13

BART WAS LYING on his bed smoking a joint, flipping through a *Playboy*, crooning *wouldn't you love somebody to love, you better find somebody to love* along with Grace Slick. He held up the centerfold. "Every guy's dream." Exactly what that girl Lucy was talking about, I pointed out. Objectification. Hadn't he been listening?

"Oh, come on, Seth. It's just a magazine. What? You never looked?"

"Well, I did, but never from a girl's perspective."

"You're not a girl. And empathy's not exactly your long suit, dude. I suppose you're gonna tell me you and your friends were saints, never talked about circling the bases?" Like I had something to contribute!

"Yeah, but now it feels kind of sleazy, you know?"

"Dude, why're you laying this whole defensive-aggressive guilt trip on me? What did Sinead want?"

When I told him, he gagged. "The campus virgin society? Was she crushed to discover your ineligibility?" Red-faced, I started toward my room, but he hopped off his mattress and grabbed my arm. "Wait a sec. All those nights behind closed doors and you never did it?" I shrugged him off. "Did you even try?"

"Of course, I tried! She asked me to stop. Didn't wanna deal with short, fat virgins."

"I doubt she said that. Plus, if you hadn't stopped, you wouldn't be a virgin anymore! Problem solved."

"Yeah, real men don't take no for an answer."

"Aw come on, man, I'm only kidding. You're a nice guy. Nothing wrong with that." I was a fish out of water. The only place I'd ever fit was on stage, roleplaying.

"Maybe you should check out the Hillel group on campus, hook up with them."

"I attended Sunday school, Hebrew school, post Bar Mitzvah Confirmation class, even the dorky Tallis and Tefillin club (mostly for the bagels and chocolate milk) looking for answers, but it was all drivel, hours wasted contemplating how many angels you could stick on the head of a pin, nothing to help me understand who I am or how I can alter the future."

"Alter the future, huh? Heavy, man." He took another hit. "Hey, you can travel back to the past and step on a butterfly. You know, the butterfly effect in Ray Bradbury's short story. This guy time travels back to prehistoric times and kills a butterfly which alters the future. Go to that fellowship dinner. You'll change one thing for sure. That Sinead's got the hots for you, man!" Really? She was kind of cute. "But don't expect me to go with you. I'm not the one looking to get laid, and anyway, like Groucho Marx said, 'I refuse to join any club that would have me as a member.'" He tucked the magazine under his mattress. "Guess you won't be needing this."

CHAPTER 14

THE NEXT AFTERNOON Ashley appeared at my door wild-eyed and frantic. "Mah daddy's comin' to take me ta' dinner, and he's bringin' his new girlfriend. Ah don't know what to do." I'd no idea her parents were even divorced. So many things I didn't know, hadn't asked, merely assumed, so focused on my own needs, and look where it had gotten me. "It's not somethin' Ah talk about. He had an affair with one of his students at Tulane. She got pregnant and he paid for an illegal abortion in a neighboring town. Couldn't risk anyone finding out. The girl got a pelvic infection, almost died, and her parents sued the university and they fired mah daddy and mom divorced him and it wasn't the first time, but she was jes' fed up and he's doin' it again and Ah can't deal with it, Seth, Ah can't deal with it. Please come with me!"

That day in Chicago I'd protected her. I'll do it again. She'll want me. "Of course, I will."

Reservations were at the Gun Club, a local restaurant favored by visiting parents, Beloit Corp execs, and frat boys looking to score. Word was they never checked ID's. The place was a Fifties curiosity, red Naugahyde banquettes studded with chrome buttons. Antique guns mounted on the walls. Cocktails and entrees with bizarre names and lots of old people, the exception being Ashley's father's girlfriend, a dumb blue-eyed, big busted blonde cheerleader-type who gazed at him with adoring eyes, hanging on to his every word like he was some kind of oracle instead of a disgusting old pervert teaching at a community college. He ordered us all Old Fashioneds. "So, Ah understand you and Ashley are an item, huh?"

"Just good friends," I grumbled.

"Real good friends, Ah'm sure." Gross motherfucker! Another old guy desperately trying to be cool, his long, thinning hair pulled back in a short ponytail, jeans so tight he walked like he had a coke bottle shoved up his ass, pearl buttons on his tight western style shirt about to pop when he sat down.

The drink went straight to my head. I felt off kilter. The whole scene so surreal. The volume of babble amping. The clatter of dishes, pots and pans. Engelbert Humperdinck crooning *Release me and let me love again* through loudspeakers. I imagined the song playing in an endless loop in Hell; something to look forward to. Probably not much different than where I was now. And it was no better for Ashley, sitting silent throughout, white-knuckled, gripping the table, staring stone-faced at her father groping a girl young enough to be his daughter in front of his daughter. So anguished. Crying out for his attention, a feeling I knew all too well. I began to understand her.

After he dropped us back on campus Ashley screamed, "FUCKIN' SON OF A BITCH! Ah hate 'im, Ah hate 'im" as his car disappeared down College Street. She grabbed my arms and shook me. "He's been fuckin' girls mah age for years! Mah age! He's mah Daddy! Supposed to be there for me, for me . . . but he wasn't. Men never are." I was just about to say I understood, we were kindred spirits, when she continued. "Why the fuck am Ah telling you this? You're jes' a child." A stake driven through my heart. Before I could utter another word she shook my hand, thanked me for being a pal, and walked off toward her dorm.

A pal! I bit my lip, bore down and pushed back. I wouldn't let her emasculate me more than she already had. "There's an anti-war rally in Madison weekend after next, a big one. Daniel Berrigan, the Catholic priest, is speaking. We should go." No response. "Well, I'm going. Some things are bigger than us. You said that." The door shut behind her.

Back at the dorm, Bart was going at it hot and heavy with some girl on his bed. Without so much as looking up he motioned me to move along. I closed my door, put Love's Forever Changes on my crappy stereo, music that spoke to me, sat on the floor with my back against the bed frame staring into a darkness so profound I wondered if I was living or even supposed to be, so lost and lonely I cried myself to sleep.

CHAPTER 15

I DECIDED TO attend the Sunday night dinner and slushed to Eaton Chapel through a mush of heavy, wet snow, the temperature having risen above freezing for the first time in like forever. What harm could it do? Being Jewish posed no barrier, though I wondered if God would smite me for cavorting amongst these Christians. I was curious, but more than that, I was increasingly isolated and uneasy with the Woodstock Generation's fluid rules of engagement. Maybe with Sinead's friends I wouldn't feel like such a loser. Maybe in a room full of losers, I'd shine like a beacon of cool! I was seeking knowledge, an alternative path to redemption and salvation. Maybe this evening would light the way. All religion drilled down to the Golden Rule: Do unto others what you would have others do unto you, and I knew I'd pay a heavy price for violating that rule. So given the choice of a Jewish rabbi who died for my sins or a vengeful God, what the fuck, go with Jesus. Maybe He was the way. And anyway, Beloit being nonsectarian, I wasn't going to face the disapprobation of a thorn-crowned Jesus nailed to a wooden cross above the altar.

A cold draft upswept through the candle-lit room as I entered the Gothic-styled chapel. Flickering candlelight spiraled the stone columns, splashed the archways and Sinead's beaming, chubby face. She embraced me, her ubiquitous camera snug between us, and led me past the pews toward the pulpit where she introduced me to a circle of kids sitting cross-legged on the raised platform who in turn blessed me and told me Jesus loved me. One of them handed me a tasty-looking bowl of steaming hot navy bean soup and fresh baked bread lathered with Wisconsin butter. Sinead pulled me down next to her. "We were waiting for you," she whispered. This was way better than sharing tepid pizza from Pizza Hut with Bart back at Haven.

Heads bowed, eyes closed, we all joined hands. One of the guys offered a benediction to Jesus for His bounty, His love, and our fellowship, everyone so at ease, comfortable in their own skins and with each other. Then we ate and chatted, just normal kids chatting about normal stuff, like whether the cover of the new Beatles *Abbey Road* album really proved Paul McCartney was dead and if "Revolution 9" off the *White Album*, played backwards, reproduced the brutal car crash that supposedly claimed his life. I flashed on Ashley and me, half naked on my bed, playing "Strawberry Fields Forever" backwards to determine if John Lennon uttered *I buried Paul* or *I'm very tired*.

We took turns around the circle thanking Jesus for something we'd experienced the prior week. Dates. Acne cures. Good test scores. Whatever. Sinead thanked Him for bringing me into the light and I experienced the same queasy unease as that first night in John and Max's room, this merely another skin I'd explore that wouldn't fit. I mumbled thanks for everyone's hospitality and great food, figuring to beat a swift retreat back to Haven, but then something happened. Something unexpected. A guy started strumming guitar chords. It was "Amazing Grace." A girl came in on the melody line. I closed my eyes, listened a moment, found the harmony line and joined her, disquiet forgotten, and afterwards, they said I sounded like David Crosby and asked me to sing a song. Pleased, I racked my brain for something appropriately Christian that would show my voice to full advantage. The Byrd's "The Christian Life" off their *Sweetheart of the Rodeo* album. I coached them on the words, and we all walked in the Light, heeding God's call, loving the Christian life. No bolts of lightning. Embraced in the afterglow of true acceptance.

Sinead squeezed my hand really hard and pulled me up. "Come with me," she said breathlessly, leading me into a dark corner behind the confessional booth. Holy moly. Some virgin society! I couldn't believe it. She wanted me, right here, right now, in the chapel and I was rock hard, ready as anybody could be. Everything I'd been taught a lie. Jesus was redemption, Sinead His instrument. I pushed her camera out of the way. French-kissed her. Fondled her small breasts. She moaned. Then pushed me away. "No, Seth. Stop," she said breathlessly. "Accept Jesus. He'll light your way forward. Set you free, I promise. Abstinence is sacrifice, a bow to His will. He will save you from hellfire and damnation."

First Ashley and now this. I started toward the main chapel doors, she right behind, pleading with me to stay. "Maybe that'll work for you, but like I told you before, my place in Hell has already been reserved." And those kids who'd wanted to be my closest friends scowled as I walked out into the cold, dark night. They'd never again give me the time of day.

CHAPTER 16

SURPRISINGLY, JACK, THE Phi Psi I'd met at the rush party on the farm, posted a notice in the Student Union offering rides up to the anti-war rally in Madison, so Saturday morning I climbed into the back of his VW bus with recalcitrant Bart in tow, shamed into going when I questioned his Woodstock bona fides. A bunch of kids were already there, Ashley amongst them. "When you left the other night Ah thought about what you said. That's what friends are for, right? Help people see past their own problems... focus on thuh bigger picture?"

I sat next to her. "Yeah. I have a friend like that." I squirmed a bit as Bart burrowed his ass between us.

"Ah knew you'd be here. Ah would've felt guilty, like a poseur, if Ah didn't go. Ah'm sorry for hurtin' your feelings..." She reached across Bart and gave my hand a fleeting squeeze.

"It's okay. Sometimes things are really hard to deal with... like you said, that's why you have friends." I turned to Bart, who was clearly focused on Ashley. "Isn't that right, Bart?"

He ignored me. "I'm committed to the anti-war movement," he said fervently. "I was at Woodstock."

THE RALLY WAS huge, several thousand people blanketing all four lawns encircling the state capitol rotunda, a human patchwork quilt, the air abuzz with electricity. Not surprising. The University of Wisconsin-Madison had garnered a radical reputation in the wake of the infamous anti-Dow Chemical protests in 1967; stories abounded of burning draft cards, student and faculty anti-war teach-ins, bra burnings, disruption of Army recruiting efforts, but the rally was completely peaceful, the vibe awesome, the police respectful, unlike the gestapo-like cops in Chicago earlier in the fall. Off duty, the Madison police probably would've marched in solidarity with us. Jonah would have blended in here and I futilely scanned the crowd for his face.

Allen Ginsburg, wearing a white kaftan, sat cross-legged on the dais in front of the rotunda chanting the Hare Krishna while accompanying himself on the harmonium. Bald on top with long wavy black hair, he asked that we send waves of love to President Nixon. Very still, all palms open to the universe, chants of "OHM" filled the air in four or five-thousand-part harmony. Tom Hayden, rakishly handsome, one of the infamous Chicago Seven, fired us up to stay involved, continue to man the ramparts, hold Nixon accountable, hold our parents accountable as well, and demand change. Daniel Berrigan, in priest collar and black vestment, implored us to pray for peace and understanding, see "the others" point of view and be respectful of it. But it was the performance by the Mad City Mime Troupe that blew my mind. They presented a broad and biting satire that had a death-masked Richard Nixon surrounded by H. R. Haldeman, John Ehrlichman and Henry Kissinger dressed as Nazi storm-troopers tromping over the bodies of US and Vietnamese soldiers, greedy arms raised high as gold, jewels and cash rained down on them from the bomb door of a plane emblazoned "Military Industrial Complex." I was astounded. I'd been in a lot of stage plays but I'd never seen humor used to such effect. I wanted to be part of this.

CHAPTER 17

AT TERM'S END, Bart and I removed our posters from the walls, moved the furniture back to its original arrangement. We'd pledged Phi Psi and would be sharing a room in the house after the holiday recess. I was in a foul mood for several reasons, including the prospect of two interminable weeks at home with Jerry and Mitzie. Bart, sounding too much like Larry, casually asked what was going on between me and Ashley, and I asked why he wanted to know. "Just making conversation. You still love her?"

"Yeah . . . unrequited."

"Come on, dude. Lots or girls out there. What about Sinead? What happened at that dinner?"

"Jesus intervened."

"We're in the middle of a free love explosion, and you act like you're cloistered."

"Apropos to Sinead. Any other questions or would you like to mind your own fucking business?"

"Aren't we touchy. You're a textbook example of an obsessive compulsive. I'm studying OCD in Psych 100 and with you as a roomie, I've been living it. Tell you something else. Taking all that White Cross is only feeding your obsessiveness."

"Why? Because I'm not a slob? Because I make my bed? The White Cross's just a study aid."

"Dude, you made my bed every day, even after we separated rooms, and the way you organize your books and LPs, always moving furniture about . . ."

"Stuff gets out of position. Haven't you ever heard of Feng Shui?"

"Yeah, I've ordered it at Chinese restaurants. You expect people to be perfect, Ashley for example. You turned her into the Virgin Mary, for God's sake. You suffocate people. Everything's black or white. You always have to be in control. You're never in the moment. Betcha that's why you can't get high ... or laid."

"Anyone ever tell you a little knowledge is a dangerous thing? Wait'll you study Freud. You'd have a heyday with this recurring dream I have."

Bart stopped packing. Got this weird glimmer in his eyes. "Did it start at puberty? That's when recurring dreams often begin. Maybe something happened when you were a kid, something so painful your subconscious mind won't let it surface?" I squeezed my eyes shut. A barely discernible image of a deep, dark forest loomed in the back of my head. "Looks like I've struck a chord. Something scares you and you don't want to face it."

I took a note from my back pocket and waved it in his face. I'd show him what was bothering me. "Remember that stuff with the theatre department head? Here, read this! It was in my mailbox today. But don't you ever tell a soul. Understand?"

I nervously fidgeted with my ring as he started to read it. "*Your beautiful blue eyes devastate me ...*"

"No, not that, read further down."

"Why? You do have beautiful blue eyes."

"I'm serious, Bart. Stop making fun of me."

He continued reading. "What the fuck! *I long to hold you in my arms, press my face against your blue jeans, feel your ...* Who sent this to you?"

"It's gotta be one of the guys in the department."

"Why in the world would you assume it's from a guy?"

"Did you read the rest of it? *I've never felt this way about another guy before* ... seems pretty clear to me."

"I swear, Seth, you're all melodrama. Save your acting for the stage. It's either from a girl who wants you, which I'd assume you'd be pretty stoked about, or someone's idea of a joke. You're letting your OCD control you. Ignore it." He didn't understand. I was in theatre department every day and now I had to worry about some guy wanting to fuck me! Why was I such a loser? And what was that shadowy image in my head?

CHAPTER 18

SHORTLY AFTER WE moved into the Phi Psi house, one of the brothers, Fat Freddie, got a package from Hawaii containing several Thai sticks, marijuana buds tightly wrapped around bamboo stems and tied with thin twine. Everyone was super excited and gathered on the floor of his room in a circle, like the chapel virgins, only here anticipating the second coming of the righteous high. I'd joined in to be companionable, unable to get stoned no matter how many times I'd tried, always warding off unwanted thoughts. Maybe Bart was right. Control issues. He removed the twine while greedy eyes looked on, pulling the sweet, pungent grass off the stick, crumbling it between his fingers until it looked more like cigarette tobacco, careful to save any errant seeds for future botany experiments. He sniffed and licked his fingers, then closed his eyes and nodded, as if he'd moved to a higher plane and he hadn't even lit up yet. "This stuff is killer, absolutely zonker dope!" Freddie rolled a fat spliff, took a long toke, passed it to me. "This will blow your mind." I took a hit that barbequed my lungs, but otherwise felt nada though I wondered how I'd even know as I'd no idea what I was supposed to feel, not that it mattered because the second and third hits provided no further illumination.

Everyone flinched when the hallway phone rang but no one got up to answer it, too wasted, staring into space, giggling, listening to a Fireside Theatre LP on Freddie's super deluxe stereo, stoner comedy for stoners by stoners and I wondered if they'd all entered another dimension of time and space or some secret society I hadn't been invited into until finally, after four or five rings that seemed to intensify to a crescendo, I reluctantly answered it and heard a little voice speaking through the receiver. Oh my God. A little person inside the phone chattering away! I recoiled and dropped it, the receiver dangling at the end of the flexible metal cord. How could anyone fit inside a telephone receiver? I ran back into the room, shared this remarkable discovery with the guys, and a wave of hilarity ensued though I hadn't said anything funny. Then I had an epiphany. They already knew about the little person, and now I did, too! Tears of joy streamed down my cheeks. I was wasted and it was so fucking dynamite. No longer on the outside looking in.

A few nights later I returned from the library to find Bart, my brothers and other house friends, maybe twenty-five people in all, in the living room in a state of palpable excitement. Bart handed me a pill, put one in his own mouth and said "Swallow it," but never having taken anything non-prescription other than White Cross I hesitated. "It's called MDA. Just take it. *Remember what the Dormouse said! Feed your head.*" The anti-drug movie was right. Pot was the gateway, but I popped it into my mouth because I wanted to see what was on the other side. Wanted to be a risk-taker, like Hemingway.

We hung out in the living room listening to a Sons of Champlin LP, waiting for whatever was going to happen to happen, everyone joining in a chorus of *Get high, get high, get high* and KABOOM I'm a blossoming flower on an ever expanding vine of truth entwining us all in a flourish of swirling fluorescent colors and psychedelic patterns spiraling up toward Heaven and God, a kind and gentle merciful God . . . and it's Gandalf the White Wizard, and He's gathering me to His bosom, bathing me in His brilliant light as we corkscrew ever higher atop a mushroom cap and I know *All you need is love, love is all you need*, and tears of joy stream down my cheeks as I look about me and see family, real family, the only family I've ever had, and I love them all and want to hug and kiss them, bursting with unabashed joy, basking in His warmth, secure in the power of His love and forgiveness for my sin, and I run out into the frigid night and climb into this humongous circular ball of interlinked inner tubes with all my friends and brothers and barrel down College Street spinning round and round like clothes in a dryer, bouncing off the rubber walls and each other with no way to stop, but who cares? I'm awash in God's love and true knowledge.

Hours later the ecstatic high waned, and I fell as from a great height back into myself, but I had discovered the key that freed me from the shackles of obsessive thoughts, amorphous fears and the utter futility of seeking love in all the wrong places. Freedom to leave my bed unmade, clothes scattered about, books and LPs out of alphabetical order, schoolwork undone. Even go commando! No more caring, no more analyzing, controlling; just being. From that moment on I smoked or ingested anything in a vain attempt to recapture that heavenly high now just frustratingly beyond my reach and Bart, my personal drug guru, was chastising me, actually chastising me, for excessive drug use, saying I was out of control and needed to find balance, a middle ground, before I flunked out of school like Tex and Mex. Talk about irony! Fuck balance; fuck control. I wanted to be a Woodstock man.

In the middle of second term, I was placed on academic probation.

April 13, 1970

Dear Seth,

We received a personal note from your academic advisor Professor McCauley. Your grades have dropped from straight As in your first term to Ds. What the hell is going on? Your mother and I are very disappointed. We never thought we'd have to write a missive like this. That hippie school was not our choice, nor your decision to major in theatre. You could've gone to the School of Industrial and Labor Relations at Cornell, worked hard toward a law degree, to becoming a productive and useful member of society, but we allowed you your choice and we expect you to make the best of that bad decision. You are in college to mature as a person, figure out what you want to do with your life, and study hard, not waste your time and our money fucking every girl in sight. Do that at home while earning a living at a menial job since that's the direction you're heading in. It's time you dealt with the realities of life. We will not continue funding your education if these are to be the results. You had better turn things around before the end of the term or you will not be returning in the fall. Perhaps a stint in the Army is what you need! Am I making myself clear? We still believe you capable of better things.

Your parents

Capable of better things. What great expectations! Still the afterthought, the lesser child, not wonder boy Jonah. I wanted to be the new me, free and easy, but was torn asunder, so needy for their approval, so desperate to prove I was as good as him. If I stopped taking drugs the old Seth would reemerge like clematis vine left unchecked in a garden, and though I hated myself for doing it, I obsessively grasped onto schoolwork and gobbled White Cross like M&Ms (they weren't a drug; merely a study aid) and virtually moved into the library to avoid the myriad distractions of the house, and unwanted thoughts.

I studied my lines for Mercutio in *Romeo and Juliet*, drew maps of Europe from the Fifteenth through the Nineteenth centuries reflecting shifting balances of power over that time span. A term paper for Sociology on Emile Durkheim's groundbreaking treatise *Suicide*. An analysis of Locke's view on tabula rasa. Clean slate my ass. I was born covered in bloody slime. Ask my real parents, who discarded me, Mitzie, who couldn't bear to touch me, Jonah who'd suffered for my jealousy. But no matter. I had a shitload to do if I could just stay focused. Goddam it, I wasn't going to be the first boy on my block to come home in a box!

The problem was me. Always had been. Always would be. I was out of step with my times. No amount of partying was going to turn me into a Woodstock man. I was terrorized by something I couldn't see. The idea of a loving God purging me of my sins an acid-induced delusion. Yet I was desperate for someone to talk to, someone who'd understand, so I went to Ashley's dorm room and knocked on her door adorned with peace signs and hippy-dippy poems by Khalil Gibran about suffering the pain of too much love, but she wasn't there.

Distraught, I returned to the house hoping to quell my neurotic mind getting wasted with Bart but froze just outside our door. Ashley's voice, clear and unmistakable. With Bart! Visions of them coupling assaulted me like a battering ram. My lady of the island! Months spent reverently decorating a cake available by the slice for anyone but me! I clutched the door jamb to steady myself. Pulsing red dots obliterated my vision. Black spiders scuttled up my neck and swarmed over my face. I bashed my head against the door to smash them, mute the anguish. Ran to the stair landing as Bart poked his head out and yelled "Shit! Seth, wait!"

Once outside, I turned my face to the starless sky and screamed at God, at the unfairness of it all, and ran off campus past Geri's burger joint to the nearby liquor store, begging an upperclassman to procure me the cheapest possible liquor, a fifth of peppermint schnapps I chugged as I entered the graveyard a few blocks away and hunkered down in front of a gravestone inscribed LOVE. Salty tears and mucous mixed with the noxious minty liquor. What a fool I was. Nothing had changed. The sun was already over the horizon when I opened my eyes, discombobulated, head throbbing, stomach cramping, and spewed over nascent crocuses heralding the return of spring.

CHAPTER 19

BART SOUGHT ME out in the library, pulled out a chair and sat down. "You sleeping here now? You haven't been back to the house in two days. You look like shit. Don't smell too good either."

"Bart, if you're not here to study, go psycho-analyze yourself."

"Why? With the cornucopia of neuroses you provide? We need to talk."

I buried my face in the Spanish language edition of *Don Quixote* while he sat quietly, waiting for me to engage. Well, he could wait until the cows came home. Did they really come home? I would've asked Sinead, a Wisconsin girl, but we weren't exactly talking. "Seth, the book's upside down." No matter. The book was indecipherable. "We need to talk about Ashley because you've got it totally wrong. She's not interested in me. I wish she was, but we're just friends..."

"Thought you were only interested in Playboy bunnies? I never should have trusted you... or anyone."

"She was looking for you; asked if I knew where you were. Needed to talk to you. She was so sad, Seth. I don't think she'd ever expected anything good in her life until you came along. She wanted to know if you still had feelings for her."

"Bunch of fuckin' bullshit."

"You're such a downer, man. Always assuming the worst, jumping to conclusions. Organizing everything and everyone into neat little categories. Well, here's a news flash, buddy. People aren't inanimate objects and sometimes things get fucked up and that's just the way it is. You're like the narrator in that Dostoyevsky novel you have, you know, *Notes from Underground*. You take perverse enjoyment in being self-destructive; I think this has to do with your brother..."

"LEAVE MY BROTHER OUT OF THIS!" He was the best big brother ever. He took me on hikes, carried me on his shoulders when I was tired. He took me out for secret milkshakes, played spaceship with me and took me to the movies. The only one who paid attention to me and protected me.

"See your reaction? Something's wrong, Seth. If you won't talk to me, see a professional. You need help."

"You're trying to change the subject from you and Ashley."

"I'm not, goddam it. There's nothing to talk about. It's you, and I care. Your self-hatred is going to destroy everything good around you, don't you see that? You wallow in it. You're like those flagellants roaming medieval villages during the Black Plague scourging themselves. Jesus Christ," he sighed. "I don't know what else to say."

After he left, I tried to get back to work but couldn't concentrate. I paced about the library, my sanctuary, and dear Mrs. Nichols the librarian, busy at the front desk insuring everything was as it should be, updating index cards, alphabetizing everything by author and subject, noted my distress, approached me and asked if everything was okay. So nice, so sweet and caring, I wished she was my mother. I wanted to fall into her arms, be hugged and kissed and assured everything would be okay and there really was a me, more than an amalgam of characters played for pathos or laughs. But who was I kidding? So I sucked up all the pain and turned my distress into jest because fat boys were expected to be jolly. "I'm practicing my role in a play. Projecting anguish. Can you feel it?"

"Listen dear, you know where I am if you want to talk."

After she returned to the reception area, and I sought solace in a couple of Three Musketeers bars, a can of Pringles and several tabs of White Cross. Shielding my face with a textbook, I pushed back that amorphous darkness that gnawed at me and hounded my dreams. And formulated a plan.

PART TWO
THE BOOK OF ISAAC

CHAPTER 1

BART LOOKED ANXIOUS as I calmly crated my dynamite collection of LPs. Asked what I was doing. As if that wasn't obvious. "I'm gonna sell them. Finance a trip to Mexico. Find my brother, beg his forgiveness. Maybe then God will give me a second chance. I can't live with the mark of Cain on me."

"I knew this was about your brother! Listen, Seth, let's go talk to my advisor, Dr. Iverson. He'll help you. I'm worried about you, man. You keep this bottled up it'll destroy you."

"Wanna help me? Carry one of these crates out to the quad."

A pretty big crowd gathered, rummaging through my LPs. Vultures picking the flesh off Seth's carcass. One kid excitedly turned to his girlfriend. "Holy shit! He's got *It's a Beautiful Day*, the original LP, for only five bucks." He handed over the money. "I just stole that."

She flipped through my Procol Harum albums and asked why I was selling my records. Seemed impressed I was going to Mexico alone, keeping a travel journal. "That's so cool," she said, handing over three bucks for *Shine On Brightly*. She interlaced her fingers with her boyfriends', a simple, intimate gesture of togetherness that rent my heart. "We should do that."

I sold most of my albums that day, like Janis losing a *little piece of my heart* with each sale but netted several hundred dollars, nowhere close to their deep personal value. LPs that told Seth's life story. But that was the point. Seth was dead. His story over. I was starting afresh.

CHAPTER 2

I ACED MY second term finals and flew home with no intention of returning. Leaving on my own terms, not Beloit's, not Jerry's or Mitzie's. Anticipating a confrontation, I called my cousin Joel and asked if he'd pick me up at LaGuardia and let me spend the night at his house.

A decade my senior, he was a glamorous figure from the late-Fifties when big stars like Bobby Darin, Ricky Nelson and Dion ruled the AM Radio airwaves. He'd often take Jonah and me joyriding in his cherry red Corvette Stingray, treat us to movies and McDonald's. I watched him compete on Dick Clark's *American Bandstand,* his wavy black hair slicked back, dancing the Lindy Hop with a pony-tailed girl in a poodle skirt and cardigan sweater. For his time, he'd been the essence of cool. "Aren't your parents picking you up? We've got people showing up for a dinner party."

I made no attempt to mask my disappointment. "No worries. I'll hitchhike."

"Geez, kid, you should have called us earlier. Ah, what the fuck. I'll pick you up in front of the American terminal. Give you a chance to see our new digs and I'll drive you home tomorrow."

SEVERAL LATE MODEL sports cars, as shiny, new and expensive as his cherry red Porsche 911 S sports sedan, lined the blue cobblestone driveway of Joel and Marsha's massive Georgian colonial in West Meadow Estates. I was floored by the faux Corinthian gilded columns in the foyer, the gleaming white tile floor, the postmodern Scan-designed table, but especially the suit of Medieval armor on the pink marble pedestal guarding the entry, a multi-epoch pastiche of elegant excess. They'd really outdone themselves.

Marsha and three other couples lounged in the formal living room, faces flush from the fire ablaze in the massive mahogany and stone fireplace despite the ninety-degree weather. Beefy wood mouldings cross-hatched the ceiling and wainscoted walls. Every surface displayed objet de art. Everything screamed: EXPENSIVE. I fanned my face. "I know, I know," Joel chuckled, "don't even say it. She's so enamored with that fireplace I can't stop her using it. Thank goodness for AC. But what the heck, its only money, right? And to think, a year ago we were in that three-bedroom split level in Roslyn. It's all about Wall Street, baby. You can have it all, and then some. Lemme introduce you around. I'll show you the rest tomorrow."

Joel and his buddies sported tight-fitting designer jeans and open collar French cuffed embroidered shirts, casual yet snappy; the ladies in slinky dresses accessorized with diamond tennis bracelets, rings and earrings, all sparkly. Dual discussions were underway, the guys droning on about impending changes at the Federal Reserve under President Nixon, something about some guy named Martin and tight money policy and its impact on the economy, Joel insisting Nixon's new appointee Arthur Burns was more politically attuned and would pursue easy money. I'd no idea what the fuck they were talking about. Couldn't imagine spending my life thinking about such boring things. The women, however, were discussing jewelry, an attractive woman in a translucent white silk blouse holding court, her nipples visible through her lacy bra. Pretty hot for someone who must've been at least thirty. She showed off a diamond tennis bracelet glittering in the fire light. "You just have to go to this jeweler. He has the best prices..."

"Inflationary pressures are gonna be a boon to the stock market," one of the guys noted.

Another frowned. "The stock market? Who cares? Pension funds have their assets dedicated to bonds. Fixed income's the game to be in!" There was agreement all around.

"... And you wouldn't believe the stuff he has, diamonds and emeralds, and his settings, to die for."

Marsha asked for his information. "Joel wants to buy me a new tennis bracelet, don't you, honey?"

"But I just bought you this house!"

One of the guys thoughtfully scratched his chin. "She may be right, Joel. Diamonds are a good hedge against inflation in an easy money environment."

"Remind me to get his information before you leave," Marsha whispered to Ms. Diamond Bracelet.

I was my usual working-class hero self in scruffy patched jeans and a chambray work shirt, out of place in this chic assemblage. Joel placed his arm on my shoulder. "This is my kid cousin Seth. He just flew in from Beloit College in Wisconsin."

"What college?" one guy asked.

"Beloit. You know, the sound you get dropping a stone in a toilet bowl." They all stared at me blankly.

Marsha filled a crystal flute with Moet Chandon Brut Imperial champagne and handed it to me. "You must be exhausted after such a long journey."

"It's only a couple of hours..."

"Anything west of New Jersey is the wild west as far as I'm concerned," she said to general agreement. I drained my glass. It was good. Crisp and dry, with a subtle hint of fizzy creamy lemon on the tongue. Marsha refilled it. "What an adventure you're having. Are there Jewish people out there? How will you meet a nice Jewish girl if you're not on Long Island?"

"I don't want to live on Long Island."

Mr. Diamond Tennis Bracelet took affront. "Where's better than Long Island?"

Marsha refilled glasses all around. "Oh, for God's sake, leave him be. He's only eighteen and a theatre major, nu? We're used to his drama. Let him explore a bit. Then we'll find him a nice Jewish Long Island girl." She looked at the other ladies. "Am I right or am I right?"

Ms. Diamond Bracelet twitched her expensive ski slope nose like Samantha on *Bewitched*. "My baby sister is a freshman at SUNY New Paltz. So cute and such a great personality. I'll give you her telephone number, Seth. You two should date this summer."

"Listen, kid," one of the guys added, "you're too young to let yourself get caught in any net. There's plenty of fish in the sea. Just remember to bring your rod and keep casting!" The men guffawed and exchanged high fives. The ladies rolled their eyes.

JOEL SPED DOWN the Long Island Expressway the next day. "Beats that old Stingray, huh? You come work on the Street, you'll have one of these in five years, tops."

"Must be nice. Big house, the car, fantastic wife... all that stuff."

Joel grinned. "Not that you'd care. You're a working-class hero, right? Viva la revolution and all that crap! Like your older brother."

"Joel, have you heard from him? Think he's okay?"

"Look, Seth, he cannot afford to leave a trail, but I'm sure he's fine. Last summer up in Nova Scotia we met several resisters. They're all in the same boat. All wanna come home, but that's just not realistic. They'd face criminal charges and jail time, but your brother was 4F for sure. Know what I'm sayin'?"

"You don't know that for a fact..."

"Not that. Mental issues. He was manic, Seth. Always with the chip on his shoulder, something to prove. And that stuff at Columbia. Why Jerry got into that argument with him I'll never understand."

"He was an anti-war activist."

"He was a schmuck." I sat there stewing, staring out the window, and Joel reached over and ruffled my shoulder length hair. "Ever consider getting a haircut, kid, or are you auditioning for the other team too? Just kidding. Seriously, some things are beyond your control. Your job right now is to enjoy the next three years and maybe even learn something. Believe me, you'll never get them back. After that, come work with me on the Street. It's a fucking goldmine. There's nothing you can't have. Make your father look like a pauper."

"The Street? Become a corporate stooge? No way... I mean, I know you're not like that but, you know, the whole environment..."

He guffawed. "You're an 18-year-old hippie..."

"Yeah, a hippie wannabe maybe."

"Well, you're doing a helluva good impersonation. Come downtown sometime. I'll treat you to lunch and show you around the office. But maybe change your clothes. The George Harrison *Abbey Road* cover look won't fly! Then we'll see what you think when you graduate."

If I told him my plans, he'd try to dissuade me. He was getting old. Sounding like Jerry. "Okay, maybe some time."

CHAPTER 3

MITZIE MADE A show of being hurt when Joel dropped me off. Why hadn't I called them? They would've been happy to pick me up, but he wasn't a minute out the door before she exploded. "How do you think that made me look, calling him instead of your own parents?"

"Sorry for making you look bad, Mitzie. I know how important appearances are to you."

"That's not what I meant..."

"It's exactly what you meant, and that's okay. I'm shallow and superficial too. I learned from you."

At dinner, I looked at the mélange on my plate. Talk about an appetite depressant. I should have been rail thin after seventeen years of her glop. Desiccated meatloaf smothered in tomato catsup. Soggy mixed vegetables from a plastic boiling pouch. Mushy, boiled potatoes, an uptick over the dehydrated potato spuds she usually prepared. Not that it mattered. I'd no appetite. Sat grimly watching two strangers shovel tasteless food in their mouths before pushing my plate away. Best get it over with. "I'm not returning to school for the summer term. Fact is, I'm not returning to school, period. I'm hitchhiking to Mexico."

Mitzie's wine glass shattered on the slate floor into myriad crystalline pieces, rivulets of red liquid trickling through the grooves in the bluestone. She started to wail and clutched the sides of her head. Jerry slammed his fork down, splattering chunks of grayish meat and catsup on the table. "What the fuck! First you go from A student to almost flunking out, and now you're leaving school?"

"You weren't going to waste your precious money on a ne'er do well, remember? Suggested I join the Army, do a tour in Vietnam. Makes sense. You'd finally be rid of me."

"Selfish bastard! You don't care what you're doing to me. I can't take this, Jerry, not after everything. It's killing me!" Mitzie pushed back from the table, upending her chair. Left the room crying hysterically, slamming the screen door behind her.

Jerry looked at me plaintively. "You can't do this to her. She can't deal with this ... not after Jonah."

Everything was still about Jonah, even with him gone. I remembered Grandpa Matthews removing his gold signet ring after Jonah's flawless Bar Mitzvah performance. Slipping it onto Jonah's ring finger qvelling he'd be the one carrying on the Matthews name. How I'd seethed with envy. He'd studied Hebrew with him; helped him with his Haftorah portion. Regaled him with Bible stories. All in preparation for that special moment. Me? I was chopped liver, the Jewish party dish no one wanted to eat. "This isn't about Jonah, Jerry! Not everything in this fucking morgue is about Jonah."

"Stop calling me Jerry. I'm your father, goddamit." He placed a hand on my shoulder. I shook him off.

"No, you're his father. All you ever cared about. Why'd you even adopt me?"

"Where'd you get such a fakakta idea?"

"You think I'm stupid. That I don't know? Jonah told me the truth when I was ten." Eight fucking years I'd suffered their silence, waiting for them to have the decency to tell me who I was and where I came from. "See anyone else around here looks like me?"

"He lied. Lots of Ashkenazi Jews have red hair and blue eyes. It's difficult to trace our heritage; our parents were uprooted, escapees from pogroms, from conscription." All bullshit. They would have returned me to the orphanage if not for Jonah. No way he'd lie to me, and he wasn't here to defend himself. And who's fault was that? Mine. All mine! "Look, Seth, I made lots of mistakes. I should've spent more time with you, but I was trying to build a business, give you the advantages I never had ... At least that's what I told myself, but maybe I was rationalizing. Avoiding stuff. We don't get do-overs; we can only move forward." He reached out to me again. "Please let me help you."

I brushed his hand away. "You're in construction, right? Ever build a house without a foundation? Won't stand, will it? Why should I believe anything you say? What did you ever do to earn my trust, make me feel wanted or loved? You and Mitzie never even came to my plays. My special moments. The one place I felt validated. So don't give me that moving forward crap."

"I'd no idea you felt that way. You were so sturdy. So self-reliant. The one I counted on ..."

"I had to be! All I had was Jonah after Grandma Matthews died and I drove him away. I'm nothing. Nobody. It's all my fault. I gotta find him."

"Seth, that's absurd. You're not responsible for your brother's issues. He had psychological problems. Manic mood swings. We weren't trying to ignore you; we were trying to help him, and sometimes it was overwhelming. How many times were you caught in his crosshairs? How often did he say mean things to you or hit you for no apparent reason? What about the time he almost killed you with the gas oven?"

"No. That never happened. He never hurt me." I'd been playing with my Lincoln Logs when Jonah entered the family room, took my hand and walked me into the kitchen. The funny smell. The hissing noise. The lit match he thrust at me. "Go on. Light the oven," he coaxed, backing away. "Just hold the match to the pilot." An explosion. Me caroming across the room. The burning smell. Sticky wetness under me. Mitzie bursting in screaming how could I be so stupid.

"He put you in the hospital with a concussion! Eight stitches. Your hair all burnt. He was laughing when your mother ran into the kitchen. Laughing! But it was our fault. We should have been watching more carefully. I know you loved him, but you're rewriting history. Maybe shielding you from things you were too young to understand was a mistake. How 'bout the time he beat that kid up for killing a squirrel?"

A kaleidoscope of unwanted images. Darkness. Trees. Limbs. "Stop messing with my head. I don't want to hear any more."

"Your mother and I love you. She has difficulties expressing it. It's very complicated. Someday you'll understand." Someday? Why not now? I scratched at the back of my neck. Spiders. She never loved me.

"Which Mitzie, Jerry? The one who'd greet me after school with milk and cookies and then tell me I was fat? The one who stuck my nose in my own shit when I was three and had an accident, called me retarded when I got a B on a report card? The one who'd play catch with me in the backyard, or the one who'd make me remake my bed over and over until the hospital corners were perfect. Or maybe the one who kicked Grandma Matthews out of the house. But then again, how would you even know? You were never there. Mitzie had so many faces. Can you imagine what it was like never knowing which one would show up at any given time? And you talk about Jonah's mood swings!" I tried to calm myself, to keep away the spiders. "And since we're reminiscing, how about the day those detectives you hired were here. Mitzie said 'If you had to take one, why did it have to be my Jonah?' Remember that? I'll never forget it." I looked into Jerry's face. He was clueless. He'd no idea what it was like to grow up unwanted in a loveless home. "Tell me why there are no photos of me with Mitzie when I was a baby. Why she'd tuck Jonah into bed, sit with him awhile, give him her undivided attention, while I was lucky if I got a brusque peck on the cheek before she shut my door, no matter how I begged her to leave it open. She knew I was terrified of the darkness. She didn't care. She only cared about him."

He grabbed me in a bear hug and cried, "I'm so sorry, I'm so sorry," his sudden vulnerability unnerving. I'd only seen him cry once, when Grandpa Matthews died. I tried to push him away. I didn't want his help. I didn't want his money. I didn't want his love, but I melted in his arms because all I'd ever wanted was him to see me, feel me, hear me, be proud of me. I'd destroyed Jonah for it. But now it was too late. This whole conversation pointless. There was only one thing to do. Go to Mexico and find Jonah.

"That's ridiculous. You haven't thought this out. What makes you think he's in Mexico, or that you'll find him when we had professionals searching for him for six months?"

"Maybe if you'd been listening, instead of screaming at him, you would've heard him mention Mexico."

"Have you considered the practicalities? What about visa's, passports, inoculations? Your 2-S deferment's only good if you're in school..."

"Like that matters, right? Those kids at Kent State had deferments, too, and they're dead." This trip was all I had to cling onto. My world was spinning out of control. Nothing else makes sense. "I sold almost all my records. I've plenty of money, almost three hundred dollars."

"You think that's all you need? Listen to me. You're eighteen. I can't stop you and won't, but you'll have to get those documents and see Dr. Coe for inoculations. Let me help."

I finally had his undivided attention at the cost of being hollowed out, powerless, as he took control of everything. Got my uncle, a big shot with Coca-Cola Corporation, to secure me a job in their Mexican subsidiary in Mexico City. Had my absence at Beloit classified a work term experience to protect me from the draft. Told Mitzie to take me shopping and to the pediatrician.

She dragged me into Mensch's clothing store for white tennis shorts and a floppy canvas hat to protect my pale chubby face from the intense tropical sun. I stood in front of the dressing room mirror. Who the fuck was staring back at me? I wanted to pick up a chair, shatter the image. I was a pitiful dog on their leash, and I hated them more than ever.

She even refused to leave the examination room while Dr. Coe checked my vitals, and reacted vehemently when he noted my fugue-like aspect and suggested I might be suffering from clinical depression. How dare he! We were the most normal people in the world. Everything would've been just fine if I'd only attended Cornell. "Now look. He almost flunked out of school! He needs a higher dose of Ritalin, and you should forbid his going to Mexico in his condition."

"Go sit in the waiting room, Mitzie. Seth's too old to have you in here."

"You don't understand, Harold," Mitzie said as he showed her to the door. "You need to tell Jerry he can't go."

Dr. Coe sighed as the door closed behind her. "Look, Seth, I think getting away for a while is a good idea. Your family's been through a lot. Give you a chance to breathe, right? I've known you since you were ten and we've always had a good relationship. Is there something you want to talk about? Just between you and me." Yeah. Tell me who my real parents are. "Are you still taking your medication?" I sat immobile. None of his fucking business. "I'm going to refill your prescription and also another one for antibiotics, just in case you're active in Mexico." He winked. "Understand what I'm saying? Just follow the dosage."

Adults were so utterly clueless.

CHAPTER 4

ALL ABOUT ME disorder and chaos. A cacophony of noise throughout the arrival terminal. Vendors hawking Kodak film, "guaranteed" Aztec artifacts, consumables likely to give you Montezuma's revenge, their English incomprehensible. Overweight old white men in loud Hawaiian shirts and Panama hats, Bermuda shorts worn high, Humpty-Dumpty style, white socks pulled over bulging calves, imperiously barking orders at darker-skinned porters trailing in their wake weighed down with luggage. Women, helmet-haired and garishly attired in tropical dresses, oversized sunglasses and wide brim straw hats shrieking as filthy beggars clung to them like leeches, tying to suck out a peso or two. Crated animals howling. A rank smell of tortillas and fried pork in the hot, dank air.

I stood in line awaiting Customs, trying to keep it together. The lawyer my uncle had arranged to meet me had yet to show. All about me hippie backpackers looking so free and easy in jeans, hiking boots and bandanas, the way Jonah would've looked. The way I should've looked. They were staring at me. I knew what they were thinking. Check out the dork. And it was true. I stuck out like a sore thumb. A pathetic white blob in new tennis shorts and dorky hat, clutching a suitcase and the tennis racket my uncle suggested I bring. As out of step here as I'd been at Beloit. I'd let Mitzie and Jerry wrest control of my quest. What had I been thinking? Had I been thinking at all? Like waking up and still living a nightmare.

I was so relieved when my turn finally came. Finally, order amidst tumult. I handed my tourist visa and employment letter to the uniformed agent, but he waved the letter in my face, started speaking incomprehensively fast and motioned for another official to come over. I twirled the ring on my finger. What the fuck was going on? Where was the lawyer? Everything was in order. My visa came from the Mexican embassy in New York, had the official stamp and everything. People in line were grumbling now, irritated at the holdup. "This is no good. You have a tourist visa, but this letter says you have a job in la ciudad. You need a job visa. You must return to the United States now." An elderly man dressed in suit and tie and a Panama hat appeared and patted my shoulder.

"Sr. Bernalga?" He nodded. "There seems to be a problem; they want to deport me."

He nodded, glanced at my papers and sighed. "Si, yes, no problem. I'll take care of it," and proceeded to engage in a heated argument with the customs guy. I couldn't understand a word, but it appeared he was demanding me be let through. The agent motioned for security, Sr. Bernalga gestured for them to stay away. Now everyone in line glared at me. I closed my eyes. Everything's in order. Everything's in order.

Sr. Bernalga opened his billfold and counted out 400 pesos. The agent determinedly shook his head. Demanded 1000. Another discussion ensued. Finally, the agent stuffed the proffered money in his breast pocket, grinned and waved me through. As we left, Sr. Bernalga patted me on the shoulder again. "They always start too high. I'll take it out of your first paycheck."

CHAPTER 5

NEXT DAY I went to work at Coca-Cola's corporate office in the mail room, stapling papers, licking stamps and envelopes with other uneducated, unskilled native workers. My Spanish was limited to things like nosotros estamos comiendo albondigas para el almuerso or oh no, olvide mi cuarderno, really useful stuff I'd learned in high school, and they spoke little or no English, merely nodded and smiled benignly. They knew I was related to someone important in the company. Aware of my special treatment, better pay, even my daily intensive Berlitz Spanish lessons. Desperate to be my own man, I introduced myself to them as Isaac (my rarely used middle name), told them I was twenty-two years old, in Mexico to become fluent in Spanish before returning to the States to teach bilingually.

I'd practice my Spanish and they'd patiently correct my pronunciation, point to various objects about the office, have me identify them. A game for them, but an obsession for me. Determined to become reasonably fluent and rapidamente, I devoured everything Spanish. Would sit in the Bernalga's den watching Spanish television, trying to make sense of it. Attended dozens of subtitled movies. Watched a subtitled version of *Butch Cassidy and the Sundance Kid* multiple times until I could get the gist of the dialogue. Rode buses along the major avenues reading all the posted advertisements on billboards, in store windows, practicing, practicing, practicing, because otherwise I'd no one to talk to other than the Bernalga's and the senior people in the office who represented everything I was trying to escape. I'd sold my most prized possessions to find myself mired in a mindless job that would bring me no closer to finding my brother and establishing a new life and identity. Jerry would no doubt have called it a valuable life lesson, but I wanted a new life and that necessitated finding my own accommodations.

Mexico City, tucked in a valley of high plateaus, was blanketed in perpetual smog pierced daily by a torrential air-cleansing downpour at five p.m., a respite I used to walk the Paseo, acclimate to the high elevation, and search for new digs. I quickly discovered the City's squalid underbelly: slums choked with dirt floored tin huts inhabited by entire families, shared with chickens, pigs and goats, crammed so close together you could literally walk through one door into another. The aroma of garbage and human feces, laced with ubiquitous odors of tortillas, frijoles and roast pork, saturated the pollution-choked air. Starving dogs with bloated bellies scampering to and fro, whimpering, tails between legs. Pregnant Indian women barely more than children themselves squatted in the streets, faces prematurely aged, clothes despoiled by dirt and grime. They begged for money to feed babies wrapped in shawls on their backs, astride their laps and beside them in the street gutters. Their eyes, haunted by hunger and homelessness, were devoid of hope or desire. Simply trying to survive. I could have merged into this vast cauldron, but the dirt, squalor and suffering offended my sensibilities, forced me to take a broader view of the world that rendered trivial my self-importance and personal suffering, so I reoriented my search and secured accommodations in a small boarding house in the Bernalga's safe neighborhood and salved my conscience by giving pesos to every outstretched hand.

The boarding house was run by a squat, elderly woman, a doppelganger for my junior high school substitute teacher, Miss Catnack, right down to the pendulous breasts resting on her ostensible waist and the safety pin holding her blouse closed. Senora Siniestra assured me she kept a respectable house but her extravagantly rouged face, bright red lipstick, beehive of fluorescent red hair and layers of pancake makeup made me wonder if it was a boarding house for circus acts. One month's rent in advance assured my suitability and she showed me a room little larger than my closet in Huntington with a shared bathroom down the hall. The other residents included a blustery University student in his early twenties claiming kinship to the President of Mexico and a cross-dressing beautician who wore his hair coiffed in the early Beatles mop top shag style, fingers all bejeweled. Lastly, the denizen of the basement apartment. "He only ventures out at night when good Catholics are asleep," Senora Siniestra whispered while crossing herself. "He's a vampire, but his rent's always on time."

Absurd. But maybe true. One night, returning quite late after an evening spent getting sloshed on Pulque, a disgusting alcoholic beverage as viscous as seminal fluid that came in a rainbow of artificial flavors and colors, I saw a shape materialize out of the dark, unlit hallway and transpose into a man so completely swaddled in black only a pair of startled eyes stared back at me. I took a step back. Bela Lugosi had returned from the dead, only now emanating the same strong odor of formaldehyde as the fetal pigs I'd dissected in first year Biology. "Good evening," he said, holding out his gloved hand. "I wasn't expecting to meet anyone this time of night." I reluctantly shook it as he explained he suffered from a weird sounding skin disease called xeroderma pigmentosum (or at least that's what I thought I heard, being quite inebriated) and avoided sunlight. "A moon child." But I was only half listening, tapping my feet like I really had to pee, desperate to get away from him yet riddled with guilt for my unsympathetic reaction. Finally excusing myself, I ran upstairs, scrubbed my hands with soap and hot water to rid myself of his contagion and gazed into the bathroom mirror. Was he that part of me living in the shadows beneath the veneer of Isaac? I'd actively sought anonymity and disconnectedness; he'd no choice but to live it.

 I was desperately lonely. I'd left Beloit to kill the boy I was, forge a new identity, but he remained my reflection in the mirror. I couldn't open up to anyone. Share real feelings. That might unmask Isaac. Shatter everything. My friends Tex and Mex had lost control. Blown their minds on psychedelics. Experienced ego death, complete loss of their self-identities. A tantalizing thought. Unshackled. Freed of expectations. Of the need to constantly manufacture and manipulate reality. But that wasn't me. I was more like Hansel, venturing into the dark forest with Gretel, leaving behind a trail of crumbs, my LSD-laced weekends never truly uninhibited. Always tethered to Monday. I yearned to write Bart or Abby and unburden my soul, but they were Seth's friends, and I would not disinter him. The only person who'd possibly empathize had spurned me long ago and I, in turn, had destroyed him. Now I had to find him. I'd never be whole until I did.

CHAPTER 6

DROWNING IN OFFICE drudgery, Dave, one of the American salespeople working for Coca-Cola de Mexico, threw me a lifeline. He had a sales call in Orizaba in the Mexican tropics, a day's drive from Mexico City, and invited me along. A welcome respite and opportunity to see more of the country. He was from Atlanta, Georgia, corporate headquarters of Coca-Cola, had been stationed in Mexico for two years running subsidiary sales. Younger than Jerry, maybe early forties, with a blondish flat top cut that bespoke of time in the Service. The American flag tie clasp on his short sleeve button down white shirts warned me off any political discussions. His belly strained against the buttons as he sped out of the city. "How do you like Mexico so far?"

"I really haven't seen Mexico. All I've seen is the city."

"Makes no difference. It's all the same wherever you go in this stinking country; dirty and disgusting." Maybe so, but not the landscape. We climbed through a high desert pass, masses of crosses clustered at every curve in the road, the valley floor a thousand feet below. "That's where buses lost control and ran off the cliffs," Dave explained. "Bernalga told me about your problems with Customs. Typical. If they can't cheat ya, they'll kill you for a nickel."

The car danced across both sides of the yellow dashed line, eerily reminiscent of Grandpa Matthews' driving before Jerry made him surrender his license. Dave accelerated into every curve as we headed down into a verdant valley. I wanted to kill Seth, but I didn't want to die. "If that's how you feel, why'd you come down here?"

He looked me straight in the face. "Do you have any idea how much they're paying me?" I shook my head as a car came directly at us from the opposite direction, it's horn screeching. Dave, in the wrong lane, swerved to the right just in the nick of time, perilously close to the steep drop off. Completely nonplussed. "Everything's paid for: American school for my kids, the cook and housekeeper, plus I'm making twice what I'd make back home. Damn good reasons for dealing with these monkeys for a couple of years. Plus, there are some pretty nice side benefits. Nothing I'm gonna see back home. No way Jose!"

We arrived at the Hotel de Las Flores early evening; a two-story brown stucco hacienda surrounded by a riot of tropical flowers. Entered under a filigreed wrought iron archway opening into a terraced atrium. Water lilies floated lazily in a large pool. An odor of honeysuckle wafted through the air. Small lizards crawled up the sides of the building. Paradise.

I breakfasted on our balcony and, assuming the dreamlike quality of the hotel would permeate the surrounding town, decided to take a walk. Squalor everywhere. Flies buzzed about bloated carcasses of mongrel dogs in the street. Young mothers with vacant eyes squatted in the dirt abutting the outer wall of the hotel begging for coins to feed the small children at their side and babies on their backs. Shaken, I retreated to the hotel and lounged by the pool until Dave returned from his sales calls. "You want a real Mexican experience, right? Come on, get in the car. You're gonna love the place we're going. All the young guys come there; no pun intended!" The gleam in his eyes made me nervous. "There's two kinds of girls in Mexico, those you marry, those you fuck." He swerved across the dirt road, plumes of dust in his wake. "You're about to meet the second kind. Guys here only marry virgins, so unless their girlfriends take it up the ass, they've got to sow their wild oats somewhere, right? Not like all that free love crap you kids have now. They come here for a little action while their sweethearts remain pristine."

We approached a seedy looking U-shaped motel in the middle of nowhere. A broken electric sign over the entry emitted an intermittent buzz. Welcome to the Bates Motel. He pulled a box of Trojans from the side compartment. "Here. You'll need one of these for either hole."

Was this how I was finally going to lose my virginity? In a whore house? Reluctantly, I took one and shoved it in my pocket, and entered a theatre of the grotesque, casually attired men sitting in chairs or on bar stools fondling half naked teenage girls straddling their laps and dry-humping to incongruous bubblegum pop blaring from overhead speakers while disco balls suspended from the ceiling whirled in circles, bathing the club in eerie, strobe-like light. The aroma of human sweat and excretions, tequila and beer saturated the air. Men drank and joked with each other while girls jerked them off or gave them blowjobs. Nothing out of the ordinary. One guy actually pulled a girl dancing on the bar onto his lap, ripped her panties off and plowed into her until separated by a bouncer. "Saca a la puta de vuelta." The only apparent rule of the house.

One young girl, fourteen or fifteen at most, immediately straddled me, started lap dancing and demanded drinks. I pushed her off only to have another take her place, like cockroaches, impossible to be rid of. Skimpy sheer halters shimmered in the strobe light displaying barely pubescent merchandise. Fights broke out amongst girls vying for particular clients, tearing each other's clothes to enthusiastic cheers before bouncers separated them and sent them out back.

Dave knew most of the men, Coca-Cola factory employees, ordered several rounds and hoisted his glass in a salute to the Company, "the bringer of the feast," while groping a girl so young her breasts were little more than buds. Grabbing a handful of her hair he pulled her head down and shoved his dick down her throat, laughing as she struggled and gagged. Heads bobbed up and down along the bar front like engine pistons. The girl in my lap ground her sticky bottom into my crotch, mashed little pointy breasts in my face, tickled my cheek with stiff nipples. "You want suckee?" she cooed, lifting her top with one hand while rubbing my crotch with the other. I was aroused. I couldn't help it. I wanted to lose my virginity, but not this way. Not wallowing in the grossest display of sexual violence I'd ever witnessed. I just wanted to leave, but by now Dave was drunk and getting pissed off. He's brought me here to get laid. He'd already paid for that girl. Let her do her job. Impatient with my lack of enthusiasm, the girl grabbed my arm and pulled me off the stool. As she led me out back Dave shouted "And don't let that whore squeeze more money out of you and use that condom. God knows what diseases she has."

She drew me into a squalid little room for my allotted one-hour, the only furniture a thin mildewed mattress covered with dirty, cum-stained sheets and a rusty metal folding chair. Stretching out on the bed she splayed her legs as invitingly as the Panty Raid girl, but that's where the comparison ended. All I saw on that cot was a kid trying to survive. I collapsed on the chair. Told her I didn't want sex. She misunderstood, turned over and spread her cheeks. "You want fuckee this way?" When I shook my head, she relaxed and smiled like the little kid she was, probably happy for the respite between men. I heard sounds of sweaty, slapping bodies. Screeches of rusty mattress springs. Male grunts and girlish moans. Cries to satisfy egos, virgins for the umpteenth time that day. I focused on the chirps of crickets ticking off every second of an hour that lasted a hellish eternity.

Dave, drunk as a skunk, drove like a maniac back to the hotel, sideswiped several cars and ran over a dog. "Nice piece of ass, huh? I fucked my tight little bitch so hard she won't be able to sit for a week." I gawked at him. She was just a little girl. How could he treat another human being like that? "Those girls are receptacles."

Back at the hotel I quickly stuffed my few things in my small backpack and left, pushing aside his anxious attempts to stop me. "Don't worry," I spat out, "I'm not going to tell anybody," and walked to the local bus terminal under a starlit sky, letting the symphony of crickets and the scent of tropical flowers cleanse the taint as I checked the schedule for the next bus for Mexico City and ruminated on fate while compulsively twirling the ring that by rights wasn't mine. If I hadn't snitched on Jonah would our lives have taken different trajectories? Did it matter? I did what I did, what I was fated to do, and was exactly where I was meant to be. Alone, in the middle of nowhere, my teeth chattering in the cool evening air. A feral dog approached and pressed his emaciated body against my legs seeking what little warmth I had. I petted him, scratched behind his ears and he made whimpering sounds, overwhelmed by my gesture of acknowledgement. My eyes flooded with tears.

CHAPTER 7

RETURNING TO THE office two mornings later, I went directly into Senor Morales' office and quit. He protested. "We sent you to Orizaba. We're paying for your Spanish lessons. Where will you go? What am I supposed to tell your uncle?" I almost gagged when he suggested I join Dave on another sales call.

"You've been great to me, and I'll make sure my uncle knows, but I gotta go. You can tell them I'm searching for my brother."

Keeping goodbyes short, I was out the door within the hour and stood on the sidewalk jostled about by the teeming human traffic. What now? Where was I supposed to go? What about my room, my stuff? The dense humid smog pressed in on me like a wetsuit. Perhaps I'd been too hasty. Maybe Morales would give me my job back if I returned to the office right now.

Awaiting a sign, I espied a tall, athletic looking guy striding down the cross street. He had wavy black hair, a goatee and a deep tan. It was Jonah! I took off after him, brushing past people, trying to keep him in sight. Get a better view to be sure, but he had a long stride. I couldn't close the gap. I darted across the busy street, ignored the blaring horns, screeching brakes, colorful rebukes, vainly shouting his name over the cacophony of street noise. Catching up at last I grabbed ahold of his shirt, wheezing for air as thick as pea soup. "Jonah . . . it's me . . . stop." He spun around. Punched me in the gut. I fell to my knees and stared up at him. His face, it wasn't Jonah's face. The nose too small, the eyes hazel, not brown. I was crushingly disappointed. "You're not him," I croaked. Pedestrians, desensitized to the sight of bodies on the streets, walked over me.

He extended a hand and pulled me up. "What do you mean, I'm not him?"

"My brother. I thought you were my brother. You're kind of built like him and I just assumed . . . I've got to find him."

He swept his arms in a circle. "In this crazy city?"

"Somewhere in Mexico."

"Wow, talk about quixotic, eh? Everywhere I go in this fucking city someone's yelling gibberish at me, trying to steal my camera or pick my pocket. Sorry I hit you. He extended his hand. "I'm Terry, on my own odyssey."

"Can I join you?"

He snapped his fingers. "Just like that? Don't you want to know where I'm going? You got a name, or should I call you Homer?"

"It's Se... Isaac, and it doesn't matter. He could be anywhere. And I speak Spanish. Pretty useful. That's the gibberish you referred to." As on cue, he was accosted by a couple of beggars who grabbed onto him, one demanding money while the other tried to wrest the Pentax camera off his neck. I shooed them away. "No molesta, no molesta. Dejanos en paz ahora mismo."

"Christ! Those little buggers are all over the place. Mistook you for one. Your gibberish is pretty good."

He frowned. "Tell you what. We'll give it a trial run, but I may end up telling you to get lost. Agreed?" We shook on it. "Like Don Quixote and Sancho Panza, eh?"

Terry was twenty-five, from Montreal, with a master's degree in Electrical Engineering from McGill University, taking a long excursion to Tierra Del Fuego, hiking most of the way. I asked how long the journey would take and he merely shrugged. "However long it takes. I'm in no hurry. Not anymore."

I gave him my new bio, same old bullshit, glibber with each performance, and he spent the night on the floor of my room in the boarding house. Senora Siniestra demanded he pay for the night's lodging, mollified when I offered her my tennis racket and any clothes I couldn't fit into my small daypack in exchange. That was Seth's stuff. He was dead. I had two hundred dollars in my pocket. I'd figure out the rest on the fly.

CHAPTER 8

WE BOARDED THE third-class bus for Merida and settled into a dilapidated bench seat. I turned to Terry and asked why he'd agreed to let me come along. "You looked desperate. I know the feeling." There was more to Terry than he was revealing, but we all have our secrets. "And you speak Spanish, so I figured what the hell. Just goin' with the flow." He started to laugh as a suitcase ran squealing down the aisle, chased by its owners. "A mobile pigskin leather suitcase. That's something I've never seen back home."

A litany of farm animals followed. Cages of chickens and roosters, birds pecking at you through slots of metal cages as their owners brushed past. Even a goat. The old bus rocked and reeked as more people and animals boarded until every seat and the entire aisle was filled to overcapacity.

The guy behind us put his hands on our shoulders. "Amigos, when people travel, they take their most valuable possessions with them. You get used to it. My name is Manuel. Mucho gusto. I am returning home for my little sister's wedding. I live in L.A. now, own an Esso gas station there. An American citizen. In Merida, I'm a pretty big deal. I send money to my parents regularly. They live well."

I turned and shook his hand. "I'm Isaac; he's Terry. We're headed down the Yucatan coast."

Manuel and I chatted for most of the twenty-four-hour bus ride while Terry snoozed, oblivious to the squeals, clucks and barks and a driver who thought he was Mario Andretti. Hairpin turns on narrow, steep roads periodically marked with clusters of crosses. Every time I nodded off, I was startled awake by sounds of the barnyard or pecked at, but my new traveling buddy could sleep through an atomic explosion.

Manuel invited us to stay with his family and attend his sister's wedding, and we were received as honored friends of the prodigal son, the successful American entrepreneur. His family home was timber-framed, the walls stucco.

Three rooms, one for living, two for sleeping, divided by sex. Colorful hand-woven blankets adorned the walls, the floors cool terracotta, a good thing as it was incredibly muggy, the air so moist and thick you pushed your way through it. The bathroom, I was informed, was out back, but where? There were lots of chickens, dogs, cats, a goat tied up to a wooden post, an abundance of robust vegetables, tomatoes, peppers of all sorts, greens and other unfamiliar stuff, as well as oranges, lemons, mangoes and plantains, even sweet baby bananas growing in large bunches on tropical trees with fan-like leaves, but no outhouse. His mother led me over to pungent-smelling rows of big, healthy looking tomato plants. "Por favor, ve a las plantas de tomate." I held my breath and did my best to oblige, but chickens immediately attacked my poop with gusto, gobbling it up as it hit the ground. I cleansed myself with a garden hose. I wasn't going to eat any chicken. Mole sauce? Forget about it.

 The wedding was held in Merida's ornate Catholic church, all richly marbled and gilded in gold leaf. A large statue of Jesus on the Cross stared down from the chancel and I wondered what he'd think about the gross accumulation of wealth in His name when poverty and squalor prevailed outside its walls. A grand fiesta followed. Colorful lanterns strung across the plaza grande abutting the cathedral, tables laden with an array of platters, rice, beans, pork, plantains, tropical fruits and tortillas, all under spotlighted archways. Tequila flowed and we danced and drank with other men into the wee hours of the morning to a mariachi band. Young women in attendance were very proper, always in groups, giggling amongst themselves as they wafted the still air with ornate hand fans, supervised by dour-looking black-clad grandmothers who chillingly reminded me of Death in Bergman's *The Seventh Seal*. Any approach, any attempt at conversation greeted by lowered eyes and blushes, fans aflutter. Asking them to dance impossible. But something about them tugged at me. Girls so wholesome. So attractive in their comportment, doe-eyed and innocent. I felt guilty. Wished I'd never confronted the reality of those poor teenage prostitutes in Orizaba who paid the price for this purity much as I preferred to think meat came neatly prepackaged and had nothing to do with a real cow.

 I lay awake that night trying to make sense of my feelings. Mexico's sexual attitudes were horribly inequitable, totally sexist, but were they much better back home? I considered Lucy's comments. Male attitudes hadn't changed. Sexual freedom still a one-way proposition despite The Pill. I was a pig, little better than Dave, and Bart's sarcastic suggestion I join the campus virgin society may have tasted bitter, but he was dead on. And Ashley, whose feelings I'd abused, had understood me better than I knew myself. My fragile male ego would never have withstood her experience. Christ Almighty. Even uncool virginal Sinead had more integrity than me.

CHAPTER 9

ONE OF THE wedding guests mentioned he'd met an American expatriate draft dodger named Frank who lived with his wife and child in an obscure Mayan Indian village, Playa del Carmen, a half day's drive across the Yucatan peninsula to the east coast. I got excited. Maybe he'd know Jonah. I explained we planned to walk the coastline in that direction and he laughed. "Que locura!" It would be a many days' journey. And solitary. We'd encounter nothing other than the ocean, sand, jungle, abandoned Mayan ruins and the occasional, sparsely populated village. "No tienes un coche?" he asked. I shook my head. "Entonces toma el autobus. No es caro. Todara la mayor parte del dia en llegar." Maybe, but I'd no money to waste on another bus ride and no desire to let Terry know I was cash constrained, so when he asked for a translation, I told him Playa del Carmen was a tropical paradise a pleasant stroll down the coast from Progresso and a guy there might know my brother or have some idea of his whereabouts.

Expressing gratitude to Manuel and his family for their hospitality we set off for Progresso, about two days walk from Merida on a single lane dirt road through a tropical jungle. We stuck out our thumbs every time an RV roared passed, almost always American tourists with Texas plates who left us choking on their dust. My clothes clung. My blue jeans rubbed against plump thighs. Every step a painful reminder of Seth's bulk. But I persevered. What Hemingway would do.

In the late afternoon we left the road and entered the jungle, seeking shelter for the night. Like explorers, we slashed through curtains of dense jungle and hanging vines, shredding a millennium of civilization as we clambered blocks of shattered walls, broken archways and crumbling foundations. I thought about Jonah and me, our adventures in Alley Pond Park, as we threaded our way deeper, the jungle now so thick it formed a canopy overhead. Suddenly, Terry stopped and placed a finger to his lips. "Can you hear that," he whispered. "Feel that chill?" Sweating profusely, my jeans and shirt smeared with sticky residue of succulents and grime, I stood very still, ears attuned to sound of movement, but could only feel the draft of cold air. It felt good.

Continuing on warily, perhaps twenty paces ahead we almost bumped into the base of a stone wall. Pushing aside vines and bramble, we realized we stood at the base of a monolithic structure. A pyramid. It was mystical, like out of nowhere. Like the magical village of Brigadoon appearing out of the mist in the Broadway musical I'd seen as a child. I craned my neck to see the steep, narrow external stairway disappear into the canopy of trees above us. It was draftier here, even colder, and Terry pointed to a gash in the vegetation. A hole. Perhaps an entryway. "That cold draft air is coming from there."

I spread my arms wide and drank in the rush of cold air. It gave me goosebumps. I didn't want to move, but Terry shoved bramble aside and peered into the pitch darkness and suggested we check it out. What lurked there? I visualized a den of jaguars. Poisonous snakes. Spiders. Or worse. Nothingness. Like my nightmare. I could smell my own fear. I stood frozen. My heart thump, thump, thumped in my chest. "No, we can't go in. We don't have a flashlight."

Terry reached into his pants pocket and extracted a Bic lighter. "We have this," he said, flicking it and proceeding into the gap, immediately swallowed by the darkness. "Don't be a wuss. Where's your sense of adventure, eh?"

I trembled with déjà vu. My nightmare. But the thought of being left alone drove me forward, deeper and deeper into the cave-like interior. The temperature dropped precipitously. The air pungent with decay, like greens left too long in the fridge. The flickering Bic flame had a strobe-light effect, like in the old silent films. "Is this cool or what?" Terry said, standing at the base of an internal stairway that disappeared into darkness. Without awaiting a reply, he began the ascent, me scurrying to keep him within arm's length. The stone steps were narrow and slippery. Maintaining a foothold challenging. The walls, dank and matted with spongy moss, closed in on me. My pulse raced. I perspired despite the cold draft. Suddenly, the flame from his lighter sputtered and went out, engulfing us in blackness so absolute I couldn't see anything, not my hands in front of my face.

Gasping for air, utterly alone, I cried out in fear. Terry flicked his Bic again, immersing us in a nimbus of light. His face all ghost-like shadows but still there. Just a few steps ahead. I reached out and touched his corporeal back. There was a glimmer of light ahead. We continued climbing, the air thinner, the humidity less oppressive and musty. At the peak, the setting sun, a giant blood-red orb on the horizon, cast a glow on a stone table, an altar, and as I grasped ahold of it to steady myself, a vibration coursed through me, and I saw the ghosts of ancient inhabitants who'd lived and loved and died here moving about the time-eroded remains of what must have been a vast city. Nature had reclaimed all. It was humbling, like looking at the remains of sand castles after the tide swept in, or at a starlit sky of celestial bodies long gone, as we would be in but a speck of time, all our human strivings for naught. That night we bivouacked at the foot of the pyramid. The real Mexico at last.

We arrived at the coastal village of Progresso the next afternoon and were watching natives spearfish for barracuda off the town dock when I noticed a Pharmacia across the street. I went in, assuming it my last opportunity to procure aloe for my inflamed thighs, and holy shit, amphetamines were displayed at the register, not locked away, not White Cross but Dexedrine, way stronger and unbelievably cheap. Stealthily placing a bottle on the counter with the skin ointment, I held my breath, already experiencing the craving, expecting the cashier to demand a prescription. Prepared to say oops mi error! But he simply rang it up! No ID, nothing. Crazy. I quickly grabbed a second bottle, and he rang that up as well. Who knew if I'd encounter another such opportunity. Why take chances? This was what Isaac needed. I popped two tabs before leaving the store. I didn't want Terry to see; he might not approve.

We slept on the beach that night, or Terry did anyway. I was still buzzing. And next morning, with the sun spreading like amber syrup over water smooth as glass, dark shadows of palm trees shapeshifting on the sand like finger puppets against a vivid screen, we began our long journey down the coastline on a sand bar sandwiched between the turquoise sea and verdant tropical forest, heat undulating off fine white sand which in the distance appeared a molten glass lake. A hot breeze seared my pale, unprotected skin. I shielded my eyes from the brutal sun. My lips cracked and blistered. My sweaty jeans clung to heavy thighs and chafed with every step despite liberal applications of aloe. I almost regretted leaving the white tennis shorts and floppy hat back at the rooming house, but they'd been purchased by Mitzie for Seth and he was dead, so I sizzled like lard in a pan until evening when a cool ocean breeze chased the heat and we bivouacked on the beach under starlit skies, me cocooned like a burrito in a large beach towel Manuel had given me, mesmerized by the symphony of rippling palm fronds, chirping tropical birds and waves lapping upon the shore. And the next day we did it again. And again. The days passing in a sort of mindless, relaxed monotony, though I never felt more alive or energetic. We explored ancient Mayan ruins perched on the coastal cliffs. Bathed in the ocean. Ate opportunistically, mostly fresh corn tortillas purchased at tiny pueblos passed along the way, augmented by baby bananas and juice from wild lemons and limes we harvested in the jungle. Terry consumed most of the tortillas. I contentedly munched jalapeno peppers, which satiated my hunger along with the speed, though they burned on both ends. Especially the tail end. I had molted Seth's skin. I was Isaac. Adventuring into the unknown.

We reached the east side of the peninsula after a week or so and bedded down at a rather desolate spot called Kan Kun. The jungle upended. Palm trees slashed and burned. A makeshift road scarred the length of the long sandbar enclosed in cyclone fencing. Terry noticed a large sign and asked me to translate. A government of Mexico project for a new resort. Terry was glad to be making this journey now, and that night, overcome by curiosity, I asked him why he'd embarked on this long trek. He countered "What are you running away from?" A quest to find my brother. "Yeah, so you told me." He shook sand out of his sleeping back and rolled a towel for a pillow. "Who's lost, Isaac, him or you? Wasn't it Hemingway who once wrote *You can't get away from yourself by moving from one place to another*. Come on. Let's get some sleep."

CHAPTER 10

I IMMEDIATELY SOUGHT out Frank when we arrived in Playa del Carmen, but the Mayan villagers said he'd left for Merida several days earlier with his daughter to get mail. His wife was visiting family in the States. As no one spoke English I struggled to describe Jonah as best I could in Spanish. "No conozco a este hombre," one of them responded. Terry drank in the idyllic setting, the thatched huts, the white sand beach and palm forest and tossed his backpack on the sand. Ready for a vacation, he suggested we hang out until Frank returned, and the villagers, assuming we were Frank's friends, invited us to fish with them in the morning. They appeared far healthier and happier than the indigenous Indians in the City.

We bedded down that night under a canopy of stars. Terry struck a match and lit a cigarette, his eyes glowing like embers as he took a drag. Wrapped in my towel I tossed palm fronds onto our beach fire. A ring of light. Our shadows melted into darkness. Sparks, like little Tinker Bells, slowly ascended the cobalt sky as I anxiously twirled the ring on my finger, still hopped up on my daily dose of Dexedrine. Everything was too ideal, too comfortable. Too good to be true. Terry motioned to the ring. "That's a really bad habit you have. Wish you'd stop."

"Sorry. This ring is special, Jonah's most precious possession. Grandpa Matthews gave it to him the day of his Bar Mitzvah. I was eight at the time. Jonah practically worshipped him." Terry nodded. Took another draw. "He'd trekked across Europe to the States to avoid conscription in the Russian army, the Matthews family's first draft dodger! Kind of ironic. See the initials? JM. Stood for Julius, his great grandfather's name; Jonah entrusted it to me for safekeeping."

"Why; what happened to him?"

"Got into an argument with Jerry, his dad, about serving in Vietnam. He was about to graduate from college in . . ." I furiously twirled the ring. Fuck. That makes Jonah twenty-four, only two years older than me. Think fast. ". . . in

1964, when LBJ was ramping up the war. Jonah told him he wouldn't go, had a huge fight, and left."

"Why do you keep saying 'His grandfather', 'His dad,' and for God's sake, will you please stop fidgeting with that ring; it's driving me crazy."

"I'm adopted. Only Jonah ever treated me like family. The ring signifies he's still with me, alive, somewhere. It gives me hope."

Terry was incredulous. Couldn't believe so many years had passed without contact. Convinced there was more to the story. I tried to explain that draft dodgers stayed in touch through something called the War Resisters League, and maybe Frank would know something about him, but Terry insisted Jonah would have found some way to let us know he was okay. "Well, you're wrong," I bristled, sucking on my ring finger. It was bleeding. I felt edgy. "I don't wanna be interrogated."

Terry tossed more palm fronds on the fire. "Sorry. No offense meant. Go on. I'm listening."

"We'd go to the park near our house. He'd always bring peanuts. Squirrels ate out of his hand, no kidding! He had this way about him, an aura of calm, of oneness with nature, like Siddhartha. One time some teenage boys threw rocks at squirrels and killed one. He cried, told me how wrong it was to hurt other living things...."

"The second coming of Jesus, eh? Come on, Isaac! I'm sure he had his flaws. My kid brother is eighteen and believe me, we get in each other's face from time to time! You sometimes remind me of him. Think you might be seeing things through rose-colored glasses, eh?"

"No, Terry. He was the best big brother. Preferred my company over anyone's." I abruptly rose, stomach suddenly lurching, and stumbled toward the shore as a blurred image, a memory, came into focus.

Abby and me sitting on a bench in Washington Square Park feeding pigeons, listening to shaggy-haired buskers mimic Bob Dylan's *Freewheelin'* sound, Abby stoned, blathering away about getting close to the Fillmore stage for The Who concert. I'm distracted. Half listening. What's Jonah doing on the other side of the park with some guy? Out of context, him so far from Morningside Heights. Abby's prattling something about throwing her panties at Daltrey. I rise, start across the park. They're leaning against the Arch locked in passionate embrace. Maybe ten feet away I clear my throat. Loudly. Say hello. Jonah's startled. Looks directly at me. No sign of recognition. Merely curls his lips in a sneer. Turns to his lover. Murmurs something. Exits the park without so much as acknowledging my presence. Just like that. Like I didn't exist. Dizzy, I grasp the Arch for support, eyes wide shut with déjà vu. Dark forest. Gnarly limbs. Fear so tangible it's pungent. How could he? I'd kept my end of the bargain. I'd kept his secret. He was supposed to love me. A stabbing pain. A dart through my heart. The strangest tingling sensation. Spiders crawling up my spine. Black dots scurrying across my face. Blinding rage. Go away. Go away. I'm smashing my head against the Arch until they disappear.

Terry stood up and walked toward the shoreline. "Hey Isaac, you okay? Kinda chilly for an evening swim, eh?" I ignored him and waded into the water until the bottom fell away.

Abby's scolding me. Pissed I'd walked away from her mid-sentence. I'm fighting back tears, biting hard on my lip, but I can't stem them. She notices the blood. Asks if that was Jonah by the Arch. Why am I so upset? What did he say to me? Nothing. He said nothing. She reaches out, pulls my head tight against her chest and coos "It's okay, Seth, it's going to be okay" but I can't stop crying because it hadn't been okay since the day Jonah told me the truth about myself. Since the day I was born and abandoned.

Terry stood at the water's edge. Upset, he yelled "Come back to shore now. I don't wanna have to come in after you."

The Who are dynamite. Pete wind-milling his guitar, Keith ballistic on drums, but I'm watching Daltrey as he swings his microphone like a lariat, speaking directly to me, to all my pain and hurt. I'm going out of my mind, dizzy in the head, getting funny dreams again and again and suddenly with a burst of clarity I know what I will do. Must do. Make Jonah experience what it feels like to be me, alone and unloved. Invisible. Shatter his wonder boy image. Knock him down a few pegs.

I dove under a breaker so Terry wouldn't hear me crying. I'd never intended to burn down the house. I'd just wanted them to see me. To actually see me. I surfaced and swam back to shore. Stood shivering by the fire. Terry tossed me his towel. "Dry off with this. You have to sleep in the other one. Everything okay?"

"Yeah, thanks." Abby was seeing me that day. Why hadn't I focused on that?

We listened to all the noise in the silence that ensued. The waves lapping on the shore. The embers rising toward the twinkling stars. The rustle of wind through the palm fronds. "Jonah used to meet me after school at the Five & Dime for milkshakes..." Swirling in circles on the counter seat. "He'd make me promise not to tell Mitzie."

"Your mom I presume?"

"If you insist. She always harped about my weight, put me on diets. Only made me eat more. My friends poked fun of the stuff she packed in my lunch box. Jonah said ignore her and everyone else. He'd always be there for me." *You gonna drink that whole milkshake, fat boy?*

"Yet you're looking for him, eh?" Terry scrunched up the top of his sleeping bag to form a pillow. "Let's get some sleep." He rolled on his side. "G'night, Isaac."

I SAT AWHILE staring into the moonlit water. Recalled the Sabbath evening services we attended with Grandpa Matthews, his pride as Jonah, his adored grandchild, participated in his first Minyan the week after his Bar Mitzvah. Old men qvelled. Gave Jonah schnapps and honey cake. Told Grandpa he had a Jewish scholar in the making and me, sitting there invisible, so desperate for his affection I practiced my Hebrew without being nudged. Paid avid attention to my Hebrew school teachers so I'd be the best Torah student, the best Bar Mitzvah, better than Jonah, and Grandpa would take me to services and be so proud and qvell over me. But he died when I was ten and the only person who'd bear witness to my dedication, the only person who'd know I'd strived for perfection, was Jonah.

Grandpa Matthews had given Jonah his ring, the ring I now wore, to carry forward an unbroken tradition spanning generations and I clenched my fist tightly, cold metal digging into soft flesh, and flashed on the exhaust spewing from Jonah's cycle before I turned my back on him. *And it came to pass . . . that Cain rose up against Abel his brother and slew him.* God help me.

CHAPTER 11

EVERY MORNING THE village kids would excitedly shake us awake. "Es hora de pescar!" And every morning I'd rub my eyes, pee behind a palm tree and swallow two tabs of Dexedrine. Another beautiful day.

We'd grab our bamboo poles and join the line of men in the shallow water, the women bearing a huge, wide net perhaps one hundred yards away. We'd walk toward them beating the sticks rhythmically, everyone smiling, everyone singing, herding swarming fish into the net where, once trapped, they were dragged ashore, gutted, staked and smoked. Every day. Bounty from the sea, cocoanuts, bananas and other tropical fruits from the jungle, the essentials sustaining life. This was a tropical heaven unsullied by civilization where time was irrelevant, and I vainly attempted to be totally in the moment, as I had at Beloit when I was high, only now frolicking with people who lived like real hippies, so free and easy, and I saw myself as Christian in *Mutiny on the Bounty*, my best performance to date, yet still a performance. Seth kept clawing his way to the surface, through fissures in Isaac's skin, obsessively harping on Frank's imminent return and the inevitability of Isaac's demise, and as the moon waxed and waned that voice became deafening, impossible to drown out despite doubling my daily dose of Dexedrine. If I didn't leave now, while a spark of Isaac remained, he would disappear.

The villagers suggested we seek Frank on Isla Mujeres. Apparently, he had a vacation home there, a place to unwind from the stress of his utopian existence at Playa del Carmen. Lucky for me Terry liked the sound of that—The Isle of Women—and agreed. Traveling with him was dynamite, like having a big brother again, and as before, it was a several days' trek up the coast to Puerto Juarez, where we'd catch the ferry to the island. My raspberry thighs were still a painful remnant of Seth, but thanks to the speed I was no longer him. I was Isaac, fearless risk taker who braved the unknown, traversed jungles, survived on wild bananas and tortillas, ready for anything in a wide-open world. Even my jeans seemed a tad looser, though my reflection in the sea was still a fat boy's.

CHAPTER 12

BY THE TIME we boarded the early morning ferry in mid-afternoon my heart literally hammered in my chest. I bounced from stern to bow like a Mexican jumping bean, energy surging, hyper-sensitized to my surroundings—the iridescent water, its salty, herby fragrance, the azure sky, the waves lapping against the hull—and as we approached the island the whisper of tropical winds ruffling through palm fronds dotting the coastline. Upon landfall, the other passengers headed for the three small hotels in the Centro, but we immediately strode off in the opposite direction towards the cliff caves on the uninhabited part of the island, free accommodations our Mayan friends had recommended. I ambled over boulders with alacrity urging Terry to keep up.

The pounding ocean surf on the north side of the island had over millennia carved shallow caves in the rock-face and after finding a suitable one there was no changing our minds. Darkness fell like a velvet curtain at sunset. My eyes adjusted to the dim light of a quarter moon, my ears to the waves crashing against the rocks like claps of thunder. The ocean glowed with an eerie phosphorescence. The sky glittered with overlapping layers of diamonds. And I experienced it all through Isaac's eyes. Terry offered me tortillas from his backpack, but I passed. I wasn't hungry. My body was still humming.

Awakening early, I peered out from the mouth of the shallow cave that served as our shelter. The sun was on the cusp of the horizon. Several small silver-green iguanas had nestled against me during the night. Diminutive copies of terrifying creatures from the silent film *The Lost World* I'd seen on the small TV screen as a little kid, cute in a hideous way. Did they bite? I lay still. Watched the rising sun radiate shimmering gold tentacles across the sea's surface until nature demanded I rise and seek a place to relieve myself. The skittish iguanas scurried away. Head foggy, jaw aching, I worked out the kinks in my back after sleeping on the hard rock surface and swallowed two more tabs before traversing slippery boulders to find a good spot, each step over the boulders treacherous as the sun played tricks with light and shadow. Stumbling, I lurched forward and fell flat on my face, arms outstretched to break the fall, and Jonah's ring flew off my finger into a deep crevasse. Momentarily dazed, I heard a metallic clinking as the ring ricocheted off rock on its descent, and at that moment a shaft of light descended from the Heavens, merciful God casting a spotlight on the ring atop a patch of sand some thirty feet below. I impulsively descended the fissure to retrieve it, banging my head against hard rock as I clung to wet and slimy stones for hand and footholds, heart pounding in my chest. I'd sold my soul for that ring; the thought of losing it too unbearable to contemplate, and maybe five feet from bottom, so close, so tantalizingly close I could almost reach out and touch it, a thunderous roar overhead engulfed me in sea water. The ring washed out to sea.

I slowly ascended into the light. Fell to my knees and cried for my godforsaken soul. I pounded my fists on the boulders until they were bloodied. God was implacable. That ring, that coveted piece of metal, was my only tangible connection to Jonah, imbued with his spirit, something I'd desperately clung to in the hope my terrible sin could still be expunged by his forgiveness. Absent that, I had to accept it was me who was lost. Me I had to find. Me I had to forgive.

Returning to the cave Terry asked about my bruises. I told him I'd tripped on some rocks, a scant truth. I said nothing of the ring, fearing he'd go his own way if he knew my quest for Jonah was over. Leaving our stuff in the cave we walked to town to bathe in the sea water, stopping first at a small mercado for food. Terry was hungry. The vendor, busy chopping cocoanuts, looked me up and down and suggested I try one with a shot of Bacardi's rum. A Loco Coco. I purchased a fifth and two cocoanuts. "Let's go to the beach."

I poured rum on my wounds, surreptitiously downed two more tabs with a swig, the rest into the coconuts. We got totally sloshed and dozed, awakened to a distinct chill in the air and darkening sky and realized we'd never find our way back to the cave.

Perusing the beach for somewhere to crash we knocked at the nicest beach shack, an octagonal structure, and explained our situation to a guy around Terry's age, shaggy-haired and bearded, a small sunburned blond child, a scruffy looking little thing with dreadlocked hair, peering out from between his legs, her hazel eyes big and curious. I made eye contact and smiled. She hid behind the man's thigh, then peered out again, playing peekaboo with me. Could this be Frank and his small child? It seemed an unlikely coincidence. I hedged my bets and explained our situation in imperfect Spanish. "Nosotros arruinamos. Quedarse dormido en la playa. Estamos durmiendo en una cueva y no podemos volver alli."

He looked me over and responded "Cave camping's illegal. And dangerous. Big trouble if the Federales catch you . . . Well, you're stuck now; you can crash here tonight." He smiled, held out his hand and introduced himself as Frank. This couldn't be a coincidence. This was fate, and I told him we'd awaited him in Playa del Carmen before journeying here, hoping he might know or have heard something about my missing brother. He invited us inside and offered us food. When I declined, Terry quipped "Don't you ever get hungry? Man can't live on jalapeno peppers alone."

His yurt was covered with bamboo thatch, the beds against one wall, the rest an all-purpose space. Frank rolled a joint and we sat cross legged on a bamboo rug over the sand floor. He took a hit and passed it to his daughter who mimicked him, slowly exhaling before passing it on to me with a cute little grin. I shrugged, took a hit and passed it on, and so it went until his daughter passed out and he placed her in one of the beds, opened a bottle of tequila, took a swig, and said he'd had no choice but to leave the US after his draft board refused him Conscientious Objector status. He'd no intention of fighting an immoral war or going to jail to make an anti-war statement like Joan Baez's husband, David Harris. It had taken a year for his mom to convince his father a live son was better than a dead hero, that Vietnam wasn't worth dying for.

"Same with my older brother. He and Jerry fought bitterly about the war. Split a month before graduating from college. Just took off. Mentioned going to Mexico. Now Jerry's views on the war have changed and he can't forgive himself for driving Jonah away. I hope he left the country and got somewhere safe. I need to find him."

"How'd you avoid the draft?"

"Uh, guess I just got lucky. High lottery number."

Terry suddenly looked alarmed. "Isaac, where's your ring?"

"I lost it in the rocks by the cave."

"But that ring was so important to you . . ."

"It was just a ring, okay? Don't make a big deal of it." I turned to Frank and described Jonah, perpetuating the charade. "Tall, thin, dark complexion, kinda like Terry. You run into anyone like that?"

"Your opposite, huh? Sorry, man. There are so many of us. I don't know him but I'm sure he's okay. He knows the deal; you have to lay low. Sounds paranoid, but we are being watched. I hope you find him, and he reconciles with you all someday." He took a deep draw on the bottle and passed it to me. "Well, it's getting pretty late. Time to turn in. You guys okay on the floor? Got a couple of blankets in that basket."

Terry grabbed them. "Yeah, man, perfect."

I had that dream again. *Jonah and I are in our space ship exploring unchartered reaches of outer space, powering past planets and other comets when suddenly a huge meteor heads directly toward us, and we veer our craft to the left, then right, trying to avoid an imminent collision but it's too late, we go careening off course, heading for a black hole, and I reach out to Jonah but he's a jack-in-the-box, grinning and boinging up and down singing "All around the mulberry bush the monkey chased the weasel. The monkey thought 'twas all in fun. Pop! Goes the weasel" and our escape hatch opens, sucking all the air, and me, from our ship, and I tumble alone and powerless into the vast black vacuum of space heading toward a black hole and I'm so scared, so scared, so scared.*

I woke, temples thumping. Ginger Baker executing a drum roll on my head. I looked about me. Jonah next to me, asleep on the floor. I'd found him! I excitedly roused him, but it was Terry who sat up. "What the fuck's going on?"

"I . . . I thought you were my brother. I keep seeing him in this dream. We're playing spacemen and we hit a meteor or asteroid and I reach out to him, but he turns into a jack-in-the-box, and I'm sucked into space and I'm falling through darkness and . . ."

"Go back to sleep, man. It's those fuckin' jalapenos."

Maybe the dream freaked me out because it contained so many elements of reality. Jonah and I had played spacemen on Grandpa Matthews' front porch during the monthly family circle meetings. All the ancient relatives, great aunts and uncles who'd journeyed to America from the shtetls in the old country, coming together to help each other, and eat babka, strudel and rugelach. We'd imagine we were our favorite intrepid astronauts, Jonah always the captain issuing orders, me his loyal first mate responsible for powering our spaceship by feverishly working the foot pedals on Grandpa's antique Singer sewing machine, exploring galaxies and distant stars. But what was on the other side of that black hole?

Next day we returned to our cave to collect our belongings. "I'm sorry he couldn't tell you anything about your brother. Maybe he went to Canada. Lots of guys did."

"Jonah liked warm weather. And when he and Jerry had their big fight he only mentioned Mexico. Nothing's been the same since he left. Just emptiness."

"I know how you feel, man. Shit happens."

I walked over to the crevasse where I'd lost Jonah's ring. How would he possibly know? Tears trickled down my cheeks. Before Jonah stormed out of the house, he'd removed Grandpa Matthews ring and placed it on the kitchen counter. He didn't give it to me. He didn't ask me to safeguard it for him. It wasn't a gift to remember him by. I'd simply absconded with it because I coveted it.

CHAPTER 13

BACK AT THE cave, Terry was rolling up his sleeping bag. It was time to push on. A long way to Tierra Del Fuego. As I feared, he asked what my plans were now; did I think Jonah had ventured further south? I told him I didn't know. My ring finger ached. Don't amputees often feel lost limbs? "I was kind of hoping I could continue on with you, if that's okay."

"You okay money-wise?"

"No worries." I'd make it work somehow.

He unfolded a map. "The farther south we go the warmer, and I assumed I'd go through Belize, but I've also heard Oaxaca is this incredible place. Supposedly a backpacker's Mecca, but definitely a longer trip. See, look here on the map. Almost double the distance."

"Well, you said you weren't in a hurry. Let's stick out our thumbs, let fate decide."

"Fine, but this time let's bus back to Merida and try our fortune from there." Fuck. I'm going to run out of money.

Outside of Merida, a Volkswagen bug sputtering and spewing billows of blackish exhaust stopped a few hundred feet ahead. The driver, an attractive blond in bikini top and sarong, asked where we were headed, and a smiling Terry responded "Where are you going?"

"I asked first, but we're driving to Mexico City where we'll catch a plane home."

Terry scratched his goatee and turned to me. "Looks like fate has spoken. Oaxaca it is."

"We can take you guys as far as Coatzacoalcos. That'll get you more than halfway. We're gonna stop in Veracruz before hitting the City." She sized Terry. "You better sit in front. Izzy, you go in back."

A petite redhead alighted, hopped into the back seat, and I crammed in next to her. "I'm Isaac. Mucho gusto."

"Mucho gusto to you, too. I'm Izzy. Kate and I are on a two-week holiday. School teachers from Santa Cruz. Where are you guys from?"

Terry moved the passenger seat as far back as it would go, virtually trapping me behind him. "I'm Terry, from Montreal, Canada."

Where are you from Isaac?" Izzy asked.

"Uh, Beloit, Wisconsin."

Terry turned and frowned. "Didn't you tell me you were from New York?"

It was stifling hot in the cramped seat. My sweaty back adhered to it, the combination of Izzy's proximity and my morning dose sending shivers down my spine. She was super-hot. Curly red hair. A ballerina's figure that reminded me of Ashley's, and a dozen questions: how old was I, what did I do, where'd I go to college, my major, my travel plans, etcetera. A game of improvisational theatre. I responded "Beloit College, History, 22, South America" and improvised a persona to match. "It's critically important we understand the past to avoid repeating it." I'm so good at this. "Maybe we can avoid the next Vietnam. *A well-informed citizenry is the best defense against tyranny.*"

Kate glanced in the rearview mirror. "Thomas Jefferson, right?" I'd no clue. Ashley had said it.

I liked Izzy and wanted to impress her. Without a doubt their stopping for us was fate. She was going to be the one. "I came down here to perfect my Spanish so I can teach bilingually. The Latino segment of the population is growing rapidly but woefully under served."

Terry turned around, glanced at Izzy and grinned. "Impressive. Your desire to serve humanity never ceases to amaze. But I thought you'd been a theatre major in college."

"No. You have me confused with someone else. Actors don't make enough money." Turn around, asshole. Concentrate on Kate. "We're gonna be bilingual eventually. Just getting in front of the curve."

That made sense to Izzy, and the questions continued. Did I have a line on a job when I returned? Anyone special back home? "Nah. How about you?" The speed was moving to hyper-drive. I tucked trembling hands underneath my thighs.

"I was in a serious relationship that ended recently. Kate suggested this vacation. I figured what the hell. I needed a break."

Terry turned again and smiled. "Me, too. I was supposed to get married a few months ago to my college girlfriend. We'd been together for years. Never really loved anyone but her. I was so ready, had my future all laid out. Our wedding morning a letter arrived. Turned out she didn't love me enough. Couldn't even tell me to my face. I'm still trying to make peace with that. I had to get away." So that was his secret.

"So, you're going to drown your sorrows in Oaxaca?" Kate asked.

"Not exactly. More like passing through. Traveling to Tierra del Fuego. But I'm in no hurry, Kate . . . not anymore."

Kate lightly touched his hand. "Maybe you're not running away but towards something good. You know, on your return trip you might consider a stop in Santa Cruz. If you visit me I'll teach you to surf."

"That sounds cool."

I'm going to Tierra del Fuego, too," I interjected. "Made good money on summer college breaks doing construction work."

"Theatre, history, teaching, construction work; wow, you're a real Renaissance man," Izzy noted.

"A man of many talents," Terry jibed, without turning around.

"I'm good with a hammer," I responded. I'd use one on his head right now! "Hey Terry, can I see your map for a minute?" I opened it. Spread it between me and Izzy. I leaned into her. Her body toasty. Her aroma cinnamon and sugar. Familiar and soothing. Evoking happy memories of Grandma Matthews. Of love. She was definitely the one. I knew it. I just needed more time. "No way we're making it all the way to Coatzacoalcos today unless you pull an all-nighter, Kate."

"What looks like a reasonable stop for the night?"

I returned to the map. Heart really thumping. "Tabasco." Izzy agreed. She'd heard that place was really hot.

We rented two adjoining rooms in an old roach-infested motel in Tabasco on the white-sand coastline of the Gulf of Mexico. Roaches the size of mice crawled on the Terracotta floors, up walls desperately in need of a whitewash. No toilet seat on the porcelain. But for five pesos I couldn't complain. Offshore, oil rigs dovened up and down like my Hassadic teachers at prayer. Up and down. Up and down. The gulf water slick and murky brown. During dinner in a small open-air café, Izzy said she'd wanted to be a professional dancer but had weak ankles, so she'd opted for teaching. Kate had always wanted to teach. Both girls laughed when I noted you could make a good living teaching, and Kate asked me who my career counselor was before turning to Terry. "What about you? Gonna make your fortune teaching as well?"

"Perhaps Isaac intends to teach bilingual historical theatre classes. Me? I'm pure mercenary. I'm going into computer science. Gonna become filthy rich." He pushed back his chair. "Come on, Kate, let's go for a stroll along the beach."

IZZY AND I returned to the pensione and stood outside our doors chatting for a moment. I pondered making a move but chickened out. A litany of excuses.

She was so much older. I was exhausted. Crashing. Scared of being rejected again. Instead, I lay awake with a massive hard-on obsessing over all the things I should have said or moves I should have made when Izzy rapped on the door and asked if she could come in. Like she'd read my mind. My heart hammered in my chest when she sat down on the edge of my bed. "Terry and Kate have gotten extremely chummy. I need a place to crash."

I immediately tried to kiss her, but she pushed me away. "Wait! Before you get the wrong idea, I don't sleep with teenagers." So close. So close. The story of my life. My balls ached. I shifted uncomfortably under the blanket and protested I was twenty-two. She laughed and responded she was Twiggy. "Let's drop the masquerade? You're not twenty-two, you're not a teacher, and for all I know your name isn't Isaac."

"They believed me."

"They weren't listening. You couldn't keep your story straight. The only certainty is you're a natural redhead." I followed her eyes down to my crotch. The blanket had slipped. I blushed and covered myself. "How about the truth?"

"My name is Seth and I'm eighteen but please don't tell Terry. He'll send me home and I've nowhere to go and no one who cares about me. I just wanna be someone else."

"Stop pretending to be someone you're not. You are who you are and lots of girls your age are going to like you. You can't force it." Ashley. Yeah, tell me about it. Then she kissed me, but a chaste kiss. Maybe a loving mother's kiss. "I won't say anything, but you should be honest. Now move over. I'm tired."

The next day they dropped us off outside Coatzacoalcos, but not before Kate had given Terry her address and asked him to write her. He promised he would. "Last night was really special."

Good fortune shined on us again when minutes later a minibus filled with hippie kids stopped for us. They were headed for Oaxaca. Marijuana smoke billowed out the side door when it slid open. Empty jugs of Ripple rolled around the floor. Roaches everywhere, the herbal kind. Terry looked askance. Took me aside, questioned getting into a van full of wasted kids. The roads were perilous. "But it's serendipity them headed the same way, just like Kate and Izzy stopping for us." One hundred dollars was not going to get me through South America and this was free transportation. I climbed in and he reluctantly followed. Isaac was going with the flow, hopped up on Dexedrine.

CHAPTER 14

OAXACA WAS KNOWN as the Amsterdam of Mexico, a traveler's paradise. The central square abuzz with inebriated backpackers and tourists crowding the restaurants and cafes. The streets lined with palm trees, the air redolent with the bouquet of dried herbs and bountiful tropical flowers. A never-ending fiesta whose only sour notes emanated from a bandstand gazebo where a flamboyantly attired mariachi band played enthusiastically but terribly. The music rattled my teeth, contributing to my constant jaw ache, but Terry didn't care; the vibe was awesome and the beer cold. "Chill out. Have a beer." But I couldn't afford to waste money. I agitatedly twirled my ghost ring and Terry slapped my hand. It was driving him nuts. "Order something, for God's sake. You gotta be hungry. You never eat and you're losing a lot of weight."

I started drumming my fingers on the table. "Am I the only person here with a set of ears?"

"Bring it down a level, man. You're so jittery. What the fuck's your problem?"

I got up. "I can't just sit here listening to this crap. I'm going for a walk."

"Whatever. You can be such as ass. Sometimes you act as stupid as my kid brother."

I CIRCLED THE central plaza like a lone wolf, my goddam jaw aching. I jiggled my front teeth with a finger. Loose. Fuck! I moved my jaw from side to side. Clicking noises. Fingered my other teeth. Also loose. Shit! Were they all going to fall out ... or worse, jaw cancer? I pictured Grandpa Matthews with his dentures in a glass in the bathroom. Prune-faced. I opened and closed my mouth, yanked on my front teeth. Not coming out ... yet. Maybe I was imagining it. But what if it was cancer? I'd no money. Was I going to die? Who'd care?

I rejoined Terry, now sitting with a rowdy group of backpackers coddling another beer, everyone enjoying themselves. "They're not horrible," I admitted, still working my jaw back and forth, "just not very good."

He pushed a beer toward me, told me to shut the fuck up and drink. Taking a long swig, he chuckled and shook his head. "You are too much, but I'm glad you convinced me to let fate decide. I don't know what it was about Kate, but we just clicked. Maybe we were supposed to find each other, eh? I'm gonna write her. Maybe something good will happen for a change."

I ran my tongue over my teeth, counting them. "It sure seemed like she wanted to hear from you."

"So, Izzy wound up in your bed, eh?"

"Yup," I said truthfully.

I SAT THERE. Watched all the young backpackers drink. Watched them eat. Spend their pesos. Money. I needed money. Money, money, money. Damn my aching jaw. I fiddled with my teeth again, Grandpa Matthews' false teeth in a glass on the bathroom sink. His prune face. Strange little particles floated in front of my eyes. I covered one eye, then the other. Still there. Oh my God. I'm going blind. Disintegrating. No, I could still see. How was I going to get all the way through South America without money? Geez, the music's fucking awful. AWFUL! Think. THINK! Then I remembered how anxious Jonah and I had been to see *Lawrence of Arabia* when it hit theatres just before Christmas, 1962. Jonah wanted to go with me, not his friends. Made me feel so grown up. Loved. Jerry told us to earn the ticket money and Jonah said not to worry, we'd figure something out, and sure enough, Huntington was blanketed with snow overnight and we were out shoveling driveways next morning. We entered the theatre, his arm around me. "We're gonna have such a good time, buddy. Find us seats. I'll go get us a large, buttered popcorn." I waited for him through the cartoons, through the coming attractions, through the ushers coming down the aisles collecting for the Will Rogers Institute. Began to feel anxious when the lights dimmed and the curtains opened wide to accommodate the large screen, a formless dark anxiety. I started to hyperventilate, got up and walked up the aisle toward the back of the theatre and there he was, sitting with his arm around another guy, and they were kissing. Kissing! Some special brother time! Quaking, I returned to my seat, a murky void, silent tears cascading. After the movie I told him I'd seen him. "Keep your mouth shut or else." I knew exactly what he meant.

I LOOKED ABOUT the central square. The money was there, somewhere, and I alighted on a street vendor hawking decorative blankets to the George and Martha tourists with limited success. Eureka! Those RV assholes had left us choking in their dust when we were hitchhiking. They were dollar signs, ready cash to ameliorate my financial crisis. It was righteous. I perused the square for likely marks. Bingo! Two middle aged couples sitting at a table, the men in polyester leisure suits, cowboy hats and boots, the wives sporting loud dresses and shellacked hair. I jumped up, lighter than air. "Hey, Terry. I'll be back in a little while."

"Where are you going now?"

"Just checkin' something out."

I walked over to the street vendor and drew him away from the tables and pointed to my marks. "I can get those tourists to pay four times what these blankets are worth."

The vendor eyed me cagily. "Y para ti, mi amigo?"

"My cut, twenty-five percent of your take. If you don't make a sale, you owe me nada." We shook on it.

This was gonna work. I sat at an adjoining table and struck up a friendly conversation, regaling them with stories of my adventures—slashing my way through the dense Yucatan jungle with a machete, catching barracuda with my bare hands in Progresso, climbing palm trees for cocoanuts, even staring down a jaguar.

One of the women gasped "Weren't you frightened? I hear they're very dangerous."

"Nah. No way it was going to mess with me, not with my machete."

"I love Mexico," one of the ladies enthused. "If only there weren't so many Mexicans."

Her friend agreed. "They don't even speak English, for God's sake."

"If English was good 'nuf for Jesus, it should be good 'nuf for these darkies, that's all I have to say," one of the guys drawled. They all nodded in agreement. I plastered a smile on my face.

The vendor approached, offered them blankets at an outlandish price, piquing their interest, but I told them to hold on, the guy was taking them for stupid gringos, asking way too much, and offered to bargain for them. The vendor pantomimed affront and we proceeded to put on quite a performance, parrying back and forth like prizefighters, like Pepe Bernalga and the Customs official. Finally, with a dramatic sigh, the vendor caved and sold two blankets to those lucky tourists at a ridiculously high price. They were so pleased they bought me a margarita.

We performed the same act the rest of the evening, and when I reconnected with Terry hours later, another guy had joined him, about his age, but bigger and blond. Also Canadian. Terry noticed I was holding a woven blanket and asked where I'd bought it. I smiled like a Cheshire cat, jaw ache gone. "Helped make a couple of sales, got twenty-five dollars and this cool blanket. No more sleeping wrapped in a towel. Not bad for a couple of hours' honest work!"

The other guy held out his hand. "Honest might be stretching it a bit, eh? Ripping off the tourists. I'm Brian. Terry was telling me about your plans for South America. I'm heading that way myself. Might join you."

I didn't like the sound of that at all. Terry and I were like brothers now. Everything was perfect. Who needed this snake in our garden? "How's your Spanish, Brian? You must be fluent, eh?"

"Nah. Don't speak it."

"Too bad. Difficult to bargain when you can't speak the language, eh?"

Terry chuckled. "Brian's got a room where we can crash. We'll spend a couple of days here. Check out those ruins. Visit the market. See how it works out. Okay?"

I WORKED THE tourists again the next day, ignoring Brian's jibes. Ended up fifty bucks richer and got a cool hand-woven Oaxacan shirt. That evening I even ordered a plate of frijoles and tortillas, but when it arrived I only picked at it. Terry asked if I was going to actually eat anything, and when I shook my head grabbed the plate and scarfed it all. "I don't know how you survive on jalapenos but you're gonna make some gastroenterologist very rich someday."

I laughed, felt flush. Money? No problemo. I ordered a round of tequila for the table and before heading out next morning procured more Dexedrine. Legal in Mexico. But who knew about Guatemala. When you're a man in control, you've got to think ahead.

CHAPTER 15

WE HITCHED A ride in the back of a fruit truck headed to Guatemala for oranges, a long day's journey to the border, every bounce in that rickety wooden trailer bed tooth-rattling, and after settling in, Brian reached into his pack, pulled out a small baggie and dropped tiny squares of paper in our hands. Blotter acid. LSD. "Place it under your tongues. It'll blow your minds."

    I was already speeding but what the fuck, I'd never had an acid/speed cocktail and curious to see what would happen. Five minutes passed, ten minutes. Nothing! I was about to call Brian out as totally bogus when whammo bammo the top of my head explodes and he morphs into a serpent, coiled, jaws distended, his diamond-shaped eyes aglitter, ready to strike. Totally freaked out, I turn to warn Terry but he's staring at his hands, moving them in circles muttering "Oh wow" and POOF, suddenly he's pixelating and I'm precariously balanced on the edge of a precipice, below me a turbulent sea of swirling and undulating molecules cresting in tentacle-like waves of octopuses trying to suck me under and the earth belches and heaves and volcanoes erupt in plumes of glittery rainbow fluorescence and I'm trapped in a whirlpool of nothingness, helpless, crying out as I'm suddenly ensnared, my body a wriggling fish on a hook and the truck driver, whose face keeps morphing like Silly Putty, is dragging me back into the cab as I squirm and struggle and a plethora of crucifixes sway hypnotically from the rear view mirror and a naked dashboard Virgin Mary levitates and moves toward me, her eyes spewing searing fire, her legs splayed invitingly, enveloping me, her vagina a vertical smile of razor-sharp chattering teeth about to eviscerate me and a voice out of nowhere asks if I'm Catholic but my eyes are locked on those saliva-dripping shredders and I mumble "I'm Jewish, I'm Jewish" and there's a screeching sound of brakes and I'm thrown between the Virgin's legs and the disembodied voice screams "You can't be a Jew. Jews have horns. They killed Christ. They're the spawn of the devil," and I'm engaged in a life and death struggle with the driver for control of the Virgin, finally yanking her away from him with such force she flies out the passenger window, hits a tree and bursts into a plume of blood-red confetti. "MADRE DE DIOS, AYUDAME!" the driver screams, "SALIR DE MI TAXI, DIABLO," and shoves me out the passenger side door.

Shaking uncontrollably, clutching myself to keep from disintegrating, I scurry to the back of the trailer where two swirling masses slowly aggregate into Terry and a scaly-skinned serpent hissing "Who are you, who are you?" but I can't recall and stand mute and helpless while the creature twists its slimy body around Terry, about to crush and ingest him and the driver's pummeling me from behind, and I turn and grab his shirt and shake him so hard the buttons pop off and he breaks loose and runs back to his cab and takes off, leaving us mired in plumes of black exhaust in the middle of a dark and impenetrable jungle and fear, like a fist squeezing my heart, overwhelms me and I start to run fast as I can through the black haze chasing Jonah's retreating form screaming "JONAH, DON'T LEAVE ME, DON'T LEAVE ME" as footsteps gain on me from behind, growing louder and louder, threatening to overtake me, and I turn to see a small child wailing "DON'T LEAVE ME, JONAH, DON'T LEAVE ME, I'M SCARED," and it's me chasing me chasing Jonah and I'm so freaked out I run all out pursuing Jonah's retreating form through the darkness, feeling hot breath on my neck and the serpent's hissing "You're bad, you're bad, you're going to Hell" and Terry's screaming "WHAT THE FUCK IS GOING ON?" but I don't stop until the ground disappears and I'm on teetering on the edge of a deep ravine separating Mexico from Guatemala.

Lungs on fire, inhaling and exhaling humid air like fireplace bellows, my body drenched in sweat, I collapse against the railing of a bridge spanning the ravine, clutching it to stay upright, steeling myself to my fate. I try to calm my pounding heart and the pulse beating in my ears like tom tom's so I can hear the footsteps, but they've ceased and in the inky darkness Terry's form is slumped against the bridge railing, panting and wheezing "What the fuck, Isaac; what the fuck," and the serpent, now morphed into his Brian form, is hissing "He's not who he says he is" in his ear.

Cloaked in my blanket I hunker down on the Mexican side, alert to the slightest movement about me for fear Terry will leave if I close my eyes, a thought beyond terrifying. I have to stay awake; have to keep him with me. Have to regain control. Surreptitiously, I reach into my pack for the bottle of amphetamines and shake out two while imagining lemons to generate saliva, an old theatre trick, and swallow them, then pass the time taking deep cleansing breaths, meditating on the gurgling waters below the bridge, quietly singing lyrics of my favorite Incredible String Band song: *Water, water, see the water flow glancing, dancing, see the water flow,* but sounds emanate from out of the darkness, murmurs of "El diablo, el diablo" growing in intensity and I cover my ears to drown out the amplifying noise shouting *Oh wizard of changes, teach me the lesson of flowing*. I squeeze my eyes tight. It's a dream, a dream, residue of bad acid the Brian serpent gave me, but humanoid forms begin to slither out of the darkness like goblins and they're coming toward me, for me, and I smack my face repeatedly. It's a dream, not real, wake up, wake up and Terry, whose form pulses in and out of focus, sees them as well and cries out "What the fuck is going on? What the fuck is happening to me?" What's he's doing in my dream?

I stand and face the mob, my blanket falling to the ground. "GO BACK, GO BACK" I command, arms outstretched, but one creature tremulously inches forward until he's right in my face and I can taste his hot breath as he presses cold steel in my belly, mumbling "Debes salir de nuestro pueblo inmediatamente." The hairs on the nape of my neck bristle. Spiders clamber up. The man jabs the gun harder, forcefully enough to knock the wind out of me. "Un camion golpeo a nuestra vaca. Traes mala suerte a nuestro pueblo." He's no goblin. He's real and I'm not dreaming, but I am in control.

"What's he saying?" Terry asks. "Why's he got a gun on you?"

"He wants us to leave. Some gibberish about my killing the virgin causing their cow to be run over. It's that truck driver. See him in the crowd? He must've hit it and blamed us, but he's not going to get away with it. I'm not going anywhere."

I stare into the eyes of the brute, place my hand over his, daring him to pull the trigger. I'm not afraid. I'm supercharged, invincible. "No tienes idea de con quien estas tratando. Soy el diablo enviado del infierno!" His gun hand starts to quiver. I'm the devil from Hell.

Brian's serpent's eyes glow. "Let's get the fuck outta here, Terry. He's crazy."

"Don't listen to him, Terry. He's trying to confuse you, tear us apart. He's the faker. A serpent, a fallen angel. He poisoned us with bad acid."

Brian grabs Terry's arm and tries to pull him away. "I swear he's going to get us killed."

The pistol cocks. I gape at the leader, incredulous. No fucking way I'm going to let him shoot me. I wrench the gun from him and place him in a choke hold, the gun to his head, and turn to the mob screaming "NOS DEJA SOLOS QUE PENDEJOS; NOS DEJAN SOLOS U OTRA COSA!"

The mob hushes. Murmurs of "EL ESTA LOCO." Then assent. "VAMOS A LA MERDA FUERA DE AQUI!"

Pee puddles at the feet of the leader, still locked in my arm. I turn to Brian, tell him to go back to Hell as Terry weeps and begs me to put down the gun, but there's no way that's going to happen. Power surges through me. Spiders crawl up my spine, across my face, in my ears and out my eyes, and a voice in my head says "Pull the trigger, pull the trigger" and as I swat at the spiders with my forearm the gun momentarily points upward and the gunman, sensing opportunity, tries to wrest it from me, the gun discharging, an ear-shattering percussive explosion that ricochets through my head and throughout the gorge. My ears ring. The spiders disappear. The gunman shits his pants and faints and I push his inert body toward the crowd, a few brave ones inching closer, kowtowing before me like groveling supplicants, and drag him away as I follow, gun still trained on them, until they're reabsorbed by the jungle. Every fiber of my being pulses with electricity and my ears buzz as if beaten with a tuning fork and with a blood curdling scream I heave the pistol into the rushing river below. Brian hisses "He's insane; he's completely insane."

CHAPTER 16

RAYS OF EARLY morning sunlight filtered through the jungle canopy. Roosters crowed and birds cawed in symphony with the ever-present crickets and gurgling waters flowing under the bridge. I was exhausted, yet exhilarated, the acid washed from my system. I'd crossed an invisible divide, experienced a profound sense of empowerment, but also of dread. I, Isaac, had held the power over life and death in my hands, and I shuddered to think I carried within me the capacity for such violence. Terry sat down next to me; peered into my eyes. "Are you okay? Your pupils are totally dilated. Last night was not cool, man. Not cool." He remained at my side until the bridge re-opened and we walked across and queued for Guatemalan customs, the customs building a barn-like structure with a large industrial freight scale in a corner. I asked Terry to hold my place in line and stepped onto the metal platform. The clocklike dial face jangled and quivered until the arrow stopped, pointed to sixty-three and a half kilograms, but I'd no idea how that translated into pounds. I'd weighed one hundred and seventy-five pounds when I left Mexico City with Terry.

"That's about one hundred and forty," Terry explained. "You've lost a lot of weight."

I glanced at my fat reflection in a window, the scale obviously broken, and approached the customs inspector with Terry right behind me, the speed now kicking like a mule. I gnashed my teeth and ran a sandpaper tongue across them. So parched. I handed my passport to the inspector and nervously fidgeted as he scrutinized it for what seemed like forever. He studied the photo, then my face. Back and forth. What the fuck was going on? I assured him everything was in order.

"Seth Matthews?" he said. "This is not you."

Cold stones tumbled about in my stomach. My fucking passport! I furtively glanced at Terry, hoping he hadn't overheard the exchange, then leaned into the agent and whispered I'd possibly lost some weight, but Terry quickly corrected him. "Of course it's not him. His name is Isaac, not Seth."

"No, Senor," the agent said, flipping the passport over for Terry to see. "You know this boy?" Terry looked at the passport, then at me, as the agent grew impatient. "Senor, are you traveling with this boy?"

"Yes, sir." Terry gulped, glanced at the passport again. "He's Seth Isaac Matthews, just like it says, but he's lost a ton of weight and always uses his middle name, right Isaac?" He turned back to the inspector. "See, same red hair, blue eyes? It's him, honestly." The agent glanced down as I pressed two twenties into his palm. He smirked, returned my passport and brusquely motioned to the exit.

I hoped Terry would let the whole thing slide but as we boarded the bus for Guatemala City and took a bench seat, he grumbled "You better tell me what the fuck is going on. I just covered your ass, but I want the truth. Gimme that passport again." I clutched the pack to my chest. "Actually, gimme the pack, Isaac or Seth or whatever the fuck your name is." He wrenched it from me. "I don't know what's going on with you, but you eat nothing, you're really edgy and that thing with the truck driver, and at the bridge . . . Jesus Christ! You almost got us killed."

I motioned to Brian in the seat behind us and leaned into Terry. "I told you he's not what you think he is. He's the serpent in the Old Testament."

"Yeah, and you're fucking Santa Claus." Opening my pack, he removed my passport and stared at it. "Jesus Christ; eighteen fucking years old! No shit . . . same age as my kid brother. Boy, this sure explains a lot."

"This is so fucked," Brian added from the seat behind us.

I protested as Terry dug deeper into my private stuff. He pulled out a small bottle. "Jalapeno peppers, huh? I can't believe I ignored all the signs . . ."

I snatched them from his hand. Protested they were vitamins. Brian said, "Vitamins, my ass."

I pleaded with Terry, told him Brian was not human, as he dug deeper into my pack, extracted my wallet and opened the billfold. "That's it? Fifty dollars? How the hell were you planning to travel through South America with no money, Isaac . . . I mean Seth. You're delusional."

"Look what I did in Oaxaca. Trust me."

"Trust you? You're a fuckin' liar and a speed freak."

I twirled the missing ring on my finger. "It'll all work out."

He batted my hand. "Stop that, dammit! It's not gonna work out. That's magical thinking; that's the speed talking."

WE SAT ON the patio of an American-style hamburger joint near the Cathedral in Guatalama City. Terry ordered me a burger but I countermanded him. "Solo una taza de café para mi."

"Oh no. You're gonna eat a burger. I can't remember the last time you ate and I don't give a damn whether you're hungry or not."

We sat in awkward silence awaiting the food. Brian glared at me malevolently, Terry lost in thought. I felt eviscerated, my entrails spilled out on the table. He'd no right to force me to eat; I wasn't a fucking baby. I needed to keep him on my side, control the situation. "I'm sorry I'd lied but figured if you'd known my real age you wouldn't travel with me."

"Fuck'n right." He lit a cigarette and blew out a long cloud of smoke. "Jesus Christ. You haven't contacted your parents the whole time we've been traveling together."

"So what? It's none of their goddam business. I'm on my own, like you."

"No, not like me. I'm twenty-five, you're eighteen, just a kid. I'd wanna know you were okay if you were my little brother." I deflated like a punctured tire. Tears coursed down my cheeks. I wanted to be his little brother more than anything in the world. "Your parents have a right to know."

Brian watched our exchange with growing restiveness. "You're wasting your time, Terry. The kid's a nut case. No way I'm traveling with him anymore. Come on. Let's get the hell out of here."

Terry took another drag and exhaled, told Brian to fuck off, but before he split in a huff, Brian said he'd stay at a local hostel for the night in case Terry came to his senses. My empty stomach grumbled when the food arrived, but the thought of eating it nauseated me. I took a small, tentative bite. Were my teeth really loose? Would they fall out? What if I swallowed them? I pushed the plate away, but Terry thrust it back in front of me. "Eat it, all of it, and when you're finished we're going to the telephone exchange; you're gonna call your parents, let them know you're ok."

I morosely chewed the food, trying not to gag on what was probably dog meat. One careless moment, one stupid fucking careless moment and all my adult credibility dashed. The reality of Seth the nail in Isaac's coffin. Calling home, the final indignity. They'd be furious, as I was when Jonah took off like I meant nothing to him, and fucking idiot me, so certain he'd return I'd prepared a blistering rebuke for his insensitivity, adding more kindling to the fire each passing day until it hit me—he wasn't coming back. He didn't care about me any more than Mitzie and Jerry. And now I was going to lose Terry as well.

As we walked to the exchange I told him I couldn't afford an international call but he didn't care. Told me to call collect. I needed the money anyway. "I don't know what you're running away from, but I'm sure you've magnified it out of proportion, and with all that speed you've become delusional . . ."

"Speed's not a problem . . ."

"You should hear yourself. You're not thinking straight. Speed *is* the problem. You almost lost your mind on that bridge. You could've killed someone or been killed . . . and that bizarre thing with Brian! The guy's an asshole, not a serpent, and believe me, he's no fallen angel."

"Don't you understand? The speed calms me, makes life bearable."

"Calms you? Are you kidding? It's making you nuts."

"Look, I'll stop. I promise. See, I'm completely back to normal. It was the combination of the speed and the acid. That's all. Please don't make me do this."

Terry stopped and put his arms around me. "Look, I'm sorry, I really am. You can't run away from yourself. Neither one of us can."

THE TELEPHONE EXCHANGE was abuzz with jovial people making long distance calls. Despite the blazing heat and absence of snow, it was Christmastime, and they were calling friends and loved ones. I was telephoning strangers, my world imploding. I silently eyed Terry as we waited in line over an hour. Change your mind. Tell me to put down the receiver. Finally connected, Mitzie answered, but when I said hello, the operator interrupted and asked if she would accept a collect call from Guatemala.

"Seth? Yes, yes, I'll accept the charges. Seth, oh my God, Jerry, its Seth, he's alive, on the phone calling from Guatemala!"

Jerry picked up. "Where are you?"

"In Guatemala City."

"How could he do this to me," she wailed in the background. "I thought he was dead!"

"Mitzie, please, let me talk to him. Where did you say you were calling from, Seth?"

She continued to sob and chatter, something about Grandma Matthews coming to her in a dream, telling her not to worry, I was alive, while Jerry upbraided me for not calling when I left Coca Cola, leaving them hanging. "I knew you were okay but your poor mother . . . my life's been hell these past months."

I wasn't sorry and she wasn't my mother. "I've been traveling with a Canadian guy, Terry. He's headed to South America, and I wanna go with him, but I'm outta money."

"SOUTH AMERICA? What about college? And who's this guy Terry?"

"Jerry, tell him to come home right now!"

I could hear the muffled sound of Jerry's hand over the receiver. "Be quiet, Mitzie."

"He's older, twenty-five, a really good guy. He insisted I call you."

"Is he with you? I'd like to speak to him."

"What do you need to speak to him for?"

"Just give him the goddam phone."

JERRY DID MOST of the talking. I stood there anxiously, only hearing Terry's responses, mostly affirming whatever Jerry was saying. He was selling me down the river; he didn't want me either. I nervously twirled my ghost ring; decisions were being made for me, not by me, my life in the balance. Then Terry smiled, gave me a thumbs up, and handed back the receiver, my momentary elation over the prospect of continuing on to South America with Terry immediately dashed when Jerry suggested I join them for an all-expense paid vacation in the Yucatan. I glanced at Terry. He already knew.

 I didn't give a fuck about South America. I'd wanted Terry to be my big brother, but he wasn't. He had his own little brother. I felt strung out, stretched too thin, like a rubber band on the cusp of breaking. And money. The reality-check. What choice did I have? Jerry was softening the blow of the obvious. Terry was sending me packing, an adult doing the right thing with someone else's child. I wasn't an equal. Not a traveling buddy. And as much as I wanted to believe I'd arrived at a crossroad and was exercising free will, choosing my own path forward, it was bullshit. There was no free will, my journey pointless. All I could do now was put on my actor face and salvage a few crumbs of self-respect, my fleeting grasp on adulthood closing like a crocus at night. I agreed to meet them at the Merida airport on New Year's Day. But when I broached the subject of returning to Beloit, Jerry was vague. Asked if I needed money. "No. See you there."

OUR WALK TO the bus station was funereal. Neither of us knew what to say. We watched people pile luggage onto already groaning roof racks and shepherd nervous animals onto the bus leaving for Mexico. It would be standing room only back to the border crossing. Terry finally broke the silence. Asked if I really had a big brother who had disappeared. I sadly nodded. I was never going to find him. "I know you think he holds the answers you're searching for, but honestly Seth, you've got to find those from within." He reached into his billfold. Offered me some money, probably to salve his conscience, but I didn't want his blood money any more than Jerry's. I just wanted to know if he'd continue on to South America with Brian.

 "No. I'll hang around Guatemala for a bit then head back north. Traveling through South America was just my excuse for running away from things. But shit happens, man. It's inevitable. It's how you handle it that counts. Like Kate said, maybe it's better to be running toward something, so I think I'll go to Santa Cruz. See if there's something real between Kate and me."

 I mustered a smile. "Maybe my journey wasn't a total loss after all."

 "Nothing's ever a loss if you learn from it. Someday you're going to look back on all this and have a great story to tell."

"Maybe, but that day sure ain't today. Terry, do me one last favor. Call me Isaac."

Terry smiled and stuck out his hand. "Goodbye, Isaac."

I started to board, then turned around. "Give Kate my regards and . . . hey, if things work out maybe you could name your first kid after me."

"Which name?" Terry chuckled as the door swung shut behind me.

CHAPTER 17

THE BUS STOPPED for customs on the Guatemalan side of the border bridge. A posted notice required one hundred dollars to cross over into Mexico. I reached into my pack and pulled out my wallet, knowing full well I'd only forty-five. I palmed it and pressed the wad of cash into the agent's hand. "Feliz Navidad." He passed me though.

Deposited on the Mexican side of the border, I swallowed two pills and started walking along the side of the two-lane road. Heat undulated off the blistering asphalt, the stench almost overpowering. I choked on dust and exhaust as cars and RV's sped past, generating just enough saliva to moisten my mouth every few minutes. I continued on, craving the evening chill, but with darkness I shivered and prayed for morning. I'd no water, food or clear sense of direction, a starlit sky my only guide, but I soldiered on wrapped in my blanket, what Isaac would do, a thought that enlivened my step. Ignoring all discomfort, I stopped only to pop pills every few hours and by dawn Isaac was once again determined to make his own way, though still walking in the direction of Merida.

Another blazing day, the sun relentlessly bearing down on my uncovered head, lips cracked and chapped, tasting of blood I sucked for the delicious saltiness, sandaled feet blistered and bleeding, every step agonizing, but my thighs no longer chafed. The desert landscape of cacti and tumbleweed so invariable I feared retracing the same patch of road in an endless loop.

With darkness a chill closed in on me like a pressure in my chest. I had flashes of a dense, dark jungle, heard sounds of pounding feet, plaintive voices screaming. I trembled with fear of something unknown, something buried within me, more nightmarish than the cacti metamorphosing into scary creatures in the shadow of the moon. I gazed upward. An entire galaxy, layers of stars overlaying stars stretching into infinity, the Earth itself infinitesimal. Me a mere speck in time in a vastness that stretched from the past to the future. Shooting stars wove intricate cross-hatched patterns in the sky. I closed my eyes and made a wish. "Let me be Isaac, let me be Isaac, let me be Isaac." Blackness.

Light again. I'm being lifted, water dribbled over parched lips, cooling cloth pressed against my burnt face. I uttered words of thanks to forms I could barely discern. Then blackness. I'm being shaken. I sit up, look around. A van full of hippie kids. "Seth, we're here. We were worried about you, man. You slept an entire day and night. Happy New Year's." I looked at them queerly. They'd called me Seth. So much for wishes.

THE VW BUS dropped me off at the airport in Merida early the morning of January 1st where, according to another broken loading scale I weighed sixty-one point two kilograms, which again meant nothing to me. Seth's fat reflection stared back at me in the men's room mirror. All I needed to know. I doused my scorched face, a mask of dust and grime, with water from the tap, soaked filthy hair in the sink. Bore another hole in my belt with a pen knife and noticed my pant legs were riding above my ankles.

I took a seat in the lounge area awaiting the arrival of an early afternoon flight from NYC. Despite popping two more pills I dozed off, startled awake by the announcement of an arrival from JFK. I hadn't missed their plane, nor the cringe-worthy sight of them alighting, Jerry dressed for safari and Mitzie in a loud floral print dress with a broad-brimmed sun hat and over-sized sunglasses. Dollar signs, marks. I would've taken them to the cleaners. And when they passed within feet of me without recognition my heart quickened. It wasn't too late. I could still run. I urged my body to do so but it wouldn't listen, and maybe a hundred feet beyond me Mitzie clutched Jerry's arm, turned, pointed to me and ran back, embracing me with a ferocity of a mother bear protecting her cub. I let it feel good. "Oh my God, I wouldn't have recognized you! You've grown and lost so much weight. You look . . . fantastic!"

"Are you crazy? He looks skeletal, like a Holocaust victim."

"What kind of diet have you been on? Whatever it is, we'll bottle it and make a million bucks." She stepped back, spread her arms and preened. "So, what do you think? I've lost weight, too. Can't you tell?"

"For God's sake, Mitzie."

"Oh, stop it, Jerry. He looks great. You can never be too rich or too thin, right Seth?" Fucking clowns. Served me right for letting my guard down even for a second.

Jerry looked about the arrival terminal. "Go ask that customs guy if there's a restaurant in the terminal, get you a good meal."

"No. You gotta get your luggage first. You can't trust the porters. Let's go to the hotel, freshen up a bit and eat in Merida. There are lots of restaurants there."

"No. Do it."

AT THE RESTAURANT he immediately ordered me a steak but only drinks for them. Why was he in such a hurry? Mitzie raised her margarita. "Happy belated birthday. Here we are, all together, a family reunited and that's what matters, right?"

An undercooked piece of beef swimming in a noxious pool of blood and fat was placed in front of me, but when I cut into it a swarm of maggots swam across the plate. I pushed it away, excused myself, ran to the bathroom and puked. Something was very, very wrong. I popped two more tabs before returning to find them sitting somber faced amid a sea of maggots. "There's something going on. Tell me."

Maggots crawled across the table, swarming over them. Were they blind? "Tell him, Jerry."

He looked grim. Took a deep breath and didn't mince words. "You're going home; back to school. The plane leaves in an hour."

It had been a ruse. I pushed the plate of putrid meat across the table, onto his lap. "You eat it!"

Mitzie wiped blood and fat from Jerry's lap. "We did what we had to do. It's high time this little adventure to discover yourself was over."

"You'd no right. I was doing fine. I'm nineteen; you can't tell me what to do anymore."

Jerry pushed Mitzie's hand away. "I let you go on this little junket because it seemed important to you, and you abused my trust. Almost drove her out of her mind, and me to an early grave. It's over now. Time to grow up, get an education, learn how to make a living in the real world."

Isaac stood up, told them to go fuck themselves, and disappeared forever, like Jonah, but I sat there, strung out and scared. Jerry planned my trip, and now my return. I was still on the path of least resistance, in control of nothing. Nothing! I hated me. Maggots were now everywhere, crawling all over me, over them, up the walls, and they still sat there nonplussed. "Did Terry know about this?"

"No. He thought we were taking you on a vacation. Our plans were none of his business, and we weren't risking you taking off with him again."

It was too much to absorb, but they'd come thousands of miles to bring me home, that had to mean something, like maybe my disappearing had finally awakened latent love. My eyes moistened. I wiped at them. The maggots disappeared. I nodded. "Okay, I understand. When's our plane leaving?"

Jerry glanced at his watch. "Your plane. You're going home alone, and we'd better get you to the gate. After what you put us through, we're taking a much-needed vacation. A limo service will pick you up at JFK and Joel will take you to the airport day after tomorrow."

I hadn't realized there remained any pieces of my heart they hadn't broken. "You're abandoning me."

"A little lesson in responsibility," Jerry shot back. "You'll have to turn on the heat and hot water. I shut everything off before we left this morning."

"Fuck you. I'm not going back to Beloit."

Jerry stood up; his expression implacable; it looked like he'd peed blood all over his pants. "Send us a postcard from Vietnam."

"So that's it? Parental responsibility fulfilled, huh? What you're doing hurts so bad."

"Leaving Coca-Cola and disappearing for months really hurt us, too!" Mitzie chimed in. "How could you do that to us after everything with Jonah?"

Jonah, Jonah, Jonah. I needn't have searched for him. His presence was pervasive. I excused myself again and sat in a toilet stall crying. Had their wonder boy returned they wouldn't let him out of their sight for a moment despite the years of pain and suffering he'd caused them. But nothing prevented them from getting rid of me. Vietnam, the perfect solution. I removed the bottle of amphetamines from my pack, spilled a pile into my hands. Why wait? Who'd miss me, remember I'd ever existed. I shoveled them in my mouth and swallowed, but immediately gagged and vomited until there was nothing left in me, or of me. Fuck them. I wouldn't make it that easy for them. I dumped the remaining pills in the toilet and flushed Isaac goodbye.

CHAPTER 18

I RETURNED TO Huntington, the house so bone chillingly cold ghostly balloons materialized with every breath. I ran downstairs, restarted the gas furnace, listened for the puffs and hisses of steam that would circulate through the old radiator pipes like an old-timey Wurlitzer organ and prayed for blessed heat, for anything that would stop my shuddering, wishing I'd never flushed the speed down the toilet. Going cold turkey was hell. Back upstairs I opened my bedroom closet to find something warm to wear. It was empty. Empty! Only hangers. Metal hangers. Wooden suit hangers. An empty shoe bag on the inside closet door. I looked about my old room. My entire life, missing. My rock and film posters, my playbills, even my stuffed animals. I opened my bureau drawers. No underwear, socks, T-shirts. Just extra linens and towels. Even my bed spread had been replaced. She had completely erased me.

I was freezing cold. I'd have to look in Jonah's closet. I hadn't been in his room since the night before my Bar Mitzvah. I gingerly climbed the creaky attic stairs. Hesitated at the top of the landing. An air current brushed my face. Lack of insulation? Warped attic windows? No. Jonah's ghost. I trembled, flipped the light switch. Illuminated his now faded *Forbidden Planet* wallpaper, his collection of tin windup Robby the Robots, the Ferris wheel, the merry-go-round and creepy jack-in-the-box. I looked about the room. The bed's hospital corners precise, the spread atop it wrinkle-free. Not a speck of dust anywhere. Not a room. A shrine. Everything positioned exactly as I last recalled it, as if time itself had stopped the moment Jonah disappeared, but no, the smiling clown face clock droned TICK TOCK TICK TOCK.

I remembered the night before my Bar Mitzvah, how I was unable to sleep, tortured with self-doubt, knowing I'd be standing on the Bima in front of hundreds of congregants leading the service and explicating my Torah portion, Genesis 2:3, the story of Adam and Eve. Fearing I wouldn't be perfect like Jonah

I grew frantic and rushed upstairs to his room to be comforted and reassured. Instead, he told me I'd never be as good as him, I'd blow it, be a laughingstock, an embarrassment to the family and his grandfather's memory. He didn't even want to be there; they'd made him come home from college. I stared at him, this demon wearing my brother's skin. Distraught, I crept downstairs, left the house and walked to Winona beach in almost pitch darkness as there was no moon, seeking refuge on my favorite rock. I needed time to think, to deal with my scrambled emotions, but in that pervasive darkness saw dim images of a dense, dark jungle, of twisted tree limbs reaching out to envelop me. Perched safely on my thinking rock, I cried myself out, grit my teeth and returned home to dress for my performance. Every good actor knows the show must go on.

I opened his closet door. Everything still there, neatly arrayed. I grabbed a winter coat, so large it hung on me, but I wasn't concerned with sartorial splendor. I was frozen. And starving. But back downstairs the fridge was empty, the pantry bare save a box of Jonah's favorite cereal years beyond its sell by date. Another shrine. I shook it, opened it, turned it upside down and let stale crumbles cascade into my mouth before spitting them out and returning the holy box to its cabinet. Heading back upstairs, I paused at the top of the second-floor landing where I'd perched a late November night eavesdropping as detectives told Jerry and Mitzie in the living room below their search for Jonah had proven fruitless. Silent tears rolled down my cheeks now as then. I'd set all this in motion. Mitzie had wept, her head on Jerry's shoulder, his protective arms around her, my immediate urge to join them in shared anguish stymied by her words: "Dear God, if You had to take one, why did it have to be my Jonah?"

In the morning I drove to the Bayside Deli, drank several cups of tinny-tasting, high octane coffee to ameliorate the shakes coming off all that speed, then drove downtown to Mensch's where Mitzie had dragged me shopping for clothes six months earlier. Making a beeline for the fat boy department a familiar, yet unfriendly voice demanded I stop. Asked what I was doing. I turned and saw the owner eyeing me with distaste. A homeless person coming in from the cold. He visibly relaxed when I explained I was Seth Matthews and needed some new clothes. "Seth? Mitzie and Jerry's younger boy? What happened to you? Have you been sick? You're so skinny. Well, no more Husky Boys department for you!"

As he led me downstairs to the Mod room, where trendier clothes, hip threads, the kind worn by rockers and TV stars, like *The Mod Squad* and *The Monkees*, and Jonah, filled the racks, I explained I was home alone and had no money. Not to worry. He'd settle up with Mitzie later.

I recognized the pretty salesgirl, Callie Winslet, an in-crowd kid from school, a dumb blond cheerleader who'd spurned me on the gymnasium dance floor in junior high school, breaking my twelve-year-old heart. "Callie, I've got a customer for you. Eyeballing, I'm guessing a size 30, but you should measure him." He turned and patted me on the back. "I'm leaving you in very capable hands, Seth. Callie really knows her stuff."

Callie looked me over, trying to place me. "Huntington High?"

"Yeah, class of 1969. Seth Matthews."

"The actor, right? Wow, you don't look like you."

"Who do I look like?"

"Just . . . different. How can I help you?"

"I need some jeans, shirts and definitely a coat. Just got back from Mexico; I'm fucking freezing."

She grabbed a measuring tape, asked me to lift my arms, and placed the tape around my waist. Her proximity, the smell of her perfume, her big brown eyes, made my heart beat faster. I'd never been this close to her.

"I never noticed how blue your eyes are, and I'd die for your eyelashes. You can put your arms down. Mr. Mensch nailed it. You're a size 30." I protested that wasn't possible, but she countered the tape didn't lie. "And the pants you're wearing are ridiculously short, almost pedal pushers. You had quite the post-high school growth spurt." She led me to the appropriate racks and started picking out clothes for me. I'd never seen such a huge selection. "These chambray shirts will really go with your eyes. Try one on. And these pants, too." I changed and stood in front of the mirror. She smiled. "Sure beats the slim pickings in the Husky section upstairs." I gave her a reappraising glance.

Everything she selected looked cool, stove pipe pants with button fronts worn by the Rolling Stones and form fitting Peter Maxx shirts, even a faux fur coat, but not on me. I looked the clown. These weren't clothes for fat guys. "Of course not, but they look great on you, but suit yourself."

Not so dumb after all. "Come on, Callie, stop trying to sell me. I looked ridiculous. I'll just take plain Levi's and a couple of those chambray shirts, okay?" I put my overcoat on and headed to the cashier station.

"I don't know what you see in that mirror. I see a good-looking guy. What's ridiculous is that overcoat. Try on the faux fur."

I looked in the mirror. "I seem to fill this out just fine."

"Yeah, you and who else?"

"Maybe I'll find someone to share it, being so good-looking and all."

"No offense, but the homeless look is out." She unbuttoned the coat and helped me out of it. "Don't be stubborn; try this on." I looked like a grizzly bear. She zipped it up, her face inches from mine, her breath warm and sweet. "I'd hibernate with you." She kept staring as she rang me up. "So, you becoming a professional actor? You were the best actor in school."

"I guess so . . . I mean, there's so much luck involved. Who knows?"

"Well, I thought you were awesome. Wanna do something tonight? Maybe go to Hennigan's? Jeff Harrington's older brother, a big shot on Wall Street, owns the place now; some of the kids from our class hang out there."

"I'm going to my cousin's house in West Meadow. He's driving me to the airport tomorrow."

"Tell you what . . ." She grabbed my hand and wrote her phone number on my palm. "Call me next time you're in town, okay?"

I looked at the number she'd scribbled on my hand, then back at her pretty face. I'd be the butt of a funny story at Hennigan's tonight. I bought the overcoat anyway.

PART THREE
THE NARCISSIST'S TALE

CHAPTER 1

BLIZZARD CONDITIONS SHUT down O'Hare Airport shortly after my plane landed, bus service to Beloit, Wisconsin suspended. I pushed my duffel against a wall and plopped down on it, resigned to a long night in the chilly airport lounge. But not alone. Lots of kids were milling about the terminal, stranded in Chicago due to the winter storm. College girls looked hippyish in bellbottom jeans or Indian print skirts, their long straight or frizzy hair unvaryingly parted in the middle, and braless of course, as unlike the demure senoritas in Mexico as night and day. My hand-woven Oaxacan shirt, its bright, tropical colors so incongruous with the weather, sparked amusement. I looked ridiculous. What was I thinking? I wanted to disappear. I closed my eyes and slunk deeper into my faux fur. It worked when I was little, playing hide and seek with Jonah. I dozed off.

By morning the blizzard had abated, but the ride to Beloit was slow going due to hazardous whiteout conditions, snow drifts obscuring road signs. Winds buffeted the bus, whipping up a froth so blindingly white I had to shield my eyes. I imagined Terry and I were on a bus, destination Tierra del Fuego, laughing as farm animals scampered down the aisles with owners in pursuit, sobered by the crosses clustered on the highway's edge. But I struggled to recall Isaac's face, the intensity of his emotions. He'd vanished into the ether of my past, revealing the true nothingness at my core. Another discarded skin. I'd scrubbed my hands of Huntington, my so-called parents and Callie's phone number. If I'd any place to call home, it was Beloit College.

I stood in front of the Phi Psi house, the familiar faux columns and seedy looking furniture on the front porch a welcoming beacon, but something was missing, the Greek letters over the front entrance. A kid with a shaggy mane of dreadlocked hair, a wispy little beard, and an oversized, moth-eaten fur coat headed for the front door. He told me the Phi Kappa Psi letters had been removed. The college had disbanded the fraternity for excessive drug use. Was I one of them, and hadn't I stayed in touch with anyone? "No. Been off the grid."

I twirled my ghost ring as he opened the door. "I'm Umo. I live here."

"I'm Seth. Nice to meet you. I lived here last year. Guess we're housemates."

Kids milled about the living room; no one I recognized. I grabbed my room assignment off the bulletin board and walked upstairs, Umo following like a stray dog. "Cool room. We freshmen only get doubles." He peered out the window directly above the missing letters. "Awesome view, dude. You can watch the whole world go by." He flopped down on the bed, a bare mattress on the floor. "Wanna get high?"

"Got any speed?"

"Sorry man. Not into that. Got some killer weed though."

Too bad. "Maybe later. Gotta get my bearings, set up my room, you know?"

STEPPING INTO THE hallway, I bumped into Bart, thrilled to see him, but when I threw my arms around him, he went rigid and pushed me away. He hadn't expected to see me again. I'd promised to write. Been insensitive, a narcissist who dragged others down with self-hatred. "You called me a liar and shut out Ashley when she needed you."

I cringed. More damage in my wake. "I'm gonna talk to her, gonna . . ."

"That's not going to happen. She's in Abruzzi, Italy right now, working on a sheep farm, trying to pull her life together . . . with my help."

"Then I'll write her . . ."

"You're not hearing me, you blew it. Ashley's with me now. I love her for who she is." I could tell from his demeanor he was prepared for an argument. "Of all people, how could you not feel her pain? You lack empathy, man; you miss a lot living in a black or white world, expecting everyone to meet your definition of perfection."

"I'm not trying to get back together; not looking for a second chance. I'm happy for you guys. Honestly, I just wanted to apologize. You're genuinely caring. You see people as more than reflections in the mirror. Why you became my friend in the first place. Ashley's lucky to have found you."

He visibly relaxed. "Oh. Hey, sorry if I came down on you so hard. It's just after everything with Ashley and then your parents calling in the fall, crazy out of their minds. They must be so relieved." Those two clowns? The so-called parents who sent me to a house as cold and empty as Mitzie's heart? "And you're so skinny . . . geez, you must've grown several inches, too."

"I guess I grew a bit, maybe lost a few pounds . . ."

"More like half of you. Please don't add anorexia to your OCD issues.

Hold on a sec. I've got something for you." Bart returned from his room with Grandma Matthews' candlesticks. "You left these behind. I knew you'd regret it, so I kept them for you."

I leaned into him, choked with tears. Thanked him over and over while he patted my back. My only remaining connection. "It's okay, Seth. Look, I gotta run across campus to the Art building. My parents gave me a new Nikon camera for Hannukah, and I've got a dark room lesson. We'll catch up later, okay?" He hugged me. "You know, maybe your journey was worthwhile. When you can see the good in others, you can find it in yourself. I really am glad you're back, and safe."

CHAPTER 2

SO MUCH HAD changed, but not the library, my sanctuary of perfection and order. Mrs. Nichols at her usual desk, the tables and chaired all aligned, books neatly filed away in the stacks by author, subject or title. Shocked by my appearance, she came out from behind her desk and asked if I'd been ill. Had I talked to anyone? My parents maybe? Was I eating regularly, having trouble sleeping, exercising compulsively? "Don't be ashamed. Lots of young people have body image issues." I glanced at my fat reflection in the floor to ceiling plate glass windows and shook my head. My eyes grew moist. Why couldn't she be my mom? She was there for me. She hugged me and I clung onto her, absorbing her concern like a desiccated sponge, and though I didn't want to, I started to cry and she patted my back. "It's okay, Seth, it's okay. Why haven't you spoken to your parents?"

"They're not my real parents, and they've never loved me."

"I'm sure that's not true."

But it was. And I got it. I didn't deserve better. I was selfish and self-centered; my self-hatred cast its terrible shadow over everyone who came within my orbit. "Nobody loves me. It's like my life's spinning out of control and everything's changing so fast, and I don't understand the rules or girls and I'm scared and so, so lonely." I wiped my eyes and nose. "I'm sorry. I shouldn't be laying this on you. It's not your problem."

She grasped me firmly by the shoulders. "All these feelings you're experiencing? You're not alone, and not just young people, and it can be overwhelming." She grabbed an oversized book sitting atop her desk and handed it to me. "This just came into the library. You should read it."

I looked at the cover. *Our Bodies, Ourselves*. "But it's for girls."

"There's lots of good information in here for boys, too; self-image, sexual experience . . . maybe it will even help you better understand girls. Okay?"

I nodded, sniffling. "When do you need it back?"

"You keep it. I've another copy." She handed me a Kleenex and walked me to my table. She knew exactly where I sat, even pulled out the same chair facing the same view. "I'm here if you want to talk, anytime, okay?"

I gave her a hug. "Mrs. Nichols, thank you for caring." I appreciated the book but put it aside. It was Bart's comment, his concern about OCD that troubled me. He'd mentioned that before, and I did tend to obsess about stuff, had trouble letting things go. But everyone has personality quirks, right? I looked up Obsessive Compulsive Disorder in the card catalogue and found a bunch of medical journal articles. Much of it focused on specific behaviors like obsessive hand washing and things that interfered with the ability to function normally, not my problem, but I did follow set patterns like always making my bed, checking to see if the hospital corners were perfect, or wiping the toilet seat before using it, using three squares of paper per wipe, courtesy flushing after fifteen squares, but so what? And maybe I was hyper-organized, needed things in their proper place, zealous about cleanliness. What was wrong with that? But as I read further, I began to furiously twirl my ghost ring. I had so many other symptoms. Unwanted sexual thoughts, dwelling on relationships, constantly seeking reassurances, always checking things (like doors and lockers), negative body image and fears of violence. I thought back to that scene on the bridge. Oh my God. I was so fucked.

CHAPTER 3

I AWOKE TO the sound of fingertips rapping on my window, the wind whistling and shrieking, driving icy cold air through every crack in the weather-beaten wood frames. I wrapped my blanket around me, trembling as much from going cold turkey as the extreme cold. I'd copped a bottle of White Cross, easy to come by, but after all those months on stronger amphetamines it was like quaffing espresso, not enough to rev my engine or mask bad thoughts. I peered outside my window overlooking College Street. A blizzard: drifts already piled high. I sighed, imagined Terry and me in Columbia or Peru by now, under a hot tropical sun, but he'd returned to Santa Cruz to embrace love, me to a frozen tundra. To empty space in my heart.

Without so much as a courtesy knock Umo barged into my room and flopped down on my already made bed. Eyes glazed. Totally baked. "A bunch of us are going to Big Hills Park to live in Medieval times, man. Wanna come?"

"It's a blizzard out there."

"That's what Medieval times was all about, man. People versus the elements! And I've scored some Windowpane acid, dude, killer stuff. Come on, man, join us. It'll be radical."

Umo had heard stories of the Phi Psi's crazy drug use. Peppered me with questions about the good old days of last year, the alumni eater already the stuff of legends. His ratty fur apropos for a journey back to the Dark Ages; my faux fur petroleum based. I flashed on the night at the bridge. LSD and Dexedrine, a dangerous combination, but White Cross? Not so much. "Beats writing a dramaturgy on Shakespeare's *The Merry Wives of Windsor*."

"Sir John Falstaff, right? Hey, you can be him." Not fat? Yeah, right.

WHAT A MOTLEY crew we were, hirsute beings building a blazing fire that illuminated the falling snow as through cheese cloth, blood orange and red, the colors shimmering on our glowing, ecstatic faces. Linking hands, we were a halo of brilliant light, the fire dancing in our eyes as we circled the bonfire with the fluid grace of oneness and danced and danced and danced until we were drenched in sweat, prostrate in the snow, and I recognized Lucy, the golden girl from UCC class, the girl with the heart-shaped face and waist length golden tresses, the girl who embodied Woodstock. She lay beside me cast in an aura of firelight, her gossamer wings aflutter. She was Galadriel, queen of the fairies, the Lady of Lothlorien, and we'd been transported to Middle Earth, living in a pine-scented enchanted forest making endless love for all eternity on a soft bed of fir needles. I remained very still, luxuriating in her brilliant amber light, not wanting to disturb this perfect moment, but the dazzling light faded to monochrome and the fresh forest scent to human sweat and wet wool, my clothes frozen to my skin. Lucy had hightailed it to the warm van. Heading back to Beloit, she glared at me and passed judgment; I didn't know how, but she knew what I had done to my brother.

I FELL INTO familiar tracks, seeking those few matchless hours of respite from the reality of my emptiness like any junkie. I dropped acid one day with a bunch of Kahuna's (as we now called ourselves in the old frat house for inexplicable reasons), sat around the living room awhile listening to the Amboy Dukes beseech us to enjoy the pleasures of a journey to the center of our minds before wandering outside, underdressed but impervious to the elements. The snow falling so hard I imagined God amusing Himself dumping bales of chicken feathers over His children. We made snowmen and snow angels, tossed snowballs, everything so transcendent, so full of love and fellowship I would have jumped into a ring of fire with them as we floated over puffy clouds toward Haven Hall, my old dorm, and gathered in a newly coed bathroom turned make-shift steam room. And there she is, the girl with the golden hair. Galadriel emerging from the mist with a dazzling smile, her naked body aglow, gossamer wings aflutter as she undresses me, takes my hands and leads me into a shower stall. In awe, I watch her metamorphose into Kali, the Hindu goddess, her many arms now encircling me like tendrils of an ancient tree, her nipples, third and fourth blinking eyes, opening a door to my soul.

Utterly beguiled by this vision of perfection, I fall backwards, arms outstretched, and land in soft, deep snow. I open my eyes. Blink repeatedly. I'm naked, lying on cold tile floor. Where's the snow? All about me steam and hazy images, disassociated voices asking if I'm okay, and suddenly I hear Galadriel's cut through the rest. "He's tripping his brains out." She pulls me back into the shower, hands me a bar of soap and demands I lather her. Pressing my hands into her small, firm breasts, her nipples stiffen under my open palms as my body sparks. This is no dream. I'm at Woodstock, about to make love to my hippie goddess. Oh, the delicious surrender, and yet, and yet, we're not alone. There are competing voices, an angel and a devil whispering to me over each shoulder, arguing back and forth. "I can't, it's wrong" or "I can, it's time," and I'm standing there, trying to be in the moment, trying to drown them out, my penis a projectile aimed at the object of my heart's desire, so close, so close, awaiting a command while this battle rages. Finally, with a cry of exasperation, I bolt from the bathroom and building stark naked, lay my body down and snuggle under a snow comforter, my body grown peaceably numb, and I'm fading, experiencing a cold rush of purifying relief. No more pain or guilt. Never again alone or abandoned. I'm dying. I'm free. I'm happy.

"SETH, GET UP, GET UP. YOU'RE TURNING BLUE!" It's Lucy, pulling me up and wrapping her long fur coat around us as I protest and beg her to leave me die in peace. "Leave you? Oh baby, you're freezing to death."

Shepherding me to her dorm room in Aldrich Hall, she tucks me into her bed, undresses and lies atop me, drawing her down comforter over us, a prickly heat spreading through me like molasses as she rubs her warm, silky-smooth body against mine, bathing my face in salty tears while crying "Let me hold you, just hold you." I come in a rush.

Next morning, acid flushed from my system, Lucy lay nestled against me sleeping, an angelic smile on her lovely face. What she must think of me! Embarrassed, so ashamed, sticky with my own seed, it's the Panty Raid girl redux and I'd never be able to face her, not ever, and slipped from her bed and room. Why had she saved me? Why hadn't she let me die?

CHAPTER 4

BART KNOCKED ON my door. He was having a party in his room; wanted me to come. I gave him the same litany of excuses I'd used all term—too much work, play rehearsals, keeping my head down, staying focused, improving my GPA— but he immediately pooh-poohed them. "You forgot to mention tonight's hair washing night. Come on, Seth, the Kahuna house isn't a monastery; time for the curtain to come down on your role as cloistered monk."

I laughed at his apt analogy. I'd been hiding since the debacle with Lucy. Told him maybe I'd drop by, but that wasn't good enough. Why was he so insistent? Just a bunch of hippies getting wasted and blowing out their ear drums. "Because I'm your best friend and I'm asking you, that's why. Trust me, you'll be glad you did." That piqued my curiosity. What the hell, my room was just down the hall; I could always sneak out.

Entering his room, the haze of reefer smoke gave me a contact high. Bodies were crammed wall to wall like sardines in a tin. Everyone having a party in their minds. Steppenwolf's *Why don't you come along little girl, on a magic carpet ride* blaring from stereo speakers. A pretty girl, real familiar looking, sat by the window in a shabby overstuffed chair he'd procured from the local Salvation Army gently swaying to the music and snapping photos with a fancy looking camera. Her heart-shaped face and mane of frizzy black hair reminiscent of an actress who played a hippie chick named Snow White in a weird, paranoiac Sixties flick starring James Coburn. I must've been staring because she looked over, shifted in her seat, patted the empty space and gave me a come-hither smile. Intrigued, I walked over and perched on the edge of her chair. "I hear you're going up to Madison fall term to be in a guerilla theatre troupe," she said.

"Yeah, well, to try out, anyway. Probably won't make the cut."

"Don't be self-deprecating, you're a great actor. I loved you in *You Can't Take It with You* our first term, so funny in that bald wig and fat suit." What fat suit? "So, let's see, then you were Horace in Moliere's *A School for Wives*, big role for a second term freshman. Mercutio in *Romeo and Juliet*. I cried during your dying scene. Then . . ."

I felt awkward, bit my lip; nervously twirled my ghost ring. "Wow, my one and only fan!" Dammit. Who is she? "So, you a friend of Bart's? In classes together?"

"Showing him how to use the dark room. He's taking an elementary photography class. You don't remember me, do you?" Geez, who is she? "It's okay. I used to be chubby, too."

No, it can't be. "Sinead? You invited me to that Christian Fellowship dinner."

"Yup, don't remind me. What a disaster. I've a confession to make; seems so silly now when I think back on it. I was so painfully insecure." She took a deep breath. "Might as well get it out of the way. Promise you won't be mad?" I nodded. "I sent you an anonymous letter."

I almost fell off the chair. "You? Geez, I thought some guy wanted to fuck me, I mean, you weren't the only insecure one. Your letter had me walking on eggshells around the department for months."

"I'm so sorry. Please forgive me, but why'd you assume it came from a guy?" Bart asked the same question, same obvious answer. I'm an idiot. Should've read that damn book Mrs. Nichols gave me.

"You wrote '*I've never felt this way about another guy before.*' Seemed obvious to me at the time. Now I feel ridiculous."

"But it was true. I had a major crush on you, and you were interested in religion, and we were both, well, kind of out of step with things and I just thought we had so much in common. But who'd want a fat girl, right?"

"I could say the same about me."

"Oh no. Those bright blue eyes, all those freckles, the long curly red hair . . . you were so cute. I knew you were going out with that girl Ashley but then I heard you'd broken up. Never expected you'd give me a second glance but when you asked if I'd accepted Jesus as my personal savior I . . . well, I thought we were connecting." She looked at me wistfully. "Were we?"

"I assumed we'd discuss important stuff at that dinner like forgiveness of sins, the tug of war between right and wrong, not abstinence!" She was like those sweet, innocent senoritas in Merida. Such a pretty butterfly had emerged from that cocoon of fat. "I have thought about you." Was this fate?

She aimed her camera at me. "Hold it! Don't move." *Snap, snap, snap.* "I want to capture this moment forever."

"In some cultures, taking photos of people without their permission is considered rude or worse, like you're capturing their soul or something." And she was capturing mine.

"Open those baby blues wide." *Snap, snap, snap.* "The camera's my interface to the world. I'm shy; it's not. I'd feel naked without it."

I recalled Bart's insistence that I come to the party. "Our meeting today... this wasn't by chance, was it?" She blushed. "There's this movie *The President's Analyst*. You remind me of the hippie chick in it named Snow White. Would you like to see it? I could bring it to campus."

"Wow. No one's ever called me a hippie chick. Thought that got reserved for girls like Lucy." She put the camera aside and brazenly took my hand. Squeezing hard, she gave me a blistering look and asked if I still believed I was beyond redemption, and when I nodded she intertwined her hand with mine and suggested we go to my room. She was going to save us both.

I floated down the hallway, a balloon on her string, and once in my room she immediately alighted on the photo of Jonah and me and picked it up. "I know you're the little redhead. Who's the other boy?"

"My stepbrother."

"Must've been taken with one of those old Brownie box cameras so popular in the Fifties. They produced grainy images. Who took the photo? Obviously not you or your brother."

I started to get a queasy feeling. "I . . . I don't know." I squeezed my eyes shut. Don't think. Don't remember. Be in this moment.

"You once said you didn't know anything about your background."

"I don't. I was adopted. Are you still attending those Sunday dinners?"

"No, turned out Jesus wasn't the answer for me either. I joined the Christian Fellowship for the same reasons you went to Mexico. I was hiding behind protective layers of fat and I'm willing to bet you were running away from yourself. But I did learn one thing. Jesus helps those who help themselves."

About to object, she shushed me with a kiss and gazed into my eyes, into my soul. "I've awaited this moment a long time." And then she opened herself to me. A plunge into a lush pool of sweet, velvety whipped cream. And had the world ended then and there it would have been okay with me.

We drifted off before being startled awake by a sudden knock on the door. A disembodied girl's voice. "Sinead, Ken keeps calling, and he sounds pretty fuckin' annoyed. He's still waiting for you; wants you there like now."

"Oh fuck," Sinead muttered, abruptly detaching herself from me and grabbing her clothes. "I'm coming, okay!" I sat up on my elbows, confused. "I'm so sorry, but I have to go. I have an appointment. Almost forgot." The stroke of midnight. Cinderella leaving the prince, flouting my pleas that she stay, spend the night, make love again. "Really, I have to leave. I'll come back." But she didn't. She'd abandoned me like everyone else. She had a boyfriend! She didn't need me any more than she needed Jesus. She'd saved herself.

I had the dream again that night. *Jonah and I are in our space ship exploring unchartered reaches of outer space, powering past planets and other comets when suddenly a huge meteor heads directly toward us, and we veer our craft to the left, then right, trying to avoid an imminent collision but it's too late, we go careening off course, heading for a black hole, and I reach out to Jonah but he's a jack-in-the-box, grinning and boinging up and down singing "All around the mulberry bush the monkey chased the weasel. The monkey thought 'twas all in fun. Pop! Goes the weasel" and our escape hatch has opened, sucking all the air, and me, from our ship, and I tumble alone and powerless into the vast black vacuum of space toward a black hole and it's growing larger and I'm so scared, so scared, so scared.*

Bright daylight assaulted my eyes and I went through the motions of the day like a zombie, mired in a deep, dark funk. Joy turned to ash. Between classes I hid in the library to avoid everyone, especially Bart, who'd want details. And that night I wallowed in misery. How many times did I need be reminded—mine was a God of retribution, not redemption.

It was still dark when I was jolted awake. Someone was hovering over me. Sinead, naked, snapping photos with her camera. "You look so beautiful," she said. "I want to give you something very special to me. It was my grandmother's." Unclasping a Celtic pendant that rested in the valley between her milky-white breasts, she placed it around my neck. "Our beginning." A sign, something lost, something gained. I pressed it hard into my chest. It didn't matter why she'd left. She slipped under the covers and as I experienced again the thrill of her warm, pliant body, I pushed back the nagging voice: "Who's Ken?"

CHAPTER 5

I PERUSED MY copy of Beloit's Pig Book for someone by that name though I'd no idea what he looked like. Even glanced through the photography portfolio she'd left behind in her haste to get to class. No Ken surfaced, but something did that made my heart quicken, a bottle of Black Beauties! Amphetamines more powerful than Dexedrine, the obvious explanation for her dramatic weight loss. I took one, and by the time Sinead returned I was ravenous for her and tore at her clothes. After we made love she noticed the bottle on my dresser, scolded me for invading her privacy but quickly assured me she didn't need them anymore. Would have tossed the bottle in the trash had I not stopped her. I told her I loved speed and had taken one. Relief washed across her face. "They've helped me become the person I want to be, not that pathetic fat scaredy-cat; she'd never have been so forward with you. Never would've had the guts to take what she wanted. No looking back. Know what I mean?"

"I took Dexedrine every day in Mexico. Really missed the way it made me feel." I asked if she could turn me on to her dealer so I could cop some, but she shook her head. He'd stop supplying her if she told anyone else. But we could do it together. It would be special. Just between us.

"But what about your boyfriend Ken?"

She laughed. "My boyfriend?" Turned out he was her TA in advanced photography and it was really hard to book darkroom time. I recalled Bart rushing off to the darkroom; his insistence I come to his party; Sinead leaving. Why'd I always assume the worst? We coupled again and again, imbued with the power of the Black Beauties, and lying beside her, bathed in sweat and the sweet aroma of sex, I felt that surge in power I'd experienced on the bridge in Mexico. Sinead and speed were the answers to all life's questions, and for the balance of winter term my aperture on the world shrunk to her furry triangle, attracted to it like a moth to flame, and the more familiar I became with her body, the harder it was to keep my hands off her. Just being near her made me think about sex. Everything else a distraction, my classes, rehearsals, even our dwindling supply of Black Beauties.

We sought out scintillating new venues for our sexcapades. The black box theatre in Pearson Hall. The dark room in the Photography department. We even went so far as to make love burrowed inside a VW-sized soft sculpture of a woman's womb while others roamed the exhibits in Wright Art Hall unawares. And I ignored my friends, a point brought home by Bart one evening when he saw me alone. "Well look who's come out of his shell. To what do I owe this pleasure?" He pointedly looked about him. "Where's your appendage?"

"In the dark room with her photography TA, Ken. Sinead has lessons with him every few weeks for advanced photography."

Bart shrugged. "Never heard of him but hey, I'm only taking an intro class." Huh? It was a small department. No, don't go there. Trust Sinead.

"Thought we'd get a chance to hang together this term, but I'll be leaving for Vermont and interning at the state psychiatric hospital. Ashley's joining me there. She got a job on another sheep farm. When I hooked you two up, I didn't expect you'd immediately move in together. Pretty big commitment. Removes a lot of options."

"I don't care. I love her."

CHAPTER 6

FOR WEEKS SINEAD harped at me to call home. Tell Mitzie about us. Like we'd be one big happy family, and on Mother's Day, frustrated by my refusal to do so, she audaciously dialed my home number and handed me the phone. "Wish her a Happy Mother's Day. Tell her about me." I should've hung up, told Sinead to mind her own business, but love is contagious and I wanted Mitzie's. My mistake.

"Sinead? What kind of Jewish name is Sinead? Figures you'd hook-up with a shiksa tramp."

Sinead wasn't like that, but Mitzie's words wormed their way into my skull. I wasn't Sinead's first, I was pretty sure. Wasn't there supposed to be some resistance, some blood, the first time? Maybe *Our Bodies, Ourselves* would have something about that. I'd have to check. And Bart knowing nothing of a Ken in the photography department. And so many private dark room lessons, always late at night. And who'd been the aggressor that first night? Not me. She'd been just like the panty raid girl. And then left me...for Ken! Seeds of doubt germinated and I struggled to suppress them. Don't obsess, I told myself. Be happy. Be in the moment. I doubled down on my daily dose. That helped.

I never shared Mitzie's comments with Sinead. When she asked me to bring her home mid-semester break, I lied and said they were out of the country. She didn't want them thinking she was just some girl I was sleeping with, not someone special. Someone worthy of me. I switched topics to her family.

"Nice segue. You're really good at changing subjects. I'm looking forward to introducing you to my folks. They're gonna love you. I'm an Army brat. Lived everywhere, bases all over the country, never in one place long enough to call home. Always meeting new people, trying to fit in. Like I told you, my best friend's always been my camera. And you're no different. Acting's your camera. But I'm never sure what's real with you."

Her folks had returned to the family homestead, a dairy farm in Janesville, her junior year of high school after her dad put in his twenty and retired from the service. "The farm saved them, maybe all of us. Life was hell before they stopped drinking. Dad would beat Mom, and she'd numb herself with more booze, a vicious cycle, but in Janesville they found God and stopped drinking. Dad's now a deacon at their church..."

"Really. I always wondered where He hung out." She hit me with a pillow. "Sorry. It's just I assumed you were from a wealthy family with all that expensive equipment and..."

"Better not to assume, right? That camera was a big stretch for my folks, but I was so miserable that last move. It was sweet of them. My oldest brother, Josh, couldn't handle the constant disruption, got in trouble with the law, usually DUIs, stuff like that. Dad pulled strings and got him enlisted to avoid jail time, and now he's back on the farm married with a kid and I think happy. The farm, finding God, it's been great... for them. I'm here on scholarship; no way could we afford Beloit tuition and if I don't spend more time working on my portfolio, I'll lose it. I've rolls and rolls of film to develop."

I scrambled atop her. I wanted her again. Wanted to obliterate thoughts of that dark room, her TA, her leaving me that first night. But she pushed me off. "No, Seth, I want us to talk. I sacrificed for that scholarship, more than you could possibly know. Straight As and almost perfect SATs and... and much, much more." A dark shadow crossed her face. What was she holding back? "And photography's not a hobby, it's my passion, part of who I am and want to do with my life. Like you with acting."

"Acting's the only time I feel real."

"Acting is only one facet of your life. People in love open up to each other. Let me in. Tell me about your family. I've always heard adopted kids were the most loved, because they're chosen."

I told her to close her eyes. Imagine a scene out of a Norman Rockwell painting. An old whaling village with white clapboard houses, a duck pond, a working dad always home in time to play catch in the backyard before dinner, a stay-at-home mom awaiting your return from school with homemade cookies and milk, wanting to know about your day, yeasty aromas of fresh baked bread cooling on the counter, report cards proudly displayed on the fridge door. Like Donna Reed in *It's a Wonderful Life*. "That's great, if you live in the movies," she countered. "Get real with me."

Donna Reed was an actor, like me. Who knows what she was really like, if she suffered from depression or drank too much or did drugs or beat her kids. We're all veneer. "I guess you can't relate."

"Oh, I get it. I don't come from a perfect family like yours. My parents had a shotgun wedding, Mom pregnant with my older brother. And growing up in a WASPy old whaling village with money and a nice house and never having to worry about where you're moving next sounds pretty goddam nice to me. Tell me about your brother."

"Jonah? He was dynamite, the best big brother ever. My best friend. I really missed him when he went to Columbia University. He left before graduation. Said school was a waste of time. He wanted to do something real, so he's building houses now for needy people in Central America. My folks are visiting there right now, helping out."

"Were they disappointed he didn't finish school before going down there?"

"Jonah was their wonder boy. He could do no wrong."

"Your family's so different than mine. I can't wait to meet them."

"Well, like I said, they're out of the country. Won't be back for quite a while. Sinead, is Ken really your photography TA? Because Bart said he's never heard of him."

"Of course. Why would I lie to you?"

"You guys aren't involved?"

She hugged me to her so tight the pendant almost punctured my skin. "There's no one but you. Don't be so insecure." She was a liar. We were both liars.

CHAPTER 7

LEAVING OUR CLOISTERED love nest, she spent more time in the dark room while I satisfied theatre major requirements in set design and stage craft. I'd also been cast as Estragon in Becket's *Waiting for Godot*, playing opposite Thad, the actor who'd called me a sex toy. He and I barely conversed offstage. We were like rock stars who toured in separate buses, only interacting on stage, but I didn't lack for attention. Girls suddenly seemed interested in me, lavishing on me beguiling smiles I thought reserved only for cool guys like Bart (Lucy, of course, not one of them. She gave me the cold shoulder, and who could blame her). I couldn't understand all this unprecedented attention; I was the same fat poseur I'd always been, not that it mattered, attached as I was at the hip to Sinead. She had antennae, quick to take my hand if she noticed other girls flirting. Marking her territory. And less interested in sex to boot. Satisfied with holding hands, kissing and snuggling. I swear, we were down to making love once a day. I needed more; I craved it. And it pissed me off she wouldn't turn me on to her dealer, controlling our supply of Black Beauties. She was making decisions for me, and one fine Sunday afternoon, without even asking me, I found myself on a bus to Janesville to have Sunday night dinner with her family.

Her brother, John, picked us up at the bus depot and drove out to the family homestead over hilly two-lane roads that narrowed into one lane dirt and gravel as we entered their farmland. All that was missing was a hayride. I was apprehensive. No idea what to expect, or what she'd told them about me, but her brother was friendly and the homestead itself, a century old Victorian with a big front porch complete with porch swing like out of the old *Andy Hardy* movies starring Mickey Rooney and Judy Garland, was charming, Wisconsin as I'd pictured it in my mind's eye. She introduced me as her boyfriend, and with them being religious Christians and all, geez, who knew what they thought about premarital sex, much less Jews? I wondered if they saw devil's horns on my head.

We sat down to dinner at a long table laden with heaping bowls of mashed potatoes, green beans, biscuits steaming from the oven, homemade jams, fresh churned butter, baked chicken and ham, everything made from scratch, mostly home grown (made me wish I had an appetite, but I was pumped up on speed). It all had an old timey-like sensibility, holding hands around the table, saying Grace, just as we'd done that Sunday night in the chapel, and that hadn't exactly worked out too well. Or had it? I was sleeping with her; just not getting enough. Regardless, they didn't seem to be the fucked-up family she'd described. They were a slice of Americana. I could show her what a real fucked up family looked like!

Her parents peppered me with questions about growing up in the big city, as if New York City and Huntington were synonymous, surprised to discover I was Jewish, us having met at a Christian Fellowship dinner, but apparently nonplussed, so I relaxed, found the rhythm of the scene, let my dialogue flow folksier, more down home twangy. Sinead's sisters-in-law kept glancing my way and giggling, passing unspoken comments to Sinead. Her brothers, faces weather-beaten, hands calloused, discussed problems in the fields, which animals needed veterinary care, weather predictions for fall planting, upcoming church events. They were rednecks for sure, but they were putting arable land to good purpose, not building crappy little houses made of ticky-tacky like Jerry on the potato fields of eastern Long Island.

Sinead's craggy-faced dad reminded her oldest brother the combines still awaited his attention. "They won't clean themselves." Then turned to me, the city boy, and explained how once the corn and soybean crops were in the granary they had to clean and fix the combines, remove debris from the fields, clear the tree lines and get everything ready for the next planting season. He glanced at my soft pink hands and barely touched plate. "Guess this is all new to you, Seth; maybe we'll put you to work to build your appetite. It's year round here, just like going to school, right Sinead? Hard work's the only thing that pays off."

"We work very hard, Daddy."

"Hope you have an appetite for dessert," her mom said, serving up large slices of homemade apple pie. "I understand you're joining a theatre company up in Madison for your field term experience. I hope you do musicals. I love them. Do you sing?"

"He's got a great voice, Mom."

"Actually, it's guerilla theatre."

Her dad put his fork down. "What?"

"You see, Dad," Josh guffawed, tugging at the bill of his CAT tractor cap, "they perform in ape suits. Hear that's real big in Nuu York City."

Sinead shook her head. "That's G U E R I L L A, Josh, not Gorilla."

"What's the difference, little sister. Still a bunch of longhair apes. No offense of course, Seth."

"None taken." Asshole. "The theatre company stages parodies, usually focusing on socio-economic and political issues like war and capitalism. This is dynamite pie, Mrs. O'Brien, the whole meal was delicious. Thank you for having me."

"You just make sure Sinead knows when you're gonna perform in them gorilla suits," Josh added. "I gotta see that."

Sinead made a show of looking at her watch and asked John for a ride back to the bus depot, but before we could make our way to the door her mom insisted we take the leftovers, clucking how thin we were, in need of a good meal now and then. In fact, she suggested we join the family for Sunday night dinner every week and Sinead enthusiastically agreed. She'd obviously updated the status of our relationship, an assessment bolstered when Mrs. O'Brien took her aside on the front porch and reminded her to use birth control. "Be a little smarter than me, honey." She planted a kiss on Sinead's flushed cheek. "You two have plenty of time to raise a family. And that goes for you too, young man. It's not just the woman's responsibility."

Driving us to the depot John quipped "Sis, they may be born again, but they weren't born yesterday," then turned and warned me to treat Sinead right or there'd be hell to pay.

CHAPTER 8

THE WALLS WERE closing in. Sinead was trying to control my life, just like Mitzie. I was suffocating, ingesting several black Beauties a day to suppress obsessive thoughts and still barely able to hold it together. She had no strings on me, and to prove it I mustered the courage to hit on Lucy one afternoon after a theatre class. Asked if she wanted to get together some time, an offer refused, but not before she pointedly asked after Sinead and called me a jerk.

Sinead and I started to quibble, small things at first, like why we had to have dinner with her folks every Sunday night with her entire family acting like we were a fait accompli, or her harping on my refusal to introduce her to my folks. Wasn't she good enough? She'd no idea Mitzie blitzed me with letters demanding I find a less sullied, more appropriate, meaning Jewish, girlfriend. I picked at her faults like the pimples she loved to squeeze and pop on my back. She was a flag waving, support our boys in Vietnam girl with zero interest in political activism or my desire to do guerilla theatre in Madison. She suggested I temper my radicalism, show more respect for Tricky-Dicky Nixon. What had I been thinking? I was living with a goddam Republican who liked bubble-gum music, claimed subtitles in foreign films gave her headaches and thought the premise of *The President's Analyst* inane, though agreed her resemblance to Snow White was striking. After a while, things got so bad the only way I could get off during sex was fantasizing I was coupling with Lucy. I was acting like Dave, treating Sinead like a receptacle, which made me feel like a total shit, but I did it anyway. I couldn't stop myself.

I confronted her about leaving used tissues under her pillow, squeezing the toothpaste from the middle and never making the bed and she treated it all with good humor and understanding. Guys were always relationship phobic, she said. Who could compete with Mr. OCD's perfect hospital corners? And when I complained she'd filed my favorite Led Zep LP with the *Z*'s, knowing full well it belonged with the *L*'s, she huffed I should appreciate her attempt to get into my awful music. Take that shit down to the basement.

"Two can play this game, you know. You're always harping about our lovemaking; always begging for more. Jesus Christ! What are you trying to do? Set a new world record? Do you have any idea how sore I am? Sometimes I can barely walk. What? Afraid it's going to stop working? Trust me. Not a problem! And the way you drone on every night reciting lines from whatever stupid play you're in with the lights on and Cream or Hendrix blasting from your stereo. I'm trying to sleep! And I'll tell you something else. You pop my Black Beauties like they're M&Ms. You're too skinny and edgy as hell and picking fights with me over nothing and I swear to God if you don't cut back, I'll stop procuring it, understand? I'll cut you off." I was steaming, furiously twirling my ghost ring. She paused, put her arms around me. Nuzzled my neck. "Please honey, I'm not perfect but neither are you. Try to be happy without the pills; maybe it'll become habit-forming."

But with each passing day I grew more convinced things were developing in that dark room that had nothing to do with photos. Those sessions were now every two weeks! Probably explained her laissez faire attitude toward sex. I felt diminished. Wasn't I manly enough? Maybe Mitzie was right for once. I needed someone more appropriate, someone I could bring home with her approval.

TOWARD THE END of the semester, she was spending every evening in the dark room supposedly working feverishly on a portfolio she wanted to send to a photography company in NYC, hoping to score an internship for her field term, but by now I knew better. I'd been played a fool right from the beginning. Well, no more. Last night of term I decided to call her out. Marched over to Wright Arts Hall. Demanded to speak to Ken in the Photography department, confront him man to man, but was met with blank stares. What TA? Ken who? No one knew who I was talking about. And she was nowhere to be found. Distraught, I returned to the house. Stalked the quiet hallway amped on speed. Images of Sinead and faceless Ken on the dark room floor. In the back seat of a car. In his room. Sinead loving the one she was with. By the time she finally returned from wherever at two a.m., two a.m. for God's sake, I'd whipped myself into a frenzy, my spine and neck itching, spiders crawling all over me. And what does she do? Asks for my opinion of her finished portfolio. As if nothing was amiss. The audacity! "You're worse than the whores in Orizaba. They do it to survive. You know, I've wanted other girls, especially Lucy. She's a real hippie goddess!" The spiders were crawling up my neck. "I get off imagining you're her."

Tears welled in her eyes. "Go ahead, fuck her. See if I care."

"You'd like that, wouldn't you?" Spiders all over my head, my field of vision narrowing. "Make you feel less guilty for cheating." I swatted at them. "I'm only with you for the speed."

"Is that all I've meant to you?"

"You left me our very first night, a time so special, for Ken. And all those other nights you said you were in the dark room. I went there tonight. Asked for him. He wasn't there; there's no TA. I looked everywhere for you. You lied to me. You've been lying to me all along."

"You spied on me?" She dropped her portfolio and flattened herself against a wall. "You're out of your mind, fantasizing! I haven't done anything with anyone. I swear, Seth, please believe me." She reached out to hug me. "Let me help you; you're not thinking straight; the speed's making you psychotic."

I'm trembling. Can barely breathe. The spiders. The spiders. They're all over me and I'm flailing at them. My brain's short-circuiting. "Go away. Make them go away." And she's grabbing my shoulders, trying to calm me, and my arm smashes into her face and knocks her back against the wall with a thud and she's sliding to the floor trembling, covering her head in a posture of submission, terrorized, and I jerk back, look at my hands, look at the girl prostrate on the floor. Shake my head. No. This isn't me. My hands couldn't do that. Couldn't have hit her. It wasn't possible. Me, who opened doors, held out chairs, walked curbside. A gentleman. I couldn't perpetrate such a monstrous act. I lift her, clasp her to me. "It's not me, I swear, it's the spiders, the spiders," and she strokes and comforts me as I weep inconsolably, assuring me it's okay, she knows I didn't mean it, and we make frenzied love as if the world was ending.

When I woke next morning she was sitting on the floor, stone-faced, scissors in hand, surrounded by suitcases, icy blue eyes rimmed with red from crying. "All this time you were never really interested in me. You never encouraged me, understood or respected my desire to become the person I wanted to be, a person you should've been proud of. I was your Snow White so long as my pussy remained untouched by anyone except you." She quietly rose and walked over to the hotplate on our dresser. Started making a cup of tea. "Last night I feared for my life, and I watched myself forgive you, even have sex with you. I cannot believe how I belittled myself, allowed myself to be abused." Her eyes blazed with sudden fury. "I AM NOT GOING TO BECOME MY MOTHER!"

"Sinead, I'm so sorry. Please forgive me. . . ."

"You sound like my father after he'd hit her, begging her forgiveness. SHUT THE FUCK UP and listen for a change. It's so pathetic; I completely misread you. Something's terribly, terribly wrong with you and I'd pity you if you weren't such a pig. You're a stranger to me. We've shared a bed, our bodies, but not ourselves. All you cared about was adding notches to your penis and being supplied with amphetamines. We're not even friends. Just junkies. And once your pathetic insecurities were satisfied I became disposable, used goods, a piece of obsolete military hardware. White trash, not good enough to bring home to Mom and Dad much less introduce on the phone. I really loved you. You were the only boy I've ever been with, and it was so special to me!" She slammed the cup on the dresser, shattering ceramic, spraying tea everywhere. "And your absurd fantasies. You wanna know where I was last night, and all those other nights when I'd leave for a few hours?" She reached into her purse and pulled out a bottle, shoved it in my face, then opened it and sprayed me with Black Beauties. "I was getting these for you, you speed crazed junkie. Ken's my dealer, asshole, the guy supplying the speed that's driven you out of your mind. He never touched me. But you, you're a monster."

The Balrog. In my face, its contorted mouth open and laughing. I started to hyperventilate. "Why didn't you tell me? Why did you lie to me?"

"I was raped by a disgusting pervert, the reverend of my parents' church, head of its scholarship committee, the decision maker. The slimy holier than thou bastard called me in for a personal interview, complimented me, how proud God was of me, the scholarship was mine but for one little thing . . . one little thing he needed to be sure he and Jesus had made the right choice. He sat down next to me on the sofa, put his arm around me, started rubbing my back. I sat frozen with fear, like with you last night, not knowing what to do. He pushed me down, pressed his hands into my breasts, pulled my panties off. 'You want this scholarship, don't you?' I lay there, feeling nothing, doing nothing. I should have gouged his eyes out, but I needed that scholarship, my ticket out of the hell my family's life had been, payment for services rendered. I started taking speed to numb myself, to obliterate him, stop feeling him, smelling his disgusting breath. To feel alive, become someone else. I thought you of all people would understand. We belonged together. We would heal each other. I never let anyone touch me until you. I joined the Christian Fellowship to hide from men. I should have stayed hidden. That's my excuse. What's yours?"

Blood drained from my face and I grasped ahold of the dresser, stars and planets swirling about me, my trembling legs rubber. The Balrog demon edged closer, closer. Blackness. And when I opened my eyes she was gone but for the lingering trace of her lilac perfume. Pills and shredded photos blanketing the floor. An envelope beside me. Her stationery. I reflexively reached for three Black Beauties, about to shove them in my mouth, then let them fall. Oh my God. I was a drug addict. And a liar. The worst kind. Lying to myself. It wasn't an accident. Her face didn't get in the way of my arm. I hit her! I leaned back against the bureau, picked up the envelope wrestling with an impulse to tear it up, knowing it contained the fallout from monstrous acts, inexcusable violence, squandered love. I had loosed the monster, surrendered to dark impulses. I was an evil cultivating in a petri dish, mired in filth nothing would ever wash away.

Yet I harbored a delusion of hope, like a candle in the wind, she'd forgiven me, and tore the seal. She pulled no punches.

Dear Seth,

I will never understand what turned you into a monster, but that is ultimately your problem to deal with. I have to get on with the rest of my life, and you cannot be a part of it. I know I will never forget you, and never forgive you for turning our love and passion into something so ugly. You need to look inward and face your demons, however frightening. You need to figure out why you have such a reservoir of self-hatred and violence in you. You will never be a complete person until you do. You will never become an adult until you do. I can't save you, Seth. I have to save myself. I need to embark on a journey of re-discovery, figure out what is missing in me. A part of me died when I was raped, and drugs won't bring that back, nor allowing myself to be badly mistreated, accepting what's fundamentally unacceptable. I will never be a victim ever again, feel guilty ever again. What happened, happened; I cannot change that, only my response to it. I am telling you this because I know something terrible happened to you, Seth, something you are hiding behind drugs. Something that terrifies you. I saw that in your reaction, and almost felt guilty leaving you blacked out on the floor, as I truly believe you are not the violent person I saw, that you are sorry for what you did, but you did it, and that is unforgivable. I will always love you, and always hate you as well, and right now that's the emotion driving my feelings. I hope someday I will recall the good things, the loving things we did together, and be able to smile when I think of you; I hope.

I've left pieces of photographs taken while you were sleeping the morning I returned to your room. You were so beautiful; I thought I'd found the missing piece of me. I thought I would cherish those images forever. Think of them as my shattered heart, a lasting memory of an obscene act, of love squandered, because that horrible man may have raped me, and I let him, and I have to live with that, but he never broke my heart. You'll have that on your conscience for the rest of your life.

Sinead

I wept as I swept up the pills and shredded photos and tossed them in the waste basket. Never again. No drugs. No relationships. Only what I deserved. Aloneness.

CHAPTER 9

I DREAMT A different dream that night. *My hands glistened crimson with Sinead's blood, my nostrils filled with an acrid iron saltiness. Eyes bleeding, offal spilling from her mouth, she gurgled "You did this," and collapsed in a pool of muck.*

I shook my head like an Etch A Sketch pad, attempting to obliterate the horrible image, but could no more erase the past than escape it with drugs, and though I tried, I couldn't rearrange our last night together into something I could live with, rationalize the person I thought I was with my despicable actions. I didn't know who I was, but I did know this—opening doors for girls, holding out chairs, walking curbside to shield them from passing cars, did not make me a gentleman. Hitting them made me a monster.

Quitting amphetamines cold turkey, I knew my body would go through an intense withdrawal and there was nothing I could do but suck it up and drink endless cups of black coffee. Speed brought out my inner demons, turned me into someone I didn't want to be but nevertheless was, no different than the demon I'd encountered in Jonah's room. I'd tried to escape myself in Mexico, but Hemingway was right. You can't escape yourself by moving from one place to another. I thought about Sinead, about my brother, about all the collateral damage in my wake. Never again, never again. If I couldn't learn to love myself, I'd never be worthy of anyone else's. I had to carry on.

I moved my few personal possessions to the basement of the old Phi Psi house, packed a duffle bag and trekked out to the on ramp of I-90, stopping only to post a hastily scribbled note to Jerry and Mitzie advising them I could be reached through the telephone number and address of my old Phi Psi brother Jack, now in grad school at UMad, my message neither an act of kindness nor filial concern, but a manifesto. This time I was operating under my own volition and had all my ducks in a row—full credit for both my senior thesis and hopefully, an internship with the Mad City Mime Troupe. The long arm of the Selective Service Administration wouldn't reach me!

I stuck out my thumb under a late-August blue marshmallow sky and had a ride in minutes. I couch-surfed at Jack's place in Madison and perused the classifieds in *The Daily Cardinal*, the University's student newspaper, for rooms to let, and found a deal almost too good to be true; twenty-five bucks a month for a room in a four-bedroom shared house just off campus. One caveat. The owner, a UMad English professor, was looking for a Shabbos Goy, a Gentile responsible for turning on and off lights and appliances on the Sabbath, hence the low rent. I applied in person and let my looks speak for me. He seemed satisfied, noting Catholics, like Jews, understood the importance of customs and ceremony, but he didn't resemble any Orthodox Jew I'd ever encountered. Ivy League tweed and a manicured beard had replaced the payot, the tallit katan, beaver fur hat and long black coat. The deal straightforward. Every Friday night I'd light the oven, turn on the stereo, ensure the house was well-lit and disappear from 6 p.m. until midnight. His weekly Shabbos dinners were private affairs. I got the room, no questions asked, and after unpacking, careful to hide Grandma's Shabbos candlesticks in the bureau under my clothes, I ran into the other tenants, three extremely hot UMad girls. Private affairs. Yeah, I got it.

My audition for the Troupe was in two days and I practiced my monologue, a scene out of Shakespeare's *As You Like It*, on the veranda outside Der Rathskeller in the Student Union, hoping they'd like it enough to take me on as an unpaid intern for the year, but it was difficult to concentrate. It wasn't merely the cacophony of students milling about, chatting, laughing, drinking beer, swimming off the dock on Lake Mendota, taking advantage of precious few months before it turned solid ice. It was Sinead. I'd lived with this girl for months without thought for her soul, her motivations or passions. How could I have been so blind and narcissistic, treated her so badly? How was I supposed to live with myself? How could I be so maladroit when it came to understanding flesh and blood people yet so adept at plumbing the depths of characters in a script, figuring out what made them tick and breathing life into them? I drafted a letter to her begging her forgiveness, put it in an envelope, addressed it to Beloit College and stamped it, but standing in front of a mailbox knew I wouldn't post it and shoved it in my back pocket. I didn't deserve her forgiveness.

CHAPTER 10

I EXPECTED THE audition to be held in a theatre but found myself instead in a small, cluttered room in the basement of the Student Union sandwiched between the janitorial and utility rooms, a dingy, dark space redolent of ink from a hand-cranked mimeograph machine spewing blue-inked copies of flyers advertising upcoming guerilla theatre events. I stood there breathing in the intoxicating odor of duplicating fluid. Taking in the scene. Two guys armed with heavy duty staple guns were sticking the flyers in pouches, probably to plaster on utility poles throughout town. Another guy in a corner hammered away at what looked like a large box. A tall, dark-haired man who resembled Jonah, or what Jonah might look like after so many years, was gesticulating in front of a small group, their eyes fixed on him. A woman behind a desk half hidden by reams of papers brusquely asked what I wanted, her New Yawk accent so thick you could cut it with a knife.

"I'm here to interview for . . ."

"Heshy, yuh fresh meat's heah."

This guy's resemblance to Jonah was uncanny. He had olive-hued skin and intense coal black eyes that bore into you. He reached out a clammy, ink-stained hand and shook mine. "Name's Heshy. You're the actor from Beloit College, right?" His breath smelled of espresso and tobacco. I nodded, barely able to speak, so taken aback. "Ready to forget everything you ever learned about stage craft?"

"I've prepared a short monologue from Shakespeare's *As You Like It* for the audition. Act two, scene seven . . ."

"Ah, *All the world's a stage*. Great. Awesome. I'm sure it's terrific, but right now we're preparing for an Action up at the state capitol building tomorrow." He sized me up. "Hmmm, I think you'll fit perfectly." He yelled across the room. "Shelley, if you've finished that coffin, I just found its occupant, Seth, right?"

He motioned over to the corner. "Get in the coffin. You're playing Death of Democracy."

"What am I supposed to do?"

He laughed. "Die, obviously," and turned to another guy. "Military Industrial Complex. Run him through the Action." He'd no interest in my monologue. Didn't care who I was or if I could act. Didn't care if I was a bad person who beat up innocent girls. I was a body, the right size for the coffin. I'd finally killed Seth. My role easy. Every time I tried to sit up, I was pushed down by Military Industrial Complex, or Jim Crow, or Dow Chemical, etcetera. Subtle it wasn't, and quite similar to the performance I'd seen in Madison freshman year, but it made its point. I was the newest unpaid intern in the Mad City Guerilla Theatre Troupe.

Next day after the Action we all gathered at Heshy's house for dinner, a ramshackle Victorian in an old industrial area off Packers Avenue. A tradition I was told, as we were paid in food. Thank God, because I was always ravenous now off speed and only allowing myself one meal daily. Perhaps I didn't look fat to others, but the mirror didn't lie. I didn't pretend to understand that, but the thought of gaining weight was anathema.

Heshy's attractive, exhausted-looking wife Paisley, attired in ragged wide bellbottoms and an Indian print blouse, busily chased after two gleeful, rambunctious toddlers, but every time her eyes alighted on Heshy they sparkled with pure adoration. According to the woman at the front desk, the apparent source of all information, Paisley was from Neenah, Wisconsin, heiress to a paper industry fortune. She funded the Troupe's actions, fed us and played den mother.

Stacks of books, particularly tomes related to JFK conspiracies, were strewn about their living room, walls plastered with posters: Che Guevara; Fidel Castro; Eugene McCarthy. I stepped gingerly over empty wine jugs, plates and half-drunk cups of espresso, trying unsuccessfully not to frown. "Hard to keep up with things," Paisley shrugged before taking off again after the two little ones.

Heavy drapery gave the living room the closed in feel of a revolutionary hideout, which tickled my imagination. These were real revolutionaries, committed to a cause. With Ashley, I'd been ready to do whatever it took to get in her panties, but now I wanted to care about something greater than myself, outside myself, so I made myself useful as best I could, collecting and washing all the glassware and plates, trying to reassert some control over my surroundings. My mind still in turmoil. How could I have done what I did? Something I could never undo.

Heshy passed around glasses of cheap jug wine while Paisley put an industrial-sized pot of water to boil. The toddlers scampered about the room, through everyone's legs, while he rambled conspiracy theories and diced onions, garlic, and fresh tomatoes for a sauce, claiming to know what happened to JFK. A vast conspiracy involving the FBI, CIA, the Mafia, the Military Industrial Complex, even the Supreme Court. Performance art of monumental proportions. I wasn't sure about his conspiracy theories, but he definitely knew how to make spaghetti sauce. His recipe similar to Grandma Matthews'. The front desk woman shook her head and laughed as she helped herself to another glass of wine. "He's talkin' to you, bubala. We've hoid all dis before."

Rummaging through a stack of books, he picked out a thick, dust-covered tome and thrust it at me. I blew on it, briefly flashing on Beloit's 1959 yearbook. "'The Warren Commission Report,' 888 pages of complete bullshit!"

"Saved by dinner," Paisley cheerfully yelled, coming up behind Heshy with a hug.

He patted the air in submission. "All right, all right. Time to eat, meine kinder. We need our strength to tear the system apart one bourgeois attitude at a time." He raised his glass. "L'Chaim. To a better world!"

I picked up a plate and joined the line for food. Maybe they'd become a new family, like the Phi Psi's. I was ready to take on this new role, molt the past, grow a new skin, become a dedicated activist and follow Heshy with revolutionary zeal.

CHAPTER 11

I'D ARRANGED TO meet Jack Saturday night at Der Rathskeller on the veranda, grateful when he showed up with two beers and hot pretzels. I was starving. "Nothing worse than a guy by his lonesome in a beer hall with no girl and no beer. So, how's the revolution going? Will it be televised?"

I greedily gulped half the mug and chomped down a pretzel. "Let's see. I'm flat broke. I've no idea how I'm gonna pay the rent much less eat. I'm pretty sure the professor who owns the house has sex orgies with the three other tenants on Friday nights. When I returned after midnight girls' underwear was strewn across the floor with lots of noise emanating from the professor's room. I guess everyone celebrates the Sabbath in their own way."

He reached into his coat and pulling out a sealed envelope. "Now that you have your own place, give your folks your new address. Kind of feels like a check, maybe some help with the money issues."

I tore it open. A check for $200 and a letter from Jerry. He missed me, loved me, couldn't wait to see me and didn't want me starving in the interim. My immediate reaction was to rip it to pieces; the sonuvabitch was trying to buy me. But then I reconsidered. I needed the money, and maybe he did care. He didn't have to write me. Didn't have to send a check. And it was from him, not Mitzie. I folded the check and letter and put them in my pocket. Jack smiled. "Starvation's off the table. Next round's on you."

"Only if you can cash a check."

I CALLED JERRY at his office the next day, reversing the charges, thanked him for the money but made it clear he wasn't going to buy my love. "You said in your letter you missed me. Funny, I must've missed you, too, last time I was sent home to a cold and empty house. You'd never have let Jonah return home that way, no matter how much pain he caused you."

The phone went silent for a moment. "You're right. I made a mistake. I regret it."

"I was the product of a mistake. I wish I'd never been born."

"Don't be so melodramatic. What I did was wrong but I can't take it back. I'm asking you for a second chance. I fucked up irreparably with your brother. I won't let that to happen again."

"What about her?"

"I know she feels the same way but that's for her to express. This is about you and me. I'm asking you to give me a chance to be a better father. Maybe I could come out for a visit, or you could come home for the holidays?" He couldn't wait to leave last time, but that was then, this is now. "You're all I've got, son. I haven't heard from Jonah since the day he left and I've tortured myself every day wondering if I'd only done this or said that everything would've been different, but that's an opportunity I'm never going to get."

Sinead's face appeared in my mind's eye. I could empathize, but I wasn't ready to go home; I needed to find my own way, figure out who I was and how to live with myself. "My internship ends next summer. I could come home for a visit before the start of senior year."

"But that's almost a year from now."

"Maybe we can talk a bit on the phone like we're doing now. Get to know each other."

"I'd like that, Seth. You okay for money?"

"Your check helped a lot."

CHAPTER 12

HESHY HAD AN endless supply of good Action ideas, and I dove in with manic energy. I was so excited to be part of the Troupe. It was wish fulfillment, a torch I'd carried since coming up for the anti-war protest freshman year and now here I was, part of something so awesome, so much greater than myself. And with so many characters to play, so many ways and days to forget who I was and what I'd done, I found normalcy in roles of Nazi-like police troopers, supercilious white liberals, heads of multinational chemical and drug corporations, police victims, and wasted hippies trying to find their way back to the Summer of Love and Woodstock. People said my stoned-out hippie impersonation was right on; I merely mimicked Umo.

One week, I ran up and down State Street, my social security card in one hand, draft card in the other, screaming "I AM NOT A NUMBER, I AM NOT A NUMBER, I AM A FREE MAN" in passersby's faces, an idea borrowed from the greatest TV show of all times, *The Prisoner*. I was arrested for disturbing the peace, dragged away screaming "WHAT PEACE? THERE IS NO PEACE," later bailed out by Heshy's ACLU friends. He high fived me during dinner, exclaiming "Seth lost his cherry today!" I belonged.

On another occasion, when several of my compatriots were arrested for public loitering during an action, we ran through the streets shouting "WE ARE THE PUBLIC. THE STREETS ARE PUBLIC. THEREFORE, THE STREETS ARE OURS," and scattered anti-war pamphlets around the rotunda on the State capitol grounds, taunting the police to arrest us. "WE'RE NOT LOITERING; WE'RE LITTERING!" we shouted gleefully and laughed all the way to the jailhouse. And when all the Troupe's women were arrested for public lewdness after removing and burning their prop bra's, drawing the largest, most enthusiastic crowd ever, we circulated speechifying about the connection between imperialism, rampant consumerism, gender objectification and Nestle Corp's campaign to diminish the importance of breastfeeding to enhance sales of their baby formula, although I couldn't say aloud how turned-on I'd been. So many attractive girls. I missed sex as much as I still craved speed, but that was the problem. I'd been so obsessed with it I'd lost sight of Sinead's humanity. No way I'd let that happen again.

I LOOKED FORWARD to my weekly calls with Jerry. Though part of a troupe I was lonely. The hippie kids were true believers ready to change the world; I was a poseur appropriating different skins and personalities. It wasn't like they didn't make friendly overtures. There were invitations to parties and dinners or simply to hang out, but I rebuffed them at the risk of seeming put offish or full of myself. The sad truth was I didn't feel worthy of them, and reverted to my comfort zone, taking refuge in the UW Library, meandering the leaf strewn pathways encircling Lake Mendota or tooling about town on a three speed Schwinn beater I purchased for five bucks. I started calling Jerry more frequently and he always took my calls. It was like he was actually seeing me, though from a distance, and we were developing a friendship that went beyond father/son. There was give and take. He told me he'd lost his youth to World War II, a four-year struggle for survival, how Mitzie's letters and his desire to return home to her had been his lifeline to a reality beyond chaos and destruction, and for the first time I understood why he loved her. He confided he'd considered homesteading in Australia after the war but couldn't budge Mitzie more than four miles from his mother. But he became vague when I asked him why Mitzie had treated Grandma Matthews like shit. "You'll have to ask her. I wish you two would establish a dialogue." She knew where I was if she wanted to talk.

NOT WANTING TO ask Jerry for more money I attempted to stretch the two hundred dollars. When not fed by Paisley I usually took my daily meal at the Sunflower Kitchen, a nonprofit café in an old church run by cute hippie chicks eager to feed all in need heaping healthy platefuls of rice and veggies for fifty cents, refills often free. I couldn't afford to waste money on food, although occasionally Jack and I would grab a couple of pizza slices at Rocky Raccoon or a beer in Der Rathskeller accompanied by older Phi Psi brothers passing through town. Unlike me, he'd maintained friendships; I had only three, him, Bart and Umo, and I'd ignored those two for months. Now they were off campus on field terms, and I missed them. I'd taken them for granted. Wrote them long rambling letters. Umo replied with envelopes of reefer he accumulated as he made his way about the country producing a photographic essay of a countercultural phenomenon, the Grateful Dead and their fanatical Deadheads. He advised me to continue my journey through the center of my mind! Bart encouraged me to hitch down to Beloit, hang out with our Kahuna brothers and my theatre mates. Someone was always throwing a party and it was only an hour away. But he'd no idea what had happened with Sinead, and I was afraid of the reception I'd receive on campus. I was probably a pariah.

CHAPTER 13

THE WEATHER TURNED bitter cold, the icy winds off Mendota talons serrating exposed skin. Most of the Troupe kids had paired off, seeking warmth through the winter months, and I found myself dialing Jerry's office number daily just to hear a voice that was becoming comfortably familiar. Sensing my neediness, he always accepted the charges, and reiterated his offer to come out for a visit, which was sweet because, like Jonah, he hated cold weather. When I demurred, he didn't pry, didn't try to insinuate himself like before Mexico. He merely let me know he was a listening ear if I needed one and would always endeavor to be as nonjudgmental as a parent could be. A few days later I received another check for two hundred dollars.

I WAS SITTING in a dark corner of Der Rathskeller one blustery Friday evening reviewing notes I'd taken at the library, my Shabbos responsibilities completed, when Heshy plopped down in a chair next to me and pushed a beer in front of me. "So, this is where the enigmatic Seth hangs out." Heshy was expansive and kind, just like the Jonah I needed to believe in. He lifted his glass. "Prost!"

"L'Chaim" I responded, clicking his mug. "Tsu gezunt and Shabbat Shalom."

He downed his beer in one long slug, sat back, wiped foam from his mouth and beard. "So, finally after many months I know something about you. You're Jewish, like me. Funny, I had you pegged for . . ."

"Irish. You and everyone else."

"What else can you tell me, you know, the kind of things people share when they've known each other for a while, like where you're from, your interests, your family, if you have a girlfriend . . . stuff like that. I've watched you disappear into every role. You're a terrific actor . . ." I beamed. "Don't thank me yet. Most of the great actors I've known have been terribly insecure. Nothing's impeded your ability to inhabit characters because you can't locate your own center."

"There is no me. I'm looking for a skin that fits."

"What a load of crap. You're the sum total of all the skins you've ever tried on. They're all you! Wanna tell me what really going on? You don't hang out with the other kids so I'm guessing there's a girl involved." Was there a scarlet letter impressed on my forehead? "There always is at your age, plus Paisley says you've ignored every overture and she's got sensitive antennae."

"I'm doing my senior thesis on the history of guerilla theatre; I spend most days in the library reading about the Commedia Dell' Arte, the rest with the Troupe and on Friday nights I perform the duties of a Shabbos goy."

"See, now we're really getting somewhere. You're Jewish, you're studying guerilla theater, adept at avoiding uncomfortable questions, and what's with the Shabbos goy gig?"

"Twenty-five bucks a month rent so long as I don't fuck up and give myself away by lighting my Grandma's Sabbath candles or letting my landlord see me naked."

"Next Friday come over for dinner and we'll light the candles together, okay?"

I told him I'd been blown away after seeing his Troupe perform at the anti-war protest in Madison freshman year and he said he'd come back disillusioned from his Tour in 'Nam and joined Vietnam Veterans Against the War. He'd been as patriotic as the next guy, growing up on stories of the greatest generation, the fight against fascism, preventing the spread of evil Communism, but came to realize we were merely tools to corporate interests that didn't give a damn about human life, ours or our supposed enemies. The fact that he never fired the gun he'd been issued was the only reason he could live with himself. And then he ran into RG Davis who founded the San Francisco Mime Troupe and saw an opportunity to turn his anger and frustration into action, focus on the greater collective good. "After I met Paisley, we moved up here and started the troupe. She's a Wisconsin girl, wanted to be closer to home when we decided to start a family. She's the foundation of my life. I don't know where I'd be without her. In my opinion, if you wanna change the world you've got to start from inner strength. Then you can win people's hearts, and humor's a better weapon than a bludgeon."

Hearts and minds. That's what I'd told Ashley. "I was excited when you invited me to audition. Prepared a monologue, but you were only looking for a dead body."

"It was a narrow coffin and you fit. I'll get us another round." A minute later he reappeared and pushed a beer across the table. "Okay, let's hear it."

"Okay, here goes." I closed my eyes a moment, cleared my throat. "*All the world's a stage and all the men and women mere players. They have their exits and their entrances, and one man in his time plays many parts . . .*"

"What part are you playing now, Seth?"

"Can I finish?"

"No, I've heard enough. You're playacting the revolutionary, but that's not who you are. You're an observer, most good actors are, and you probably beat yourself up for it, but lemme tell you, it's the observers who write history. And I'll tell you something else. We're all actors, kid. All insecure, trying to find our way. You might want to keep that in mind. Swing by the house tomorrow. I've got lots of original source material you can use for your thesis."

CHAPTER 14

WINTER MELTED INTO spring. Jerry asked me probing questions about guerilla theatre, even postulated it was another form of guerilla warfare. "The American revolutionaries engaged in that type of combat to beat the British, and now the North Vietnamese have taken a page from our own playbook and are using it against us. You don't march head-on into battle, you come at your enemy from the side. Isn't guerilla theatre doing the same thing, fostering social change by critiquing with humor the morals and values that set a country's trajectory? You don't bang people over the head. Make them so angry they won't listen. You make them laugh, often at themselves. I read somewhere, I can't recollect the source at the moment, guerilla theatre is a struggle for a nation's very soul. It's interesting stuff. Mind expanding. Feels good learning something along with you. Makes me feel closer to you."

"I've been spending most evenings interviewing Heshy for my thesis. He worked with RG Davis in San Francisco before starting the troupe in Madison..."

"And RG Davis drew inspiration from Che Guevara's *Guerilla Warfare*."

"Heshy's been dynamite. He's placed a treasure trove of information at my disposal and I'm hoping to interweave historical data with his own thoughts and reminiscences. And he's been a great sounding board for my assumptions. And he and Paisley have been so great to me, insisting I stay for dinner and always on Friday's. And they've got two kids, Pippa and Zoey, I've grown attached to. They're such a close family."

"I'd like us to be a close family too."

WITH THE RETURN of warm weather our Actions burgeoned. The Troupe performed two of my own ideas, a gender bending adaptation of Shakespeare's *Comedy of Errors* with genders reversing roles (the sight of hirsute guys wobbling around a stage in high heels in red dresses priceless) and the anti-war parody

MacBird, which we performed on the veranda at Der Rathskeller. With my return to school looming, I worked feverishly on my guerilla theatre thesis in the UW library. But none of this took my mind off the inevitable face-off with Sinead. I wished Heshy would ask me to stay and broached that subject at dinner my last Friday night, but Paisley immediately noted I needed to finish college and the senior thesis I'd been working so feverishly on. I told them I'd rather stay with the troupe, but Heshy looked at Paisley, then back at me and said "No."

I was taken aback, his response unequivocal, and blinked back tears. Terry at the telephone exchange in Merida; Jonah in Washington Square Park. It hurt. A lot. I'd started to think of them as family. Sensing my hurt, Paisley reached across the table and took my hand. "Don't get the wrong impression, Seth. We love you and want what's best for you, but your life's so manic; you never give yourself time to just be you, and you'll never be happy until you can do that."

"Like I said that night in Der Rathskeller," Heshy added, "you've got to figure out who you are and what you want out of life."

I wanted to open up to them; tell them about Jonah and Sinead, about what I'd done, but I couldn't bear their disapproval. Black tar sloshed about my stomach like a washing machine on agitator cycle. "I'm just an actor and you've given me great roles to play, and a purpose."

"That's a shitty way to live a life," Heshy said. "You need to open yourself to others; stop playacting. We know there's stuff you're holding back. You're hiding here. Using us as a safety net. Risk exposure. Stop hating yourself. Find someone to open your heart to." Heshy reached for Paisley's hand and squeezed it. "Trust me, it will open up your world."

There was a painful silence, as if a tornado had swept through the room, dead calm in its wake. Paisley finally asked if I'd found the play I wanted to direct for my senior performance thesis. "Edmond Rostand's *Cyrano de Bergerac*."

Heshy smiled. "And you'll play Cyrano, right, a brilliant man with a physical flaw he magnified to tragic proportions, and a tale of unrequited love. A compelling choice. Let us know the date of the performance and we'll come down for it."

"I have to leave next week. I promised I'd go to New York for a visit before fall term starts."

"We've loved having you here, Seth," Heshy said. "If you still want to join the Troupe after graduation we'll talk then."

CHAPTER 15

I KNEW JERRY loved me and that made going home easier, but who knew which version of Mitzie I'd encounter. Our last unfortunate conversation regarded Sinead, so I armored myself when I exited the plane and saw her outside the gate waving excitedly. Once inside the terminal she embraced me, and despite my best efforts to freeze her out, painful memories of Merida and my return to Huntington still fresh in my mind, I thawed in the warmth of that emotional display. She'd mapped out an itinerary for the entire week, purchased tickets for the two of us for a multi-day Elia Kazan film retrospective at the Art Cinema, took long walks with me on the beach, asked me questions about guerilla theater, about Heshy and Paisley. She never mentioned Sinead, only noted I'd make a great catch for some lucky Jewish girl and handed me the keys to her old Dodge Lancer, mine to take back to Beloit. All this should have given me pause, but I was a starving puppy staring at a bowl brimming with puppy chow; I couldn't stop eating. I almost broke down and called her Mom.

During the week Joel called and reminded me of his standing invitation to visit him at work, see what it was all about. I didn't want to hurt his feelings, tell him working on Wall Street, surrounded by money grubbing Republicans who'd trash the environment and sell their mother for a dollar, was the farthest thing from my mind. We made a date for the next day.

Lehman Brothers Kuhn Loeb was housed in a monolithic structure of glittering glass overlooking South Seaport. As he showed me through the office, he told me the firm had been founded one hundred years ago by the Lehman Brothers, and later merged with Kuhn, Loeb & Co. to form one of the Street's most venerable investment banking firms. The immense forty-first floor trading room, the size of several football fields, seemed claustrophobic despite its size, the windows sheet-rocked over to prevent distraction. Artificial light illuminated the sea of blinking phone banks, people spaced three feet apart, side by side and back-to-back, row after endless row of buzzing worker bees. The firm's superstars all had private offices on the floor, "Partner's Row," and Joel aspired to be amongst them. It was the brass ring. The ultimate goal.

Sitting beside him in his tiny cubicle, I was mystified by the chatter over picking up basis points, reducing portfolio duration, immunizing risk. A foreign language. More striking was Joel's boss, Nate Rucksberg, the head of capital markets, hurling his chair through the glass fishbowl window in the center of the trading room, spraying shards over the entire fixed-income department of the firm, and me. I was shaken but neither Joel nor any of his co-workers even stirred, too focused on extracting orders through the phone from clients to notice blood trickling down their faces. They were star athletes, like Mickey Mantle, playing through pain, the atmosphere so frenetic I would've thought everyone was mainlining amphetamines.

THE NIGHT BEFORE leaving for school Mitzie informed me we'd been invited to a friend's house for dinner. I demurred, needed to pack, asked her to express my regrets, but she was adamant, had already said I'd be joining them. What was the big deal? They'd never asked me to join them before. Who were they?

"They were at your Bar Mitzvah."

"Oh, must've been the Jewish people. Come on Mitzie. What's the big secret? I'm leaving tomorrow. I've got stuff to do, and it's a long drive out to Wisconsin."

"It's a surprise, and I just gave you my car! Show a little appreciation. Surely you can do this little thing for me, plus their daughter will be there. It would be rude not to come." How could I have lowered my guard?

I slouched in the back seat of Jerry's car pondering his silence, perhaps discomfort, then recognized familiar landmarks leading to Abby Freed's house. Oh my God, no wonder. I was about to be ambushed. Spend a chilly evening with my oldest friend I'd treated like shit, never answering her letters or calling her. I almost bailed out of the car before we pulled into the long bluestone driveway leading up to their mini mansion.

Mrs. Freed opened the door, aglitter in a black sequined top. She hugged me to her ample bosom. "Look at you. So grown up! I still recall the chubby little boy sitting in the back seat with Abby going to that concert at the Westbury Theatre. The two of you so cute. So, what's new?"

"I get to sit in the front seat now; even have my driver's license."

She laughed. "Your mother said you had a great sense of humor. And so handsome." She pinched my cheek. "What happened to all your baby fat? Your mother talks about you so much I feel like you're mishpucha!" The nice lunches, the feigned interest, the films. Mitzie was Machiavellian. Mrs. Freed walked over to the stairs while I glanced about the place. Everything sleek, modern and antiseptic, from the wall-to-wall white ceramic tile floors, the floor to ceiling picture windows and Formica everything kitchen, a room Mrs. Freed never entered except with instructions for their live-in help. "Abby, come on down," she chirped. "The Matthews are here, and you'll never guess who's with them." How could down to earth Abby have sprung from her loins?

I hardly recognized the lovely, confident woman who strode down the stairs. Large charcoal eyes, perfect posture, olive-toned skin, nipples pressing the silk fabric of her summer dress in the most tantalizing way. We sat side by side at dinner, Mrs. Freed and Mitzie babbling nonstop about all the concerts we'd attended together, even reminiscing about the time I'd defended Abby's honor in middle school, which made both of us blush. If that bully Brad Taylor could see her now! I was ready to be more than just a pal. I morosely nibbled the buttery chicken biryani that Ashti, their live-in maid and cook, had prepared, and after a barely tolerable meal Abby excused us, suggesting we take a walk, both mothers chiming in unison "Have a nice time," their eyes alive with fantastical aspirations.

Once outside, I asked her if she'd known about this. "Not a goddam thing. My mother treated dinner like a state secret. Fuckin' bullshit, trying to run our lives." She reached into her purse and pulled out a joint. "You still on that getting high on reality schtick?" She lit it and took several big tokes.

"If this is reality, pass that over to me. I mean, don't get me wrong, it's great to see you."

"You, too. Finally, a chance to tell you what a complete asshole you are, my best friend, remember? All the good times we just reminisced about! You dumped me, just plain dumped me, and that really hurt. You didn't call freshman winter break, didn't write. Never responded to the letter I sent to you in Mexico. Didn't you realize I was worried about you? Didn't you realize how much you hurt me? I assumed you didn't want to know me anymore, and now this stupid charade with our mothers! Jesus Christ!"

"Could I have that joint again? Now I really, really need to get stoned."

She giggled. "Sorry. Had to get that out of my system. I've missed you."

What the fuck was wrong with me? How did I manage to fuck up every relationship with women, even friendships? "I'm sorry. I knew you were writing me because you cared, but the boy I was then didn't want anything to do with the past. I was pretty fucked up. I'm still fucked up, but hopefully more self-aware."

"Anyone special in your life?"

"Yes. According to our mothers, you."

"Yeah, right."

"Had a couple of relationships that didn't pan out. Flying solo now. How about you?"

"I have a serious boyfriend at Cornell. He's black, hence Mom's scheming."

Mask your disappointment! "Oh boy! Bet that's testing your parents' liberal sensibilities."

"Visualize Stokely Carmichael and you'll get the picture."

WE WALKED AWHILE in edgy silence through the tony development, an upper-class community of people from similar backgrounds, first generation Americans whose parents had fled persecution in the "old country" and now lived the American dream in glorious ostentation. As Grandma Matthews used to say: "Keinehora, such a great country!" I took another toke and passed it back to Abby. She laced her arm through mine. Felt like old times. I'd missed her friendship. "We could've been more," she said, "but I never got your attention. You weren't interested."

I'd failed to see a good thing when it was staring me in the face. "I spent a lot of time obsessing over our times together, whether you liked me that way, but I wasn't willing to risk our friendship. What if I was misreading signals? And you were taller than me. I guess I wasn't looking at it from your perspective."

"Apparently not. And wasn't ignoring me risking our friendship? And having to hear you'd gone off to Mexico to search for Jonah from my mother! Jesus Christ! Shouldn't you have told me? Well, water under the bridge now. Before we head back, I must ask you, did you figure out what happened to him?" I shook my head. "You always wore rose colored glasses where he was concerned. Always defended him. That day in Washington Square Park it broke my heart to see you hurt like that. Frankly, I'm sorry to say this, but I think your brother was an asshole."

"You gotta understand. Growing up, he was all I had. Without him, I faced an abyss."

"Well, you either face that darkness or let it control your life." She glanced at her watch. "Geez, we better get back before they start planning our wedding."

CHAPTER 16

RETURNING TO CAMPUS, I immediately overloaded my schedule and avoided the Arts center. As head of the film committee, I set up a great director's series, including such luminaries as Hitchcock, Truffaut, Kazan and Stevens, particularly excited to bring George Stevens *Shane* to campus, the quintessential western. I also co-chaired Students for McGovern as a way of staying involved after Madison and got a part-time job as short order cook at the Student Union grill. I tried to leave no moment unstructured, but it didn't forestall the moment I most dreaded when, on one fine September day, I saw Sinead sitting amidst the dappled leaves on an Indian mound in front of Middle College, the sight of her so devastating I had to steady myself against the trunk of a Dutch Elm. She was reading, ubiquitous camera beside her. Sunlight caressed her pretty face and large blue eyes, more prominent now she'd cropped her long frizzy black hair, sporting soft curls cut above the ears. Not the visceral memory of my face buried in her lustrous hair, but she looked healthier, chubbier. She looked up and saw me. "Any more room on that mound?" I asked.

I fidgeted about, bit my lip, unsure how to continue as she pantomimed surveying the empty space surrounding her. Sighing, she snapped her book shut and scowled, "It's completely taken. What do you want from me, Seth?"

"Forgiveness. What I did was unspeakably wrong. I can't forgive myself. Can't get you out of my mind."

"I hope it haunts you forever." She picked up her book and opened it, dismissing me out of hand. I would've given anything to change what happened, but when I looked into her icy blue eyes I realized I couldn't undo what I'd done.

"Leave me alone. Plenty of girls here to brutalize, and with speed freaks it's only a matter of time."

I fumbled for words, desperate to re-forge any connection. Told her how wonderful she looked, how her beautiful eyes stood out even more with her short hair, but she told me to save my breath. I wasn't the first glib monster she'd encountered in her life, but the only one who had destroyed her. I started to cry. She saw me as a monster. "I just need you to know I'm truly sorry. I mean it from my heart."

"You broke my heart, you bastard! You've come to the wrong place for absolution. I've dreaded this moment. I hadn't let anyone touch me after I was raped ... not until you. I thought you were so sweet, so gentle." She started to weep. "I'll never be able to trust anyone again." I reached out a hand, wanted to say my inability to trust had destroyed my life, but she drew back as from a contagion. "You never opened up to me, shared what was in your heart. I loved you. I would've helped you, whatever it was, no matter how painful."

"I'm not making excuses but maybe if you'd opened up to me it would have made it easier..."

"I know that, dammit. I know that, and that's why I didn't tell anyone about what you did. Why my brothers didn't beat the shit out of you! I protected you, maybe myself as well, I don't know, but it doesn't matter anymore. It's our dirty little secret, along with our addiction. All you'll ever get from me."

I told her I hadn't taken speed since the day she left me, but she just sneered. "Once an addict, always an addict. I know. I take it one day at a time, but look at you, rail thin. Not a junkie? You're a fucking liar."

"You're wrong. I can take it or leave it."

"Really?" she smirked. "Lucky you." She tossed her textbook on the ground. "JUST LEAVE ME THE FUCK ALONE! I hate you, and still love you, and I can't stand it ... I can't stand the sight of you. Don't approach me again. EVER. Seeing you is too painful. Too confusing. I don't want to talk to you. I don't want anything to do with you. And give me back my pendant." She was bawling now and people were turning in our direction. "Will you do that for me?" Choking back tears, I clutched it to my chest. Flashed on Jonah's ring disappearing into the crevasse. "The thought of you lying with another woman with my pendant pressed between you ... I can't bear it."

"There's been no one since you."

"I don't care. That was special between you and me. There is no you and me and never will be. Understand?" She reached out again. "Give it to me. NOW."

I unclasped it, handed it to her and watched her quickly drop it in her pack as if radioactive. She returned to her book. Tears dropped on her text.

I WAS STUDYING in my room when the phone rang in the hallway, and from the sounds of things emanating from Umo's bedroom, he wasn't going to pick up the phone imminently. He and Lena, the sorority chick he'd hooked up with, were noisy as hell. Such an unlikely pair, another reminder the world was enigmatic. "I'll get it," I yelled to no one in particular.

A man's voice asked for Seth Matthews. "Speaking. Who's this?"

"A friend of a friend. I understand you might be interested in procuring some study aids. You've already sampled them." My heart rate accelerated. I gnashed my teeth; started to sweat. Started to need. "I'm willing to give you a special return customer deal on some real Beauties. Interested?"

I should have simply slammed the phone back in its cradle, but rationalizations mushroomed. I reflexively pinched my stomach; I was becoming fat Seth again. My theatre thesis was a ball-buster. I was up to all hours writing and editing long hand, then typing, cutting, correcting and pasting misplaced paragraphs; I'd never get it completed in time. I needed help; needed the mental clarity, the incredible kick. The way it pushed negative thoughts aside. I'd been speed free for a year; proof enough I wasn't an addict. Why abstain? I'd no one to hurt. Like he said, they were simply study aids. "WELL?" The voice impatient.

"I guess so."

"All right. Cash only. Meet me in front of George Webb's tonight, say nine o'clock? And come alone. I see anyone else, I'm gone, got that?" Click.

CHAPTER 17

LENA BELONGED TO the Delta, Delta, Delta sorority, or the Tri-Delts as they were more commonly known, apt as there were only three members. Desperate to prevent the college confiscating their house, they'd initiated an aggressive campaign to recruit freshman girls and one night over dinner Lena informed Umo and me we'd "volunteered" to cook and serve dinner at the house Sunday night, adding some boy appeal to their rush efforts. When I demurred, Lena kicked Umo in the shin and jerked her head in my direction. He passed me a joint. "Come on, Seth. What's the big deal?"

I took a hit and coughed. "Sorry. Too much work."

"All you do is work," Lena scolded. I liked Lena but sometimes she sounded eerily like Mitzie. "You need a break. I can't believe you won't do this one little thing for me. Umo will be sleeping alone if you don't." Like that supposed to bother me? Their lovemaking drove me up a wall. Umo grabbed his Allman Brothers *Eat a Peach* album from a pile of LPs he'd left scattered on the floor. "It's just one night for God's sake, a few hours. You've been ogling this album. I'll give it to you."

"And you always cook dinner for us anyway," Lena added. "I doubt you'll find it that onerous. Think of all the praise you'll get from a bevy of cute girls hand selected by me. You'll just have to cook a little extra."

I placed the album in with the *A*'s. "Starting your own Pig Book, Lena? I thought only us guys were chauvinists. I'll do it this once, but don't act like I'm there all the time. I don't want to meet anybody. Don't want any entanglements. I just wanna be left alone."

"No worries. I'll tell them you play for the other team . . . And by the way, it's The Allman Brothers Band. Shouldn't you put it with the *T*'s?"

UMO AND I spent all day Sunday in the Tri-Delt kitchen prepping dinner. So much for a few hours. I cooked; he rolled joints. Lena flipped LPs on the stereo and poured glasses of cheap jug wine. The dope and wine took the edge off the speed, her music all R&B, Aretha Franklin, Dionne Warwick, Sly and the Family Stone taking us higher and higher. I mellowed out for the first time in weeks and the sight of those cute freshman girls traipsing into the house reminded me how starved I'd been for female contact, my eyes immediately drawn to this one petite redheaded hippie chick who remined me of Izzy. What was she doing here? Woodstock, maybe, but a sorority gathering? My ruminations were cut short by Lena making introductions. "This is Umo, my boyfriend." She placed a protective arm around him. "I met him right here at the house." She'd actually met him selling her an ounce of pot. "Hands off, girls!" They all giggled. "And this is our roommate and chef, Seth." Heads swiveled in my direction like a pack of raptors. "Practically lives here; loves to cook, and even does dishes; how sexy is that! Oh, and he's so lonely." She blew me a kiss. "Aren't you, baby blue?"

My annoyance was ameliorated by profuse praise as we served the spaghetti, garlic bread, salad and glasses of wine. The pretty redhead had bright green eyes that sparkled like emeralds and an enigmatic smile that reminded me of Botticelli's *Birth of Venus*. Pert little breasts stretched her tight-fitting Vanilla Fudge concert T-shirt in the most wonderful way. I'd attended that concert with Abby at the Fillmore on January 4, 1968, a handy excuse to strike up a conversation. "Hi. I'm Seth." I pointed to her chest. "You know, I was there."

She looked down and giggled. "I'm sure I would've remembered."

I blushed. "I . . . I meant the concert."

"Good show?"

"Dynamite. They're from Long Island, like me. When'd you get into them?"

"One of my younger brothers bought me the shirt back home in Portland . . . that's Oregon, not Maine. Thought the name was funny. I'd never heard of them but went and bought one of their records." She nudged her neighbor over a bit. "Wanna sit down?"

"Sure, thanks. Which LP?"

"The one with the psychedelic cover design."

"Their first. Came out in the summer of '67. My favorite song's a cover of the Supremes' "You Keep Me Hanging On." They definitely made it their own."

"That's my favorite, too."

Her aroma, cinnamon and sugar, flooded me with happy memories of Grandma Matthews. And hadn't Izzy prophesized I'd find someone special my own age. Maybe she was right. I watched the pretty redhead mash her spaghetti into a hash and demonstrated twirling it with a fork and spoon, the way I'd learned back home in New York.

"I'm Erin, by the way. So, like this?" Concentrating, two prominent front teeth pressed her lower lip. A constellation of golden freckles bridged her nose. And those green eyes, speckled gold and grey in one, gold and brown in the other, changed in the light. A girl with kaleidoscope eyes. Her hair fell to the small of her back in a haphazard braid. An oddment of tomato skin clung to her metallic braces. A cute little bunny rabbit. She nudged her neighbor over a bit more. "Your spaghetti sauce is excellent. Lena said you made it from scratch."

"You must like it 'cause you're taking a bit home with you."

She covered her mouth with her hand and blushed. "I hate these stupid braces," she stammered, rising, but I gently clasped her hand, drew her back down and flicked the piece of tomato into my napkin. "There, all gone. If you left, the evening would be ruined. So, you really liked my spaghetti?"

"I said so, didn't I? I can taste fresh herbs, thyme, oregano and marjoram, I think. Garlic, red pepper, a touch of red wine? Any secret ingredients?"

I leaned in close to her elfin ear studded with a little gold peace symbol. "Pot," I whispered. Her eyes flashed like headlights. "Only kidding. Too many people here. That's for special occasions back at my apartment. This is Grandma Matthews recipe, only she called it spaghettis, counting each strand. She was the greatest cook ever, but English was a second language. I'd sit in her kitchen and watch her for hours. That's how I learned. Everything was dynamite. You remind me so much of her." My eyes grew misty. Visceral memories of her soft ample lap, her comforting scent. Cuddling or feeding me, guiding my first tentative steps. "You smell like her."

"That supposed to be a compliment?"

"I loved her more than any other woman in the world."

"That... that's so sweet," she whispered breathlessly. I brushed away unbidden tears, hoping she hadn't noticed. "Living off campus with Lena and Umo must be kind of weird, you know, being the odd man out. I stayed with her last spring when I visited Beloit; she was so nice. Invited me tonight and I couldn't refuse, though sororities aren't my thing."

"The Tri-Delts are pretty cool, not your typical sorority types. Probably why there are only three of them... four if you join."

She introduced me to the girl she'd nudged over to make room for me, her roomie Kelsey, a busty brunette in a UC Santa Cruz banana slug sweatshirt, her ponytail sticking out the back of a UC Santa Cruz baseball cap. Kelsey asked if I really was at the house all the time, and when I said I could be, they looked at each other and giggled. "So what's your major?"

"I'm doing my senior thesis on guerilla theatre."

"That's so cool," Erin said. "A bunch of us took a bus from Portland to San

Francisco for a Student Mobe rally and saw the San Francisco Mime Troupe perform. Guerilla theatre as social action goes all the way back to the Commedia dell' Arte. It's a great teaching device. Helps people see things differently without beating them over the head. Of course," she said, smiling self-consciously, "I don't have to tell you that."

"I think you just did. So, what are you gonna study at Beloit?"

Her eyes bore into mine. "How to save the world ... one person at a time."

Lena poked me. Suggested it was time to bring in dessert, and I reluctantly excused myself. There was something about Erin. I felt at ease with her. She promised to save my seat.

Umo and I had decided to serve bananas flambe, and making a grand entrance, we cautioned everyone to stand back. I doused the sliced bananas with an entire bottle of cheap brandy, then lit them with a kitchen match, anticipated a big swoosh. Nothing happened. We looked at each other quizzically and flailed away, match after match, while the girls tittered amongst themselves. Finally, I looked about the room, hoping to turn this lemon into lemonade, and asked if anyone wanted to make me banana bread. Giggles but no takers.

AFTER DINNER UMO and Lena snuck out, leaving me with the entire cleanup, but Erin lingered and offered to help. Scrubbing pans in the sink, her T-shirt soaked through within minutes. She'd have gotten my vote in a wet T-shirt contest. I crooned *Set me free, why don't you babe, get out of my life, why don't you babe.*

She smiled. "Wow. You have a great voice."

You really don't want me, you just keep me hangin' on ...

She giggled *"Ooh, ooh, ooh, ooh."* So did she.

You really don't need me, you just keep me hangin' on. I was finding the groove now. *Why do you keep comin' around, playing with my heart? Why don't you get out of my life, and let me make a new start? Let me get over you the way you've gotten over me-e-ee ...*

Yeah, yeeeaaah.

Set me free why don't you babe, get out my life, why don't you babe ...

Ooh, ooh, ooh, ooh ...

You really don't want me, you just keep me hangin' on ...

Yeah, yeah, yeah ...

I moved next to her, grabbed a dish towel. So turned on. *You really don't need me, you just keep me hangin' on ... You said when we broke up, you just wanna be friends, but how can we be friends when seeing you only breaks my heart again, and there ain't nothing I can do about it ...*

Wha ooh, wha ooh, whaohaa, she warbled, a wood spoon her microphone.

You know I really love ...

Set me free, why don't you babe ...
Talkin' 'bout love ...
Get out my life, why don't cha babe ... ooh, ooh, ooh ...
You don't really want me, you just keep me hangin' on ...

Caught up in the moment, I'd unintentionally enfolded her in my arms, and she made no move to separate us, merely looked up at me and smiled. Oh my God. Holding her felt so good. I wanted her so bad, but I quickly detached from her. I didn't want to feel the warmth of that embrace, validate my yearning for physical affection. No entanglements, remember? "Thanks for your help," I said, as casually as possible. "It made cleanup go by fast." I stuck the bananas in the fridge and, noting the hour, offered to walk her to her dorm.

CHAPTER 18

TWO NIGHTS LATER, having popped a Black Beauty, ready to pull an all-nighter, I was re-reading *Cyrano de Bergerac* for the umpteenth time, working out production staging and casting details, when someone knocked on the door. It couldn't be a friend. They'd just walk in, there being no lock. A second knock, a bit louder. "Okay, okay, I'm coming, I'm coming." Play in hand I brusquely opened the door and standing there, holding two loaves of bread, was the cute little redhead sporting the same Vanilla Fudge T-shirt and a long Indian print skirt, her hair unbound and so voluminous it overwhelmed her petite body. Damn, what was her name? She held them out to me. "I made these for you, Seth."

"Whoa, cool, thanks! I shoved the play under my armpit and took the breads. "Wow, still warm; they smell great. Thanks for dropping by. I got a lot of work, so. . . ."

"I see you're reading *Cyrano de Bergerac*. I've always wanted to read that."

"I'm directing a production of it for my senior performance thesis. I'll play Cyrano as well."

"Isn't your nose too small?"

"I'm a pretty good makeup artist. I'm working out the casting, the sets, all sorts of stuff. Kind of overwhelming. I usually just act." What the fuck's her name?

Lena suddenly appeared. "Erin! I didn't hear you arrive." No surprise with the racket she and Umo were making. "Don't just stand there; come in, come in." Passing me, she whispered, "Idiot".

I held out the loaves. "Look Lena, those bananas weren't wasted after all."

"How sweet. Let's make tea and try some. Looks delicious."

"It's a recipe from my friend Connie, Erin said, "only she calls it bananas bread because it's made with more than one banana." She glanced around the living room. "Wow, you guys sure keep this place tidy."

Lena pointed at me. "Not guys. Guy."

I walked into the kitchen, placed the breads on the cutting board and put the kettle up for tea. Erin followed me into the kitchen, about to slice the bread with a paring knife when I stopped her. I handed her the bread knife, pointing out the serrated edge. "Just a small slice for me," I said, patting my stomach. "You were wearing that T-shirt Sunday night. A favorite, huh?"

"Seemed you liked it. You kept staring at it."

I reddened. "And you're from Portland, Oregon. Never been there. End of the American frontier. Land of Mark Hatfield. South of Scoop Jackson..."

"You always view geography in political terms?"

"When you're at war, you need to know the good guys from the bad." Turning toward her, I inadvertently bumped into her, sending a tremor through me. A pleasurable sensation. Something unquantifiable was happening, a subtle shift in the Earth's alignment. I sensed she was the answer to questions not yet asked, and I was momentarily discombobulated. "When did they put ovens in the dorms?"

"I used the kitchen in the Tri-Delt house. Lena was nice enough to let me bake there this afternoon."

We took the banana bread and tea sat into our cozy living room, Umo and Lena on our ratty couch, Erin and I pressed together, gently rocking in the oversized threadbare armchair rocker, our bodies a perfect fit, her physical proximity and enthralling scent soothing the amphetamine buzz revving my internal engine. Lena stuffed a wedge of banana bread in her mouth and pronounced it delicious. I took a small bite and placed the plate on the side table. "It's almost as good as Grandma Matthews'."

Erin looked disappointed. "But not good enough. You don't have to eat it."

"Oh no, I really like it; it was so sweet of you to bake them. I'm just not very hungry right now. I'll save it for later." It was the sensation of her body next to mine I hungered for, and I asked her over for dinner Thursday night, knowing nothing would come of it, but I had to see her again. "We're having some friends over. I'll let you borrow *Cyrano de Bergerac*."

"We are?" Umo asked.

Lena elbowed him in the side. "Yes Umo. You remember."

"I'd love to. Maybe I can help you with your lines, you know, take the girl parts."

CHAPTER 19

TEN OF US CRAMMED into our living room, the tranquilizing aromas of roasting turkey and marijuana comingling. Erin was a no-show. I gazed forlornly out the kitchen window toward Commons, replaying Tuesday evening's conversation in an endless loop, searching every word and intonation for nuance I'd either missed or misinterpreted. I'd probably insulted her, taking only a small bite of her banana bread. I was disappointed. There was something about her that left my troubled world behind. Lena walked in, put her arm around me and gently massaged my back. "Erin?" I nodded. "You like her, don't you?" I nodded again. "Funny. You're deeper than I thought. Most guys would've made a beeline for the busty ponytailed brunette next to her, not a frizzy-haired, flat chested redhead with buckteeth."

But I wasn't like other guys. "I think she's gorgeous, not that it matters. She's not here."

"She's insecure, probably figured you were being polite. You hardly touched the banana bread; didn't even remember her name." She pushed me out of the kitchen. "Go find her. I'll carve the turkey."

SHE WAS STANDING in the dinner line at Commons next to a pipsqueak freshman boy vying for her attention with nonstop chatter about *Star Trek* episodes. "... But my favorite of all times has to be 'The Trouble with Tribbles'..." and seemed genuinely surprised when I butted in and asked why she hadn't come over.

"I . . . I didn't think you really meant it."

The pipsqueak was annoyed. They were in the middle of a conversation. I ignored him. "I wouldn't have invited you if I hadn't meant it. I figured you were blowing me off."

"Oh no. I'd never do that!" I placed my hand on her shoulder and took her out of the line.

"But Erin," the pipsqueak whined, "I wanted to tell you about . . ."
"Bye, Henry," she said, her pretty Irish face aglow as we walked away.

I'D ASSUMED LENA was working the Tri-Delt angle, but she exuded genuine warmth toward Erin and introduced her around. We once again commandeered the armchair rocker, pressed together with plates in our laps. I had to restrain myself from nuzzling her swan-like neck. Told her I loved the perfume she was wearing. "Then I'll keep wearing it," she said, pronouncing my chutney stuffing delicious. Gesturing to my full plate, she asked if I ever ate anything, and pooh-poohed my explanation that the act of cooking made me full. She'd known several anorexic girls in high school who made the same claim. Luckily, I was a boy.

"Boys suffer from anorexia too, athletes mostly."

"Not much of an athlete either. Ask the guys on my summer baseball team back on Long Island."

"You don't have a New York accent."

"The benefits of a theatre education, but I can imitate one. Whataya tink? Ya wanna heah 'bout it? How funny is dat? Am I right or am I right?"

She laughed, snorting wine up her nose. Told me her father, the family chef, was also finicky about knives, but that's where the similarity ended because I did dishes. "That's girl porn."

"Well, if you're painting, you'd use the right brushes, right?"

"True." About to take another bite of stuffing, she paused, asked if this was a special occasion. I laughed, said it was, but only put pot in spaghetti. She had a problem with pot, the only drug she'd ever tried.

"Do you always make banana bread for guys you don't know?"

"You're the first, but I'm glad you didn't know to heat the brandy first. Gave me the chance to make you Connie's magical bananas bread. Who knows what might happen."

Walking her back to her dorm, she told me she'd been on an Outward-Bound trip during the summer with people my age or older. Boys like Mr. Star Trek were simply too immature. My age, however, was perfect. I sighed extravagantly. And she really liked my moustache. "The tomato soup residue on my upper lip? Took me forever to grow it. You know, I also took a trip when I was eighteen. Traveled around Mexico with an older guy, but it didn't turn out too well, unlike your experience."

"I'd love to hear about it. I'm interested in everything about you."

"Really?" There was something so special about her. I'd never met anyone like her. I loved her scent. Loved the way she looked in the Indian print blouse with red fringes and silver swirls worn as a mini dress, the way her shock of copper penny hair set off her emerald eyes. And though the voices inside my head said walk away, you'll only end up hurting her, I knew none of this would have happened had the bananas flambeed and that means something. Maybe it was fate. If I didn't see her again I'll regret it forever. "Would you like to see *Shane* with me at the Student Union tomorrow night? It's my favorite Western, the only truly authentic Western every made. I'd love to share it with you."

"I'd love to."

CHAPTER 20

I DROPPED BY her room late Friday afternoon. Kelsey, still wearing the banana slug sweatshirt, opened the door. Turned out her boyfriend was at UC Santa Cruz and she wore it to feel closer to him when she was lonely, which was all the time. "You're kind of early. Erin's down the hall taking a shower. Come in. She should be back momentarily."

I looked around the room, and was immediately drawn to a black and white group photo hung above a desk captioned *Outward Bound: Montana Expedition Summer, 1972*. "Those guys are really buff."

"No shit." She pointed to two of them, both seniors at Reed College in Portland, and jokingly wondered why Erin hadn't bagged one of them as a trophy boyfriend. On the desk was a plastic S&H Green Stamps portable record player, the kind I'd had as a small child, alongside a pile of haphazardly stacked LPs, many out of their cover sleeves. Incredible String Band; Vanilla Fudge; Pentangle; Cream. Even Led Zep. Someone knew their music, but not how to take care of LPs. "Those are Erin's," Kelsey said, as I compulsively restacked them alphabetically. I picked up Pentangle's *Baskets of Light* LP and winced. Scratched and filthy. Found the cover sleeve and was about to put it away when Erin entered wrapped in a towel, her hair a mass of wet ringlets. Startled to see me, she reflexively pressed her hand to her chest to hold the towel in place. Not much else to hold it there. "What are you doing here?"

"We've a date, right?"

"Yeah, you just surprised me is all. Give me a few minutes to do something with my hair."

"Why? It looks dynamite. All frizzy and curly, kinda like mine. What'd you do to it?"

"Nothing. That's the problem."

"I think it looks really sexy. Definitely you. But you should keep your LPs in their cover sleeves." I slipped Pentangle in place before Peter, Paul and Mary. "It's bad for the vinyl."

Kelsey chortled "Goodbye soup cans, iron and blow dryer."

"Lemme get dressed, Seth. Turn around, okay? I did, but in my mind's eye I saw the rosy glow of her skin fresh from the hot shower, the copper red pubic hair.

I quickly jammed my hands in my jean pockets. The whisper of cloth brushing her alabaster skin was giving me a hard on. "You know, a couple of years ago I brought Pentangle here for a concert. Funny story. I'd just dropped acid with a few friends at the Kahuna House, place I used to live until the administration kicked us out, another long story, but anyway, their manager called; they were in transit from Madison to Chicago and were free for the evening. Could do a concert for five hundred dollars, totally in our budget. I emceed and got to meet them all, John Renbourn, Danny Thompson, Jacqui McShee, Bert Jansch. Tripping so hard my microphone turned into a snake! I was like totally freaked out."

"We saw lots of rattlers on the Outward-Bound trip."

My skin tingled as she brushed against me. I turned around and found myself at a loss for words. Her eyes glimmered like sparkling gems, set off by her emerald green mini dress. Kelsey said we could pass for siblings, but I wasn't having brotherly thoughts.

We walked across campus to the Student Union smoking a joint, at least I was. She was fake toking. I explained how director George Stevens had visualized an authentic western right down to the smallest detail. "Shane is facing off against this young gunman who's trying to establish he's top dog by killing him, and all Shane wants to do is put his past behind him and live peacefully . . ." She seemed really interested. ". . . And they're firing their weapons again and again, missing wildly, you see, because the guns back then weren't remotely accurate, but extremely loud, not at all like Gunsmoke, where Matt Dillon only needed one shot to take down the bad guy, which was obviously historically inaccurate."

"You're really into this, aren't you?"

"Did you know James Arness went to Beloit College? He played the sheriff on *Gunsmoke*. His brother went here as well. Peter Graves. He played Mr. Phelps on *Mission Impossible*."

"So many luminaries out of Beloit's theatre department. Guess you'll be one of them, too! You know, a man coming to terms with his past is a universal theme."

"That's what makes the film so iconic. You totally get it. That's dynamite!"

AFTER THE MOVIE, we strolled toward Commons holding hands, our frizzy red curls interweaving in the gentle breeze. I lit another joint and passed it between us, though she still fake-toked, and I sang *Guinevere had green eyes, like yours mi' lady like yours.*

"Your voice is so clear and sweet, an Irish tenor. Anyone ever tell you that?"

"I like to sing James Taylor songs, too."

"I'd love to hear them, but you said you'd tell me about Mexico."

"Aw, I just needed to get away, figure stuff out. Not worth talking about."

"But I'm interested."

"I used to fake toke, too. Didn't like the sensation of losing control. Of course, it ultimately didn't matter 'cause the more things I tried to control, the less control I had, if that makes any sense at all. Why do you do it?"

"Not for such a convoluted reason. I've almost passed out a couple of times." She took a big toke, held it in for a few seconds and exhaled a cloud of smoke. "So, did you figure things out?"

"Figure what out?"

"The things that compelled you to go to Mexico."

"They were merely symptoms of bigger things I still haven't figured out, but let's not talk about it."

"It's healthy to talk about things. Maybe I can help. I'm a good listener and I've got some things figured out, I mean, what I want out of life. I suppose that's something, but it's not very women's libby! If I told you, you'd laugh. Think it's stupid."

"Bet you say that to all the guys."

"Oh, so true. I shoo 'em off me like flies." She made a grand sweep of her arm, then wobbled and clutched mine. "I knew that weed would go right to my head . . . Seth, did you really mean it, what you said about my hair? All the cool girls have straight hair."

"I think you're totally Woodstock cool. I'm serious. So tell me."

She blushed. "I've never shared this with anyone. If you laugh at me . . ."

"Swear to God, I won't."

She took a deep breath. "Okay then, here goes. I want lots of children. I'll cook them healthy organic meals, sew all their clothes, teach them to be peace-loving, caring, environmentally conscious human beings. I want to live in a big old fixer-upper house on a tree-lined street where the children can play and ride their bikes and . . ." I'd closed my eyes. Visualized the perfect mother, Donna Reed in *It's a Wonderful Life*, only Erin wouldn't end up a spinster librarian when I disappeared. She was a prize.

"Who gets to play the husband in your dream?"

"Are you auditioning?"

I tried to imagine myself returning from work to a home redolent with the aroma of fresh baked bread, eager to share my day, hear about hers and our ginger-haired children's. I imagined tucking them in bed. Singing them to sleep. Falling asleep ensconced in her warm embrace and sweet scent after making passionate love. I wanted to believe that could be my future, but I knew better. My eyes welled up and I turned away, grasped for a flippant response. "Will your dream house be *a very, very, very fine house, with two cats in the yard*?"

"If you're finding it so funny, why are you crying?"

I wiped my cheeks with the back of my hand. "I'm not. Something got in my eyes and I'm just a sap for mushy sentiment. Your imagery is excellent; you should major in Creative Writing."

She pressed her palm to my chest and told me to trust my heart. I blinked repeatedly. "See, all gone. I'm just a very good actor. Wanna come back to my apartment and listen to an album?"

"Okay."

LOUD LOVEMAKING NOISES emanated from Umo and Lena's bedroom down the hallway. Erin blushed, looked uncomfortable. Privacy was at a minimum. She nervously fidgeted about the kitchen picking things off the counter and examining them, ordinary things like oven mitts and spoons, as if they were unique items she'd never seen, her front teeth pressed into her lower lip. There was anticipation in the air, something I sensed but couldn't quite define. She swept her finger across the countertop. "You keep everything so neat and clean. Do you fold your toilet paper into little squares?" Doesn't everyone? "I like those candlesticks. Antique?"

I took them off a shelf. "They were Grandma Matthews Shabbos candlesticks. Mind if I light them? It's after sundown and all but it's kind of a tradition."

"I think it's sweet. Traditions are important. I often ate Friday night dinners at my best friend's house, and they lit candles and said the blessings over bread and wine. I always wished my parents had traditions like that, but they're agnostic, think God's a human construct, and I'm not sure what I think to be honest."

"I believe in some overriding presence, I guess, you know, a moral center to the universe, but don't go thinking I'm some kind of ultra-religious nut."

"I'll worry if you start talking to Her." But I did talk to Him. I lit the candles and placed them atop the dresser in my room and turned off the lights. Flopped down on my mattress and patted the space next to me. She sat as far from me as possible, babbling on about my tidy room, the perfect hospital corners, as we watched the candlelight dance across the walls and ceilings. "I've two younger brothers and they're total slobs. Thought all boys were."

"You're not the first to tell me I'm not like other guys." I placed *Stand Up*, a Jethro Tull LP, on the turntable and cued the tone arm to the second song on side two. "The album's from 1969. This song blows me away. He's talking to me." *Don't want to be a fat man. People would think that I was just good fun . . .* "You see, no one takes fat guys seriously. We're just the shit clowns following in the wake of the parade."

Erin threw her arms around me and we tumbled back on the mattress.

CHAPTER 21

WHEN I OPENED my eyes next morning, she stood gazing out my east facing window. Her petite body, muscular and yet so smooth, was enveloped in a golden radiance, her forehead resting lightly against the windowpane, naked but for my blanket wrapped around her. An indecipherable expression on her face. I imagined her traipsing through the field at Yasgur's farm in a diaphanous gown with a garland of flowers in her hair. Warmth surged through me, emotions new, complex and confusing. Mixed with guilt. Droplets of blood dappled the sheets. I hadn't meant it to happen. I hadn't meant to love her, knowing I'd only make her cry, turn her sweet dream nightmarish. Oh God, if she didn't leave now, I'd never be able to let her go. She picked up the framed photograph of Jonah and me. "Look at you, so chubby and adorable! Who's the other little boy? He's nothing like you."

I fidgeted uncomfortably. My room pressed in on me. The sun was directly in front of her now, outlining her lovely body in molten gold. It was too much to bear. I snatched the photo from her hand. "Don't you have to leave? I've got lots to do today; I'm sure you do too." She winced. Sweat trickled down my face. Breathing became difficult. She would fill my empty heart and break it. "It's my fault. This shouldn't have happened. I'm sorry. Please forgive me."

"But it did and there's nothing to be sorry about. I'm not sorry. Don't you like me?"

"Yeah, I like you a lot. That's why you have to leave."

She sat down and took ahold of my trembling hands. Her skin so white, so soft, I wanted to melt into her. "That makes no sense. You don't really want me to go. Tell me about the photo."

"It's my brother, but it's kind of personal."

She furrowed her brow; looked at our naked bodies. "More personal than this? Can't you feel our connection? I sensed it the moment we met. Knew it was real when you put your arms around me and sang to me." She rose, went over to my bureau, opened my top drawer filled with neatly folded, color-coded T-shirts, took one out. "I like this one. It's so funny: 'Wanted Dead or Alive for Over-acting' and . . . oh my God, is that your mugshot? Where'd you get it?"

"I was arrested up in Madison during a guerilla theatre performance and Heshy, the guy who runs the Mad City troupe, had it made for me after I was bailed out."

She sniffed it. "Hmm. Eau de Seth. I'll keep wearing this scent, too." It hung to her knees. She looked devastatingly cute. "Are you hungry?"

"No, not really. Listen, Erin . . ."

"Well, I am. Let's make something to eat." She walked into the kitchen like she owned the place and opened the fridge. Placed veggies on the counter. "You can tell me more about your brother."

"I've got a paper due tomorrow. I'm sure you have lots of homework, too."

"Do you have any rice?"

"Uh, in the pantry, but . . ."

She turned around, took my hands and stared into my eyes. Into my soul. "I'm not leaving. I shared my dream with you. Now it's your turn to share." She put rice up to boil, chopped vegetables and placed them in the cast iron frying pan. "How old were the two of you in that photo?"

"Jonah was eight. I was three. We're not biological brothers—I'm adopted—but I loved him so much. He was carrying me home after hiking in Alley Pond Park. Our special place. That photo's my very first memory."

"That's sweet. Where is that?"

"In Queens on Long Island. Near where we lived when I was little. It was a vast forest, trees so tall they blocked the sky. At least it seemed that way to me. We played hide and seek. Searched for pirate treasure along the shoreline of this immense pond. Took a secret road through the park with bridges and a castle."

She stopped mid-chop. "Sounds magical. The trees out where I live are three or four hundred feet tall. Sitka's, Douglas Fir, even Redwoods in the southern part of Oregon. But surely your mother didn't let an eight-year-old take you to the park alone."

A momentary wave of disquiet washed over me. Who took the photo? I shook it off. "It was a long time ago. I'm sure it was much safer then. Like I said, it was our special place."

I heard Umo and Lena's voices in the hallway, the apartment door open and close, the kitchen now alight with late morning sun. A heady aroma of steamed rice and sautéed veggies permeated the room. I watched her plate food, humming *Where have all the flowers gone*, her brilliant copper penny hair almost down to her waist, bare but for that oversized T-shirt. I felt overwhelmed by the confluence of events that had brought us to this moment. It felt so right, so like fate, but so wrong. She'd no idea I was a monster.

She carried two plates into the small living room, settled into the overstuffed rocking chair that fit us like a glove. Beckoning me, she handed me a plate. "Eat," she commanded. "Where's Jonah now?"

I shared my canned story, the same one I'd used to deceive others, but now I choked on the words. "I'm lying to you. I've been lying for years."

"Then tell me the truth. You can trust me."

How often had Mitzie abused my trust? Why would it be different with Erin or any other girl? If I tell her the awful truth she'll flee, but better now than later. Before she breaks my heart. Before I break hers.

"They weren't fighting about Vietnam. Jonah was home because I outed him to Jerry and Mitzie. They'd no idea he was gay and Jerry went ballistic. I knew he would. I counted on it. At first Jonah seemed relieved, tired of hiding his true nature, hoping they'd accept him and love him as they always had, but that didn't happen." His expression of hurt and abandonment. How I'd gloated. "Jerry demanded he start treatments, see psychiatrists, undergo shock and conversion therapies, whatever it took to 'cure' him, all the while Jonah staring at him as if seeing him for the first time. He walked out the door. Just quietly got on his motorcycle and left. He wasn't ashamed. But I was, still am."

"You couldn't have known how they'd react."

"Oh, but I did. I'd so much anger bottled up, so much jealousy, so much need. I wanted them to see he was no better than me. I wanted the love and attention they lavished on him."

"We don't always do or say the right things when we're angry. One time my mother refused to buy me an expensive pair of designer jeans all the girls were wearing in high school, jeans I absolutely couldn't live without, and I told her I hated her, wished she was dead."

"How can you possibly compare the two situations, and anyway, she didn't die, did she? No harm done. But if she had you'd understand, Jonah's gone, maybe even dead, and I set it all in motion. I'm so ashamed. I destroyed his life, and Jerry and Mitzie's too. Consumed with guilt, they became obsessed with finding him and I became even more invisible. Understand now? I obliterate everything good, everything that could bring me happiness. Look at us together—it's so beautiful, but it can't be. I'll hurt you and you'll hurt me. Please leave."

I expected her to run screaming from the room. Thank God for her narrow escape, but she hugged me tight, told me she wasn't going anywhere, and I melted into her, purging tears dammed up for five years.

"It's going to be okay," she cooed, gently massaging my back. "It's going to be okay." That afternoon she placed her toothbrush next to mine.

CHAPTER 22

FOUR NIGHTS LATER she noted the stack of unopened letters on my desk and hesitantly asked if they were from a girlfriend. From my adoptive mother, I explained, unopened because their content never varied, but as I opened my desk drawer to put them away, mentally kicking myself for having left them in the open, she saw a photo and snatched it before I could stop her. It had been taken at a Pulqueria where I'd gotten sloshed with office friends from Coca-Cola in Mexico City. "Oh my God, this is you?" What had possessed me to keep it. "Now I get that Jethro Tull song." She glimpsed again at the photo. "You know what I see? A cute boy. You were chubby, big deal. Who said you were fat anyway?"

"Mitzie. Always putting me on diets, haranguing me for not being thin and perfect like my brother."

"No one's perfect, and you are thin. You realize that don't you?"

"I tried so hard, so she'd love me like Jonah, but my room was never clean enough, the hospital corners never tight enough. My grades not perfect. She even put me on Ritalin."

"No wonder you needed to get away. That's too much pressure for anyone to deal with."

"My life was spinning out of control. Thought I could run away from me, become someone else, but you can't. You can't hide from God. He will never forgive me for what I did to Jonah. And without punishment there'd be no moral order to the universe. I'm going to pay for what I did. It's as simple as that and only a matter of time unti . . ."

"You actually think God's up there on Her golden throne looking down on Seth Matthews; isn't that kind of narcissistic? Fatalism is an excuse for not taking responsibility for your own actions."

"But we don't control our own lives. I learned that in Hebrew school.

There's even a High Holiday prayer: *Who shall live and who shall die, who by fire and who by water, who by sword and who by beast* . . . on Yom Kippur our fates are sealed by God!"

"And I thought Catholic dogma was a bunch of hooey!" Replacing the photo in the drawer, she espied my bottle of Black Beauties. "Seth, what're you doing with amphetamines?"

"They help me study and maybe they suppress my appetite a little. Kind of like the Ritalin."

"They're bad for you. You should stop taking them. You're not chubby but I wouldn't care even if you were." Really? I'd seen that Outward Bound photo with those hunky guys. I needed my Black Beauties. They calmed me, my drug of choice, not Mitzie's or Dr. Coe's or one of the many crazy shrinks she made me see. Nobody could tell me what I looked like. I could see myself in the mirror. I simply needed a better place to hide the speed. And I'd spend more time in the pool, at least a mile of laps daily, lift weights, do sit-ups and crunches, limit my diet to rice and veggies.

CHAPTER 23

MIDTERM BREAK WE drove up to Devils Lake with Umo and Lena. We had all the camping and hiking essentials, sleeping bags, my homemade granola, carrots, apples and coffee, a baggie of dynamite grass and a bottle of Crown Royale liberated from Umo's dad's liquor closet during summer break. And I'd found the perfect hiding spot for my Black Beauties, the glove compartment of my car, easy access for my daily dose.

Absent a tent, our shelter was a canopy of trees, our light the sun, moon and stars. The weather was lovely, a mere hint of impending winter in the air. I inhaled the potpourri of crushed, decaying leaves, crumbled earth and moss, so crisp, clean and dry. The trees a riot of earth tones, rust, yellow, burnt orange and reds mingling with stalwart green, the ground blanketed with leaves crunchy yet soft to the step and faint with mildew.

Erin chafed at the bit to go rock scrambling. I'd gone once before, the climb fun with a great view from the top. Days so short now, we dashed to the base of a wall of rocks, vestige of the last ice age, packing a couple of joints and the Crown Royale. Erin looked up, scoffed and called it an ant hill. Lena took one look and slowly backed away, pulling Umo with her, and told us to have a good time. I looked longingly after them as they disappeared into the dark shade of the burnt amber forest through a gentle rain of cascading leaves, along with the Crown Royale and the joints. "Let's do something a bit more challenging, Seth." She pointed to a mountain of boulders across the lake. "That looks interesting."

"That looks way steeper. This scramble looks interesting enough."

"Sure, for kids. Nothing compared to what I did this summer."

"But we're not prepared. We don't even have gloves."

"We won't need them. You're climbing boulders, not vertical rock face. Just follow me and do what I do. You're not going to fall. Come on, Seth. Geez, why'd you even bother bringing me here? I keep forgetting I'm not with my

Outward-Bound buddies." I ground my teeth. Her Reed buddies, real men, not wimps like me.

She started ambling to the other side of the lake, me following a few paces behind. "Knew you'd change your mind. It'll gonna be so much fun, Seth, a no brainer." Yeah, a no brainer all right.

With an impish grin she started the ascent, assurance in every step, as natural as breathing, and I tried to mimic her moves, looking for every hand and foot hold in the rock, staying as close to her as possible. As she climbed, she described her family's Chicago origins, how her parents' wound up in the Pacific Northwest when her dad was offered a faculty position at Reed College out of grad school. "My brothers and I were all born in Portland. We've no other family there, although Connie and Ted are almost family."

I tried to keep pace, heart pounding in my chest, hands freezing, the rocks so cold. "Ah, the bananas bread lady."

"Uh huh. We still have family in Chicago, Dad's brother. We stayed with them when my parents drove me to Beloit; it's hard to stay connected, being so far apart, probably why I'm so close to my parents and brothers. We do lots of stuff together, you know, camping and hiking, cross country skiing. Mom's folks followed us out west, but they've passed on. Grandma McGuire's still alive, living with my uncle and aunt in Chicago, but her memory is fading. Didn't remember me at all when we saw her in late August, before school started. Mistook me for my mom. Called me Carol."

"My family's not particularly outdoorsy, except for summer trips to the shore."

"But you are. Look how well you're doing." I looked down. Big mistake. Fifty feet from the forest floor. I was hyperventilating, armpits clammy, beads of sweat tickling my face I couldn't wipe without letting go of the rock. I started thinking about Jimmy Stewart in *Vertigo*.

"It's so beautiful out west, Seth. I can't wait to show it to you. We've hiked all throughout the Cascades volcanic range that runs from British Columbia to California . . . it's mind blowing. And Glacier National Park, and the Canadian Rockies. You've never seen anything like it." Would I ever see anything ever again? "And we boogie board in the Pacific; water's so cold we wear wetsuits."

"Your mother, too?" Mitzie's idea of outdoor adventure was walking across the parking lot at Macy's for a sale. My hands were cramping now; I wanted to shake them, get some blood flow, sorry I'd taken speed today. My jaw ached, my temples throbbed like tom toms, Erin's idea of fun the equivalent of ingesting five Black Beauties.

"Yup. Mom, too."

"Are we there yet?" I squawked like a little kid in the back seat of a car.

"We've got another fifty feet or so."

Fifty feet! Dear God, please don't let me die. Not now. Not like this. I needed to distract myself. "What are your brothers like?"

"Ryan's a total jock; high school sophomore. You can tell the season by the competitive sport he's playing. Pretty happy go lucky; total slob, unlike you. Liam's thirteen, in seventh grade, and so cute, like you. When he was eight, he informed us he was going to be a famous film director. Had his Academy Awards best director speech written! He's very serious. When he sets his mind to something there's no stopping him."

"You're like that."

She stopped, casually turned to me as if terra firma weren't seventy feet below, inelegantly wiped her brow with her forearm, and smiled. Just another stroll in the park. "That's right. I go for what I want."

"You and your mom close?"

"Very, but we've different goals. She's convinced if a woman's not a professional, she's not fulfilling her destiny; got her master's in library science. Head librarian at Reed now. She expects me to be a feminist like her and break through the remaining barriers, but first I want to have a family, like Connie."

I thought back on the UCC class freshman year. "Most women today agree with your mom, Erin."

"So what? I'm my own person. I'm an Outward-Bound woman." Looking for her Outward-Bound man. A good country and western song. Me the old lover left behind.

"Think we can keep moving? My hands are going numb."

"Don't be such a wuss. This is child's play. You should've been with us this summer." I was suddenly seized by a horrible thought. How would we get down? "Anyway, Connie's like a big sister. When Mom first advertised at Reed for a mother's helper I was annoyed. I was in middle school and didn't need a minder. But Connie became a member of the family, really. Taught me so much. Understood me in ways Mom didn't. We'd read the women's magazines together, clip recipes, cook and sew, things I loved to do, but Mom frowned upon. She met Ted through Dad, while taking his Philosophy 101 class; Ted was Dad's TA. Connie went gaga over him, made him bananas bread and brought it over to his off-campus apartment. Of course, it only works on someone who's receptive. Sound familiar?"

"She must be a sorceress. That bananas bread cast a spell on me. Hope I survive to meet her."

"You will if you come home with me for the holidays. Please! I really want you to."

"Will we have to climb any volcanoes?"

"Hmmm. In December?" She was actually considering it! "Nah, too much snowpack."

I was ready to fall to my knees and kiss the ground when we made it to the top but couldn't let on. The view was dynamite, miles of humpbacked hills flowing into verdant farmland, the autumnal sun casting a psychedelic sheen of reddish gold, purple and magenta on the rock-face, but we'd little time to tarry. Darkness would descend like a velvet curtain. We went down the same way we came, a harkening back to my recurring dream, plunging helplessly into a bottomless void, but my feet landed on solid ground, Erin awaiting me with open arms.

She moved the rest of her things into my apartment when we returned, an invasion of pink. She purchased all manner of dry goods at the local food coop. Mason jars filled with grains, beans, whole wheat flour and rice now lined the kitchen shelves, things that bespoke of home and hearth to her; she even organized them alphabetically for me. She canvassed the campus cajoling kids to register to vote, for McGovern of course, and persuaded Lena to let us use the Tri-Delt house for a Sunday night McGovern spaghetti benefit. She fascinated me; Earth mother, social activist and adrenalin junkie, naivety, sureness and rashness all in one unique package, with a seemingly unshakable faith in me. Everything was too perfect, too Playa del Carmen. Letters postmarked Huntington kept arriving, unwelcome reminders of the fragility of happiness. I stuffed them into the desk drawer without a word.

CHAPTER 24

I HAD JUST finished my daily laps, drying off by the side of the pool when Lucy walked in. I hadn't seen her in nearly a year and immediately apologized for being such a pig that day after theatre class. She was gracious. Water under the bridge. On a deadline to finish her senior playwriting thesis, a psychological drama set in a nursing home. Had spent her field term working in one. "Got a lot of good material. Eerie place. I'm hoping my play makes the cut for a fall production, and there's a role for you."

When I asked her to describe my character, she refused. I'd have to wait to find out. "I see you've been busy. Another Irish lass, huh? Whatcha do, promise your parents you'd only bed girls from the Emerald Isle, the whole Erin Go Bragh thing, or is it Erin Go Braless? She sure doesn't need one." The kettle calling the pot black. "I've been busy, too." She held out her hand. "Check it out." A diamond engagement ring.

"That's dynamite, Lucy. I'm really happy for you."

"Thank you. Met a med student specializing in geriatrics at the nursing home. Alex said it was love at first sight but being the only woman under eighty the competition wasn't too fierce. We spent the summer together on Martha's Vineyard. I thought I was attracted to redheads, but it turns out I prefer my men tall, dark and handsome . . . and Jewish." I told her I was also Jewish and if she didn't believe me she could check out my circumcision.

"Already did, or have you forgotten? You had your chance. It really hurt when I woke up alone that morning. And after saving your life, too! Didn't you know how much I liked you?"

"Hey, I've got a role for you as well. I'm student directing *Cyrano de Bergerac* as my performance thesis, and you are Roxane."

"Nice segue. I'm flattered but I don't know, with my own play and all . . ."

"Mine's not going into production until winter term, so let's make a deal.

You be my Roxane and I'll take that mysterious role in your play." We shook on it, and she invited me and Erin to a McGovern victory celebration party she and her roomies were having.

ALREADY PITCH DARK when I left the pool house, wintry gusts buffeted me from all sides. Lord knows, it had to be minus ten degrees without the wind-chill factor. Icicles formed on my wispy moustache. The old Dutch elms stood stark naked, gnarly limbs claws scratching at the charcoal sky, funnels of dead leaves undulating in the snow-scented air. I shivered, picked up my pace, anxious to come in from the cold and cuddle with Erin.

A faint sniffling noise greeted me from the kitchen; Erin fixing herself a cup of tea, Umo and Lena elsewhere. As I hung my furry jacket in the closet, I glanced at the hallway mirror to discern if I was getting buffer. "Preening in front of the mirror?" she bristled. "Geez, can't you toss your coat on the floor or over the furniture like every other guy?" I ignored her tone. Probably her time of the month. I playfully grabbed her from behind and fondled her warm breasts, chasing the chill from my hands. Her nipples responded immediately but she jerked away. "Stop it. Your hands are freezing and you're making me spill my tea."

"I ran into an old theatre mate at the pool. Lucy. Hadn't seen her in a year. She's written a play, hoping to go into production next month and wants me to star in it. Isn't that cool! She's agreed to be my Roxane and invited us to an election night party."

"I thought I was going to be your Roxane. I've been the one practicing with you."

"And I really appreciate it, Erin, but Lucy's a real actress." I nuzzled the back of her neck, planted little kisses up and down her spine, under her chin, even licked her earlobes, something she loved and really turned me on, but she pushed me away.

"Guess that's one more thing I'm not," she muttered. I'd no idea what she was talking about. Definitely her time of the month. I asked if she needed anything for menstrual pain. "Just because I don't feel like hopping in the sack doesn't mean I'm having an affair with Mr. Tampon! Not that you'd want me anyway. Blood on the sheets is so messy. You'd never go with the flow!"

Good pun, if a bit sarcastic. Where was that coming from? "Is there anything I can do for you?"

"Oh sure, why don't you help me with my calculus assignment. After all, you took Medieval Philosophy to satisfy your math requirement. Or maybe with Quantum Physics. Didn't you take Physics as Natural Philosophy?" So much for cuddling.

"So, maybe I'm right brained. Let's see who winds up making more money."

"Money, material possessions, status, security, Jewish girlfriends ... that's all you New Yorkers think about, isn't it?" What the fuck? Jewish girlfriends? "For some of us it's about following our dreams."

Enough. I headed toward our room, but she reached out and grabbed my arm, frenetically scratching the back of her head with her other hand. "Don't you ever, ever walk away from me. The world is going to hell in a hand basket. My world is going to Hell! Don't you care about anyone or anything besides yourself?"

I didn't know what had set her off, but I didn't need this crap. I should've simply let the storm clouds pass, but instead added fuel to the fire, suggesting she go shave her legs or armpits or something. "Oh really? Wanna Judy Doll? Check out the advertisements on back page of the DC comics. Right next to the adverts promising to turn ninety-nine-pound weaklings into Outward-Bound men." She started to cry.

"Erin, what the fuck is going on? Please tell me what's wrong?"

"Wanna know what's wrong? I'll show you," and pulled me into our bedroom where open letters lay scattered about the mattress like dead leaves. She tucked herself into the corner, engulfed in Mitzie, clutching one in her hand. I dropped to my knees beside her. "For weeks I've watched that pile grow. You wouldn't tell me anything. You were keeping something from me." Mitzie. Always Mitzie snatching happiness from me. "Letter bombs, and when this one arrived today, I finally imploded." She handed it to me.

Dear Seth,

You haven't answered any of my letters but I'm sure you're just too busy with schoolwork. I was so thrilled when you came home this summer. Just knowing that you and Abby are together makes me so happy. And it makes so much sense. You've been best friends since you were little children and have such a wonderful foundation to build a future on. And for both families to have our children so close to us, what can I say. I feel blessed...

I didn't need to read further. My mouth so dry I could barely swallow. "Erin, let me explain..."

"What? Why you lied to me? Maybe you can explain this, too." It was Abby's high school graduation photo. "I found it in your drawer. I assume it's your Jewish girlfriend." I tried to convey she had it all wrong, but she cut me off. "I thought I knew you, thought we wanted the same things. You loved my dream, and I loved you for loving it 'cause it's not a dream, Seth, it's what I want out of life. I opened myself to you completely. You made me believe you were that man. You used me. Someone to fuck until you went home to your real girlfriend."

"Abby and I have been friends forever. Period. She's seriously involved with another guy. Only reason her mother's scheming with Mitzie is he's black."

"So she means nothing to you?"

"I didn't say that. We're best friends."

"So, she does mean something."

"Geez, Erin, am I on trial? You becoming a lawyer?"

"It's a simple question, yes or no. Are you together with her? In love with her?"

"What? Are you just gonna believe Mitzie?" I'd been so happy that week at home, until the last night. Mitzie had seemed interested in me. In the things I was interested in. Not what she wanted me to be. I allowed myself to believe things were different, but they're never different, and now I was walking a tightrope between Mitzie and Erin with no safety net. "You'll never understand."

"Oh, I think I've got a pretty clear picture. You're hedging your bets, having your cake and eating it too. Explains why you've never evinced the slightest interest in anything about me that came before you, my friends, my childhood, the Outward-Bound trip. I'm a placeholder, someone to warm your bed; what more do I need to know?"

"That's not true; I want to meet all the important people in your life..."

"Then why act like I don't have one, like I've simply merged into your life story?"

"I told Mitzie that Abby and I were only friends and would never be more than that, and I didn't show you those letters because I knew this was how you'd react. Mitzie gets fixed ideas in her head; me going to Cornell, becoming a lawyer, marrying the daughter of one of her friends in the Sisterhood, living happily ever after in Huntington. There's always been a price tag on her love. Mistake I made was not throwing them out."

"Doesn't take a degree in psychology to figure this out. You're desperate for her love. That's why you've kept those letters. I never believed you when you said you hated her."

"Doesn't everyone want love? Didn't your parents love make you feel safe and secure, help shape the person you've become, Look at me. I never had that, not until now, and I don't want to lose you."

"Then trust me enough to be open with me. Respect me enough to let me decide how I'm going to react to things. And I'll tell you something else, I won't tolerate that woman breathing down my neck."

"I swear to God, Abby's not."

"Not her, Seth. Your mother!"

CHAPTER 25

NIXON WON IN a landslide, McGovern taking one measly state. The country had gone mad. Erin, Umo, Lena and I were sitting in the living room screaming at the TV set as if the little square box could relay our anguish to the world when the phone rang. Jack calling from Madison. There was going to be a huge rally at the state capitol. Send a message to Nixon—end the fucking war! We should go. Erin was ready to go. She wasn't going to sit around and mope. The FBI had established a direct link between Nixon and the Watergate break-in. People aren't paying attention. This was supposed to be a democracy. "If we don't stand up now, we'll wind up in a totalitarian state."

"Won't be the first time," I concurred. "George Santayana said, 'Those who cannot remember the past are condemned to repeat it,' but it's often attributed to Winston Churchill." I'd looked it up. Erin seemed impressed. Actually smiled at me. A first in several days. Benefits of a liberal arts education. I turned to Umo, busy rolling the customary joint. "You guys wanna come? Jack'll put us up."

"Nah, you guys represent us."

LUCY'S McGOVERN VICTORY party appeared funereal. I recalled a line John Steinbeck had lifted from an oft quoted Robert Burns poem: *the best laid plans of mice and men often go awry*. Everyone was bummed out. Lucy greeted us at the door with a platter of brownies. "Unbelievable, huh? Another four years of Nixon. It's crazy. How could McGovern not win? Everyone I know voted for him!" Dismayed, she looked at a poster of an extremely pregnant woman captioned *Nixon's the One*. "Prophetic, huh? Now we're all fucked! Anyway, have a brownie. They'll take your mind off him."

Erin took a big one. "They look delicious. How long have you and Seth known each other?"

"Since freshman year." She elbowed me in the ribs. "UCC class, remember, Seth?"

"How can I forget. You tore me a new asshole."

"You acted like one." She turned back to Erin. "Friends since sophomore year. Pretty funny story actually. A bunch of us dropped acid and went to Big Hills Park in the middle of a blizzard pretending we lived in the Middle Ages. Seth was so wasted he thought I was Galadriel, queen of the fairies from *Lord of the Rings*. We dropped acid again a few days later and Seth transported me to Middle Earth."

Erin took a large bite of her brownie. Wryly noted our acting hadn't been confined to the stage. Lucy gave my arm an affectionate squeeze. "Well, with actors, all the world's a stage, right Seth?"

"How often did you guys drop acid together?"

"One time too many . . . for Seth. It was kind of scary. One minute he's lathering me in the shower and the next running naked out into the blizzard. I found him half frozen in the snow outside Haven Hall making snow angels. He was completely out of it. Almost carried him to my dorm room. Took an hour to warm his body. I saved your boyfriend's life."

Erin took a larger bite. Her face was chalk white. Placed a hand to her forehead. "Phew, is it me or is it really warm in here? Excuse me for a moment. Where's your bathroom?"

"Just down the hall and to the right."

Lucy and I chatted about her play, now titled *Blue Ladies*, and I lost track of Erin until spotting her in a corner of the living room munching the rest of her brownie, while engaged in conversation with a short-haired girl with a camera slung across her shoulder. Sinead. I was so fucked. "Lucy, what is she doing here?"

"I guess one of my roomies invited her. Go say hello. It'll be an Irish reunion." I walked over. Sinead was talking, Erin listening, perspiring despite the chill in the drafty apartment. What was Sinead telling her?

"Hi Seth. I was just showing Erin my great grandmother's pendant. You remember, don't you? Thought she'd be interested, being Irish and all." Erin's face now ghostly pale. "Nice talkin' to you, Erin. Good luck." As Sinead walked away Erin started to sway and clutched my arm. Her eyes rolled back in her head. Fell like a tree in a forest, hitting the wood floor with a loud thunk. Her eyes fixed and dilated, trance-like. I freaked out. Knelt beside her for what seemed an eternity. Sinead must've told her what I'd done. That I was a monster!

Gasping, she lurched up, blinked spasmodically, took in all the concerned faces hovering over her like medical interns in a surgical theater, and turned crimson. Sinead leaned over my shoulder and stage whispered, "Say hi to Ken for me," and left the room.

Lucy looked down at Erin with studied bemusement. "Could've been the hash brownies, but I only used a few grams, and everyone else is fine."

"You put hash in them without telling us? She doesn't have a high tolerance."

"Obviously, but how was I supposed to know that? Relax, Seth. She's coming around."

"Too strong for a little girl like her," someone murmured.

She felt woozy. I asked Lucy if I could take Erin into her bedroom and let her lie down for a while. "No problem. Just don't do anything you didn't do with me, okay?"

I lay Erin atop a pile of winter coats and sat next to her gently caressing her face. Embarrassed, she pressed her face into my chest and cried, "I can't go back out there. Everyone'll be looking at me. It's high school redux."

"You think this is bad? First time I tried a Power Hitter I was at a party given by one of the Kahunas off campus. Standing next to one of those floor-to-ceiling plant racks at the top of a flight of stairs, you know, the kind with lots of plants in clay pots hanging from it. Well, I took a humongous hit and next I knew I was at the bottom of the stairs lying in potting soil, surrounded by broken clay and plants, everyone looking down at me. It was awful. I was mortified, not to mention totally paranoid, and left immediately, so maybe that wasn't the best story to tell you." She giggled. I was on pins and needles, waiting for her to bring up Sinead. "No one's gonna make fun of you, Erin. Everyone liked you."

"I'm not so sure about Lucy. She wanted me to know you two had history together. What did she mean with that comment about not doing anything you and she didn't do? There's energy between you. She's your Woodstock dream girl, isn't she? A perfect hippie goddess. Sounds like you were a lot more than just friends, and how bad can an acid trip be when you wind up in bed with a girl who looks like the woman on the cover of your *Electric Flag* album? Admit it. You're still crazy about her."

"And you look like the chick on the album cover of *Blind Faith* . . . smokin' hot."

"The barely post-pubescent one with the flat chest and frizzy hair? Geez, thanks."

"I'm telling you, Erin. Nothing happened. We didn't have sex."

"Well, as Lucy described it, it sure sounded like more. And sex is just a physical act. Making love is about feelings, and I'll wager Lucy's got a totally different take on that night. Maybe even unfinished business. You never look outward; everything's in relation to you."

I changed the topic. Asked what she and Sinead had been talking about.

"Why do you care?"

I told her we'd once been involved, that things hadn't ended well, and she scoffed, asked if I had any other surprises in store, and who was that Ken guy? "Just someone I used to know. Let's go home."

CHAPTER 26

THE MADISON RALLY started in front of Memorial Union at 10 a.m. and wound its way up State Street to the to the Capitol Rotunda. Jack warned us to watch out for the jocks and frat guys. Things got rowdy after Badger home games and the jocks versus freaks thing was still big in Madison.

The lawns surrounding the rotunda overflowed with protesters. The air sparked with electricity. Chants of *One, two, three, four, we don't want your fucking war* echoing around the capital lawns. Anti-war luminaries Tom Hayden and Jane Fonda exhorted us to stay involved, man the ramparts when necessary, not wallow in the aftermath of the disappointing election results. Joan Baez sang "Joe Hill"; Country Joe McDonald sang his anti-war rag "I Feel Like I'm Fixin' to Die"; Phil Ochs his iconic "I Ain't Marching Anymore." Maybe we could change the world. This was power. The legacy of Woodstock. Erin, wearing her *Stop Bitching and Start a Revolution* sweatshirt, hugged me and thanked me for bringing her to the rally. It felt better to know we weren't alone.

After all the speeches a crowd had congregated in one corner of the rotunda cheering and laughing. Mad City was staging a guerilla theatre event. I pulled Erin through the sea of humanity. Heshy noted my presence. "The prodigal son returns bearing lovely gifts."

After introductions he warmly embraced Erin and held up five fingers. "Now I know five things about your enigmatic boyfriend. He looks more Irish than Jewish; that's one. He's an excellent actor, on and off stage, that's two..." He counted off with his fingers. "He's evasive, likely to answer a question with a question to protect his secrets. That's three. Bet you've already experienced that one, huh? He was a Shabbos goy, and lastly, he has excellent taste in women." Erin was charmed. "So, what's happening with *Cyrano*?"

"I'll start working on it winter term. Right now, I'm cast in another student's play and starting rehearsals soon. It opens in December."

"You seem different, Seth. Happier. What's changed?" Looking directly at Erin, he continued, "Or should I guess?" I grinned and clasped Erin around the waist. "Looks like you found somebody to love. You've got to stay for dinner. Paisley and the kids are going to want to see you."

"Geez, Heshy, I don't know, we have to get..."

"Absolutely. We wouldn't miss it," Erin interjected. "We just have to get the car. It's parked near the campus."

ERIN CHATTED NONSTOP as we walked back down State Street. "Funny how we both got involved in the anti-war movement in 1969. Did I tell you I went to the March on Washington demonstration with a bunch of Reed students?"

"In November of 1969? You would've been fifteen. Your parents let you go?"

"They couldn't stop me. I marched because I needed my voice to be heard. Five hundred thousand people standing united on the Mall sent a message, you know, we weren't going to tolerate politics as usual, all that 'bringing democracy to the world' and 'fight against Communism' bullshit. Like Phil Ochs just reminded us: *It's always the old to lead us to the war, It's always the young to fall.*"

We passed a hippie boutique displaying a Renaissance-style dress in the window display. Flared gossamer-like sleeves, tight laced bodice and a long, flowing skirt of pale forest green and cranberry. Erin stopped and gawked. "Oh Seth, that dress... it's the most beautiful thing I've ever seen. Do you mind if I go in and look at it? Just for a minute." They had it in petite. "I'm going to try it on. Just for fun, okay?"

I stared out the display window while Erin was in the dressing room. Watched crowds bearing placards stream past, talking, laughing, chanting anti-war slogans. Would their enthusiasm wane, like after Kent State? Erin's wouldn't. She wasn't playacting, part of the scene. She was the real deal. A true believer. Unique. And when she emerged minutes later, viewed herself in the full-length mirror, the dress undulating as she tossed her head, shifted her pose and twirled about, I knew I'd found my true hippie goddess, the woman of my dreams. And I wasn't even tripping.

The salesgirl said Erin was born to wear that dress, but after glancing at the price tag, Erin sighed and returned to the dressing room to change. I quietly asked the salesgirl if they had another in her size, and they did, but after sizing me up in my torn, patched jeans, frayed chambray work shirt and long unkempt hair, noted it was pretty spendy. Ninety dollars. The food budget for a month. I quickly drafted a check, handed her my driver's license, asked her to please hurry and had already stuffed the dress in my backpack when Erin returned and handed the dress back to the sales lady. It just wasn't her after all. The sales lady winked at me. Once outside, Erin lamented "That dress was so perfect. All I needed was you, a blizzard and a roaring fire and I would have been your Galadriel."

Closer to campus, as forewarned, the bars were packed with frat types sitting street side in the chilly late-autumn afternoon, leaning back in their chairs, feet up on the rails, drinking beer, hooting and catcalling all the pretty girls walking by. A stark contrast to the scene at the rotunda. One big guy in a Phi Psi football jersey slurred, "Look at the lil' hippie chick. What a dollie! Hey Red, come 'ere. I've got a nice warm lap jus' waitin' for ya." He guffawed, high fived the guy next to him. Erin flashed him the finger. He stood up, swaying, stumbling into the rail. "You lil' bitch, I'll show you wha' I can do wi' a finger."

"Jus' 'bout same size, too," his friends howled. Mr. Phi Psi turned red, about to jump the rail separating him from us when I high-fived him, whispered the secret fraternity password, gave him the secret handshake. That changed everything. He handed me a beer, was only kidding around with my "Dollie." Erin placed her arm through mine and reminded me we had to split if we were going to get to Heshy and Paisley's on time.

Entering Heshy and Paisley's chaotic house, Pippa and Zoey jumped me before I could remove my coat. Where'd I been, was the pretty lady my wife, where were our babies? I laughed and tickled them and told them they were my favorite babies, but Erin and I would work on providing more. I tumbled on the floor and ran through the house with them until Paisley scolded me for working them into a lather. I'd missed everything about this house, the chaos, the life, the overflowing love. Even as Paisley admonished me, I was warmed by the affection in her eyes. I carried the children to the couch and read them *Good Night Moon* several times until Zoey was asleep in my arms and Pippa contentedly sucking her thumb.

At dinner, Erin noted their house reminded her so much of her own. Paisley asked if she wanted kids. "Seth was made to be a daddy. He's a Pied Piper; I've never seen the kids get attached to someone so quickly."

"I can't wait to have children." Heshy predicted a bevy of redheads in our future.

After dinner, Erin helped Paisley with the dishes while I read the kids more bedtime stories, tucked them in and kissed them goodnight. This is what life was all about; what I'd never had. Before we left Heshy admonished Erin to take care of me, keep me out of my crazy head. I promised to let them know about the *Cyrano* performance. Driving back Erin leaned against me. Kissed my cheek. "You were wonderful with those children."

"Kids from difficult family backgrounds often swear they'll never bring children into the world, but not me. Children need unconditional love, need to know their parents will always be there for them, no matter what. How else can you learn to be open and trusting?" I gave her hand a firm squeeze. "I want to be that kind of father, and with you I know I'll be."

I was at my desk taking staging notes for *Cyrano* as Erin readied for bed. I'd already popped a pill, ready for an all-nighter. She drew back the down comforter and gasped. The dress was spread out, waiting to be filled by her. Genuinely touched, she threw her arms around me. "I'm going to wear it every day, thinking how much I love you."

CHAPTER 27

THAD, MY THEATRE nemesis despite our effective collaboration in *Waiting for Godot*, knocked on my door in mid-November and asked if I had time in my busy schedule for another play. I demurred, still smarting over his calling me the department head's sex toy. *Cyrano* was a big project and I'd already committed to Lucy's play *Blue Ladies*. But he already knew that. She'd asked him to direct. Needed someone with "real vision" for her project. "Personally, I wouldn't have cast you." No surprise there. "It's a disturbing psychological thriller involving a psychopathic nursing home attendant and an elderly patient, and with your looks you're more the Andy Hardy type, all gosh and golly." If he only knew. "But casting is the playwright's prerogative," he sighed. "I just need to know if something's going on between you two. I can't have personal stuff interfering with my production."

"We're friends. When do we start rehearsals?" He made a big show of looking at his watch. "You mean tonight? No notice?"

"She said you'd already promised. See you in two hours."

WE SAT IN one of the black box theaters, just Thad, Lucy and me, reading lines, Lucy cross-legged on a metal folding chair in a loose Indian print top that gapped every time she leaned forward. I averted my eyes, looked toward the exit and asked after the rest of the cast, but it turned out to be a two person play. Thad appeared apprehensive. Was there going to be a problem? He was sensing sexual tension. "The play's all about sexual tension, Thad. Seth and I are Method actors."

Lucy had written a dynamite script but was clearly miscast, taxing my skills as a makeup artist. I had to transform this gorgeous girl into a wrinkly octogenarian. And I kept flubbing my lines during a pivotal scene where I had to lift her half-naked out of bed and carry her out of the room with evil intent; she wore the same see-through fishnet top every rehearsal. I recalled her admonition during UCC class. *Just because some asshole gets aroused by me doesn't mean I magically control him or should be required to cover up my body.* Maybe, but she was stretching the limits of my acting skills, and laughed when Thad fumed and demanded we repeat the scene several times. "I'm not buying it, Seth. SELL it to me! And Lucy, you're supposed to be terrified. You're ruining the entire scene!" He called for a five-minute coffee break and demanded we have the scene nailed when he returned. "You're not taking it seriously. Go practice. And listen, Seth, I need you to show more psychopathic sexual tension." He exited the theatre.

"There's always been sexual tension between us," Lucy said. "I wrote this role specifically with you in mind. Come on, let's work on the scene."

"You're a cruel woman, Lucy. Give me a few minutes alone." I needed to get deeper into my character and walked outside coatless despite the frigid night, arms folded across my chest, trembling as I strolled past the Indian Mounds where Sinead called me a junkie and then proved it. Who had I been kidding? My one-year respite from speed had proven nothing, my lack of self-control sickening. I'd abused Sinead's love, lied to her, objectified her, used her as a rite of passage and physically hurt her. And now I was hiding my drug use from Erin, lying to her about my sexual desire for Lucy. And I'd taken sadistic satisfaction in outing Jonah and destroying his and Jerry and Mitzie's lives. My narcissism and obsessive compulsions had savaged everyone I'd ever come into contact with. Yeah, I was a monster. Exactly the kind who'd physically assault a helpless old woman. I re-entered the theatre. "Let's do this," I hissed.

After the scene, Lucy was in tears, streaks of aging makeup running down her cheeks. Thad had watched in silence, almost in shock, then sprung from his chair, overturning his coffee. "THAT WAS FUCKING DEMONIC. THAT'S EXACTLY WHAT I WANT."

ERIN SAT IN the front row opening night, the black box theatre filled to capacity. No sets. No props. No costumes. We had to make the audience buy into the fantasy we were creating. This was real acting. I thought the performance okay, not quite in the pocket, but opening nights were often like that. The audience's response so enthusiastic Lucy literally jumped into my arms, kissed me smack on the lips right in front of Erin and thanked her for lending out her boyfriend. She'd written the role specifically with me in mind and I hadn't disappointed, though she'd tired of me talking about Erin all the time. Would've made her jealous if she wasn't already engaged. "Lucky for both of us you are," Erin mused, and walking back to our apartment she glowered, "She's every bitch I hated in high school."

CHAPTER 28

ERIN KEPT PESTERING me to join her in Portland for Christmas break and I agreed, knowing full well Jerry's disappointment and the flak I'd receive from Mitzie. I acted like I was enthusiastic to meet her family and Connie and best friend Beth, see the exotic Pacific Northwest, but the plain truth was I feared she'd reconnect with those Reed guys from Outward Bound in her beloved city, see them in a more romantic light and never return. Lord knows, between Lucy's play and the Mitzie/Abby debacle she had to be wondering was I worth the bother. Insisting I call home, she sat beside me for "moral support" while Mitzie went off. What was I talking about? I'd told Jerry I'd come home. They were expecting me. Didn't I want to see Abby? "I'm living with Erin, a freshman from Portland, Oregon. Her folks invited me." Erin gave my hand a firm squeeze.

"Erin? What? Another Irish shiksa? Why am I only hearing about this now?"

"Remember our last conversation about girlfriends? Anyway, I've never been out west..."

"There's nothing out west."

"You're such a New Yorker! Portland sounds cool, and her family celebrates Christmas. We just sit around and mope, go to a Chinese restaurant and a movie, wishing we were Christians for a day."

"Does this shiksa know you're seriously involved with a lovely, Jewish girl here in New York who, by the way, has been in love with you for years?"

"Her name is Erin, not shiksa, and Abby's engaged, Mitzie. You've fantasizing. She's been living with her boyfriend since sophomore year. And she knows about Erin. We write each other. I appreciate you getting us reconnected ... as friends. Maybe it could have been more once upon a time, but I lacked the sensitivity antennae to pick up on it, like you right now. Can't you be happy for me?"

"Let's be brutally honest, okay? You don't know what love is; you just can't stand an empty bed! If you'd listened, you'd be at Cornell right now with Abby and we wouldn't be having this conversation. You've left me no choice. Do not bring home any more gentile girls. It's high time you started thinking with your brain instead of your penis. You need someone you share more than sex with."

"I completely agree. That's what I've been trying to tell you." Without Erin I'd still be wandering that stark desert landscape in Mexico, lost and alone in an uncaring universe. Maybe I still desired Lucy, but risk losing Erin. No way.

Mitzie babbled on, her plaintive words disassociating into noise. She hadn't heard a word I said. Fine. I wasn't asking her permission and obviously not getting her blessing. I was simply informing her of my plans. "This conversation is not over," Mitzie declared. But it was. I hung up the phone. Moments later, the phone rang again, Jerry reminding me to bring a map, use the emergency gas credit card, and call when we arrived in Portland. "No more Mexico's, okay? And Seth . . . I'm glad you found someone who makes you happy. Give my regards to your young lady and her family." He really did care. And a map was a good idea.

WE PLANNED TO spend the first night in Chicago with Erin's aunt and uncle, three girl cousins and grandmother, and driving down I-90 she detailed the many virtues of their restored turn of the century Greystone a few short blocks from Wrigley Field. "It still has its original leaded glass bay windows framed with opalescent stained-glass panels, you know, with all the ripples and imperfections that really bring out the true beauty of things. The architect was Louis Sullivan; I looked him up. I assume he designed the stained glass, 'course it could have been Tiffany. I want stained glass windows in our house someday, although refracted light from clear leaded crystal is also attractive." I knew nothing of Sullivan and less about old windows, but her enthusiasm was a total turn on. I wondered how she knew so much about this stuff, and what the heck was opalescence? "Opalescence simply describes the milky look of the glass that gives it its iridescence. I've always been interested in architecture. Wish I was smart enough to become an architect." Ridiculous. She was dynamite. There was nothing she couldn't do. She was an Outward-Bound girl. Maybe Beloit offered architecture courses. We'd check it out when we returned after break.

"What does your uncle do for a living? Their house sounds expensive."

"Ah, there's the misogynistic New Yorker I know and love. My uncle AND AUNT are both lawyers. He's the District Attorney. She works from home doing defense consulting work with other attorneys. And by the way, since it's all about money, she makes more than him. My grandmother lives on the third floor, though there's been talk of moving her downstairs. She suffers from dementia."

There were two cars parked curbside, one a late model Mercedes with a license plate inscribed *GUILTY*, the other a Volvo wagon likewise emblazoned *NTGUILTY*; easy to tell which belonged to whom. A large Christmas tree dominated the west-facing front parlor, presents wrapped and awaiting Christmas morning. Surprisingly, a Jewish star topped the tree, with dreidel ornaments interspersed with traditional ones. Late afternoon light illuminated the opalescent stained-glass, casting shimmering prisms of light on the walls. It was lovely. Erin's cousins were all redheads, but Mrs. McGuire looked semitic, more like the Matthews clan. Mr. McGuire, a redhead like his daughters, gave off an odd sense of déjà vu.

After the girls absconded upstairs with Erin, leaving me with the senior McGuire's, Mrs. McGuire offered me a glass of juice and went off to the kitchen while Mr. McGuire stared at me, puzzled. "You look so familiar. First time in Chicago, Seth? Have we met before?"

"I was here once freshman year for a protest rally in the Civic Center. Turned into a real fiasco."

He slapped his knee. "I knew it! I never forget a face. Fall of 1969. You were square dancing for peace, right? Got into a hubbub with our famous police force. Seems to me you were chubby, just a few wisps of whiskers, but I'd never forget that carrot top or those eyes. I remember thinking if I'd a son he'd probably look something like you."

Oh my God. He was the guy who tried to stop the cops from beating us, and now, leaning forward and parting his hair, showed me the scar from the eight stitches on his scalp. Small world, or was this fate? He was about to launch a follow up when the girls reappeared with Grandma McGuire in tow, and we headed into the dining room. She was ancient; after introductions, she called me Quinn. "No Mom. Seth is Erin's boyfriend, not Dad," and over dinner, the interrogation continued. "Erin, how do you like Beloit so far?"

"I'm really happy I went there." She squeezed my hand under the table.

"Anything particular you're focusing on?" The McGuire sisters looked at me and giggled. She flashed me a quick smile and said architecture.

"She'll be a dynamite architect," I interjected.

Mr. McGuire looked at his wife and grinned. "An explosive testimonial. What about you, Seth? You graduate this year, right? My brother told me you were a Theatre major. Any idea what you're gonna do?"

"Either getting a Masters in Performing Arts or Film school."

"Will you stay at Beloit after Seth leaves?"

"I'm not making plans, Uncle Sean. Just playing it by ear." Just playing it by ear! One sentence. One measly sentence and my glass heart shattered. I spiraled, as in my dream, toward a black hole, alone. Abandoned yet again, and I struggled to maintain my composure, fought back the vision now dancing before my eyes: Erin back some day visiting with husband and children, her uncle asking whatever happened to that redheaded boy you dated in college? "Seth?" she'd say. "Lost touch years ago." She'd affectionately squeeze of her husband's hand. "A momentary fancy." Smile. You're an actor, remember? I spent a restless night on the parlor room couch staring at the colored lights of the Christmas tree.

CHAPTER 29

WE LEFT CHICAGO the next morning with a bag filled with sandwiches, fruit and cookies, as well as a large Thermos of coffee. Provisions for the trip out west. Mrs. McGuire couldn't help being a Jewish mother and assumed I'd relate to the concept, but she didn't know Mitzie. I wondered if there was some special "How To" book Mitzie had failed to read. Mr. McGuire asked if we had blankets in the car in case of emergencies, but Jerry had provided those before I'd driven the car out to Beloit. I figured it would take two or three solid days to reach Portland, and we'd put those blankets to good use (perhaps not quite as Jerry had in mind) in rest stops when I tired of driving. The back seat was compact, but so were we, and usually slept atop each other anyway.

It would have been a grand adventure but for Erin's pronouncement. I struggled to keep my emotions in check, the endless miles of bleak barren landscape only intensifying my gloom. I wallowed in it. Why had I trusted her; why had I opened up to her? I tried to erect an invisible wall between us. Me on Death Row, Portland my gallows, Erin my last meal. That first evening I made love to her in the frigid back seat with inexhaustible passion, knowing each coupling might be our last, and Erin had her first orgasm. Something to remember me by. We continued our journey the next day, stopping only at HOJO's along the way to use the bathrooms and refill the Thermos. But late that second afternoon I saw a faint blueish shadow on the horizon that morphed, as we got closer, into a huge mountain range. "The Rockies," Erin exclaimed. "Aren't they magnificent? I knew they would take you out of your funk."

I was incredibly excited but made like it was no big deal. I wouldn't allow her to dispel my gloom. We had the Catskills back home. Erin thought that hysterical, like comparing Mount Everest to that scramble at Devil's Lake. "Imagine how it must have felt when pioneers in covered wagons first saw these mountains and climbed into the unknown. The men out front leading the horses, the women under the canopies, nursing babies and shushing toddlers, real risktakers, like us. Falling in love is risk-taking like that."

I glanced at my perfect girl. Could this be a new beginning? Could I be coming home to a place I'd never been before? I put an arm around her. Please God, let this be real. Let this be forever. Let me be happy. If only she wasn't not making plans, playing it by ear. If only.

HER FAMILY RESIDED a block from Reed College on a street lined with turn of the century houses dwarfed by majestic evergreens and maples. I'd never seen trees so tall. Most of the houses were bungalows built in the craftsman style, her family home no exception. It had a large covered front porch with columns supporting the overhanging roof. Hiking boots and waders were scattered about the wood plank flooring. Rain gear slung over wooden benches, no umbrellas in sight. The solid oak front door massive, with wrought iron trim. "It's a classic bungalow," she said, noting many of the houses in the area had been purchased as kits from the Sears Roebuck Company at the turn of the century. I was nervous, flashed back on my experiences with Sinead's family on the farm. God, how they must hate me. I grit my teeth. "All right. Let's get this over with."

Erin bolted up the sidewalk to the front door. "Relax, Seth. Just be yourself; they're going to love you." But which self?

Once inside, the McGuire house reminded me of Heshy and Paisley's, only more adult-like, and I relaxed a bit. Books and magazines littered every surface, stacked high; comfy looking furniture was covered with handmade throws; mismatched ceramic cups half filled with tea or coffee perched on end tables and the fireplace mantle arrayed with scented candles. Creative disorder. A decorated noble fir, perhaps eight feet tall, dominated a corner, taking advantage of the high crown-moulded ceilings, topped with a peace symbol. Her dad, in apron, burst from the kitchen trailing yummy aromas, hugged and kissed Erin, and warmly shook my hand. Erin inquired after her mother and her father motioned to the kitchen where a pair of legs stuck out from under the sink, the Wicked Witch of the East minus sparkling red slippers. "Stupid damn disposal," a disembodied voice grumbled, then "Got it," and Mrs. McGuire came out from under, wiping hands on her apron. She held Erin at arm's length for a better view, commenting on how much she'd changed, imperceptible changes maybe only women notice in one another. Small and compact, she had Erin's face but even paler skin, blue eyes and jet black thick wavy hair, black Irish like Sinead. She turned to me and gawked.

"You're right, Erin. Liam in a few years. Seth, you must have some Irish blood in you." I wouldn't know.

Dr. McGuire clasped his hands together and asked if we were hungry.

"Starving," Erin responded. "I've been telling Seth what a great cook you are, Daddy."

He tossed me an apron. "I hear you're pretty handy in a kitchen, too. Let's get to work; this meal won't cook itself."

The kitchen had a huge butcher block large enough to accommodate several cooks. A hanging pot rack filled with copper bottomed pots and pans of all shapes and sizes above it. A wood block was stuffed with an assortment of knives. An old gas double oven with a four-burner stove top and center grill dominated one side of the room, an immense hood fan overhead. Serious equipment showing signs of active use. Dr. McGuire motioned to several onions and garlic cloves and asked if I minded mincing them. Happy to have something to do, I noticed the chef's knife was missing from the knife block. Dr. McGuire passed me his. "You do know your way around a kitchen."

While we prepared dinner, Erin explained her mom was the Mrs. Fixit of the family, always working on something, be it appliances, creaky doors or plastering walls; her dad added he was good with a paint brush, but not much else. "That's Mrs. McGuire's territory. I just try to stay out of the way . . . but I'm the chef!"

Erin started telling her folks about our overnight visit with the Chicago McGuire's, but her dad cut her short. "Sean called and told us, honey." He turned to me. "Small world, his having met you three years ago, Seth. You made quite an impression, taking control of that volatile situation . . ."

"What are you talking about?" Erin looked from her father to me. "You'd met my uncle before?"

"Well, not officially introduced or anything. Remember I told you about the square-dancing incident at the Civic Center when I was a freshman? Turned out your uncle was the guy who interceded, the one who got hit over the head by the police."

"I knew we had a connection the day I met you."

IT TOOK SEVERAL calls from the kitchen to pry Erin's two younger brothers, Liam and Ryan, from their Strat-O-Matic Baseball game in the adjoining family room. They both had red hair, Ryan's eyes green like Erin's, Liam's blue like the senior McGuire's, a younger, thinner version of myself at his age. I hoped his life a happier one. Dr. McGuire's hair was salt and red pepper. Mrs. McGuire stood out, as I did back home. Setting the dining room table for six, I romanticized that sixth seat had always been mine, another child home from school, embraced in the bosom of my family.

At dinner, Mrs. McGuire casually passed around the salad, immediately admonished Ryan for snarfing half the dinner rolls and told Erin Connie and

Ted were on the east coast showing little Tony off to relatives and would call when they returned just after Christmas. "Connie sent me photos, Mom. He's adorable. Wish I could've been here for the christening."

Dr. McGuire and his sons attacked their food with gusto, already requesting seconds when Dr. McGuire noticed my full plate. "Seth, you've hardly touched anything. If you don't like the chicken . . ."

"Oh no. It's delicious. I tend to eat slowly." Heck, we'd just sat down.

"Don't be insulted, Daddy. He eats at a glacial pace if at all. Subsists on coffee and . . . love." She grasped my hand. Ryan looked up. "Gross."

Beth, Erin's best friend, had also called. She was spending Hanukah with her grandmother in San Francisco, back hopefully by the 28th. Erin looked disappointed. "She'd better be. We're leaving on the 29th." That perturbed Mrs. McGuire who'd assumed we'd stay through New Year's, but Erin explained we were celebrating New Year's with friends in Madison and figured it would take three days to get back with me insistent on doing all the driving. Insistent? She had a driver's license?

"Of course. Since I was sixteen. You never asked, and besides, it's your car; I figured you didn't want me driving it."

"She's a very good driver, too," Dr. McGuire added. "I taught her."

"Daddy, Seth thinks I'm Athena, sprung fully grown from his head. That's a variation of the Biblical Genesis story, Seth, you know, like in your Haftorah. Eve fashioned from Adam's rib, Athena springing from Zeus' head . . . most religions have similar allegories." Dr. McGuire laughed but Mrs. McGuire was unamused; suggested we men were lucky there was no axe on the table. Another generation of males perpetuating the myth women existed in a nebulous ether until men came into their sad, lonely little lives to fulfill them.

"In case you didn't learn this in Hebrew school, Seth, Zeus' head was split open with an axe and out popped Athena, the goddess of wisdom. And, of course, as everyone knows, Eve made Adam self-aware. One could say men would still be dumb, docile animals without us. What do you think, Mom?"

"One could say they still are." And I'd been chastised for saying women had all the power in UCC class!

Dr. McGuire guffawed as he took a second helping of mashed potatoes. Wondered if we had any plans beyond studying comparative mythologies? A crash course in Feminism perhaps? Mrs. McGuire glared at her husband. "If they offer that class at Reed, dear, you should audit it."

"I wanna show Seth around town, do some Christmas shopping. Maybe a day trip to the beach, one to Mount Hood." She turned to me. "Ever been snowshoeing, Seth? It's just a stroll on snow. If you can put one foot in front of the other, you can snowshoe."

Dr. McGuire seemed concerned. "The snowpack's deep this year. Do you have chains, Seth?"

"Only the ones he's forged in life, Daddy. But now he has me, so there's still hope for redemption!"

Liam brightened. "Hey, that's from *Scrooge*. When Marley visits him in his sleeping chamber." The 1951 version; my personal favorite. I noted Alastair Simms almost declined the role that defined his career.

"Chains... for your car tires?" Dr. McGuire continued. "You can't count on the road conditions staying good this time of year. Take the Volvo, Erin. You can show Seth your driving skills; chain up outside Sandy."

Erin winked at me. "Liam, Seth's head of Beloit's film committee. He selects all the films shown on campus. He showed me *Shane*, the most important western ever made, our very first week together."

Ryan looked up from his third helping. "Since when do you like westerns?"

"It's not just a genre film, it has a universal theme. A man coming to terms with his past. And don't chew with your mouth open. It's gross."

Ryan sneered and stuffed a chicken wing in his mouth. Liam enthused, "I wanna go to Beloit, too."

"Then I suggest less Strat-O-Matic Baseball and more reading," Mrs. McGuire said.

I'D BE BUNKING with Ryan and Liam and after dinner walked down the hallway lined with family photos. Toddler Erin with her Grandma, Mrs. McGuire's mom; grade school Erin looking totally nerdy with buck teeth, her head a mass of untamed frizzy red hair, accepting an elementary school science award. Boyish figured early teen Erin bodysurfing on the coast; hanging upside down from monkey bars; shooting rapids in an inflatable kayak. A photo taken at the pinnacle of Mt. Hood attached to a certificate commemorating her achievement as the youngest person ever to summit the mountain, sunlight reflecting off a mouthful of metal. Her artwork was framed on the wall as well, several framed sketches and a trippy painting that seemed to undulate, intricate and technically precise shapes that chillingly reminded me of interlocking spider webs. So many aspects to her! Posters lined the walls of her room: *Make Love, Not War*; *Shower with a Friend*; *Flower Power*; *Eugene McCarthy for President*. She even had the same jack-in-the-box crank toy as Jonah. Everywhere I looked I was bombarded with evidence Erin had lived a lifetime before me, experiences I hadn't shared and would never know but for these photos and posters. I'd viewed her as an extension of myself, but she wasn't. She was her own person with free will to choose how she wanted to live her life and with whom. To my shame, I found this very unsettling.

She walked into the room and took my hand. "When Beth and I saw that *Shower with a Friend* poster, we laughed our twelve-year-old heads off. The very idea of showering with someone! We were so goofy." She walked over to her dresser and cranked the handle of the jack-in-the-box. '*Round and round the mulberry bush . . .*' it twanged. I shivered with dread and she placed her arm around me. Stay in the now. "I'd no idea you'd actually summited Mt. Hood."

"There are lots of things you don't know about me. Perhaps you could express some interest."

"Don't most Catholics have crosses, like the Jews have mezuzahs on doorways?"

"We're lapsed Catholics. And anyway, you don't need organized religion to know to do unto others as you would have others do unto you. But we respect other's traditions, like you lighting Sabbath candles."

"There's a story from the Passover service about a heathen back in Roman times asking Rabbi Hillel, this famous Talmudic scholar, to teach him the entire Torah while standing on one foot and Hillel said almost those exact words. That was the whole Torah, he'd explained, the rest was commentary, but of course, being Jews, a whole lot of commentary. Do your parents mind you going with a Jewish boy?"

"All they care about is whether you're a good person. It's your mother we're going to have to work on." I fought back a rush of sadness. I'd no doubt she meant every word . . . for now. But she wasn't making plans; just playing it by ear.

Love permeated Erin's house. There were no hidden agendas, no taboo topics, nothing muted the light that shone from every heart. I wished I could be like them, wished I could've grown up in a house that wasn't a morgue. I wished they were my family. I wished my head wasn't mired in its own chamber of secrets. I wished I knew what lurked in the darkness.

CHAPTER 30

WE EXPLORED PORTLAND and the environs, hiked about ten miles on a trail that ran right through the city. Saw a herd of huge deer Erin laughingly informed me were elk. We went to Multnomah Falls, stood on a bridge watching the water cascade down two levels, then continued up through a primordial forest of majestic evergreens and ferns of such epic proportions I expected to encounter dinosaurs.

The next day we journeyed west to the ocean, and I was as humbled by my first glimpse of the Pacific as I had been atop the pyramid in the Yucatan. Like the ocean water off the coast of Mexico, the transparency of the Pacific's water reflected the many moods of the sky. Growing up on Long Island, I was accustomed to murky water, to the odors of salt, decay and sulfur, to the clusters of condominiums that dotted the beaches and taxed natural resources, oblivious to Mother Nature. Here, beaches were wild and pristine, shaped and reshaped by strong winds and pounding surf. Here, forests of Douglas fir, spruce and alder loomed above the coastline, the sweet odor of evergreen pervasive. Skeletal remains of massive trees, trees that had stood for hundreds of years before succumbing to time, lay supine in the fine sand, and as atop the Yucatan pyramids, I was again reminded the forces of nature would wash away all our human striving. We were merely a temporary blemish on all its beauty.

We hiked three miles out a peninsula that jutted straight into the ocean at a place called Cape Lookout experiencing several climactic conditions—rain, fog, sun, mist—as if the land couldn't make up its mind. Eventually we reached the edge of a cliff overlooking the ocean several hundred feet below, gazing into the horizon with awe and a sense of wonderment. Erin took my hand. Couldn't imagine living anyplace else, and why would she? Everything she wanted out of life was here.

We drove east to Mount Hood the next day, stopping at a chain-up area to put snow chains on the tires, or Erin did anyway, as I'd no idea how to deploy them, humiliated when some asshole in a pickup and CAT tractor hat rolled down his window and drawled, "She bait your hooks, too?" We drove a winding beehive road buffered by walls of snow twenty feet high or more to the parking lot at Timberline Lodge, six thousand feet up Mount Hood, higher than Mount Katahdin in Maine, with the pinnacle looming another six thousand feet above us. The Lodge a vast rustic structure built during the Great Depression with vertical and horizontal wood cross beams larger than any tree trunks I'd ever seen. Massive multi-sided stone fireplaces on all three stories with enormous logs ablaze in all of them. Entranced, I suggested we hang out, but Erin pushed me out a back exit and pointed to a tiny speck up the mountain I could just discern through a veil of snow. "That's Silcox Hut. Clamp on your snowshoes. We'll stop there and warm up before returning."

I was panting by the time we reached the Hut. The pulse in my throat throbbing from the combination of speed and physical exertion. I felt pretty chipper. I'd done it. I'd earned my mug of hot chocolate by the blazing fire in the dark, timbered hut, and was mellowing out, grooving on the companionableness of all the Outward-Bound types surrounding me, feeling like one myself. But not for long. Erin extracted two ice axes and Hefty trash bags from her backpack. "They're for sliding down the mountain, Seth. Snowshoeing down two thousand feet would be stupid. We'll use the axes as brakes. We have to be back home before dinner."

I followed her outside and looked at the long, steep decline. She had to be kidding. I didn't care how unmanly it made me look. No fucking way I was sliding down two thousand feet. "That's about the dumbest thing I've ever heard," she huffed, and I cringed. Others could hear her. "If you're going to insist on walking what's the point of my sliding down. Jesus!"

"You might have mentioned this before we snow-shoed up here."

"You're right. My bad. I'm used to hanging with a very different crowd." I grit my teeth, clamped on my snowshoes and started down the hill, Erin bitching we'd never make it back in time for dinner. My second humiliation of the day. Silently staring out the passenger side window the ride home I awaited an apology that never materialized. I was no Outward-Bound guy.

CHAPTER 31

WHEN CONNIE CALLED, we immediately drove to a place called Ladd's Addition, a maze-like development of century old bungalows interspersed with roundabouts of rose gardens. We knocked at a small bungalow door and Connie answered, an infant attached to her breast. "Erin, look at you. So grown up!" They hugged gently so as not to dislodge the baby. "It's wonderful to see you." She detached the baby so Erin could see his face. Her nipple was stiff. Leaking droplets of milk. "Tony, this is your Auntie Erin."

Erin said he looked like Ted with more hair and they both giggled. Slipping her arm through mine, she drew me into the hallway. "Connie, this is Seth, the man I wrote you about."

"It's so nice to meet you, Seth. Hang your coats on the hooks. I promised Ted you'd stay until he gets home. He wants to see you, Erin, and meet you too, Seth. Erin's like our little sister."

Connie's kitchen, a small utilitarian room with ancient-looking appliances, had dozens of Ball jars filled with grains, beans, rice, flours, and other bulk items I recognized from our tiny kitchen at 848 Park. She brewed herbal tea while Erin held the baby, mesmerized. I pictured her nursing babies, but not mine. Someone else's. Maybe one of those Outward-Bound guys' babies. A warm draft of sweet yeastiness permeated the room when Connie removed a cookie sheet of hot scones from the oven, plated them, grabbed a jar of honey off a shelf, and placed them on the mission style dining room table.

I nibbled one so as not to be rude, the speed humming though my system. The girls chatted away as if they'd last seen each other yesterday. The same closeness I shared with my cousin Joel on those rare occasions we saw each other. I looked about the place. The front rooms wainscoted, paneled ceilings and thick mouldings framing the small parlor and living room. A large loom dominated the parlor; a built-in bookcase filled with balls of earth-colored yarns. The small dining room had floral wallpaper, "Original William Morris wallpaper," Erin informed me. Every cluttered surface, the books, magazines, pillows and throws, created a sense of harmony, of comfort amidst chaos, the same feeling I'd experienced at Heshy's and again at the McGuire's, counter-intuitive to the rigid perfection that had dominated my childhood home and ruled my life.

Erin showed off the dress I'd bought her in Madison and Connie insisted she see the clothes she'd bought at a vintage resale shop in Cambridge. Erin, the baby asleep in her arms, asked me to take him for a minute. I was apprehensive. I'd played with Heshy and Paisley's kids, but this was an infant, small and fragile. What if I held him wrong and hurt him? She placed him in the crook of my arm. "Yeah, that's right, and honey, it's okay to breathe. He's not made of glass."

They disappeared into Connie's bedroom and as luck would have it, baby Tony opened wide his curious eyes, alarmed at the sight of this stranger. Unsure what to do, I resisted the impulse to run into Connie's room and hand him back. Instead, I sang him my favorite lullaby, "Sweet Baby James," and he cooed, actually cooed! I thought my heart would burst. Southern light streamed through the stained-glass windows splashing rainbows on the walls and us and by the time I was singing *and rock a bye sweet baby James* he'd fallen back asleep in my arms! What it must feel like to be so secure and trusting. Sensing eyes on me, I looked up. Erin and Connie were standing in the hallway watching and listening. Something passed between them. A nod, a knowing smile. Erin reached out her arms for him but I balked; for the moment we were all doing fine.

CHAPTER 32

I RECOGNIZED BETH from the Outward-Bound photo, as muscular and zaftig as Erin was petite, her large eyes charcoal brown, her lustrous dark chestnut hair parted in the center almost down to her waist. A guy magnet according to Erin who had been relegated to go between for boys too chickenshit to approach Beth directly. "Thank goodness you like frizzy haired, flat-chested girls."

Beth had obviously heard quite a bit about me. Needled me about living with a shiksa, the sacrilege of preferring theatre or film to law school. "Oye Vey! Your mother must be dying!" She suggested we go to a neighborhood coffee house popular with Reedies, a dark, smoky all ages venue with live music. Two of the Outward-Bound guys were there, Randy and George, yelling "YO ERIN" from across the room before bounding over; the same jocks I recognized from the black and white photo, only now, in living Technicolor. One of them had long, curly red hair and blue eyes like mine, and as he picked her up and twirled her about as if she were light as a feather, she giggled with delight, hugged him and exclaimed how much she'd missed him, missed them both. Acidic tar sloshed about in my stomach. I gnashed my teeth. Plastered a smile on my face.

The redhead, slow to let go of her, asked if she was enjoying life in the flatlands and pointedly told her how much he'd missed her too. Erin's eyes blazed with light. "Wisconsin's okay, but it's no Portland. Randy, George, this is Seth."

Randy got right in my face, intimidating me with his bulk. Took my hand in a vise-like grip and shook it 'til it hurt. "Nice to meet you, Sam. Welcome to Portland, the spiritual center of the universe." Erin didn't correct him or mention boyfriend status or any special attachment. She was playing it cool, keeping options open, and I had a sudden epiphany. I was a type, her type, nothing more, replaceable at whim. My neck started to itch. "I hear you've been in town for a week and didn't call us. I'm crushed."

"We've been pretty busy. This is Seth's first time out here, and with family stuff and all . . ."

"Do anything exciting?"

"Snow-shoed up to the Silcox Hut but Seth insisted we walk down."

George guffawed. Why would anyone walk down when you could slide? She should have called them. They would have taken her helicopter skiing. She thought that sounded awesome. Randy slapped me on the back. Hard. "You East coasters gotta get with the program, Sam." Translation: He was the Outward-Bound guy. Me the ninety-pound weakling. Spiders skittered up my spine. "Pretty awesome here, isn't it Sam?" Once again, no correction from Erin who agreed there was no better place on Earth.

I started to say my name was Seth but Randy cut me off. "Speaking of better, we're planning a two-week reunion hike on the Pacific Crest Trail this summer. Whataya think, Erin? You up for it? I've got a tent and equipment for both of us."

"Up for it! Are you kidding? Count me in!"

A ROCK BAND had set up on a small stage toward the back and started playing loud. Erin and her buddies continued to chat about the Outward-Bound trip and helicopter skiing, things I knew nothing about. I was clearly out of my element. I couldn't make out much of their conversation through the din, but it was pretty damn clear they were happy to see each other and definitely making plans that didn't include me. Could that asshole have been more obvious, or she more eager? Spiders were crawling up my neck and I slunk off to the bathroom unnoticed. Stood in front of the mirror, hands on the sink taking deep breaths, willing the spiders to disappear. Go back out there and punch the motherfucker. That'll work.

The noise level suddenly elevated as the bathroom door opened, *Hey, hey, he, he, get off of my cloud*, and a dude with long Rasta hair entered. He smelled like sheep. "Fuckin' hot out there," he said, lighting a joint. He took a few puffs and passed it to me. I took a couple of big tokes but when I tried to pass it back he said "Keep it. You look like you need it," and left the bathroom. I took a couple more hits, splashed cold water on my face, squeezed my eyes shut and told myself everything was going to be okay. When I opened them, the spiders were gone.

My return went also unnoticed. I listened to their chatter. George had a class with Dr. McGuire winter term and hoped he wouldn't be a total ballbuster. Erin promised to put a good word in for him. Randy would send her information on the summer hike. He turned to me. "Thanks for minding my girl, Sam." My girl! I furiously twirled my ghost ring and as they disappeared into the crowd Erin turned to Beth, palpably excited about the reunion hike.

"Me too. You know, I hadn't written you about this. Figured I'd tell you in person. George and I have hooked up, and you know how close those guys are, kinda like you and me. Poor Randy."

Erin's eyes widened. "Come on, I wanna hear all the gossip. Seth, mind if we go outside and catch up a bit? You can hardly hear yourself in here." She squeezed my hand. "Everything okay?"

"Dynamite. I'm going to get closer to the stage."

The band struck up my favorite Paul Revere and The Raiders tune, "Kicks," lyrics that were dead on, eerily consistent with Hemingway's philosophy of life. No matter what I did, no matter where I went, I'd never escape myself, and now I was paying the heavy price for having tried. My so-called girlfriend was making plans that didn't include me.

We dropped Beth off and sat in the car outside Erin's house. My jaw ached. I was stewing over that upcoming trip, over the way Erin had virtually ignored and belittled me. "Wasn't it cool running into those guys? I'm so glad you got to meet them. And that hike! What a blast; I've been wanting to do the PCT like forever." She moved her hand to my crotch and playfully asked if Mr. Penis was lonely and wanted some attention.

I brushed her hand away. "Guess I'll have to do now your hunky friends aren't here." I flung open the driver's side door. "Don't worry. I grew up sloppy seconds. Thanks for the reminder." She winced. Grabbed for my arm but I jerked it away. "Maybe I'm not an Outward-Bound guy, but I was trying my hardest to please you." I stomped off toward the house.

CHAPTER 33

I LAY AWAKE that night, staring at the ceiling, the brothers sound asleep, obsessively replaying the events of the evening until I thought I'd lose my mind. I tried to still the voices, wanted to believe Erin loved me and wouldn't eventually leave me for my doppelganger, but kept thinking about Bart and Ashley that night in the Phi Psi house, his assurances in the library there was nothing going on between them... at that moment. To quell the internal noise, I stole out of the house in the early morning, opened the glove compartment and ingested two Black Beauties; told myself a real Woodstock man wouldn't care, would enjoy the moment, and recalled a quote from the famous psychotherapist Fritz Perl: *If by chance we find each other, it's beautiful. If not, it can't be helped.* If only I believed that crock of new age shit.

Dr. McGuire gave Erin one hundred dollars and told us not to be foolhardy; blizzard conditions were predicted in the Gorge. I thanked the McGuire's for their hospitality, promised to drive safely. I'd thirsted for parents like them and tried to memorize everything about them. I'd never see them again.

The highway paralleled the Columbia River, snaking through cliffs looming a thousand feet on both sides, a perfect wind tunnel when the winter storm struck the Gorge. The car was buffeted from all sides. The ascendant sun blasted through a veil of snow, enveloping us in glittery, tinsel-like fire. I'd never experienced road conditions like this. Long haul trucks lined the emergency lanes, signals flashing, waiting out the weather. Temporary highway signs blinked red through the white curtain warning of worsening conditions ahead. Signs for areas to chain up. "Maybe we should turn around or you should let me drive," Erin suggested. "I'm not trying to insult your manhood, but I've driven through conditions like this." When I ignored her, she continued, "Jesus Christ. I don't know what the hell is with you, but if you're going to insist upon being so pigheaded pull into the emergency lane and chain up."

I followed instructions she issued from the comfort of the cab and continued east, now wet and filthy as well as miserable, visibility so abysmal I could only judge the passage of time by the sun's journey from windshield to rear view mirror. Wind gusts buffeted the car while I obsessed about Erin and Randy's upcoming summer plans and their presumably shared tent, so hyped up on speed I gnashed my teeth in rhythm with the repetitive crunch, crunch, crunching of the metal chains on the snowbound highway. We could have been driving to the moon, or not moving at all, maybe even stuck inside that fucking Timberline Lodge snow globe she'd given me for Christmas, an ornament never to be hung on next year's Christmas tree.

Crawling out of my skin, white knuckled, jaw aching, constantly making steering adjustments to stay in lane, I glanced at my perfect girl now contentedly clipping articles and recipes from women's magazines Connie had given her for the trip back, humming "Where Have All the Flowers Gone." I was mulling if she'd prove as inconstant as Mitzie when a chunk of ice slid off the top of the truck in front of us and smacked against our windshield, jolting her. She closed her magazine and again suggested we exit the highway and return to Portland, the weather too awful to drive through the night, but the weather was nothing compared to the storm brewing in my head. I continued on until somewhere in southern Idaho a beacon of light in the distance slowly resolved into a Stuckey's highway stop. She demanded I stop. Needed the bathroom, and if I wasn't going to turn around, she'd inquire for the nearest motel. I filled up, then downed a cup of black swill that swooshed about my acidic stomach. I also removed the chains; they were driving me crazy.

Erin returned to the car. There was a Motel 6 a few miles up ahead. We could stop there for the night. But when I drove past it, she dropped the stack of magazines on the floor and glared at me. "You've been acting weird since Chicago, in a total funk last night. I'd write it off to your usual moodiness, but this is dangerous. Pull over. We need to talk."

"Leave me alone. There's nothing to talk about."

"You think silence isn't hurtful? Don't pull that crap on me. I know you. You've got some crazy convoluted monologue going on in that fantastical head of yours, and it's getting the better of you."

"Says the girl not making plans; the girl playing it by ear."

"Jesus. Is that what this is about? You misinterpreted my words and now you're over-analyzing them like your Hebrew school teachers parsing the Torah, coming up with hidden meanings. There are none. I was saying I wasn't sure whether Beloit was the best place for me. We, you and me, are a given."

"Couldn't help noticing Randy's curly red hair and blue eyes. Gonna share your dream with him next or have you already?"

"Maybe I do prefer a certain type. So do you. Me, Sinead, Lucy, Ashley. Like so what?"

"And you're not making plans, huh? What about your upcoming summer junket with Randy and George? Guess I know whose sleeping bag you'll be sharing!"

She bared her teeth, scratched the back of her head with both hands. Started to shake. "Oh! Now I get it. How dare you! I'm not your possession; we're not attached at the hip, and I don't have to ask your permission to do something with other friends, things you've no interest in anyway. I mean Jesus Christ, I'm always with your friends, hearing stories about your life, about you and Lucy tripping together, showering together, making love, performing together, and I'm supposed to be totally fine with all that because it's about you, but when we're hanging with my friends, and Heaven forbid, it's about me, that's different."

"That why you belittled me in front of those guys? To get even? Kinda passive aggressive, don't you think? Couldn't you have just screamed at me or punched me in the nose? Would've hurt a lot less."

"I didn't mean it that way . . . well, maybe I did, a little, but I'm not one bit sorry. Consider it a wakeup call. I need you to be as interested in me as I am in you."

"You're gonna leave me and I'll have nothing, be nothing, just like before. I can't go there again, not after you, not after feeling truly alive for the first time in my life. I'd rather be dead."

"Seth, I'm not leaving you."

"It's only a matter of time." Mucus dripped down my mustache and I wiped it on my sleeve.

"Oh, gross. Stop being so melodramatic." She rummaged through her bottomless purse. "I'll get you a fuckin' Kleenex. Even now you're making it all about you. Hold on a sec. Dammit, I must have used the last one. Lemme check the glove compartment."

"NO!" I lunge across her to stop her but too late. The car swerves to the right. I skid on a patch of ice. Plow into a snow embankment, my head contacting the steering wheel. Whack. Blood sprays my face. Erin tosses sideways against the passenger door. Sounds of bone-crunching. Yelps of pain. The compartment flips open and the bottle plops into her lap.

I flipped the emergency lights, the red glow pulsing through the dark cab, lighting Erin's face, alternating red and white as she stared at me, apparently in shock. I shouldered my door open against gale-force wind that punched me in the nose and penetrated the cabin, her clippings flying about like confetti. Dripping blood from my nose, I ran to the passenger side and opened her door. She sat rigid, clutching her hip, her right leg at a weird angle, her face contorted in pain. A trucker pulled up behind us, got out of his cab and asked if we were okay. "My girlfriend's hurt. I need to get her to the nearest hospital."

"Closest one's Twin Falls. About an hour from here. Your nose looks broken. Can you see okay? I can call for help."

Erin grimaced. Her bottom lip was bleeding. She'd bitten down on it. Couldn't move her leg. Carefully closing her door, I quickly surveyed the minimal damage to the front of the car, lucky to have hit an embankment of snow and not the guard rail. I started the engine and shifted into reverse, the wheels spinning for an instant before lurching back. I waved to the trucker and signaled my move back into the right lane, blood freezing on my cheeks as I pressed the side of my face against the cold side window. I had to stay alert. Had to avoid being mesmerized by the hypnotic cadence of the windshield wipers ineffectually slap, slap, slapping at the irrepressible snow. I could only breathe through my mouth. Erin, in obvious pain, grimly clenched the bottle of amphetamines with a white-knuckled hand, and I saw Sinead on the floor of my room staring at me in abject terror and must have mumbled, "I'm so sorry Sinead," because Erin's voice rang out, "I'm not Sinead but I'm beginning to understand," then rolled down her window and heaved the bottle into the storm. "You stupid, stupid boy. Your pupils are completely dilated. You're speeding right now, aren't you? You realize you could've gotten us killed?" She emitted a long stream of vapor and furiously scratched at the back of her head. "I'm so angry with you. So angry. This is what happened with Sinead, isn't it? You were hopped up on speed." I saw the reflection of the grinning monster in the windshield, its mouth yawing open. I lurched back against the seat. Trembled involuntarily. "Seth, what the fuck is going on with you?"

"I don't understand. It relaxed me, calmed the voices. I was in control . . . and then I wasn't."

"You hurt her, didn't you?"

"I swear, I didn't mean to. It was all misunderstandings, misassumptions . . . I thought she was cheating on me with a guy named Ken, but it was all in my head."

"Then why are you doing it again?"

"Because you're gonna leave me. You weren't making plans, you said so. Everyone leaves me."

"Dammit, you're not listening! You only hear what you want to hear. You cling to your fatalism as if it defines you. Well, let me tell you this. Touch speed again and I will leave you. Get me to the goddam hospital."

I sped through the raging blizzard, headlights piercing the grey gloom like a candle through lace, emergency lights flashing red. The disillusionment in her voice was unbearable. I wasn't the man she hoped I'd be, the man of her dreams. I'd never touch speed again. Never. And swore to God I'll set her free before she ever came face to face with the monster.

I pulled into St. Luke's Emergency Room entrance. ER personnel rushed out and placed Erin on a gurney and wheeled her into X-ray. Her hip fractured, a freak accident, turned at just the wrong angle when it smashed into the unpadded metal door handle. She told the hospital staff the car skidded on ice, omitted we'd been fighting, convinced her parents would be furious. She'd have surgery as soon as Dr. McGuire flew in from Portland. An emergency room doctor reset and bandaged my nose, black rings already encircling my puffy eyes. The nurses kindly let me spend the night in the chair besides Erin's bed and I held her hand while a nurse gave her something for the pain. I lay my head on her bed and wept. What was wrong with me? Why I was hell bent on destroying the best thing that ever happened to me?

Exhausted, I dozed off. *Jonah and I were in our space ship exploring unchartered reaches of outer space, powering past planets and other comets when suddenly a huge meteor heads directly toward us, and we veer our craft to the left, then right, trying to avoid an imminent collision but it's too late, we go careening off course, heading for a black hole, and I reach out to Jonah but he's a jack-in-the-box, grinning and boinging up and down singing "All around the mulberry bush the monkey chased the weasel. The monkey thought 'twas all in fun. Pop! Goes the weasel" and our escape hatch opens, sucking all the air, and me, from our ship, and I tumble alone and powerless into the vast black vacuum of space toward a black hole getting larger and larger and I'm so scared, so scared, so scared.*

I woke with a start, my head in Erin's lap, a blanket covering me. She appeared preternaturally calm. Ruffled fingers through my hair. Her eyes glazed. "Daddy called from the airport. He'll be here soon. Surgery's this afternoon. They gave me something. I feel like I'm floating."

I awaited Dr. McGuire's arrival with foreboding. I'd promised to take good care of his daughter, and now, a day later, she was in a hospital bed. He'd hate me, take her away, never give me the chance to demonstrate I was worthy of her love, despite my unworthiness.

The surgery went well, and afterwards he took me downtown for dinner. He was solemn, as if he had a particularly unpleasant task to perform, and I could feel every beat of my heart, like when I got too stoned, each one another second ticking off my impending doom. Excusing myself, I ran to the men's room, leaned over the sink and took deep, calming breaths. Returning, he asked if everything was okay, but how could anything ever be okay again? I almost killed his daughter. "Tell me exactly what happened, and no bullshit."

"It was my fault. The weather was awful. She told me to stop or let her drive, but I ignored her. We argued. I took my eyes off the road for a split second, skidded on ice. Lost control."

"Why the hell didn't you listen?" I blew my nose and grimaced, the napkin bloody. Tears coursed down my cheeks. "Look, I know you didn't mean it, but it happened, and she's returning home with me. Thank God she'll be okay." I looked at the burger placed in front of me. Flashed on the scene in the Merida airport. I was the foul meat, the maggots inside me. I was being abandoned again and deserved it now just as I must've deserved it before. "I booked us a double room at a motel near the hospital. Tomorrow morning you can say goodbye and head back to Beloit. It's still about fifteen hundred miles on I-80 but there's a break in the winter storm pattern. Take advantage of it. Don't be stupid again and try to drive straight through." He reached into his billfold and handed me one hundred dollars. "Spend a night in a motel."

Blood money, payment to go away. "Dr. McGuire, I'm so sorry. I really love her; I can't imagine life without her."

"Neither can we. C'mon, let's eat dinner and get some sleep."

Next morning, I held Erin in my arms, probably for the last time, and hit the road.

CHAPTER 34

I SPENT THE next two days with naught to do but listen to Top 40 on the AM radio and micro-analyze my miserable life. But to what end. Erin was back in Portland. Her parents despised me and Randy wouldn't have to miss her any longer. I'd trashed the best thing that had ever happened to me, love enough to fill the vacuum in my heart. Love enough to overwhelm the darkness, ease the burden of guilt I'd carried for five years. I kept thinking about the conversation I'd had with Bart. About Dostoyevsky and *Notes from Underground*. I had committed another loathsome act that could not be undone. Something that would gnaw at me, embitter me, but relieve me of the responsibility to take control of my own life. Dr. McGuire had been right to take her away. I'd have done the same in his place. I returned alone to the empty attic apartment and a pile of letters postmarked Huntington. Letters from someone as narcissistic as me, the one person who'd be pleased by this turn of events. I placed her unopened letters in the drawer by my bed and yielded to established patterns of behavior to avoid dealing with my demons. I crafted another awesome film schedule, worked out, continued to write my senior thesis, memorized my lines for *Cyrano*. Picked up additional hours at the Student Union. Drank bottomless cups of coffee. But I didn't touch speed.

January 2, 1973

Dearest Erin,

Leaving you was the hardest thing I've ever done in my life. The thought I might have killed or permanently injured you devours me. I don't know if I'll ever forgive myself, much less be forgiven by you or your parents. It was my fault, and I am so, so sorry for what happened. I miss you so much. The apartment feels devoid of life without you. The few months we shared were the best of my life. You gave meaning to it. You're the only person who ever penetrated my many guises, and for that brush with happiness I'm eternally grateful. I checked the curriculum for architecture classes but found nothing beyond the physics and math classes I assume you'll have to take, but I'll stop by the Administration office and see if I can find out anything else. Erin, I don't know why I didn't throw the speed away, why I lacked the strength to have faith in us and risked squandering something as precious as your love. I swear to God I will never do it again. I hope this is not the end of our story; I hope we'll write new chapters together, but I can only hope.

Please wish your family a healthy and happy New Year.

I will love you forever.

Seth

CHAPTER 35

LUCY CAME INTO the Student Union during one of my grill shifts. "So, what's up, Rocky Raccoon? Did your woman run off with another guy?" She stuck out her lower lip and pouted, "Did she hit poor Rocky in the eye?"

"Very funny. Nose actually. Seeing's how I'm working in the local saloon, what can I get you?"

"Maybe you won't need a prosthetic protuberance for the part of Cyrano." I turned in profile. "Sorry. You'd need several more breaks. How about whipping me up some corned beef and cabbage, or maybe Irish stew with a side of Irish Soda Bread!"

"Come back St. Paddy's day. I do make the world's greatest grilled cheese ... with the works!"

"Sounds good. So, word around campus is you and Erin had a car accident and she broke her hip, huh? Back home in Portland. I assume that explains your raccoon face. That why I haven't seen you doing laps?"

I placed her sandwich on the griddle. "Yeah, the chlorine really stings. Erin's surgeon said if she's diligent with her rehab, she'll be fine, and knowing her, that won't be a problem. Whether her parents will let her return midterm ..." I shrugged. "They were pretty pissed off at me."

"Well, I'm really sorry. Puts you and Erin in the same boat as me and Alex; too far apart."

I plated her grilled cheese sandwich and rang her up. "I'm gonna start swimming again this week. The fries are on me."

She took a bite. "Hmmm. Yummy."

I'D BEEN BUSY working on my guerilla theater report, cutting, reordering and scotch-taping handwritten paragraphs on a yellow legal pad sheets now several feet long before typing it on my Smith Corona when there was a knock on the door. My heart leapt; Erin standing in the doorway holding banana breads. No, Lucy, holding a casserole dish, looking as Peggy Liptonesque as ever in that fishnet top and bellbottoms. "Expecting someone else?"

"For a second I thought you were Erin."

"Not too disappointed, I hope. Am I interrupting anything? I thought we could have dinner together, something healthier than the fare at the Student Union. I hate eating alone."

My stomach's gurgling noises reminded me I hadn't eaten a thing all day, and I was suddenly starving. "Looks good. I could use a break. Running out of correction tape anyway. Got my only B in high school in tenth grade typing class." I grabbed two plates, divvied up the rice and veggies, poured two glasses of Bolla Bardolino. We sat facing each other on the living room couch.

"Seth, you're staring, again."

Those perfect breasts. "You don't exactly make it easy. You and Erin are so alike."

"We don't look anything…" She followed my eyes down to her chest. "… Oh. Jesus, you're still a misogynistic pig, but since you brought it up, how about answering that question I asked at the pool last fall. Why didn't you want to be in a relationship with me?"

"I did, but I was scared and, to be perfectly honest, inexperienced."

"As was I." No way. She embodied everything that symbolized Woodstock. "You were so wasted that night. I wasn't expecting some macho performance. I just wanted to be with you. Thought we had all the time in the world. Every little girl has romantic dreams of being swept off her feet by a knight in shining armor and when you called me Galadriel, I thought you were mine. But that was only a fairytale; the real world doesn't work that way." She looked at me earnestly. "Could I have made my feelings for you any plainer?" Could I have been any blinder?

"Have you started memorizing Roxane's lines?"

She sighed, took my hands and gazed into my eyes. "*Alas. How many things have died and are new born. Why have you been silent, all these fourteen years? This letter, and the tears, were yours.*"

"*It is my fate, to be prompt and be forgotten. I spoke for Christian 'neath your balcony: So I have done in all things all my life. While I stood hidden in darkness down below, others climbed to kisses and to fame …*"

"Do you still have feelings for me, Seth? I can stay if you want me to."

In my mind's eye I saw the blazing fire reflected in my goddess' eyes as she danced amidst the blizzard and emerged from the mist, but it was Erin's face I saw, not Lucy's. I took Lucy's hand. "I'll always have feelings for you, but I'm in love with Erin. I hope we can still be friends."

For a moment her bright eyes clouded over, but she mustered a faint smile. "It's funny. You chose a tragi-comedy so eerily like our own story, but there was a moment, wasn't there?" I nodded. Fate had other things in store for us. "So, laps tomorrow? We've the pool pretty much to ourselves, and there's a dance at the Student U Saturday night. Don't make your friend go alone." She took our plates into the kitchen. "You love to dance. It'll be good for both of us to get out."

January 20, 1973

Dear Seth,

Sorry for the delay in my response to your sweet though overly fatalistic letter, but there are a few things I have to tell you. I'm truly sorry for hurting you that night at the coffee house. It was immature of me, but you deserved it. You've never truly respected me as an individual, always viewed me as an extension of yourself, so we need to establish some ground rules for a healthy and happy relationship. Let me start by saying I love you and I know you love me, but this isn't the nineteen-fifties; you don't own me any more than I own you, and if I want to do something with other people I expect you to act maturely and trust me. And I expect you to remain speed free FOREVER.

I've also had some pretty big decisions to make. I'm not returning to Beloit . . .

I put the letter down and started to weep; she was leaving me. I knew she would.

. . . for my sophomore year. A liberal arts school isn't right for me. You were right. I love science and math; I love drawing and old houses. With your encouragement I've decided to become an architect, combine all my nerdy interests, and the University of Oregon in Eugene offers undergraduate degrees in architecture. Tuition wouldn't be free like at Reed, but at least its in-state and UO also offers graduate degrees in both Theatre Arts and Cinema Studies. Maybe you could come west after you graduate and we could both go there. What do you think? . . .

I put the letter down again and wiped my eyes with relief.

I miss you so much, an aching longing nothing can fill. I think about you constantly, picturing you in our apartment (oh God, it must be absurdly clean), wandering around campus, in the Student Union, all those cute girls making special requests, and especially those play practices with Ms. Hippie Goddess playing your unrequited love interest. How's your written thesis coming along? You better keep me up on all those play rehearsals with Lucy or I'll skewer you with Cyrano's scabbard! I'm not even going to ask you about your promise—I KNOW you're keeping it. Have you received any more letters from your mother?

All my love,

Erin

I was so fantastically happy I immediately sat down and wrote back.

January 28, 1973

Dearest Erin,

Wow! That's a pretty big decision. When you first said you weren't making plans, I made it all about me, the same damn thing Mitzie does, which drives me crazy, and then I go and do the same thing. You've every right to call me on it. I'm sorry. I didn't mean to disrespect you. I'll try to do better. You're the best thing that ever happened to me, but I never felt I deserved you after the bad things I'd done. Thanks for still believing in me. The West coast is so far from everything I'm familiar with. I think I'd prefer to head East, get a job, make some money. I'm not sure what I want to do, but I don't want to be a lawyer. Maybe I'm simply afraid of the unknown. I went to Beloit's career office and noticed the northeast has lots of schools that offer undergraduate degrees in architecture, including NYU, Columbia, Harvard, MIT, all great schools. Maybe you could check them out as well. Boston's only a five-hour drive north of New York. I miss you so much. I keep imagining you partying with all those Reedies; all the guys hitting on you! Please don't worry about Lucy. The play's been my salvation. I love acting, losing myself in another character, breathing real life into fiction, but with you in my life its acting, not my life. I can't wait for break, to drive out to Portland and pick you up, knowing you'll be with me when I graduate. I miss you so much.

All my love,

Seth

February 14, 1973

Dear Seth,

I've been so angry with my parents. Dad said your picking me up was a nonstarter, refusing to see the accident as a fluke, and while they haven't come right out and said it, I think they hope this separation is a natural ending to our relationship and see no point in my being on campus this spring since I won't be returning to Beloit for sophomore year. They prefer I take classes at Reed and apply for admission to either Reed or other West coast schools. This led to a big row, the worst I've ever had with my parents. We've never really fought over anything besides stupid stuff. But this is my life and they've no right to try to run it. I'm almost nineteen, an adult, and can make my own decisions, even if they disagree, but I do love them, and it hurts to see them so upset with me. Anyway, the discussion is ongoing, and I still intend to be there with you when you graduate.

    I dream I'm running my fingers through your curly hair, kissing all those cute freckles, feeling your body pressed against mine. I miss the excitement in your voice when you talk about films, the passion you bring to theatre, but mostly I miss that special look in your eyes when you see me, and all the love that shines through and how you make me feel beautiful. That's how I go to sleep every night. I love you so much. Happy Valentine's Day.

All my love,

Erin

February 28, 1973

Dearest Erin,

I cannot blame your parents for the way they feel, though it hurts deeply as they're parents I would've wished for. They truly love you and care about you. You've no idea how precious that is. Please don't damage your relationship with them over me. I'm not worth it. Everything you said in the car that day was true. But I still hope your parents will change their minds and give me another chance. It would mean so much to have you with me when I graduate. Everything at school is okay. I've got all my lines memorized and the staging directions all set. The written thesis is looking pretty good. Heshy's input has proven invaluable. I'm working the grill at the Union about twenty hours a week, which along with everything else, keeps me pretty busy, but not so busy that I don't think about you every minute of the day. And I'm speed free.

I love you,

Seth

March 5, 1973

Dear Seth,

Now that I've decided to leave Beloit Beth's put on a hard-court press for me to matriculate to Reed. Behind my back she and mom planned a little dinner party and invited George and Randy. That really pissed me off. I knew exactly what she was up to, and mom, well, she's still furious over the accident. Anyway, the dinner took place and Randy asked me out. Told me he'd liked me all summer and couldn't get me out of his mind. I'm not going to say I wasn't flattered; that kind of stuff never happened to me in high school. But when I told him we were a couple and I didn't want to go out with anyone else he seemed genuinely hurt and it felt so strange to have that kind of effect on someone. Kind of thrilling, too. I know how it feels to be rejected, and I told him I really liked him and maybe if I hadn't met you and fallen in love things might have been different, but I did meet you. Needless to say, this led to another fight with my parents, and I told them I was coming back to Beloit at the break to be with you and nothing was going to change my mind. If I'd wanted other people and experiences I would've made those choices, but I chose you and I'm applying to east coast schools. Most of them have graduate programs in film studies and theatre; maybe you should apply to them as well. As a concession, I did agree to fly back, so I'll let you know when my flight's expected. You can pick me up at O'Hare. I am making the right decision, aren't I?

I love you and can't wait to be with you,

Erin

She was coming back for me, giving me a second chance to make things right, and I wasn't going to blow it. I went to the school library and signed out every book I could find on architecture, including biographies of architectural luminaries. No longer registered for classes, she'd have a lot of free time on her hands, probably on pins and needles awaiting responses from the east coast schools. I applied to two graduate programs in film and drama as well, but half-heartedly. I'd always thought I wanted that, but were I being completely honest, despite my negative preconception of Wall Street, the excitement and drama of working on a trading floor populated by ADD-addled, obsessive-compulsive drama kings really appealed to me. I'd be a professional actor and make money at the same time. Jerry would approve and that meant a lot. Erin not so much. I didn't share these thoughts with her.

CHAPTER 36

WHEN I CARRIED her up the three flights of dark, rickety stairs to our apartment and kicked open the door, she looked about with mock dismay. How would she uncover evidence of Lucy's presence? The place was spotless but for a pile of books on the couch. She hobbled over, glanced at the titles, then turned to me with tears in her eyes. "Now I know I made the right decision. Thank you, Seth."

That night, after a dinner of rice and veggies, we made passionate love over and over until we were exhausted and fell asleep in each other's arms, a Playa del Carmen happiness that lasted all of one night. Returning from classes next day, Erin was sitting in our little living room clutching a packet of now opened letters from Mitzie. She'd been crying. I slumped on the sofa next to her. What was wrong with me? Why hadn't I tossed them? "How could you let her say all those horrible things about me? She doesn't even know me. You never even told them about my accident. Don't you think they would've wanted to know?"

"I didn't want to give her the satisfaction."

"Of what? My being hurt?"

"Of you being out of the picture."

"Yet you kept them, knowing I'd read them. That means something, Seth, and you've got to figure it out, like why you insist on going back East after graduation."

NOT WANTING TO risk dealing with Mitzie on the phone, I waited until my shift break at the Student Union and called Jerry at his office. He was furious I'd waited so long to tell him of our accident. Not mollified by my assurances the car was fine. How could I have been so thoughtless? He would have called Erin's parents. Made sure she was okay. Asked if there was anything he could do. He asked for the McGuire's address. He'd write them, apologize for not having contacted them sooner. None of this had occurred to me. "Is there anything I can do for Erin now?"

"Yeah. Make Mitzie's nasty letters stop."

He assured me they would, and the very next day, returning from my first tech rehearsal for Cyrano, I found a beaming Erin. A dozen long stemmed red roses were perched atop our kitchen countertop in a pretty glass vase. She handed me the card that had come with the flowers:

Dear Erin,

We were so sorry to hear of your accident, but happy you are on the mend and back on campus with Seth. We look forward to meeting you at Seth's graduation.

Fondly,

Mitzie and Jerry

"Isn't that sweet? Thanks for calling them. These flowers are your mother's way of saying she's sorry. A fresh start, you know?" I doubted Mitzie knew a thing about them, but Erin always looked for the good in people and I wasn't going to suggest otherwise. I just wanted to be happy. The weather was warming, fresh buds on the trees, kids emerging from cocoons of heavy down and wool, the Indian Mounds once again alive with music, meandering philosophical discussions and the aroma of reefer, frisbees buzzing from all directions. There was an air of expectancy, everyone entering the great wide open, and with Erin by my side I cautiously dipped my toes into the waters of happiness and worked hard.

She was such a trooper. Never complained about her hip, managed her way up and down the stairs, met me after my evening shifts on the grill at the Student Union. She'd pop a nickel in the juke box and watch me wipe down tables accompanied by Roberta Flack's "Killing Me Softly," one of my favorite songs. Now in final rehearsals for *Cyrano*, she'd await me in the theatre lobby and we'd walk home engaged in lively discussions about Victorian, neoclassical and modern architecture, stuff gleaned from the various books I'd procured her. I skimmed them so I could engage intelligently with her. I wasn't going to repeat the mistakes I'd made early in our relationship.

I was nervous as hell the day of *Cyrano*'s performance. This was it. The culmination of four years of work and my last chance for the A I needed to graduate with honors. I wanted Jerry to be proud of me, and Mitzie to see me walk down the aisle Cum Laude, proof I was as good as Jonah, her wonder boy. The performance was in the main theatre with an opening night capacity audience including Heshy and Paisley, who'd made the trip down from Madison. Tech rehearsals had gone well. The sets, inspired by Erna Kruckemeyer's adaptation of Rostand's play, looked great. Having achieved a rapprochement with Thad during *Blue Ladies*, I'd cast him in the third major role of Christian, the love struck medium through which Cyrano expresses his passionate unrequited love for Roxane. We were ready.

Erin, still elated over the flowers she assumed from Mitzie, sat in the front row engaged in animated discussion with Heshy and Paisley, another bouquet of flowers in her lap, these from Paisley. I waved at them and blew Erin a kiss as the lights dimmed and a hush descended over the audience. I could almost hear the sounds of silence, the errant cough, the rustle of clothing, and retreating to the wings, I took deep breaths, drew my sword from its scabbard, slashed the air several times, took several leaps and bowed with the elegant grace a cavalier to ensure my prosthetic nose stayed in place. I was Cyrano. Poet. Wit. Swordsman extraordinaire. Love-struck fatalist. Lucy whispered "Break a leg. Just don't lose your nose."

After our performance the audience, many of whom had been moved to tears, gave us a standing ovation. We'd imbued a raw power and emotional depth to Rostand's words, perhaps because this was Lucy and my swan song, the culmination of a four-year tumultuous relationship, and I couldn't have been happier, especially when Erin threw her arms around me and declared I was her Outward-Bound man, having scaled the heights of acting. I coasted on an adrenalin high as we left the theatre.

A few days later, nearing the end of my evening shift in the Student Union, she hadn't arrived for our usual walk home. At first I wasn't concerned. After all, she was still on crutches and the weather was lousy. So I waited, almost an hour, with growing concern, and started to imagine the worst. A fall. A mugging. Rushing home, I found her sitting in our little living room. Relieved, I asked why she hadn't met me, but she merely stared blankly at the wall, clutching a letter. I couldn't figure out what was wrong. She'd been so happy.

Without a word, she dropped the letter on the couch and hobbled toward our bedroom. I picked it up and read it. It was addressed to me, from Jerry, wanting to make sure Erin had received the flowers he'd sent from his office, assuring me he'd talk to Mitzie about the nasty letters. I followed her, attempted to put my arms around her, said I'd hoped the flowers were from both of them, but she pushed me away, told me I was being dishonest. "Why, Seth? Why doesn't she like me? I'm a really nice person. Adults always like me. And you're no better than her. You're so desperate for her love you'd sell me down the river. All those fucking letters and not a word of protest from you. I stuck up for you with my parents! Think that doesn't hurt? Want to write a play with real pathos? Write one about a boy who's so desperate for his mother's love he can't see true love staring him in the face!"

"That's not true. We're here, together. I love you."

"But you're not seeing me. You think it's fun being stuck here? Had you given it a moment's thought? I can't do any of the things I love . . . things I'm really good at. Me, the Outward-Bound girl, remember? I can't even go on that hiking trip, you know, the one where you had me sharing Randy's sleeping bag! Can't imagine that bothers you one goddam bit." I cringed, guilty as charged. "I'm the homebound girl, the crippled girl, while you go off and star in plays. I've never felt so helpless. I can't shop, can't cook. I hate you doing everything for me, and I'm in love with someone so damned obsessive, so controlling, you probably think this is a fairy tale. Me, Rapunzel, being rescued by my prince!" She yanked open the top drawer of my bureau and spilled the entire contents, all my socks so carefully color-coded, on the floor. "I hate it, I hate it, I hate it!" Then, opening the closet, she grabbed half my clothes, all neatly hung, and flung them about the room. "I'm returning some disorder to this fucked up universe. I'm so frustrated. All I wanted was to be with you, share this precious time we'll never get back. You're gonna graduate, adult responsibilities are gonna pile up. This moment is so brief, and it's slipping through my fingers; you're slipping through them. . . I feel like your dog waiting to be petted, fed and taken for walks. Believe me, pooping outside can't be much worse than in your door-less bathroom!" Shuffling over to our bed, she leaned on her crutches, carefully sat down and tossed them against the wall. "I hate these fucking things!"

"Erin, you have to believe me. I've never loved anyone as much as you in my entire life, except Grandma Matthews . . . and Jonah."

"AND LOOK WHAT YOU DID TO HIM!" Wide eyed, face chalk white, hands over her mouth, Erin tried to walk back those words as I sat there stunned. The image of distraught Jonah leaving the house, tears streaming down his face as he boarded his motorcycle and rode away forever, flashed before my eyes. She hadn't meant the way it came out. She'd gotten carried away. She was frustrated. Needed to know I was as committed to her as she was to me. But she was right. I was a narcissist. I didn't deserve her.

CHAPTER 37

BEFORE THE PREMIERE of new shows I tended to puke, probably to relieve nerves, the built-up anticipation, mostly out of fear the new skin would flake off in front of an audience, leaving me naked in all my nothingness. I retched now, in anticipation of Mitzie and Jerry's imminent arrival for graduation. I'd assured Erin that once my mother met her in person she'd love her, more hopeful wishing. I'd no idea which Mitzie would show up.

Erin nervously hobbled about our apartment in my *Off the Pigs* T-shirt and blue bandana searching our immaculate, but shoddy, apartment for something to do. I embraced her. Kissed the nape of her swan-like neck. Suggested she take a relaxing shower and wear her renaissance dress to dinner. I'd made reservations at the Gun Club, a good choice if dinner erupted in pyrotechnics.

I could hear Mitzie complaining about the grungy stair landing as they clomped up three flights. Jerry's response nostalgic. Reminiscent of their first apartment, a third story walkup in Queens after moving out of Grandma and Grandpa Matthews house. "Yeah, very romantic," Mitzie said. "You could pee out the window. I had to schlep down three flights of stairs to an outhouse."

"I would've held onto you."

"Not the way we were bickering. More like oops! Got rid of that pain in the ass. Time for a new wife!" A missed opportunity, Jerry.

When we greeted them at the door, Mitzie brushed passed Erin as through an apparition, noting how thin I was, asking if anyone was feeding me. And I thought there was no such thing as too rich or too thin. I took Erin's corporeal hand. "I'd like you to meet Erin."

Jerry hugged her. Mitzie merely glanced about the apartment and pronounced it a pigsty. "Forty-eight bucks a month," I responded, "and all the mice we can eat. I call that a good deal." Mitzie shuddered, but I told her not to worry.

They only scampered about at night. "Found a dead one on my pillow. Opened my eyes and there it was, inches from my face."

"Was I back in Portland then, Seth?" Erin asked.

"Yup. A little protein for my veggie stir-fry. So, you guys all settled in at the Plantation Motor Inn? It's Beloit's finest accommodations."

"Barely adequate," Mitzie hissed through clenched teeth, staring pointedly at Erin.

"Best thing about the Plantation is the twenty-four hour diner. One night, or to be precise, early one morning, I ordered a rare burger, remember Erin? It came well-done and I sent it back. Next one, same thing. Third time, a frozen patty on a bun, the cook standing by the kitchen door, watching. I took a big bite and pronounced it perfect. Pretty funny, Mitzie, huh?"

"I presume my son has to carry you up the stairs?"

"I've climbed volcanoes, Mrs. Matthews; this is a cakewalk."

Driving to the restaurant, Jerry sat in front with me, Mitzie in back with Erin. She brushed hair from Erin's face. "Ever consider having it styled?"

"I love Erin's hair," I interjected, scowling at Mitzie through the rear-view mirror. Erin merely smiled, complimented Mitzie on her pearl necklace and displayed the heart shaped pendant I'd given her for her nineteenth birthday.

"How nice," Mitzie responded blandly. "Perhaps someday you'll meet someone who'll give you real jewelry." I looked grimly at Jerry. He sighed and lifted his brow. We pulled into the parking lot.

An elderly waiter came to take our order. "Here for graduation, I presume?"

"Yes. My son is graduating from Beloit College tomorrow," Jerry responded proudly. "With honors!"

"How nice for you. Your order please?"

"I'll have the filet, rare," I said.

Erin's eyes grew wide. "Oh my God. They have lobster. I had it once. Most delicious thing I ever tasted." Jerry handed his menu to the waiter and ordered lobster for the two of them. Erin protested it was too expensive and Mitzie immediately concurred. Something cheaper would be more appropriate. But Jerry wouldn't hear of it. A special weekend deserved a special dinner.

The waiter impatiently tapped his order pad with a pen while Mitzie parsed the menu like the Torah seeking either enlightenment or God's dining suggestion. "Hmmm. Veal Scallopine? Wonder if they have many Italians out here? Oh wait, there's fried chicken. Maybe I should get that. But I don't know. My stomach's been acting up so maybe a salad." She asked the waiter if the chicken was any good and he sighed. "It's chicken. They fry it."

"She'll have the fried chicken," Jerry said.

"I don't know, Jerry. It may give me heartburn later." She was giving me heartburn now.

Jerry asked for the wine list and was informed they served red or white, but when he asked what types of red, the waiter merely shrugged. "Alrighty then; we'll have the red."

The waiter departed muttering, "Every year the same thing. Damn Beloit kids."

Two large lobster platters appeared just as Jerry started asking me my future plans, affording me a moment to collect my thoughts while the waiter returned with an unlabeled bottle and unceremoniously plopped it on the table. Jerry poured glasses all around, raised his and said "I'm very proud of you, son."

Words I'd hungered for, and I tried to contain my emotions with a quip. "Erin, that lobster looks like an alien, a lobsterman from outer space."

She giggled, cracked a claw, neatly extracted the meat and dunked it in the hot butter. "Able to survive an atom bomb," she intoned in a resonant TV announcer voice, "only to drown in melted butter." But when Mitzie harrumphed, Erin looked to me for help, for a guffaw or something. I downed the glass in one gulp and held it out for a refill.

"I read Seth's guerilla theater thesis," Erin declared, squeezing my hand under the table. "It's brilliant. He's applied to grad schools for an MFA in theater or film. He could become a professor. He'd be fabulous."

Mitzie dramatically dropped her fork. Film or drama. Stupidest ideas she'd ever heard, not that it mattered. I was going to law school.

"He's not stupid," Erin flared. "He's brilliant and only twenty-one. He should follow his dreams."

I drained my glass again, thinking about the call at the telephone exchange in Guatemala. This time I added my own two cents. I wasn't sure what I was doing. It depended on where Erin ended up.

Jerry expertly extracted the lobster tail from its shell. He appreciated Erin's enthusiasm, but she was very young. Didn't know how the real world worked. I had no connections in the film industry. There was so much luck involved. He clearly disapproved and although I was disappointed, I wasn't surprised. Maybe he was right. Loving films and making a living in the film industry were two different things. I knew no one in that field, but I did know someone on Wall Street. Images of that trading room floated through my head. The adrenalin rush. Everyone hyperkinetic, like on speed, only safe and legal. And I'd still be acting. Simply on a different stage. I wouldn't get that kind of rush reviewing films or teaching. I put my fork down, picked up the bottle to pour myself another glass. Fuck. Empty. I furtively glanced at Erin. "Maybe I'll check out Wall

Street. Joel thought I'd be really good when he showed me around his trading floor last summer."

Dead silence. Jerry mulled the idea as if savoring a fine wine; Erin so appalled she forcefully cracked down on her lobster tail and green goop spurted on the white tablecloth. "You'd have to cut your beautiful hair!"

"I've disguised myself for many roles."

"Discussion over," Mitzie pronounced. "Seth is going to law school. I've already signed him up for an LSAT review course." The only way I was going to be a lawyer was playing one on TV, like in *Perry Mason*. "And what's this business about waiting to see where Erin winds up? She's leaving Beloit?"

"I am, Mrs. Matthews. Beloit's not the right school for me."

Mitzie, suddenly all smiles, patted Erin's hand like she was a good puppy. "That's very mature of you. I'm impressed. You go back home, be amongst your own kind, you know, the West coast type. Study basket weaving or numerology or whatever fakakta things you people do out there."

Erin maintained her cool. "I want to study Environmental Architecture. I'm concerned about our ecosystem, our responsibilities to the earth as well as ourselves." Mitzie guffawed, and I immediately grabbed Erin's hand, but too late. "Probably not something people on the East coast concern themselves with, Mrs. Matthews, you know, limiting our impact on the environment. The air we breathe, the food we eat, the water we drink, silly West coast stuff like that."

"These new environmental policies are stifling my ability to do business," Jerry added.

"Can't eco-friendly construction practices be reflected in your pricing, Mr. Matthews?"

"Yes, but it's a competitive world out there, and please, Erin, call me Jerry."

When I raised the empty bottle in the direction of our waiter, Erin bristled I'd had enough. And Mitzie stayed on message like a horse with blinders. Erin could go to Reed for free. Her parents so pleased to have her close to home. She'd hate the East coast. "Back east women are more fashion conscious, more conventional, less assertive and intellectual. Right now, Seth thinks he wants something different, exotic, but that's not what he's used to and comfortable with, and once he realizes it, you'll suffer for it."

Talk about damning with faint praise! Tears welled in Erin's eyes, and I blurted out "Any news of Jonah?" knowing that would smother the sparks flying between the woman I loved and the stranger who raised me, though it pained me to see Jerry's distress, but Mitzie still managed to get the last word before we left. Abby was so sorry to miss my graduation. She'd make it up to me as soon as I got home.

I sat on the living room couch watching Erin apply the many elixirs she massaged into her face every night as she mimicked Mitzie. "Oh Jerry, what do you think? Should I have the fried chicken? I hope it gives her the worst case of heartburn ever!" I laughed. Told her Jerry liked her. "He's sweet but patronizing. Expects women to be arm candy. Now I see where some of your Neanderthal attitudes come from." She hobbled into the room and sat down next to me. "I don't know why your mother doesn't like me, Seth. I didn't almost kill YOU in a car crash!" Ouch. "Can't she see I love you? Maybe the lobster joke wasn't funny, but I was so nervous; you always joke when you're nervous. And that 'Abby's so sorry' bit. Your mother's A BITCH. I'm starting to understand the kind of fucked up home you grew up in. And what's with that McGovern goes to Wall Street garbage you pulled out of your ass? I'm not trying to pressure you, but I think you could use all your intensity for something better than working in a den of thieves. "

I hugged her close. "You should've seen Joel's house, Erin. There's nothing he and Marsha can't have." Though I questioned a few of their decorating choices. "I want to give you everything, too."

"I'm not expecting you to give me anything, caveman. I'll love you whatever you do. We're partners."

CHAPTER 38

IT WAS DRIZZLING when we met them for breakfast at the Plantation diner. From the open kitchen the cook yelled "Hey Red, another rare burger?" I laughed, too early in the day, but I'd love his famous blueberry pancakes with two eggs over real easy, a request seconded by both Erin and Jerry. He turned to the waitress. "Think we have enough eggs?"

Mitzie frowned, glanced around the room buzzing with graduating seniors and their families while polishing her silverware with a paper napkin. She suggested we eat elsewhere, but Jerry, clearly exasperated, snapped she needn't eat if she didn't want to. Chastened, she quietly ordered toast and coffee.

Leaving the diner, the drizzle became a rain as persistent as Mitzie's bitching about the humidity ruining her perm. It started to thunder, a low rumbling series of crackles that escalated into a sound and light show worthy of the special effects at the Fillmore East. The sound ricocheted off the wood floor of the basketball court, reverberated through the gymnasium. The team banners undulated. The floors trembled as families packed into the cramped athletic facility and by the time commencement began the air was redolent with the odor of wet wool and sweat, and after enduring an abysmally forgettable speech suggesting one third of my graduating class would have Alzheimer's by the time we were seventy, the provost called us to the dais to receive our diplomas. We tossed our mortarboards in the air with a hue and cry.

People milled about at the reception, chatting, drinking sparkling soft beverages the college had provided, occasionally peering outside to see if the downpour had abated. I kissed Erin long and hard, then hugged Jerry. Mitzie had disappeared. Glimpsing Bart and Ashley talking with Bart's parents from across the gym floor I grabbed Erin's hand, walked over and congratulated them on their engagement, then spotted Lucy talking to an older guy, presumably Alex, nudged Erin and suggested we go over and say goodbye.

"Gladly," she smiled, placing her arm through mine. "Lucy really was great as Roxane. The chemistry between you was amazing."

Lucy smiled as we approached and introduced us to Alex, her personal physician, who immediately noted Lucy had said I was a great actor. "Only as good as the people you perform with," I added. He asked if I was going to New York to wait on tables until I was "discovered." I laughed. Close. I was going to audition for a role on Wall Street. Why not be a well-paid actor?

"Perhaps inspiration for another play!" Lucy chimed in. "A psychopathic Wall Street guy, investment banker by day, lady killer by night. What do you think?"

"I was born to play that role."

THE HEAVY RAIN overwhelmed downspouts, spewing torrents of water into the street, along sidewalks and downhill toward the town. Mitzie, standing beside an open door, stared through a wall of cascading water lost in reverie. I stood quietly beside her. She seemed diminished, engulfed in sadness, and muttered, "If only we could have celebrated your brother's graduation from Columbia." Even now, during my moment, his presence lingered. I handed her my diploma.

"You have no idea how sorry I am for what I did."

She sneered and waved it in my face. "You actually think you're responsible for your brother's disappearance? You give yourself too much credit. Our self-proclaimed student revolutionary was expelled from school one month before graduation, one fucking month, because he thought it a grand statement to rampage through school buildings. The draft board notice arrived within the week." She thrust it back at me. "Your so-called earth-shattering disclosure was shameful but not enlightening. I was his mother; I knew he was gay. Give your stupid diploma to that little shiksa you're schtupping. Maybe she'll return it when she finds someone better, and believe me, she will. I just want out of this godforsaken hell hole." I wanted to plead with her to brush aside the past and try to be happy for me, if only for the moment, but what was the point. I merely blinked back tears and walked away.

CHAPTER 39

JERRY WARMLY EMBRACED Erin as he and Mitzie prepared to leave for O'Hare. He looked forward to seeing her again, was keeping fingers crossed for good news from the schools she'd applied to. He wanted her parents to know she'd be with family for Thanksgiving. Was happy to see me so grounded. How good we were together. Touched, I threw my arms around him. I had a real father. "Thanks, Dad."

"Jerry, I'm sure Erin will want to be with her own family and friends on the West coast."

"Actually Mrs. Matthews, I only applied to MIT, Harvard, Yale, Columbia and NYU, so wherever I wind up I'm sure I'll make Thanksgiving. It's sweet of you to invite me."

A LETTER ARRIVED welcoming Erin as an incoming sophomore for the MIT Class of 1976. She'd have to take two science and math classes during the summer at Reed. I was excited for her but also despondent. She'd be in Portland all summer. Who knew what could happen in three months? Various scenarios, all bad, played in my head.

I drove her to O'Hare Airport and waited with her at the gate for her boarding call. She asked if I was really going to interview on Wall Street, not being the Wall Street type, which she defined as a supercilious preppy, silver spoon in mouth White Anglo Saxon Protestant eager to rape and pillage everyone and everything for a buck. Talk about generalizations! That didn't describe my cousin Joel and he was doing great. "I seriously doubt anything will come of it, but I'm curious and he offered to get me an interview with his company's professional training program. I'm a good actor, and pretty competitive..."

"Well, you might as well go. I'm just worried you'll get the job before you hear back from the grad programs you've applied to. You'll succeed at anything you set your mind to." She hugged me. "But if going to Wall Street makes you happy, then I'm with you all the way. If you need my support, call me, okay?" For a brief moment I imagined us driving out West together, starting afresh, unfettered by unhappy memories and ties. Instead, I gathered her to me one last time, fortified myself with her essence, hoping it would saturate every cell of my being and help me withstand the assault I knew was coming. The loudspeaker blared "Final boarding call for flight 217 to Portland," and she gently pushed me away. "You have to let go or I'll miss my plane. It's only for the summer, Seth. We'll be together before you know it."

Hobbling toward the gate she turned, blew me a kiss. I yelled, "Whatever happens I'll always love you!" but she didn't hear me, had already disappeared behind the closing plane door. "I'll never love anyone but you!" What was I doing? Why was I going East? But I knew the answer. I didn't want to go to grad school. I craved that adrenalin rush I experienced on Joel's trading floor almost as much as I wanted Mitzie's love.

CHAPTER 40

I ARRIVED HOME to an obsequiously affectionate Mitzie. She fawned over me, suggested I sit down, maybe I was hungry; did I want a cup of coffee or a sandwich? Someone else might have been bewildered by this sudden about face but not me. I simply waited for the next shoe to drop, and it came almost immediately. "Your LSAT review course starts next week. And go on over to Abby's house. She's awaiting you."

"Did Abby's mom happen to mention she's engaged?"

"To that schvartzer? So what?"

"Please don't use words like that. It's disrespectful. He's a black man. And just so you know, I've no intention of taking that review course or becoming a lawyer. And I'll tell you something else. I'm going to be with Erin."

"Really? I must be imagining it's you standing in the kitchen with me. You're actually in Portland, Or-e-gone with that little shiksa!" She laughed in my face. "Let's cut the song and dance, Mr. Thespian. You're here on Long Island because this is where you belong and you're going to take that LSAT course and become a lawyer because that's who you are, and I'll even bet that little shiksa suspects it. And that job interview? What a waste of time. Not that there's anything wrong with Wall Street. Jonah would've been fabulous. It's you, bubala! You're not an earth-shaker. Neither a risktaker nor an intellectual. You're a plodder, like your father. Match your dreams to reality. You'll become a lawyer. You'll have comfort and security, enough money... and marry a woman who's presentable and live right here on Long Island and there's nothing wrong with that. You on Wall Street? Like a turd on a dining room table."

"I don't care what you think, Mitzie. You're not going to tell me what to do or whom to marry, understand? I'd rather kill myself."

She clapped. "Bravo! You really are a good actor, a bit melodramatic, but almost believable. Look, we don't need to argue. It was your last year in college and you had a little fling. Why not enjoy yourself, I mean, she was legal, though you'd never know it from that flat chest and those braces. And those hairy legs! How could you stand it? Jewish girls come with the same equipment, only better displayed. Time to put childish things behind you…" I started to walk away but she grabbed my arm and twisted it. "Let me tell you a few hard facts about life. People like you and me, we settle; we don't reach for the stars. Love is great, but it fades real fast. And you know what you're left with? A good job. A steady wife. Money! That's a future! And I know several Jewish girls right here in Huntington who'll make excellent wives. You'll choose one and raise a nice family. Who cares if you love her? You'll learn to love her." I stood there gaping. "That little shiksa, that baby, she reminds me of a bunny rabbit hopping through a carrot patch! No poise. No manners. Thinks she's so smart with all those stupid, radical feminist ideas from the West coast. And the way she dresses!"

"Why, because she's smart; not afraid to speak her mind? You don't know her; the things she wants out of life, her dreams. Get this through your thick head. I love her."

"You don't build a future on love. You're dealt the cards you're dealt, and you make the best of it, just like I did. That's the way the real world works."

"Why do you think I went to school so far away, why I disappeared in Mexico, why I stopped coming home? You've always tried to suffocate me, control me, mold me; but you never held me, hugged me, or loved me! Erin makes me feel whole. Like a complete person. Can't you be happy for me and nice to her for my sake if not your own? You already fucked up once. You tried to shape Jonah into what you wanted him to be. No wonder he kept his personal life so hidden."

She squeezed my arms so hard her whole body quaked. "You little bastard! First you try to make amends with that stupid diploma and now you're guilt-tripping me. It's not my fault he got expelled. I'm not the one who outed him to your clueless father. I'm sick of being a victim. Tired of people talking behind my back, whispering poor Mitzie with the faigelah son, feeling sorry for me. I don't want anyone feeling sorry for me anymore, not ever, understand? I don't want pity. I'm as good as anyone and I'm not going to let that shiksa take you three thousand miles away and leave me with nothing. You'll become a lawyer and be successful and marry a nice Jewish girl and come to Temple with me so I can show off my grandchildren."

"Stop calling her a shiksa!"

"I'll call her anything I damn well please. And I'll tell you something else. If you felt that strongly, you'd move heaven and earth for her. You wouldn't let anything or anybody stand in your way, but you let others make decisions for you, always worried what others think, how you look; you bemoan the cruel unfair world and do nothing about it!" She drilled into my eyes, nodding. "That's right.

That's what I'm talking about, and I'd respect that strength, even if I disagreed, so don't go getting all high and mighty with me."

I gawked at her. I didn't want to believe her, but my heart did. I could envision my future with stark clarity. I'd lose Erin to the clarion call of the Pacific Northwest, live and die in Long Island purgatory in a loveless relationship forged by Mitzie with no one to blame but myself. My need for Mitzie's love was pathetic. I craved it as a baby needs its mother's breast. I hated myself for it almost as much as I hated her.

PART FOUR
THE BOY WONDER

CHAPTER 1

THE WOMAN WHO ran Lehman Brothers professional training program, a Ms. Smythe, had her office on the forty-fourth floor, and after a distinctly chilly greeting that telegraphed this interview had been foisted on her, abstractedly perused my resume for a minute or two, dramatically sighing and shaking her head while I sat there like an idiot. Did she see a turd sitting on the other side of her highly polished mahogany desk? I awaited her acknowledgement. Ask me a question, any question. I could already hear Mitzie's "I told you so."

She finally dropped my resume on her desk, cleared her throat and informed me that she, representing the venerable firm of Lehman Brothers Kuhn Loeb, had the awesome responsibility of hand selecting trainees with the utmost of care, culling the crème de la crème from the finest schools, young men and women from institutions like Harvard and Yale (though I bet even Cornell would've elevated me in her estimation), kids who'd rise to the top of their profession to the glory and profitability of the firm. Sadly, I was not one of them, but at least she disparaged me with some class.

As she rose, signifying this aberrant interview over, her hands automatically smoothed any creases in her mannish dressed for success outfit. She offered me a bon mot, suggesting I try one of the wire houses whose standards, as she put it, were several rungs lower. Before I had the chance to thank her for her time or ask what a wire house was, she curtly barked "Best of luck," and turned on her heels.

I watched the elevator light blink as it made its way to the forty-fourth floor. I couldn't go home, not like this, my tail between my legs; I was as good as any of those kids she'd hire. Hell, I could've attended Cornell but chose not to. I was worthy and no one was going to say otherwise, not even the little mocking voice inside my head. When the elevator door opened, I quickly pressed floor 41 instead of 1. Someone was going to listen to me, goddamit, I was an actor, this merely another role, the bright young go-getter out to conquer the world. I closed my eyes. Found my center. I didn't need a script. I'd channel all those guys I watched on the phones, blood dripping down their faces. I could do this. I rushed past the receptionist and knocked on the first partner's door I approached. "Come in," said a man's voice.

Act One, Scene One: Young go-getter framed in the doorway. "Sir, my name is Seth Matthews and I want thirty seconds to tell you why you have to hire me."

He ushered me inside just as the angry receptionist grabbed my arm and threatened to call security. "No need. There's no problem here. Have a seat, Seth, right? You've got your thirty seconds; make 'em count."

Gold-framed investment banking tombstones lined his walls, plastic encased ones littered his desk. The nameplate on the door said Harrington. Why'd that name ring a bell? "Mr. Harrington, I'm smarter and hungrier than any of those kids you'll hire out of some fancy MBA program. They've been so mollycoddled, they'll never be able to deal with rejection; never go through the wall for you or truly appreciate this opportunity like me. I didn't go to some fancy school where I picked up bad habits or other people's ideas. I'll do things the Lehman Brothers way!"

"What exactly do you want to do?"

"I want to be in your professional training program." I stayed on the offensive when he asked my age. I didn't want to be dismissed as too young and underqualified. I played a hunch. "Did you go to an elite business school and get an MBA?"

"No, came straight from college, but it was easier back in the Fifties. Firms were having a hard time recruiting. Now, everyone wants in, so we're pickier, hence the MBA requirement."

"Well, it looks like you've done pretty well for yourself." Bingo! That salesgirl Callie at Mensch's mentioned some Wall Street bigwig named Harrington owning Hennigan's Tavern. What the fuck; I'd nothing to lose. "Sir, did you by any chance grow up in Huntington on Long Island?" He nodded; sat up straighter. Wow! Small world. Keep going. Turned out I went to high school with his younger brother.

He warmed noticeably. "So that would make you, what? Twenty-two? New college graduate?"

"Yes sir, Beloit College in Wisconsin. I'll be twenty-two in December. I majored in Theatre."

"Interesting. Are you acting right now?"

I looked him square in the eye. "Yes, sir. How am I doing?"

He roared and slapped his knees. "Well, you've certainly got moxie! I've hired a bunch of people from Huntington, never anyone as young as you. Do you know Laurie Schloss? Works in commercial paper." Girl down the street Jonah's age. Mom had tried to coerce him into calling her. "So, you must know . . . ," and it went on and on, back and forth. I got excited. I knew younger siblings of several people he'd personally hired. Things were definitely looking up. He put his elbows on the desk. He was going to run me through the gauntlet, introduce me to all the partners on the Row. See how good an actor I really was. "Convince them to take a shot on a kid straight out of a non-Ivy League college and you've got my vote! By the way, they'll all ask how much you expect to be making in three years. The answer is $100K, got it?" Sure, and I'll walk on the moon! But three hours and seven partner interviews later I had an offer for twenty-six thousand dollars! The program started next week.

CHAPTER 2

I PACED ABOUT the kitchen repeatedly checking the time. I needed to call Erin, but with the three-hour time change . . . Plus I needed permission to make a long-distance call. Mitzie, eyeing me, demanded I either stop fidgeting or tell her what was going on. "I gotta speak to Erin."

"Poor baby. She gonna kiss your booboo? I told you that interview was a waste of time. You still have time to take that LSAT course." But when I smirked, she was taken aback, put down her cup. "You mean to tell me Joel actually got you a job? He must be a bigger shot than I thought."

"He doesn't even know. I did this on my own. I start at Lehman Brothers Kuhn Loeb next Monday in their professional training program. Twenty-six thousand dollars starting pay. And I'll tell you something else, Mitzie; I'm gonna take that job and make partner someday!"

"And someday I'm gonna wake up a size ten!"

Dad came in from the front porch and I told him. Flabbergasted, he noted I'd never evinced the slightest interest in finance. Asked if I'd read the *Fortune* article on the marijuana business he'd sent me. No, but I'd smoked a lot of it.

Mitzie looked at Jerry like he was delusional. Reminded him the LSAT review course started this week. I was supposed to become a lawyer. "That's for him to decide, Mitzie. It's his life, not yours."

"But he could take over your business, handle contract negotiations, the banks. He'll be tougher. Expand your business."

"Why? You lacking for anything? Your ego and Seth's future are not synonymous."

"Everything here is ancient, not like at Sylvia Freed's house. You saw her kitchen. Formica, new appliances, that gorgeous white ceramic tile. Not to mention the live-in help. Maybe if you'd been more successful I'd have those things, too."

"I couldn't even pry you from that crazy old oven which, by the way, cost more to convert to electric than buying a brand new one! Why are you so focused on what others have, Mitzie? Does everything have to scream 'Look at me, I'm a success' to make you feel secure? It's ridiculous and I'm sick and tired of it. I want it to stop—NOW!"

I'd never seen Jerry stand up to Mitzie like that. I was so proud of him. "Dad, it turned out the guy who hired me was from Huntington; said I could be making one hundred K in three years. I'll be the only one without an MBA from an Ivy League school. I can't wait to tell Erin."

"You accept that offer. You're gonna do great. But I'll be proud of you whatever you do. I mean that."

Mitzie looked at us, shaking her head in disbelief. "Make your call but keep it short. It's long distance."

ERIN PICKED UP the phone. "I was hoping it was you! I miss you so much." The sound of her voice made me so happy, and so sad. I told her I'd been offered a job starting at twenty-six thousand dollars per year.

"OH! MY! GOD! I don't know how you pulled that off, Seth Matthews, but I am truly impressed. I had no idea you could make so much money on Wall Street. I'm so blown away I don't even know what to say."

"Should I take it, you know, being Wall Street and all? I was so pumped when I left Lehman but on the train back to Huntington, I started having doubts. I mean, what would Heshy think? From guerilla theatre to Wall Street. Am I selling out?" I couldn't picture myself a capitalist pig. "I haven't heard from any of the grad schools yet."

"Try it for a while, see how it works out. It's not a life sentence. You can always change your mind and go to grad school next year."

"You think so? It feels so right, like I instantaneously absorbed the environment and knew how to play the role."

"Well, you are a Method actor, right? You always talk about putting on new skins. Consider this performance art. The twenty-six-thousand-dollar question is whether you can work on Wall Street and still let your freak flag fly ... Wait, please don't tell me you cut your hair." Did it just the other day. It was getting kinda long. "I'm not sleeping with a Republican."

"With that kind of money, I'll be able to drive up to Boston, take you to restaurants, concerts, buy you nice clothes ..." The line appeared to go dead. "Hello? Erin, you still there?"

"Yeah. Just thinking; accept the offer."

"Thanks, honey. I'd better get off the phone. Mitzie's shooting daggers at me."

CHAPTER 3

I HAD LUNCH next day with Joel at Harry's at Hanover Square, a popular eatery and watering hole for the Wall Street crowd run by a Greek restaurateur Harry Poulakakos, who greeted people at the door. "Joel," he gushed, "so nice to see you! How's everything at Lehman Brothers?"

"You tell me, Harry." They both laughed. "Harry, this is my cousin Seth. He's starting at Lehman next Monday in our professional training program."

Impressed, Harry vigorously shook my hand. "Well, you come here after work. We put out a nice buffet for our friends. Cost you the price of a drink, but in your case bring ID! Your usual table, Joel?"

We walked through the bar area of gleaming wood veneers, shining brass, with bottles of every imaginable liquor lining the back of the horseshoe-shaped bar front. Well-dressed waiters and bartenders bustled about, serving patrons in expensive Brooks Brothers suits or the latest in Italian fashion, splayed collar shirts, many two-toned with French cuffs and expensive links, silk ties costlier than my new suit from Mensch's. The place reeked of money. And as Harry showed us to Joel's table he told me the building, which dated back to the mid-nineteenth century, had started off as a private club for rich city merchants who dominated the commodity trade and the site of the first commodity market in the United States, the New York Cotton Exchange. Turns out the original Lehman Brothers had made their fortune right here. We were seated at a window table with full view of the bar and its denizens.

"You just had your first important lesson on Wall Street," Joel noted. "Pick a place you like and make it your regular. Be sure the owner or maître d knows you by name. A little cash helps their memory. Have a favorite table; it impresses clients. Everyone wants to be with someone connected. It isn't just about what you know, it's the whole package."

"Joel, I don't even know what a price earnings ratio is! I am so over my head!"

"Lehman didn't hire you for what you know! You don't know jack shit!" Two glasses of white wine appeared before us. "You're a twenty-one-year-old kid just out of college. You had the balls to force your way into a partner's office and demand he hear you out! Do you have any idea how rare that is? I'd no idea you had that in you!"

"I'm an actor. I wanted this role. I simply sized up the situation and acted on it."

"Right! And they're betting you'll keep doing that for a long time." Joel lifted his glass and clinked mine. "Here's to an incredible career full of enlightened self-interest. You just became a high-class whore!"

"No way that's gonna happen. Wall Street's not gonna change me."

"Oh really?" He ruffled my newly shorn hair. "What ever happened to letting your freak flag fly? You're already turning to the forces of evil." He chuckled. "Okay, lesson two. You're a kid, you're poor..."

"But I'm making..."

"Shit. Twenty-six K sounds like a lot of money to you, but good luck trying to find an apartment for less than 100% of your annual salary! Look, you're young, single, have no one to worry about but yourself. Let Harry feed you. Network. Talk to the older guys, become a protégé. But keep your own counsel with your peers. They'll kill you given half a chance. This program lasts four months. Lehman will keep a few of you, the rest, sayonara!" Two plates of fried calamari appeared. "Do you understand what I'm telling you? Don't look so overwhelmed. This is a dog-eat-dog world. Eat your lunch. They make the best Peach Melba dessert!"

"There's something else. I'm in something of a pickle. My girlfriend Erin is home in Portland for the summer and Mitzie's busy trying to arrange a marriage for me on Long Island. She hates Erin."

"Erin's Catholic, right? Sorry, buddy, I'm on Mitzie's side. Lots of nice Jewish girls here."

"But I'm in love with her. I don't want to meet anyone else."

"Sure, and you'll find yourself the Jewish dad of a Catholic family." My God, he sounds as old as Jerry. "Just being pragmatic, kid. Go on a few dates. What about Marsha's friend, the one with the younger sister she wanted you to meet? Who knows? Lightning may strike."

"It's already struck. I'm looking for advice, not a date."

"Seems to me you're gonna get fucked either way, and keep in mind a bird in hand is worth more than some bush three thousand miles away. But seriously, trust me, it will resolve itself, though knowing Mitzie I doubt you'll have much say in it." He pushed his empty plate away. "Let's order that Peach Melba now."

CHAPTER 4

I ENTERED THE conference room, Daniel in Ms. Smythe's lion's den, only this lair hosted a pride of MBAs, older and better attired than me, their smug faces reflected in the highly burnished mahogany table. Crystal decanters filled with iced water refracted the overhead light, prisms of primary colors dancing on the mahogany-paneled walls. A gold Cross pen and leather-bound binder embossed with our names and the Firm's logo at each seat. Aromas of wood polish, leather and after-shave, the air pungent with expectancy. The elite fifteen!

Ms. Smythe cleared her throat. "Okay, let's go around the table and introduce ourselves." She turned to a lanky guy, about six feet two, straight limp hair, Brooks Brothers suit, private school tie, his blasé expression heralding an air of entitlement. Quintessential prep. "Worthington, why don't you start." Worthington? Erin's gotta hear that!

"Thank you, Ms. Smythe," he drawled, stretching his ego to fill more of the room. "Please everyone, call me Worthy. Only Grand Mama calls me Worthington, and it's so stuffy. I'm actually the seventh, so you can imagine! Haw-haw." Everyone sat stone faced. "The usual curriculum vitae; went to Princeton, family school, then Harvard B. Family's been in the investment banking business since the Mayflower. We undoubtedly financed the voyage. Haw-haw!"

All eyes then turned to the only female trainee, a drop dead gorgeous Asian American beauty. "Hi everyone. I'm Ellen Masterson, first generation American on my mom's side, attended Columbia University undergrad and business school on full scholarship..." And so it went, blue bloods dominating the mix, almost everyone sticking to the family business, except Ellen and me.

"What about you, Seth? You certainly come via a different path!"

I flashed my most engaging smile, but when I told them I'd just graduated from Beloit College in Wisconsin, Worthy guffawed, "Guess we know whose daddy works for Lehman Brothers!"

"No, no connections. Convinced the partners to hire me on merit, just like you, Worthy!" Ms. Smythe's face reflected a hint of amusement.

IT WAS A four-month marathon through four institutional departments on the trading floor, fixed income, commercial paper and equities, all one-month rotations plus classroom time and prep courses for the Series 63 and 7 licenses required for employment in the business. At the end of the program departments would bid on us. Multiple bids and you had a choice; if none, well, check out the wire houses.

Nate Rucksberg, now ensconced in a shatter-proof glass fishbowl in the nucleus of the trading room, had a panoramic view of everything, brokers under constant scrutiny, the entire system designed to maximize paranoia and competition. Guys would arrive at the office by 8:30 perfectly coiffed. By ten suit jackets were rumpled and hanging off the back of chairs, by eleven sleeves rolled to the elbow, ties askew, brokers roaming the aisles as far as their telephone umbilical cords would allow, gesticulating, cajoling, beating fists on desktops, pulling their hair, chain-smoking, periodically pumping the air with success or slamming the phones down, a sea of sweat and unbridled testosterone allayed only by the extremely attractive female sales assistants occupying every third desk. In a room of two thousand, the number of female brokers could be counted on two hands. I looked around that vast room. Two thousand raving maniacs with attention deficit and obsessive-compulsive disorders mainlining the amphetamine-laced atmosphere. AND THE DRAMA! They were all actors, like me. Adrenalin kicked in just watching them. This was the drug I'd been looking for.

Weeknights, after a beer and Harry's buffet, usually in the company of Ellen and Sandy, the two trainees friendly to me, I studied Ben Graham's *Security Analysis* on the Long Island Railroad commute to Huntington learning about PE ratios, Price to Book, Debt to Capital, Price to Sales, Price to Call, Yield to Maturity, ad nauseum, best cure for insomnia ever. It was a long, sweltering ride, my damp back pressed into the faded, worn leather seats, mesmerized by the chug a chug a chug a chug a of the train on the track, watching signs flash by, drowsy by Jamaica Avenue, jolted awake by the conductor's sing song "Mineola, Mineola, Mineola," arriving at Huntington Station in time for bed.

THE SATURDAY MORNING after my first full week at Lehman I went down to Winona Beach and swam out to the third float to bask in the sun, taste the salty brine on my lips, relax to the Zen-like roll of the float as waves lapped against it, and watch recreational boats leave the protected harbor for the bay, which opened into the oft turbulent Long Island Sound. A quarter mile offshore a flag flapped atop of the old lighthouse in the gentle breeze, a distance I'd swum many times to sit on its rocks in quiet contemplation.

A group of teenagers sailed a flotilla of Sunfish to Sand City, site of an abandoned cement factory, to party. From a distance they appeared a school of fish zigzagging its way across the water, periodically tacking and jibing to maintain full sails. I envied them, so carefree, yet I relished the crushing exhaustion of a frenetic work schedule that left no time to think or obsess about anything other than beating the competition for a permanent job at Lehman.

I lay back, closed my eyes and enjoyed the brief respite before meeting Mitzie and Dad dockside at his boat for an afternoon cruise that turned into an ambush the moment I saw the Bienstock's, friends of Mitzie's from the temple, on board with their obnoxious daughter I'd detested in Hebrew School. Both mother and daughter were smearing gobs of baby oil on their olive skin, Mrs. Bienstock in a one-piece black suit, wide brimmed sun hat and big oval sunglasses, her cherry red lips and long manicured fingernails and toes matching perfectly, daughter Susan in a silver bikini leaving a lot less to the imagination, accented with lots of gold jewelry, hair coiffed and makeup perfect. Her silver-toned manicure and pedicure reflected the sunlight. The annoying girl I remembered had transformed into a full-fledged Jewish American Princess with an expensive movie star smile and the perkiest ski slope nose money could buy. "Hi Seth. It's been like forever. I hope you like my new swimsuit. I bought it special for today." Her bikini top barely covered her nipples, and there wasn't much fabric covering her bottom, either. My groin stirred. I was only human.

Off we went, cruising at five knots; I could swim faster. I tried to avoid staring at Susan's baby oil-glazed body (not easy on a boat barely thirty feet long), and within ten minutes Dad had ducked into the placid waters of Cold Spring Harbor and secured anchor, never having left the protected bay. Mitzie disappeared into the galley to prepare ham and cheese sandwiches with Susan. Dad opened the small refrigerated bar cabinet on deck, pulled out fixings for martinis, but couldn't find the ice. "It's in the freezer compartment, dear," Mitzie said, turning to Susan. "The Matthews men! They'd be so helpless without us."

Us men sat portside eating ham sandwiches, slurping martini's, reading *The Times* and the *WSJ*, discussing stocks and growth opportunities in Mr. Bienstock's hospital supply business, a very successful business he had me know. The women sat starboard, carefully removing the carb-laden bread from sandwiches they'd just made, discussing whether Susan should keep her maiden name or go by her husband's after she married. "It all depends on his name," Susan noted, smiling salaciously at me as she smeared more baby oil under her bikini top. "For example, I prefer Matthews to Bienstock, no offense, Daddy, but Bienstock is sooo Jewish." Fellini should have directed this scene. I suggested Baum; she could name her first boy child Adam, and she took a moment to consider it before crinkling her excavated nose. Were the Baum's members of the temple? "No matter," she continued, "still too Jewish." The mothers concurred. Unbelievable. Time for a swim.

"Susan, wanna go for a dip?"

"You mean like in the water? Get my bikini wet? No way. And I just had my hair done."

Mitzie urged me to lather on more sunblock. Such a paleface. I'd burn. I couldn't recall such motherly concern all those summers ago at the Rockaways, when I regularly burned to a feverish crisp. "He shouldn't swim alone," Mrs. Bienstock added. "Too dangerous." Susan placed her oil-glazed hand on my arm. Made little circles with talon-like nails. It tickled. "Let's go relax on the front of the boat and catch up. I hear you're working on Wall Street now. You must be making so much money."

Mrs. Bienstock clamped her hand on Mitzie's arm. "Remember the Swernoff boy? I hear he's making a fortune trading commodities or futures, I can't remember which, or maybe it's stock options . . . or whatever. Point is, there's lots of money on Wall Street and with the new electric rail lines on the LIRR commuting to Manhattan from the north shore is a breeze."

"And the houses in Great Neck are to die for," Susan added. "Country Estates in Roslyn is also nice."

"If Wall Street doesn't work out, I'm certainly looking for a bright young man to come into my business," Mr. Bienstock added, "just so long as it stays in the family."

Susan squeezed my arm and pushed her chest out, exposing the rim of her nipples. "What do you think, Seth?" Impure thoughts. I pulled my arm free, stepped onto the swimming platform on the back of the boat and asked if she was coming. "No way." She leaned back in her seat and maneuvered a tinfoil reflector under her face to magnify the damaging rays of the sun. "This is the life. Am I right, or am I right?" Only Dad appeared forlorn, stuck with Mr. Bienstock, probably wishing he could jump overboard, too.

I swam to the lighthouse rocks and pondered whether Erin was likewise being pressured to date more appropriate guys. The McGuire's would want to keep her in Portland, and they'd been pretty steamed over the accident. Maybe she'd miss that backpacking trip, but nothing stopped Randy from making another run at her with Mrs. McGuire's encouragement. Perhaps Dr. McGuire was introducing her to his favorite young protégés, as he had Connie to Ted, hoping something would stick. What better way to keep her on the West coast than have her fall in love with some Reedie.

June 12, 1973

Dear Seth,

I started classes this week. Real ballbusters. Thank goodness I've always had a facility for memorization, almost photographic really, and it's coming in handy with all these equations. Reed has a strong reputation in the Sciences, well earned from what I can see, and if this is any taste of what MIT is going to be like, I'll be one busy girl, which is good because otherwise all I do is pine for you, wonder what you're doing, wonder if you're missing me as much as I'm missing you! This separation is even worse than the winters. I got so used to you being with me all the time, shopping and cooking together, singing and making love and sleeping nestled against each other. How is everything going with the training program? Do you like the other kids? What's it like being on a trading floor? What exactly is a trading floor? Is work at Lehman hard? Tell me more about your fellow interns. Has your summer league started yet? What position are you playing? Let me know how your games go. Did you hear from NYU or Tufts? I know this must feel like twenty questions, but is Abby still engaged? Is your mother trying to find you another nice Jewish girl, and are you fending her off? Do tell in your next letter. I'm doing really well with the physical therapy. Trying to spend time every day off the crutches. Just walking around the campus is a workout for me right now, but I'm determined to be off them before I see you. The therapist says I'm his best patient ever! Please send my regards to your father (and don't forget the promise you made me).

I love you, I love you, I love you,

Erin

June 16, 1973

Dear Erin,

I miss you so much! That's great news about your rehab. I'd never doubted my Outward-Bound girl would be off those crutches in no time, what with your drive and self-discipline! I can't believe it's already been two weeks! I'm so busy, the days so long I try to stay in the city weeknights (out of Mitzie's line of sight). Sandy, one of the two trainees I like, has a studio apartment on the upper Eastside and lets me sleep on his living room couch. Most of my evening meals are complimentary at Harry's. I usually order a beer, cheaper than hard liquor, and devour the buffet. Not the healthiest meal plan, but way ahead of Mom's mystery meals, and easier to digest without the constant hassling and laundry list of Sisterhood daughters she insists I call now she's finally accepted Abby's out of the picture. Last weekend she tried to hook me up with the daughter of friends from the Temple, a total princess I hated in middle school. To give you an idea, she wore a skimpy new silver bikini but refused to get it wet! I'm playing in a summer baseball league with my high school buddies. We call ourselves the Intoxicons and play Saturday nights, then go to Hennigan's after the game. I feel an obligation to spend my beer money there, seeing how Mr. Harrington helped me land the job at Lehman. Besides schoolwork and physical therapy, what else are you doing? Hanging out with your Reedie friends? Are they still going on that hiking trip? Fill me in. I can't wait to see you at the end of the summer. Fly here and I'll drive you up to Boston, help you set up your dorm room. I did hear from both schools. Accepted by NYU Film school. Rejected by Tufts. Guess it really doesn't matter now.

I love you and miss you so much (and I'll never break that promise).

Seth

CHAPTER 5

WHEN I ARRIVED home Friday night there were several letters from Erin sitting in a pile on the kitchen table, Mitzie in her usual spot coddling her ubiquitous cup of tea. "Look what the cat let in, the prodigal son." She handed me several messages from Susan Bienstock I immediately crumpled up. "I'm just trying to protect you. When Erin dumps you, you won't know what hit you. Her father's a professor at Reed and she lives right near campus and is taking courses this summer, right? How long before some nice Reed boy asks her out, before she discovers there's a world out there bigger than Seth Matthews? What's special about you? You think her needs and desires are any less powerful than yours? Plus, Susan's right here and she obviously likes you. Her father owns a multi-million-dollar business. You could do a lot worse." She handed me the letters postmarked Portland, Oregon. "There's a 'Dear John' letter coming. Maybe it's in this pile. Don't read them in front of me. I don't want to see the crushed look on your face!"

"Why would you care? You don't give a fuck about me." My stomach churned as I grabbed the letters and went upstairs. Please don't let her be right.

> June 21, 1973
>
> Dearest Seth,
>
> Happy Solstice! I'm so excited. Mom and Dad rented a beach house in Oceanside for the July 4th weekend. That's the little town where we ate lunch, the one that looks like an Italian hill village. I wish you could fly out here. I checked the tide chart and there should be a big minus tide. We could walk around the capes, maybe through that tunnel you thought was so cool the day we were there, looking at all the starfish and sea anemones. I'd still be on crutches, but I can walk short distances without them, at least until the hip pain

gets too intense. I know it's a pipedream; you've neither the time off nor the money. I'm still doing physical therapy and swimming in the Reed pool. I'm going to be off these things and in good shape before the end of the summer. That's my goal and I'm going to make it. Is Mitzie still after you to go out with Ms. Silver Bikini? Has she hooked you up with any other eligible Jewish girls? Are you finally going to tell her to fuck off, that we're together? Tell all, in your next letter. And remember your promise!

I love you so much,

Erin

I imagined guys ogling Erin the way I'd stared at Susan. I knew what they'd be thinking, what they'd be wanting. She was going to get hit on. How long before she said what the fuck, what am I waiting for?

June 25, 1973

Dear Erin,

I miss you so much. I'd give anything to fly out for July 4th but it's impossible and I doubt your parents would be very pleased to see me anyway. Being here is such a drag. Other than hanging out Saturday evening with the Intoxicons, Mitzie spent the weekend yammering about the Bienstock girl and telling me you were going to dump me. I'm not stupid. I know plenty of guys are going to hit on you; I would if I were them. I think about how angry your parents were after the accident and the zillion other reasons I don't deserve you, and it's hard, just hard, because I couldn't blame you. Be honest with me. Do you still love me? Are you going out with other guys? Do you want to? If only I could hear your voice, know you're real, but long-distance calls are so expensive. All I can do is hope someday we'll look back on this time together and have a collection of love letters, a written record of what we were like when we were younger. That's a positive way of looking at things, isn't it? Making lemonade out of lemons, something I struggle with, but I swear to God, Erin, I'll never do speed again. Believe me, I don't need it. The whole Wall Street atmosphere is like swimming in it!

I love you so much,

Seth

P.S. I don't want anyone but you.

June 30, 1973

Dear Seth,

DO NOT LISTEN TO HER! I'm not interested in going out with anyone else. I love you. Don't doubt it, ever. Your comment about our looking back together someday was so sweet; made me feel all tingly inside. I liked that! I'm so happy you're trying to look at things in a positive light. Don't stop!!! I'm fortunate Beth's home for the summer. We go to free concerts in the Washington Park amphitheater, usually local bands, although we saw Big Brother and the Holding Company, minus Janis, which was a bummer. I had no idea how much they sucked! We go to coffee houses, too, all ages places like the Gallery, and hang out at the Student Union a lot. I didn't think it possible to miss someone as much as I do you. Beth is going on that Outward Bound reunion trip on the Pacific Crest Trail and has been taking long day hikes with Randy and George in the gorge in preparation, which sucks for me. Everyone feels sorry for me, disappointed I can't join them, but it's all they talk about. UGH! We do hang out together but Randy's well aware I'm committed to you and is dating other girls. We're just friends, like you and Lucy (only WE didn't spend a night together). And as far as other guys are concerned, they can eat their hearts out! I've already got my guy. Tell me more about Ellen. I imagine women on Wall Street must be pretty glamorous, there being so few of them. I imagine you swimming at Winona Beach, accosted by pretty girls in bikinis vying for your attention, but I know you're being a good boy. Tell that bitch mother of yours to leave you alone or she'll have to answer to me.

I love you so much,

Erin

July 4, 1973

Dearest Erin,

I'm trying hard to ignore her, to make light of it all, but it does bother me. She won't leave me alone. Every time she hands me one of your letters she says it probably starts "Dear John." I arrived home Friday night to find her latest ambush, Sabbath dinner with some people named Spevak (from the Temple of course), and surprise, surprise, they had a daughter Mara who just so happened to be eligible for Mitzie's scheming. Boobs the size of grapefruits (a waste as far as I'm concerned). I don't know how I'm going to make it through the summer. This girl was entering her senior year at Stony Brook University and hung on my every word like I was already a Wall Street oracle, which is hysterical because I don't know shit. Insisted we drive her shiny new Karmen Ghia, a present from Daddy, to Winona Beach. Told me high finance really turned her on and tried to go down on me. I pushed her away and walked home. It doesn't matter how many times I tell Mitzie I only want you; she doesn't care. She's arranging potential economic alliances. Mara's father runs a big plumbing company and does business with Dad. You have no idea how lucky you are, growing up in a house filled with love and security. I want my children to have that. I don't want them growing up like me. This summer is starting to feel like purgatory. I want you so much. I miss you. Mr. Penis misses you!

All my love,

Seth

July 9, 1973

Dear Seth,

We just returned from the beach, and I found your letter awaiting me. Here's what I want you to do right now. Go into your bedroom, take off all your clothes, get into bed and close your eyes. Imagine you and I are on Oceanside beach, looking out at the Pacific Ocean, listening to the roll of the waves on the rocks, smelling the piney scent of the Douglas fir and spruce trees hanging suspended in mid-air over the eroded cliffs, roots dangling like tendrils. Imagine I'm slowly removing my clothes, pressing your hands into my breasts. Can you feel my nipples stiffening? Now imagine my pressing your fingers into Ms. Pussy, then licking my love juices off each glistening finger before I kiss you all the way down to Mr. Penis, slowly, languorously, and I take him deep in my mouth. Does that feel good? And now imagine we're rolling on the fine beige colored sand, ocean water washing over us as we make love like Burt Lancaster and Deborah Kerr in *From Here to Eternity*, the water so clear and clean, and oh, the warmth of you inside me. Remember the night you showed me that film, how we returned to 848 Park so mad for each other we made love all night long? You were unstoppable that night and I had multiple orgasms. That's what I think about; that's what gets me through these lonely nights without you. Goodnight my love. Sweet dreams, sleep tight (and give Mr. Penis a hug for me).

I love you,

Erin

PS-Maybe this is the one letter we won't save for posterity. Can you imagine the shock if our children found it?

July 12, 1973

Dear Erin,

After your last letter I made my very first stock investment, ten shares of Kimberly Clark (maker of Kleenex). I miss you so much. I went to Jones Beach with Joel and Marsha on July Fourth, the ocean water on the South Shore all milky brownish grey, not pristine like the Pacific, but you can swim in it without a wetsuit (and make love in the surf, which I can't wait to do with you). It must've been hard walking in the sand with crutches. Were you able to go through the tunnel to the other beach on the other side of the cliff? Did your parents take you to that café in Oceanside with the yummy angels on horseback? Dad and Mitzie took me out for lobster last Friday night. I was leery at first, afraid Mitzie would spring another eligible Sisterhood daughter on me, but the only thing awaiting me was a big crustacean. I don't get what the big deal is. They're so messy, all that yucky green stuff all over my hands, and worse, we're given bibs. Place looked like it was filled with babies. Only the highchairs were missing! Without butter they're tasteless. Best part's the side of fries! The Intoxicons all got together for a beach BBQ Saturday night. Everyone got sloshed. I tossed my cookies, but I wasn't the only one.

Mr. Penis and I both send all our love,

Seth

The pattern continued. Weekdays at Lehman Brothers, nights decamped on Sandy's couch, returning to Huntington Friday nights to find another Sisterhood offering at the Sabbath dinner table awaiting my approval, a succession of veiled dancers strutting their wares before me like I was Moses in Jethro's tent, a modern day middle eastern bazaar. How many heads of cattle or herds of sheep would transfer hands after the shidduch was made? Which father would hold up the blood-stained sheet stripped from the matrimonial bed to evidence the good bargain? Mitzie was wearing me down, feeding my insecurities with her relentless speculation over how many boys Erin was dating and schtupping since she clearly hadn't saved herself for marriage. When I complained to Joel, he said I was "Fighting the tape," long distance relationships didn't work, there were lots of nice Jewish girls right here on Long Island. I knew Erin loved me with all her heart, but hearts were such changeable things.

CHAPTER 6

MITZIE STORMED INTO Hennigan's early Friday evening and lambasted me in front of my friends. "Figured I'd find you here. You were supposed to come directly home, remember? It's Sabbath, and I prepared a special dinner. Do you have any idea how you've embarrassed me and insulted our guests? The Simon's are over with their lovely daughter Amanda, and everyone's been patiently awaiting the appearance of his royal highness. Are you coming or not?"

I should've told her to go fuck herself but instead followed her docilely, tail between my legs, my mortification compounded when the Intoxicons, recalling my lead role as Tevye in our high school senior class production of *Fiddler on the Roof*, broke into a hearty rendition of *Matchmaker, matchmaker, make me a match*.

An awkward silence pervaded the dining room when I entered, but before I could utter an insincere apology, I was rendered speechless at the sight of the pretty girl with frizzy red hair, green eyes and freckles dotting the bridge of her obviously original nose. My heart skipped a beat. So like Erin. No glitz, no fancy jewelry or makeup. Mitzie looked like the cat that just ate the canary.

I sat quietly during dinner, but afterwards, taking a stroll down to Winona Beach, felt compelled to inform Amanda I was seriously involved with a girl who could be her doppelganger and not interested in dating anyone. I was doing it for my sake, not hers; I didn't trust myself. The mere sight of her made me happy. I explained Mitzie had been casting her net into the Temple Sisterhood pool all summer long, parading girls in front of me like a shtetl matchmaker, whereupon she immediately corrected me. The word in Yiddish was shadchani, and Jewish parents had been doing it for generations. "So, I'm guessing this other girl is neither Jewish nor from Long Island."

"She's Catholic, well, agnostic really, and from Portland, Oregon."

"Hmmm. I get where your mother's coming from."

"But I think it's offensive. Treating you like chattel. For God's sake, this is 1973, not 1900."

"On the contrary. You're the one being objectified. She's parading you in front of me. Bet you never looked at it that way. Guys can't see beyond the tips of their circumcised penises. You probably don't remember me because I'm two years younger, but I was at your Bar Mitzvah. You were chubby back then, lots of freckles and red hair, like me, with a sweet voice and outsized personality. I saw you in all the high school productions, too. And now on Wall Street. You're obviously still an actor."

She had a quick wit, like Erin, and I drunk her in like a man with an aching thirst. We made plans to go see *Jeremiah Johnson* at the Village of Northport movie house next Saturday night, and when the Simon's left, Mitzie kvelled, "I had a good feeling about this one. Flat-chested. Brainy. A real plain Jane, but that's obviously your taste. Her father's in the cesspool business. Huge growth with all the development on the Island."

If she was trying to cement a relationship, this one would go down the same sewer as the others. "Before you start fantasizing again, we're just going as friends."

July 27, 1973

Dear Erin,

Mitzie finally went over the top. She stormed into Hennigan's on Friday night, scolding me in front of the guys for being late for dinner. Pretty embarrassing having to walk out to a chorus of Intoxicons singing "Matchmaker, matchmaker." I actually had planned on skipping this week's edition of pick the eligible harem girl whose millionaire father does business with Dad, but she was nice, had no idea she'd been entangled in Mitzie's web, and what's weirder still, I swear she could be your twin! A Jewish Irish girl! You'd like her. I told her right off the bat I was seriously involved, and she was totally cool, just looking for friends to get her through a summer at home with the parents. We're going to see a movie next week in Northport village. I'm telling you so you'll know nothing is going on behind your back, at least not by me. Mitzie, well that's another story. If anything like that happened with you, I mean, you'd tell me, wouldn't you, like you did that dinner last winter with Randy? Fill me in on everything. When does the term end? Will you be able to fly up here before the end of August? Meeting your doppelganger only makes me miss you more!

I love you,

Seth

CHAPTER 7

THERE WERE NO letters from Erin when I arrived home Friday night. "I told you it was only a matter of time, bubala," Mitzie smirked. "Absence does not make the heart grow fonder." Joel had said the same thing.

Saturday night, early for the show, Amanda and I walked along Northport's waterfront pier. Gentle waves splashed against the dock in the protected harbor. Sailboats swayed, sails flapping in the wind, bells atop masts chiming to the accompaniment of a cacophony of squawking seagulls. Amanda chatted about school, her upcoming junior year at Vassar, her ambition to become a psychotherapist. So like Erin down to every physical detail I couldn't stop myself from lusting in my mind, imagining her in my arms, my face buried in her coppery-hued hair, hands pressed into her small pert breasts. She was an elixir for my love-parched soul. "My first college roommate Bart is becoming a psychologist. Said rooming with me reaffirmed his decision every day; thought he should have gotten school credits."

"Why? You wanna talk about it?"

"See, that's exactly what I mean. You sound just like him. Guess you're on the right track."

At the end of the pier, she took a deep breath and stretched her arms skyward to salute the brilliant setting sun, her radiant curls afire. Her breasts pressed against the thin material of her summer frock. "It's so gorgeous here, so New Englandy. The briny scent, the chorus of gulls. Don't you just love it? I can't imagine being anywhere else." Sentiments shared by Erin in the Pacific Northwest.

"All I've ever wanted was to be somewhere else." With Erin.

"But you're here, aren't you? You simply need the right reason to stay." She tentatively grasped my hand. "You won't find another Wall Street out there." It was so weird. Like she'd read my mind, and her touch, it felt so good. Too good. I quickly snatched my hand back. Should've reminded her Erin was my girlfriend, I was committed to her, but I remained silent. There'd been no letters. Joel's comments layered over Mitzie's. Was Erin succumbing to the entreaties of her own parents and her best friend? Was she experiencing similar feelings for Randy? Would our love recede into the ether as we found succor in the arms of others? Was that our fate?

Walking down Main Street I started singing *Just yesterday morning they let me know you were gone*, but Amanda cut me short. James Taylor was insipid and depressing. Did I know Blood, Sweat and Tears' "You've Made Me So Very Happy?" Speaking of insipid. When I reminded her she loved James Taylor she retorted, "You have me confused with my doppelganger."

CHAPTER 8

I ROTATED TO the institutional equity department. I loved storytelling, persuading with words, not mathematical equations, and was assigned to sit with the only institutional saleswoman, Risa Friess, an extremely attractive single woman in her mid-thirties. "Well, what have we here? The boy wonder everyone is talking about."

I tried to ingratiate myself; compliment her, offer to get her coffee, but she unleashed on me, nostrils flaring like a racehorse tired of coming in second. "Look, let's cut to the chase, okay? You want to know how I do my business, right? I'll show you." She unbuttoned her blouse just enough to expose her décolletage, her nipples visible through her lacy, translucent bra. "Just low enough to play peekaboo with all those horny, married money managers; leave them wanting more, wondering how far I'll go for a ticket. Usually, I'll start with a hand job, maybe a blow job if the commission dollars are big enough. For a really big trade, they can fuck my brains out. Whatever it takes." I flashed on Joel's high class whore comment.

Relishing my shocked expression, she took a moment to appraise me. "You're pretty cute; quite fuckable. Here's my best sales advice. Get accounts with lots of women analysts and portfolio managers. Learn to use your tongue for something more worthwhile than the crap we spout, and you'll make a nice boy toy, really rack up those votes and commission dollars. Any other questions? No? THEN FUCK OFF!" She turned back to her Quotron screen and phone bank without another word.

My face was on fire. Everyone on the sales desk staring, laughing, even the sales manager who'd referred to me as Chris Harrington's "Grand experiment" and sarcastically labeled me "The Boy Wonder." He suggested I sit with one of the older guys who'd come over to Lehman as part of the Kuhn Loeb merger, a burly Irishman named Kevin who immediately took me aside with sage bits of advice like "A salesman's job is to walk down corridors of indifference shedding light on the obvious," and "Never pass a bathroom without using it," then dumped a thick stack of research reports in front of me. "Start reading."

The reports were amorphous, almost incoherent, absent a uniform analytic approach, but I quickly found a key to analyzing them efficiently and effectively by reducing each one to critical points justifying the conclusory recommendation. I swear, it came as naturally as organizing socks in my bureau. I could juggle multiple ideas, cut to the heart of each without skipping a beat. I was thrilled! On Wall Street my OCD was a virtue. Inner demons, blind ambition, pathological fear of failure all catalysts seeding success. If there ever was a narcissist's dream, this was it. My desk at Lehman the key to a kingdom where I'd get rich and no one got hurt. I was going to be unstoppable. A star. Make partner. It was merely a matter of focus. Fuck those inner voices. To hell with what transpired in Portland. I was going to show Mitzie what I was made of!

CHAPTER 9

ANOTHER FRIDAY NIGHT. Still no letters. Mitzie, sensing my despondency, went for the kill. "Stop kidding yourself. She's dating other boys. Go on, call Amanda and ask her out to dinner. You know you want her. And I know for a fact she's expecting your call." She handed me the phone. "Bet you a hundred dollars Erin's got a date, too." She slipped me a hundred-dollar bill. "Take Amanda someplace nice."

Amanda answered her door dressed to the nines in a low-cut emerald-colored mini dress that set off her mascaraed green eyes and displayed her cleavage to advantage. She looked ravishing. Sophisticated. High heels. Diamond posts in her elfin-like earlobes. No hippie goddess but the very essence of "presentability" as defined by Mitzie. Maybe like Erin if she wore makeup. I liked it. A lot. More than I wanted to. Was Mitzie right? Was it time to put childish things behind? This Amanda was different, more assertive. She kissed me full on the mouth, pulled me in front of a mirror and gazed at our reflections. She brushed back my hair; straightened my tie. It felt good to be fussed over. "We belong together," she said. Perhaps we did. Erin had obviously forgotten me. I'd been her momentary fancy, just as I had feared.

We drove to Linck's Log Cabin for their Friday night special shore dinner, Amanda's favorite food lobster, just like Erin. About to order fried clams, she cajoled me into giving lobster another try. When the large insects arrived, she immediately dug in, cracking a large claw, neatly extracting the meat and dipping it in the butter. Recalling Erin's quip that night at the Gun Club I intoned, in my best Fifties sci-fi voice, "Lobsterman from outer space, able to survive nuclear attack only to drown in hot liquid butter." She didn't laugh. Not even a giggle. And I thought it was pretty darn funny. I tried another tack. One that would have Erin in stitches. I held my lobster by its claws and danced it across the plate humming "Puttin' on the Ritz." "I'm Fred Astaire," I explained, "and your lobster's Cyd Charisse; let's dance," but Amanda furtively glanced about us to see if other tables had noticed my inappropriate antics and chided me to stop playing with my food. It was immature and embarrassing. A finger had snapped; I woke from a hypnotic trance. I pushed my plate away. I'd no appetite for the large insect, or her. I didn't want someone more presentable, fashion conscious and conventional. I didn't want arm candy. I wanted Erin, and Amanda was right, she wasn't Erin. Only Erin was Erin!

Amanda's eyes teared up. "I assumed if you really cared so much about that Portland girl you wouldn't be here with me, but I'm wrong, aren't I? I'm just a proxy. When you're with me, you're thinking about her. You're still in love with her. It doesn't matter how much I like you."

"Amanda, you're a really nice girl and maybe if we'd met . . ."

"Spare me the platitudes." She pushed out her chair. "Please take me home."

Mitzie was sitting in the kitchen, playing Solitaire and drinking her ubiquitous cup of tea when I walked into the house. I slammed the hundred-dollar bill on the kitchen table. She looked up, startled, about to say something but held back. I could see the disappointment in her eyes. "Bet's off." I headed upstairs without another word. If I let Mitzie make my decisions for me, they'd all turn out to be lobsters.

ON FRIDAY, AUGUST 13th I finally received a letter from Erin. At the office. I thought I'd be sick. The long-dreaded Dear John letter. I left my desk. Went to the bathroom. Into a stall. Away from prying eyes. After two months at Lehman I knew better than to show any sign of weakness. The wolves would pounce at the first sight of blood, and I was about to be shattered.

August 8, 1973

Dear Seth,

I'm worried about you, honey. You haven't answered any of my letters. I called you twice after receiving your last one and asked you mother to give you the messages to call back, but you haven't, and now it's been two weeks and I know something's wrong; I can sense it. You've become distant. You've let Mitzie get to you and all I can think about is my doppelganger. Be firm and tell Mitzie to stop trying to run your life. I swear to you, she'll come around. She loves you and deep down I know she wants you to be happy. I know how obsessive you are, how driven, but maybe you on Wall Street is like trying to fit a square peg in a round hole. There are so many other things you can do, and you'd succeed at any of them!

And you'll always have my full support. With those work hours, I doubt you're getting enough sleep, and what a horrible commute! I know you're lonely, honey; I am, too, but we'll be together soon. Classes have ended and I'm now studying for next week's final exams, and the week thereafter I'll fly to New York, giving us a whole week before MIT classes begin. Please Seth, don't be wishy washy with Mitzie; believe me, she'll come to love your Irish lass from Portland. I love you so much. Please write back so I know you're okay, that we're okay.

Yours forever,

Erin

What letters? What calls? I re-read the letter; guilt tempered with mounting anger. She'd been trying to reach me for weeks! No wonder she'd written me at the office. Mitzie had twisted my fate to her own advantage. Watched me writhe in angst for weeks, biding her time until I acclimated to Amanda. She was as cold-hearted as my birth mother. Playing with my heart like that. I'd been so, so wrong, trying to forge a path between the two of them. Love was a trapeze act with no safety net, only the faith that someone would catch me in mid-air, and that person was Erin.

CHAPTER 10

I BOARDED THE train home that night physically and emotionally exhausted but armored and grimly determined to do battle with Mitzie once and for all, and after the stifling hour and a half train ride, my suit drenched with sweat, who should I see sitting in the Huntington station waiting room but Amanda! But no, not Amanda. The bedraggled and wan girl with the suitcase clasped between her knees, crutches balanced precariously against the wall behind her, was Erin. Stunned, I stood motionless amidst the bustle of tired, overheated commuters pushing and shoving passed me. "Erin! What are you doing here? Aren't you supposed to be in Portland?"

"Plans change, and my professors let me take my exams early."

"But how'd you even know I'd be on this train?"

"I didn't. I've been sitting here for hours watching for you, fighting to stay awake. I must look a total mess!" She did, the most glorious mess I'd ever laid eyes on, her emerald eyes rimmed with red like sad Christmas ornaments, her frizzy copper hair matted, clothes all wrinkled. She'd lost weight; looked so fragile, a baby bird with clipped wings. "I got in around midday. Had to ask like ten people before anyone would even stop to give me directions out to Long Island. How can you tolerate living here? I've never seen so many aggressive, obnoxious people."

I pulled her up and hugged her. Buried my face in her hair, inhaled her wonderful scent. "I can't believe you're here . . . that you're real." To hold her, to touch her. It was rapture. This was home. "When I hadn't heard from you, I assumed I'd never see you again. I only received your last letter at the office today. Why didn't you let me know you were coming today?" She stood mute. Her eyes ablaze with fire. "And look at you! Standing without crutches!"

"Injuries heal. Mending a relationship someone's hell-bent on destroying is harder."

"How . . . how're your folks, your brothers?"

"Glad to see the back of me; everyone's been walking tippy toes around me. Look, it's been a really long day; I need a cup of coffee, to freshen up a bit. I haven't been sleeping well these past few weeks. Let's go to your parents' house."

I could see Mitzie in the kitchen right now, busy preparing yet another special Sabbath dinner despite the clear message I'd delivered last Friday night. What if Amanda was there? I wasn't ready to face it. "Mitzie's gonna freak out we didn't give her advanced notice. Let's stop for some coffee . . . I'll call, let them know you're here. Better yet, let's get dinner first, okay?"

"But its Sabbath dinner, right? Eligible Jewish girl night? Tonight's BYOG night! Bring your own gentile. It'll be a surprise."

A surprise I wanted to delay as long as possible, so I took the longest possible route to Huntington Bay. I showed her the Duck Pond at Heckscher Park, the Revolutionary War period clapboard houses dotting the Village Green. Described the touch football games the Intoxicons used to play there, one of which resulted in my jaw being dislocated. Erin remained quiet throughout, taking in the idyllic scenery while I mused over the changes in her. She seemed more assured, her set of mouth more determined. This was not the same girl I'd left at the airport three months ago. Finally, arriving at East Shore Road, the narrow two-lane road overlooking the Harbor, she sighed, thanked me for the fifty-cent tour and suggested I show her Winona Beach as well.

Happy for the further delay I turned onto the one lane road leading to the beach and parked in the empty sand lot. I came around to her side and handed her crutches she immediately brushed away. She had a mischievous grin. Surprised nobody was there. We slowly ambled over to the shoreline where a wall of large boulders formed a little secluded alcove demarcating the harbor from the bay. I pointed out my special rock, a large flat boulder jutting out into the water, and she limped towards it, leaned against it and stripped. Her body hair all gone! "Erin, if someone comes down here and sees us . . ."

"They'll get a thrill." She beckoned me, my red-haired siren, drew me in and drowned me in her body, carving deep blue ripples in the tissues of my mind. Then pausing for a moment, she held me at arm's length. "You're Odysseus long at sea and I'm Penelope, your faithful wife, awaiting your return with intense physical longing." She pulled me deeper into her. A gentle wave washed over us. Home.

ERIN HOBBLED TO the kitchen screen door and knocked. "May I come in, Mrs. Matthews?"

Mitzie's mouth dropped open. A raw chicken hit the Marmoleum floor with a splat. She bent down to pick it up, then nervously wiped her hands on the front of her apron. What was Erin doing here? I'd never said a thing. Erin reminded her I didn't know. Someone hadn't given me her letters, or messages. "May I come in or are you expecting special company for Sabbath dinner?"

Mitzie blanched. "No, no, come in, please. But you're supposed to be in Portland."

"I was, but then my plans changed." Erin placed her crutches against a wall. "I took my exams early and caught the red eye to New York..."

"But just for the weekend, right? I mean, you are going back..."

Erin shook her head and hobbled over to the stove that almost killed me, a Forties antique with strangely humanoid features, large dial eyes and wide chrome mouth that appeared to be smiling despite Mitzie's cooking. "I love your stove, Mrs. Matthews. It's got real personality. Actually, everything here shows real individuality, and your Marmoleum flooring is really cool; I hate that sterile white ceramic everyone seems to want now, and it's easier to clean with kids running about. Is that countertop original? The chrome accent is really neat. Was the house like this when you bought it?"

"No. I did a lot of renovating. Tried to keep everything to period, which luckily is easy to do in Huntington. The town's loaded with resale and consignment shops. You wouldn't believe the things you can find. I'd no idea you were interested in antiques. Most young women want everything new these days."

"We passed several driving through town. I'd love to see them. I love antiques. That's one of the reasons I'm interested in old architecture. The craftsmanship was incredible."

"You're so right. See this Dutch table? Found it rummaging through my favorite store. Needed a little TLC but it's hand carved. I just love the lines. So graceful, and made here, not in overseas sweat shops."

"You've a great eye, Mrs. Matthews. Did you refinish it yourself?"

Mitzie seemed to relax. Actually smiled. "Thank you, Erin. That's sweet of you to say. I've got a workshop in the garage. I'll show it to you later if you like. But you look tired. Maybe you should get off your feet. Please, take a seat."

"Thanks." Erin eased into the cozy booth tucked into the corner with the bay window view of the backyard. She peered through the window. "This is nice. A safe place for children to play."

"I miss watching them out there," Mitzie sighed. "Wish I'd taken more time to enjoy those moments. They're so fleeting. Everyone rushes around like chickens without heads these days, accomplishing nothing. Speaking of which, I'd better get this one in the oven or we'll be eating it raw."

"I'm sure you'll have many more moments like that with your grandchildren."

"You want children, Erin?" Mitzie asked, closing the oven door.

"Oh, yes. I've always dreamed of a big family. And a house like yours. We passed some gorgeous Federal and Colonial style houses from the Revolutionary War period on the way here. Houses built in 1900 are considered old in Portland. Too bad Huntington is so far from Wall Street, but that's where Seth works so I imagine we'll be looking for a house closer to the city."

"Don't you want to be closer to your family in Portland?"

"Won't I be close to family here in New York?"

Mitzie's face brightened. "After dinner, I'll show you around the rest of the house. It was built in 1928. The fixtures are original and almost impossible to replace, all the windows single pane leaded glass. Drafty and not particularly energy efficient, but I love the refracted light. And maybe we can check out some of the consignment shops in town while Seth's at work. There are three hundred years' worth of antiques."

"I'd love that." Erin grimaced as she shifted position on the bench. "I'm very interested in how to maintain that beauty in an environmentally responsible way."

"Yes. You mentioned that at graduation. Are you in a lot of pain, dear? Can I get you anything?"

"I'd love a cup of coffee. It's been a very long day. Thank you, Mrs. Matthews."

Mitzie prepared coffee in the Farberware pot. While it percolated, she checked on the chicken, boiled potatoes and prepared a green salad. Then, grabbing two coffee cups from a cabinet, she poured them both cups and sat down on the other side of the table. "Erin, I'm so sorry we got off on the wrong foot. It's my fault. Can we start over?"

"I'd really like that, Mrs. Matthews."

"Please call me Mitzie. Can I get you anything else?" Erin caressed my hand underneath the table and shook her head. I asked if Jerry was on the front porch and left to find him. The entire interaction between the two women was too puzzling. He was lounging in his wicker chair, feet up on an ottoman, pre-dinner Pernod on the side table. He gave me a sly grin. "Sounds like Erin and Mom have found some common ground."

"Why didn't you come in and say hello?"

"Best seats in the theatre are often toward the back."

DINNER WAS SERVED on the front porch. Following Mitzie's lead, Erin shielded her eyes as Mitzie lit the Sabbath candles, the gesture not lost on Mitzie, surprised Erin was familiar with Jewish customs. "I grew up in an agnostic household, but my parents taught my brothers and me to live by the Golden Rule and respect other traditions. My best friend Beth is Jewish, and I had Friday night dinner at their house often, so I'm familiar with the candle lighting custom and the prayers over the wine and bread . . . well," she smiled, "the transliterations anyway."

"I don't speak or read Hebrew either," Mitzie noted. "Never had the opportunity to go to Hebrew school or services." Why don't I know anything about her family?

"That's a shame. I think parents should instill young children with some religious structure and tradition, even if they ultimately chose a different path." Mitzie concurred.

Dad regaled Erin with his one brief stopover in Portland, returning from action in the Pacific theatre during World War Two. Turned out he and Mitzie had met at a USO function for Jewish soldiers at Temple Emmanuel in New York City. She was picking raisins out of her Danish pastry. He didn't like them either.

"He was so dashing in uniform." MItzie placed her hand over his. "But handsome as he was, I didn't know I wanted to marry him until I met his mother. She became mine. Taught me so much. We lived with his parents while he found his bearings and started his construction business and I became pregnant with Jonah, Seth's older brother." She furrowed her brow. "Grandma Matthews was good to me, better than I deserved." Was this remorse shtick for Erin's benefit? "You would have liked Grandma Matthews and she would have loved you. Most of my home aesthetic came from her."

"Seth says I remind him of her. Except she was a better cook."

I pushed food about my plate. Dad suggested having dinner at Patricia Murphy's tomorrow night. Erin would love their shore dinner. Lobster, clam chowder, steamers and fries. What was Mitzie's angle? Why was she being so ingratiating? She was a conniving spider, entrapping prey in her web to be ingested at her leisure. An attack was imminent. Had to be. And yet, their interaction was such an about face. Was Erin's innate goodness contagious?

After dinner Dad and I sat on the porch. The two ladies chatted away like old friends while doing dishes in the kitchen. I asked him to explain what I'd just witnessed. "Détente," he said.

CHAPTER 11

WHEN I WENT upstairs Erin was not in my room, but the attic light was on. I unhappily continued up the creaking stairs to Jonah's cold room. Found her winding up the Robbie the Robot. "Just like mine, and it still works." It marched jerkily across the bureau emitting sparks in its wake. "Same jack-in-the-box, too. My parents took me to see *Forbidden Planet* when I was pretty little. The special effects were scary. Gave me nightmares for weeks. I'd no idea they'd turned it into wallpaper for kid's rooms. The Balrog demon is still pretty frightening." She plugged in the black light, illuminating the room in fluorescent planets and stars, the Balrog inching ever closer. "Whoa, far out." She looked up at the smiling clown face clock. "Tick tock, tick tock, let's make love to the clown face clock."

"We can't. It's forbidden on this planet."

"Very punny. They won't hear us; but we 'd better do it on the floor. No way I can replicate your mother's perfect hospital corners." Try for an hour nonstop. She undressed and lay on the carpeted floor. Her nipples immediately stiffened. Goosebumps all over her luscious body. "Brrr, it's drafty up here. Ms. Pussy's cold without her fur. Meow, meow. Come warm her up." I didn't move. My heart thump, thump, thumped in synchronicity with the TICK TOCK TICK TOCK of the clock. I started to tremble, and she sat up on her elbows, eyes full of concern. "What's wrong, honey? Something's bothering you, I can tell. Is it this room? Did something happen here? Talk to me."

I stared at the glowering image of the Balrog demon. It seemed to inch closer. I gulped. "The night before my Bar Mitzvah I was really nervous and came up here seeking reassurance from Jonah, but he was awful to me. Like his body had been inhabited by a demon. I remember it like it was yesterday. But there's something else. Something happened to me I can't remember and need to remember it but I'm afraid to remember and I don't know why but it scares me."

"Wow. That sounds ominous, and convoluted. Something up here triggers those feelings, right?"

I pointed to the Balrog and the jack-in-the-box. They're in this nightmare I've had for years."

She sat up, her arms around her knees, immediately interested. "This nightmare. Always the same one? That has to mean something."

"Dreams are weird. They don't make any sense. I hate being up here, Erin. Can we please go back downstairs to my room?"

I DROVE ERIN up to Boston the last weekend in August, her folks having already shipped her stuff there. During the five hour drive she spoke reverently of architectural luminaries like IM Pei, Eero Saarinen and Alvar Aalto who'd designed the campus buildings, translating mathematics into flowing form and structure. She talked of them as if they were rock stars, openly discoursing about things she'd never have discussed in high school for fear of sounding nerdy. It made me glad to think I had something to do with her newfound confidence.

We walked through the lobby of the dormitory designed by Aalto as through a church, in silent awe. No wonder MIT had been her first choice. And she immediately hit it off with her new roomie, Sheryl, another sophomore, from the DC area, a Jewish girl who propitiously had a car and a boyfriend in grad school at Stony Brook University on Long Island whom she visited monthly, only too happy to offer Erin a ride in exchange for the company and gas money. I left them engaged in a discussion of the summer reading list. Bart and I had discussed the merits of Hemingway versus Dostoyevsky. Their exchange more obtuse, merging science, philosophy and mathematics. My brilliant girlfriend had found her path.

CHAPTER 12

I RECEIVED MULTIPLE bids, my employment at Lehman Brothers assured once I passed the licensing exams. It was time to get my own place. My overprotective father waited up for me weekend nights, unable to sleep unless his twenty-one-year-old chickie was tucked safely in the roost, ridiculous but sweet. My relationship with Mitzie edgy, her turnabout with Erin too confusing. And as Joel correctly surmised, Manhattan rental agents laughed me off the phone when I shared my salary information, though one kindly gave me the number for a large apartment complex in Douglaston, Queens rumored to be going coop. Apparently, renters would get first dibs on purchasing their apartments at an insider price for a potential profit and Douglaston, being only a half hour from Penn Station on the electric LIRR line, would shave an hour off the Huntington commute. It was too good a deal to pass up.

Fortuitously, a two-bedroom unit had become available. I walked through the apartment with the rental agent who has assured me the place simply needed a little TLC. It was a dump. Kitchen cabinets falling apart, linoleum flooring cracked, scratched and filthy. Bathroom riddled with mold, patches of wall tile missing. A screened in porch overlooking the busy road, a special feature, was missing sections of screening. The hallways reeked of overcooked meat, rotting cabbage, roach spray, mothballs and treacly old lady perfume. But there was ample hot water and you couldn't beat the rent. As regards the potential coop conversion the agent merely grinned. Good enough for me. My move in was a snap, my worldly possessions handily fitting in my old beater: my suitcase stereo, some LPs, a duffel bag of clothes, two suit bags, an exercise mat, coffee pot, twin mattress and a case of empty Ball jars awaiting Erin's presence.

September 10, 1973

Dearest Erin,

You wouldn't believe this place. Everyone in the building is 150 years old. The old lady directly below, Mrs. McBride, is already banging on the ceiling with a broom every night while I exercise. No one says hello or makes eye contact. Most look like they'd already expired. So much for the good news. On to the apartment! I'll have to excavate the kitchen, and let's not even talk about the bathroom! But I won't be lonely; there are hundreds of cockroaches living with me, maybe thousands, swarming all over the place. Fearless little buggers join me for breakfast, trooping across the table with a confidence borne of knowing they'll inherit the Earth long after the human race destroys itself. If the coop conversion actually occurs, it might turn out to be a good investment after some needed renovations. But the commute's a breeze, a half hour into Penn, fifteen more minutes down to Wall Street; that's dynamite, especially as I'm now up at 5 a.m. to make a cup of coffee and catch the 5:35. The station's just a block away. I can't wait to show it to you!

All My Love,

Seth

September 20, 1973

Dear Seth,

Having a place of our own sounds so great. Can't be any worse than 848 Park! How many cockroaches equal one mouse? And it's temporary. By the time I graduate you'll be a Wall Street tycoon making one hundred thousand dollars a year and buy me a beautiful house in some really neat place.

    The kids here are so weird, like walking slide rules. I haven't met anyone who isn't a genius. Everyone is so uncool, it actually creates a new definition of cool, if that makes any sense to you. I don't stand out here, like in high school. I'm just normal! Scary, huh? When are you coming up? I miss you so much. I ache to be with you, lay with you, press my perky breasts into your back (this better be giving you a hard on)! Truly, what I miss most is listening to you breathe as you sleep. You do snore, by the way. I feel so incomplete without you; you're my missing limb, yet just knowing you're in my life makes it so much easier to concentrate on my schoolwork. And I'm especially comforted you're sharing your bed with creatures I approve of. Give the roaches a big hug and kiss for me!

I love you,

Erin

I accepted an offer from the institutional equity department and drove to Boston Friday night to celebrate, putting off all the cleaning, scraping and painting needed in the apartment until after I passed the licensing exams. Three other trainees had made the cut as well, Ellen joining me in equities, Sandy and one other guy going into fixed income sales. I was assigned as associate for Kevin Egan, the brawny Irishman who'd given me all that sage advice during the rotation. Worthington Blah Blah the Seventh and the rest of the blue bloods were washouts. I arrived at MIT amidst an official school party, geeky looking people clutching cups of what I assumed was purple passion. Erin stood out like a diamond in the rough, several guys clustered around her, attentively ogling her. I hugged her and planted a big kiss. "Seth, this is Harry, Bill and Mark. Guys, this is my boyfriend, Seth. He works on Wall Street." I noted their disappointment with pleasure. "We've been discussing topology, you know, how properties of space can be preserved under continuous deformation, like stretching and bending without cutting or gluing things together. I know I'm simplifying it, guys, but Seth was a liberal arts major." They knowingly nodded their geeky heads, all eyes glued on Erin's luscious breasts.

Harry, sporting a pocket protector, held out his hand. "That's the gist of it. Nice to meet you, Seth." Mark was wearing thick black specs taped at the broken bridge. Definitely not topological!

Erin handed me a cup of the purple liquid. "Honey, I got stuck hosting, and the party ends at 11 so I can't hang out until then. I gotta get back to the kitchen and bring out more platters of cookies." I took a sip. It actually was purple passion, even here at MIT, nerd central.

Watching her tight little ass wriggle its way back to the kitchen proved distracting for all of us. I cleared my throat to regain their attention. "So, what's with this topology stuff?"

Mark asked if we'd heard the one about the topologist who ate a coffee cup. "He thought it was a donut!" They all cracked up. Nothing to worry about here. Compared to MIT guys I was the essence of cool.

Saturday morning, we strolled along the Charles River toward Harvard Square. A glorious fall day, golden sunlight rippled on the water as sculling boats advanced downriver, diamond specks shimmering in their wake, the coxswains' commands echoing across the water like skimmed rocks. Leaves were turning that wonderful array of colors that presaged decay, Erin's hip so improved she danced her way along the riverside path, her coppery mane catching the sunlight, untamed, glorious and irresistible, as she illuminated how math was a universal language, connecting ideas, getting from point A to point B. "It's everywhere, Seth! It explains the world." But it couldn't explain why she still wanted to be with me.

CHAPTER 13

WE SURVIVING TRAINEES started a weeklong review course for the Series 7 and 63 exams, took practice tests every day, flunking the first few but catching the rhythm of it as the week progressed. Ellen and I decided to get together to study Saturday at her apartment in Brooklyn, my place still a disaster.

Crossing the Kosciuszko bridge into Brooklyn was entering a third world country, the BQE littered with detritus, tires, burnt out car frames, mildewed mattresses and sofas, even an old toilet; the tin shed villages on the outskirts of Mexico City Disneyland by comparison. I passed areas of dilapidated brownstones and tenements, corners populated by unsavory types of all stripes and colors, even a run-down neighborhood of Hassidic Jews who looked like my Hebrew School teachers. Small wonder they were so fatalistic; the borough God chose for them left much to be desired. Things gentrified the farther south I traveled, small mom and pop storefronts, bodegas and churches, and by the time I reached Carroll Gardens I was in Italy.

Ellen's apartment on Clinton Street was one of six in a subdivided mid-nineteenth century brownstone. The beefy mahogany mouldings were water-stained, evidence of old leaks in the blistered ceiling plaster, badly scuffed solid oak floors, broken or missing pieces in the stained-glass windows. I assumed the other units had similar issues, but at one time this must have been a grand family home. "Erin would love this. She's really into architecture and renovating and old stuff."

Ellen handed me a mug of strong black coffee. "Excepting you, the old stuff that is, not the renovating." She giggled. "Here's some rocket fuel. I don't know how you drink this all day long, but I made you a full pot." Her dressed for success business attire had been replaced with an oversized Columbia University sweatshirt and torn jeans, her long silky black hair swept up in a bun crisscrossed by chopsticks. "The neighborhood's convenient to downtown Manhattan. Only seventeen minutes to Wall Street, and so cheap! I'm gonna buy a place before it gets discovered. You should think about it."

We spent the day studying in her living room, a small parlor with a non-working fireplace that just managed to accommodate a couch, coffee table and easy chair. I sat on the easy chair, legs dangling over the arm, she sprawled on the couch, and took test after test until we were both scoring in the high-eighties and feeling pretty good. Bleary-eyed, she stood up, did several yoga stretches and pulled me up from my chair. "I can't take another test today. Let's pick up a couple of bottles of Italian red and make spaghetti or something. I know just the place to shop."

We walked over to Court Street to Cappuccino's Fine Foods. Bells chimed as we entered. "According to Zuzu, every time a bell rings an angel gets his wings."

Ellen basked in the smells and asked if Zuzu was an old girlfriend. "No, a little girl in *It's a Wonderful Life*. She has these rose petals that fall off their stem and her father, who's distraught and wishes he was dead, places them in his pocket and then gets his wish. The petals disappear. But when he's given the gift of discovering what life would have been like had he never been born, he realizes the positive impact he'd had; all the love and fellowship he'd created. He prays for another chance at life and gets it. The petals reappear in his pocket."

"Why's that so important to you?"

"Who wouldn't want a second chance?"

"Well, I can't speak for Zuzu, but this is heaven on earth." Wheels of dry Italian cheeses hung from the ceiling, hot trays filled with sausage, peppers and onions, Arancini and fried veal cutlets, as well as tubs of fresh mozzarella and ricotta behind misted-over display cases. "I gain weight just looking at this stuff."

An elderly man greeted Ellen from behind the counter. "Signorina Ellen, il mio piu bel cliente!"

"Giuseppe, I'm not sure what you said but it sounds delicious."

"I think he said you're his most beautiful customer."

"Thank you, that's so sweet! I was telling my friend here you make the best mozzarella in New York."

"Same way my father made it before me." He reached into the glass display and spooned out a piece, insisting I taste it. I told him it was delizioso and suggested making lasagna. "Okay, so maybe a little sausage, crushed tomatoes, mozzarella, ricotta. What time you want me over for dinner? I've got a nice chianti, too."

I pointed to the glass display and asked if the Cannoli were homemade. Giuseppe mimed affront, then insisted I taste his ricotta. "Bello, eh?"

"Mejor que he probado."

"Tu parli Italiano?" He seemed surprised.

"Spanish Italian. Solo lo basta para sonar ridiculo." Ellen looked impressed. "I spent a half year in Mexico and the two languages are very similar."

"What were you doing in Mexico?"

"Trying to kill myself."

She looked askance but didn't pry. Heading back, she gave me a quick tour of the Italian social clubs, Catholic parishes, pork stores, pasta shops and espresso bars, then opened the first bottle while I boiled water for the pasta, crushed garlic into a pan of simmering olive oil, added minced onion and let the mixture caramelize before adding the chopped sausage, crushed tomatoes, fresh basil, dried herbs and touch of red wine. Handing me a full glass she asked if I was actually serious about killing myself or being melodramatic.

I added the lasagna noodles to the boiling water with a tablespoon of salt. "Yes, well, metaphorically speaking, but I have Erin now. I'll kill myself when she eventually leaves me. Every moment with her is precious because it won't last." When she frowned, I explained "I believe in fate. Don't let my nice guy act fool you. I destroyed my brother's life in a jealous rage. I outed him to my parents."

"Wow, a shitty thing to do, but still a choice, one of multiple pathways we can chose as we go through life. I don't believe in predetermination. I'm guessing he must've done something horrible to you."

My field of vision contracted. I started visualizing dark, impenetrable woods and squeezed my eyes shut to push back on the murky image. "I'm just saying don't dig too deep. You won't like what you find."

"But Zuzu's petals? His second chance?"

"That's a movie, not real life." Was that true? Hadn't Erin come back to me?

"Well, on the bright side you picked the right career path."

"No kidding. I fit right in. All the drama, intensity and narcissism, it's like mainlining speed, and I really liked speed . . . too much. It didn't like me. Think *Dr. Jekyll and Mr. Hyde* and you'll get the picture."

"Ah, the endless cups of coffee. Bet that's how you maintain your svelte figure, huh?"

I mixed the ricotta with a beaten egg, grated parmesan cheese and sliced the mozzarella. "I'm not so sure you fit in to the Wall Street scene."

"Don't rub it in. My father's a Port Authority policeman. Mom's a salesclerk at Lord and Taylor, waiting on rich women like your mother and all those other pampered kids in the training program. I'm this year's social experiment, waiting for the shoe to drop."

That wasn't what I meant. I drained the noodles, layered all the ingredients and put the casserole dish into a 375-degree oven. "I'm the one without an MBA and I didn't go to an Ivy League school like Columbia. You're a good person, too good for the viper's nest we work in, but I'm glad you're there."

By the time I removed the lasagna from the oven we'd polished off the first bottle of chianti. I uncorked the second and we joked about Worthington and the other stuffed shirts in the training program while she set place settings for two on her little kitchen table. But when I poked fun of Ms. Smythe she bristled. I'd no idea what it was like being a professional woman in a men's-only club. "Women get fucked over big time! Remember your encounter with Risa Friess?"

"And her unforgettable career advice?"

"Take it as a compliment. But seriously, imagine what it's like guys always asking if it's your time of the month, whistling as you pass their desks, pinching or patting your ass like you're up for grabs. Ever have a guy come up behind you and give you a little shoulder squeeze or massage or put his arm around you?" I flinched. "Right. Now you get it. We're disrespected because we're women, so we have to be smarter, tougher, and more aggressive than any of you guys!"

"But it is what it is . . ."

"That's your inner male chauvinist pig talking. I've got as much right to be there as any of you." She took another gulp of wine. "When I get rich, I'll tell you all to fuck off! By the way, your lasagna rocks." A career path if male prostitution didn't pan out!

I was feeling pretty tipsy and Ellen suggested I spend the night, assuaging my concern for the safety of my car by assuring me no self-respecting car thief would be seen in it. She put a pillow and blanket on the parlor room couch, left a fresh blue towel in the bathroom and apologized for not having an extra toothbrush. I fluffed the pillow, took off my jeans and T-shirt, left my undies on for propriety's sake, got under the covers and dozed off immediately, but sometime later, still dark, I sensed a presence and bolted upright, covering myself with the blanket. Ellen was standing there in flannel pajamas. Crying she'd never be good enough. I made room for her on the couch. Put my arm around her, her head on my shoulder. Two bottles of chianti had cracked her cocksure public façade. She was insecure like me. Maybe we all were. I was deeply moved. We were actors, polished wood veneers over cardboard hearts. We fell asleep and woke up next morning even closer friends.

CHAPTER 14

OF THE FOUR surviving trainees, only Ellen, Sandy and I passed the regulatory exams and the following Friday we were invited to dine in the Partners elegant dining room on the forty-fourth floor. The burnished oak paneled walls, sterling silver cutlery, bone china service, sparkling lead crystal stemware, the natural light streaming through floor to ceiling windows, illuminating everything in rainbows of refracted light. Awe inspiring. But what thrilled me was the rarified air. Rubbing elbows with the best of the best. I swore to myself I'd be one of them.

Billecart-Salmon Brut Rose champagne accompanied a smoked salmon appetizer. Coquilles St. Jacques and Filet Mignon in a demi glaze were matched with Chateau Pichon Longueville Baron Bordeaux, and we three, sole survivors of a grueling rat race, got sloshed as we were briefed on the tremendous opportunity that lay before us. No one was going back to work after this meal, and it wasn't even over. After the main course cleared, aged cheeses were accompanied by old Port and a humidor of expensive cigars circulated, Don Diego, Dunhill, even illegal Cubans, nothing too good for the elite of the elite. All around the table partners clipped the ends off cigars and lit them, toking away until the room was a fog of smoke, and I watched with fascination as these incredibly wealthy men, as there were no women partners, stuffed handfuls more in their suit pockets. I grabbed a Don Diego for Dad. Ellen was bypassed and shot me a look that could kill.

Sent home in a limo, a first, drunk on an elixir of expensive wine, power and infinite possibilities, I exchanged my suit for sweats and began the arduous task of making the apartment livable for creatures other than cockroaches. I stripped the floors, nuked the oven with Dow cleaner, same stuff used to defoliate Vietnam, and scrubbed out the fridge. Late Sunday afternoon I called Erin and chatted for an hour, fuck the cost. I'd be making a hundred grand in three years! I needed to hear her voice, tell her about the Partners' lunch and Ellen's neighborhood in Brooklyn, and after scolding me for using napalm, said she'd come down the weekend after next. Mitzie had invited her. Missed our presence in the house, or Erin's anyway, and had a surprise for her. What did Mitzie have up her sleeve? I placed a door key in the mail in case she arrived late and asked her to bring clothes she didn't mind dirtying.

When not studying her social life apparently consisted of writing me and hanging with Sheryl. They'd discovered a really good Mediterranean restaurant on Commonwealth Avenue and a super cute place in Harvard Square called Grendel's that made the best lamb biryani. "I've been attending Sabbath dinners at the Hillel house on campus with Sheryl, and I've memorized the blessings for the candles, the bread and wine. I'll demonstrate my proficiency when I see you. Is there a prayer I can say before jumping your bones? I miss you so much!"

"I should have asked that English professor in Madison. You do realize that those feelings can be broken down to pure science, to the influence of hormones like oxytocin and pheromones..."

"Oh, how impressive. Do you have any idea what you're talking about?"

"None. I read it in an article in *The New Yorker*. Erin, you know stuff about dopamine, right?"

"Ah . . . yes, I've studied neurotransmitters. Why are you asking? Since when are you interested in science?"

"Well, the article mentioned people with ADHD don't produce enough of it. And you know I was on Ritalin in high school and maybe need more..."

"NO! ABSOLUTELY NOT! This is about cocaine, right? Doesn't take a rocket scientist to figure that out." Everyone did lines in the bathroom. It gave them a lift. Enabled them to reach right through the phone for orders. "It's really bad, especially for someone like you. It actually dulls the dopamine receptors... a real catch 22. You need ever increasing amounts just to stay in stasis, exactly what happened to you on amphetamines. Remember that Paul Revere and the Raiders song? *Kicks just keep getting harder to find*, and let's face it honey, they sure didn't bring you peace of mind, so I'm not interested in a repeat performance. Say thanks but no thanks. It would bring out impulses you can't control. Working on Wall Street provides enough excitement."

"But the excitement must wear off; why else would they be doing it. They're okay."

"Maybe Wall Street's definition of okay. DO NOT USE COCAINE. PERIOD. Am I making myself clear?"

CHAPTER 15

EVERY AFTERNOON KEVIN and a cadre of old timers gathered at Harry's for a drink or two before heading home to the 'burbs, midtown, the upper eastside, or wherever. They'd adeptly weathered the ebbs and flows of the Wall Street economy like experienced sailors' shifting from port to bow, avoiding the turbulent economic waves sweeping their peers overboard, and the water was pretty choppy right now. Occasionally, this survivor's club invited me along, regaled me with stories of the glorious past, and paid for my shots of Glenfiddich.

Kevin drank Irish neat and hoisted his tumbler. "Well, gents, here's to another day before youngsters like Seth here put us out to pasture!" Refills appeared almost immediately. "And lest we forget, to Kuhn Loeb, that once great firm humbled by Lehman Brothers!"

"Here, here." Everyone tossed back their drinks, me included. Around the table they went, naming firms I'd never heard of, either defunct or merged into new entities. The whiskey flowed and the room started to remind me of early films of the German Expressionists, shifting proportions and bizarre angles. I planted my feet solidly on the ground.

"Here's to Goodbody & Company," said another who worked at its successor, Merrill Lynch; we drank to that as well. I thought about Clarence Goodbody finally earning his wings.

"What about you, Arthur?" Kevin asked. "Where'd you go after HB Collins liquidated?" The senior member of the group, Arthur was a popular voice of the Street, his sage quotes appearing regularly in the financial press. With his sparkling blue eyes, red-veined nose and thinning hair combed over a largely bald dome, he was a walking advertisement for St. Patty's Day, which for him, Kevin and the rest of this crew, was every day. Kevin turned to me. "HB Collins was liquidated in 1913!" The guys hooted.

"Very funny, very funny, Kevin," Arthur retorted. "Seth here is a pretty sharp kid. Looks to me like you're training your replacement!"

The bartender had opened a new bottle of Glenfiddich when I arrived; now it was three quarters empty. I staggered up and made it to the men's room in time to toss my cookies. I think. I've no recollection how I made it back to Douglaston, but next morning my head was resting against the toilet bowl, not a good pillow. Amazingly, fifteen minutes under a scalding shower, another offering to the porcelain god and a mug of rocket fuel achieved the improbable, the 5:35 into the city, although the rocking motion and chuga chuga chuga churned my stomach and I barfed again in the foul men's room in Penn Station. It would mark the first time I hadn't arrived at the office before my national sales manager and Kevin pulled me aside after the morning meeting. The national sales manager had given him a message to deliver. Late again and someone else would have my desk, and I wasn't even late, just not early. "No one cares what you did yesterday. You don't get credit for good behavior. You won't even get credit for what you do today. You're only as good as the business you bring in tomorrow."

"But when tomorrow comes..."

"That's right. Now you get it. On and on until the day you retire... or get fired, and if you don't think that's fair, become a teacher. And drink a liquor you can hold; try vodka, its clean and clear. You're not ready to pound Scotch. Got it?" He patted me on the back. "And know your limit. By the way, you look like shit warmed over."

CHAPTER 16

FRIDAY NIGHT, EXHAUSTED from the long work week and hours spent peeling through layers of grime in anticipation of Erin's late arrival, I fell asleep. *Erin lay with me, one leg draped across my groin, swollen breasts pressed into my back, nestled by several little redheaded lumps with tushies up, breath sweetened with mother's milk.* "Our Woodstock," *she whispered.*

She was indeed atop me when I awoke, her body pressed into mine, slowly rocking back and forth, breathing heavily until she cried out and collapsed into me. I shared my happy dream. "That's a lot of Bar and Bat Mitzvah's to pay for," she noted.

In the morning Erin looked about the kitchen and noticed the empty Ball jars. She threw her arms around me. "You've been waiting for me, haven't you?" I nodded. "That is so sweet. You know, I think with a little paint and wallpaper, maybe some furniture, we'll have this place looking downright homey before I move in for the summer. I've been offered an internship with the NYC Department of the Environment on the recommendation of my environmental studies professor. Isn't that fantastic?" The prospect was both thrilling and terrifying.

Mitzie called; invited us for lunch. Over bagels, lox, and crumb buns Erin discussed the apartment, the improvements needed, decorating ideas. Mitzie immediately offered her all the extra furniture and kitchenware stored in the basement, happy to help Erin set things up, insinuating herself deeper into our lives, an intrusion I didn't relish. Erin invited them to be our first dinner guests. The two ladies disappeared upstairs, leaving Dad and I sitting on the front porch drinking coffee and discussing the market, but shortly thereafter, Erin came bounding down, her face flush with excitement. Mitzie had given her a strand of emeralds that matched her eyes.

"Well, we're off shopping. See you guys later," Mitzie chirped, and as the front door closed, I turned to Dad, pondering how the shiksa had morphed into beloved daughter whose worth was measured in emeralds.

"Aren't we suspicious. Can't your mother simply want to do something nice?" That'll be a first. "She and Erin share interests and passions, the most important being you. Things change, Seth, people change, and the girls have had several months to get to know each other. Mom's acknowledging Erin presence in our lives, letting Erin know she's welcome, and your mother's not stupid; she's hoping the furniture, jewelry and motherly attention will anchor Erin here in New York because wherever Erin is, you'll be."

"Erin's my girlfriend. We're not married. Those emeralds must be worth a fortune. You can't expect she'll simply return them when she dumps me."

"You really don't understand women at all, do you? That girl's in love with you. Anyone can see that, and you adore her."

Perhaps my fear of abandonment wasn't logical, but it was visceral. Something had happened to me. Something I couldn't remember. "I sometimes feel I'm on the edge of an abyss, staring into darkness. I know something's lurking there. When I was in Mexico, I had this bizarre waking dream. A toddler version of me was chasing me chasing Jonah through a dark forest. I was pretty wasted at the time, but that image felt so real. It meant something. But I haven't figured out what. Do you know something I don't?"

"Well, like you said, you were pretty wasted. Don't look for excuses to avoid life. You've got to be open to love, even to risks . . ."

"Not risks, Dad, certainties. We're all assigned roles at birth and we've no choice but to play them out. I learned that in Hebrew school."

"I went to Hebrew school too, you know. You've misinterpreted what you heard. Think about it. If we were all under a compulsion to act, what would be the point of the Commandments, of Torah? We have free will to act for good and bad, and when we sin, and we all do, the opportunity to repent. What you and Erin have is real and she'll be your equal in every way; you need that in a life partner. It's uncanny. You and your mother, both hiding behind walls, pretending not to feel. I wish you'd both drop your guards and actually communicate with each other, but that's your journey regardless of what I say. However, you made a wise choice in Erin."

"I never decided anything."

"Well, according to your fakakta philosophy of life, neither did she!" He put his arm around my shoulder. "Let's go downstairs and take a look at that furniture."

CHAPTER 17

I READ EVERY research report and interviewed all sixty analysts, prepared spread sheets tracking their recommendations over time. Common sense said this wasn't baseball where batting five hundred made you a superstar; on Wall Street it made you unreliable. I wanted to market analysts who were either predominately right or unerringly wrong because you could make good money either way, long or short.

The morning research call, the platform for analysts to come up with new investment ideas or provide additional information for pre-existing recommendations, was a cacophony of babel. Sixty analysts, each with their own style, their own approach to delivering information. There was no uniformity. And worse, analysts labored under the misassumption it was the salesperson's responsibility to figure out the key elements of their calls, as if we were mind readers. I wasn't exactly a stock market savant. As Joel had so aptly pointed out, I didn't know shit, but I knew from stage acting you had a limited window to grab someone's attention. Clients were barraged with too many ideas, and if you rambled, if you couldn't cut through the chaff in thirty seconds, it was game over. I'd spent years working off scripts, and I deployed that approach here. Start with the investment conclusion, rattle off the five critical points that supported it, and reiterate the conclusion. Keep it simple. Make it easy for them. Every call, every idea, the same uniform approach I was convinced would garner client mindshare. I discussed this with Kevin, and he agreed but counseled me to keep my head down and focus my approach solely on our clients. Wall Street egos were huge, and it was too easy to step on toes. Wall Street was famous for shooting messengers.

Kevin's clientele was based in Hartford, Connecticut and Boston, Massachusetts. I made the morning research call to the buy side analysts, freeing Kevin to focus on transactional ideas with portfolio managers, the decision makers. My calls were thirty second shots, time enough to leave voicemail on their answering machines or maintain clients' focused attention; like us, they suffered from attention deficit and information overload. It wasn't rocket science, just efficient, bottom-line oriented and consistent, and positive feedback from clients came in top tier rankings in the Mclagan broker polls, which translated into higher commission dollars. I brought research home every night, fearful of falling behind and losing my seat in the game. I'd taken his warning to heart. One slip up and someone else would own the three feet of real estate with my name on it. If I was still killing it in the spring Kevin promised to take me on the road and introduce me around, really show me the ropes.

When Erin came down for my twenty-second birthday in December, I informed her I couldn't go to Portland with her over the holiday. Disappointed, she suggested I throw in the towel. This wasn't the career for me. It fed my obsessive tendencies. I should go to grad school, become a theatre teacher, find a position at a good private school, maybe a university, become active in community theatre. A great way to raise kids. "I don't need material things, fancy cars or big houses or lots of clothes . . ."

"But you like those things. Don't tell me you don't." I'd found a place where my OCD worked for me. And the applause! The thrill of putting big numbers on the scoreboard! This was an actor's dream if there ever was one. I couldn't risk it. I wouldn't. No matter how much I wanted to mend fences with her parents.

"Like is one thing. But I need you."

"I'm gonna show Mitzie I'm as good as her wonder boy!"

"Oh, come on, Seth. If you won't be forthcoming with me, at least stop hiding behind lame excuses. This isn't about your mother." She tapped the side of my head. "It's about avoidance. Stuff you're repressing. Maybe you should talk to Bart."

"Honey, I've got so much research to catch up on. I won't be able to work on the apartment with you this weekend."

"Don't worry, Mr. Evasive. I've already planned out a full day painting and wallpapering. I think I'm going to build a wall unit in the living room, too. Look sweetheart, I just want you to be happy." She reached over to the crate I used as a nightstand, opened her backpack and pulled out an expensive bottle of cabernet sauvignon. "Tonight you're mine, not Lehman Brothers!"

CHAPTER 18

IN MID-JANUARY I had my first annual review with Jake Winters, the square-jawed national sales manager, a handsome middle-aged man, dapper in his Brooks Brothers tailored suit, two toned dress shirt, French cuffs clasped with solid gold bull and bear links, and silk tie, an outfit exceeding my net worth. He'd been a standout wide receiver at Stanford, almost pro but for a career ending injury and spoke in football metaphors. I'd dreaded the meeting, expecting the worst. He'd laughed when Risa gave me that work "advice" and threatened me when I was merely on time for the morning call.

He ignored me while perusing Kevin's McLagan report, statistics that compared and ranked all the Wall Street firms by salespeople and each institutional clients (there was a direct correlation between salesperson rank and commission dollars). I nervously scoped his office, his massive mahogany desk, his Stanford undergrad and Wharton MBA diplomas framed on the wall behind him. Photos of him making spectacular catches, many autographed by football luminaries. I was so out of my league. Finally, after what felt like an eternity but probably only minutes, he looked up as if surprised to still find me there. "I'll be blunt. Given your age and educational resume I was extremely dubious of your ability to perform up to Lehman Brother standards...," My stomach cramped. Here it comes. Mitzie's smirking face dancing in front of my eyes, "but numbers speak for themselves. You've been gaining impressive yardage, really grinding it out, blocking and tackling for Kevin."

Convinced I'd been about to get fired, I bit my tongue to keep from weeping with relief. "Yes, sir. Thank you, sir."

"Lehman took a big gamble with you, over my objections, mind you, but it's paying off, so I'm giving you a two-thousand-dollar raise to twenty-eight grand!" He contentedly sunk deeper into his butter-soft leather armchair while I absorbed that. Two thousand dollars! Kevin's fourth quarter commissions up almost thirty percent in a crappy market environment. It should've been twenty thousand dollars! Whatever. It beat getting fired.

Game face time. "I appreciate your confidence in me. I'll keep breaking through the line, pounding out more yardage. Take our team all the way to number one!" The douchebag enthusiastically clapped me on the back as he ushered me out of his office.

Kevin put his phone down. Asked if I'd received the rah-rah you should be paying us for this privilege speech. "In so many dollars."

Kevin chortled. "Did he tell you to fight for every yard, never lose sight of the goal line?"

"I told him I'd be a key lineman on his team."

"Smart, son, very smart."

CHAPTER 19

BY SPRING ERIN had transformed my hovel into something she'd be willing to live in all summer. Roaches still crawled out of the fridge lining but that was unavoidable. Erin's mason jars now held beans, rice, nuts, flour and sugar. A bookshelf spanned the length of the living room, space for my growing collection of LPs and, not letting that raise burn a hole in my pocket, a new two-thousand-dollar killer stereo system that rattled the walls and would've put the ancient denizens of the building into shock were they not so hard of hearing. There was ample room for our collection of books, magazines and Erin's knickknacks. I was super impressed with Erin's work as were all my relatives, Joel and Marsha particularly; they used a service to change light bulbs and water plants.

Kevin was good at his word and took me on the road, our first excursion a sales-only visit to Hartford and Boston. He showed me how to schedule meetings with precision timing, introduced me to all the buy side analysts, mostly guys in their late-twenties to early-thirties. Gave me face time with the portfolio managers, old guys in their forties and fifties. One asked Kevin if I shaved yet. Kevin had an idea ready for everyone, knew the names of clients' wives and kids, personal stuff that made him flesh and blood. I took mental notes.

After a full day of meetings in Boston, Kevin invited Erin and me to dinner. She was nervous but he was charming, disarming and effusive. He'd told me a good salesman drew people out to talk about themselves, everyone's favorite topic, and he deployed this on Erin. "I'm finally meeting the Irish beauty behind this guy! I understand you're studying architecture at MIT, first architecture school in the country if I'm not mistaken. Any thoughts on what you want to do?" I was impressed he'd taken the time to look that up.

"Environmentally friendly design, considering surrounding parameters like impact on natural habitats. We're not doing that very well right now."

"Sustainable practices add significant cost, barriers to profitability for companies."

"So I'm told, but aren't they part of the cost of doing business? I mean, I'm no expert but it seems logical if costs go up you either pass them through to the customer or readjust the valuation metrics you use to analyze the investment merit of companies. Isn't it just simple math?"

"Sounds like you have a better idea of what we do than you let on, Erin."

"Well, Seth and I discuss this, on those rare occasions he's not working."

"My wife Cathy has the same complaint about my work hours. This is a tough business. You work really hard, and it stresses relationships, but that's the price of admission for the opportunity to make the kind of money most people only dream of..."

"Money isn't everything."

"You're right. Family is everything, but money doesn't hurt. What would you like to order?"

"Is it okay if I order the lobster roll? The menu only says 'Market price' and we can't get lobster in Portland."

She looked agog when Kevin asked if she'd ever had a three pounder. "You see, that's what money's for, Erin, and this is a special occasion." Kevin ordered lobsters for both of them and a bottle of Sauvignon Blanc. The waiter quickly glanced at Erin and me. "And three glasses." I stuck with fried clams. "Someday you two are going to have a family and I must say you'll have gorgeous children, and you'll want to give them everything, things you never had, and this is a career that can make it happen."

"And I love what I do, Erin. Doesn't that count?"

"Of course. It's just most girls worry about other girls stealing their boyfriends. I worry about Lehman Brothers!" She finished the entire lobster.

CHAPTER 20

ERIN MOVED INTO the apartment in late spring. We hadn't lived together in over a year, and only for a short time at that, but it felt seamless. She was a confident woman with a bead on her life and desires, not the dependent girl I'd carried up the steps at 848 Park. And I was on the road now, two days every other week to Hartford and Boston, usually with an analyst in tow hawking new recommendations.

Every morning I'd brew a fresh pot of coffee before catching the 5:35 and leave Erin a cup and a love note. Her schedule typically nine to five, her office an easy walk from Penn Station, although she traversed seedier parts of Manhattan investigating lead paint poisoning compliance issues in city tenements and compiling statistics. It was dangerous work, but focused as I was on my own stressful high wire act, I gave it passing thought, and the Coop filing finally came through, the forty-eight thousand dollars purchase price almost double what I was making. Dad lent me the money. I promised to repay him.

We did our shopping Saturday mornings at the Big Apple Supermarket on Springfield Boulevard, Erin on a first name basis with everyone, atypical in the stratified New York social structure. Whether in the produce section, at the deli counter or cashier line, Erin asked after their days. Always said please and thank you. She'd patiently take a number and await her turn at the deli counter until called, then exclaim "I am not a number; I am a free woman." Bill the deli man, a big fan of *The Prisoner*, would laugh and add a little extra for the pretty Irish girl from Or-e-gone.

We shared the cooking, sang together as we had the night we met. I recalled favorite dishes I'd watch Grandma Matthews prepare in her Woodhaven kitchen, or maybe at our house, I was a bit fuzzy on that, and reproduced her blintzes and kreplach from memory. Sampling them Erin would always say they were almost as good as Grandma Matthews. "The Jehovah's Witnesses believe that at the end of days all your relatives come back down to Earth. You can challenge your grandma to a cook off." I didn't think our apartment could handle the crowd.

We'd jog through tony Douglas Manor weekend mornings, home to several Mafia Dons, one of the safest communities in Queens. On sweltering days we'd drive out to Robert Moses State Park, surf the small waves with beginner surfboards, and stop at Jordan Lobster Farms on the way home. You couldn't get lobsters in Portland. I'd steam and shell them, mix the meat with mayo and celery and pile high in hot dog buns accompanied with chilled chardonnay or sauvignon blanc on our screened in porch overlooking Douglaston Parkway. I still didn't like lobster. All that yucky green stuff got on my hands. But the pleasure it gave Erin made it all worthwhile.

We only argued when she suggested hiking in nearby Alley Pond Park. She wanted to see Jonah's and my special place, the locus of my cherished photo. For weeks I came up with a variety of lame excuses and alternatives, always with the bribe of lobsters. A nagging voice in my head said "Don't go there," and I flashed on the waking nightmare I'd had in the Mexican jungle with Terry and Brian. But once Erin got an idea in her head there was no changing her mind.

The vast pond I remembered, where we'd floated makeshift boats on clear, sparkling water, was little more than a puddle coated with phosphorescent greenish scum. The dense, dark forest of humongous trees that dwarfed the sun merely a patchwork of scrawny-looking trees. I again experienced the unease of being in Jonah's room. Of something unknown. Of something I needed to know. Of something I didn't want to know. I pushed back at it.

The trail leading to the remains of the Vanderbilt Parkway was as I recalled, but now mired in English ivy, strewn with broken tree limbs and weeds, replete with a detritus of broken glass, beer cans and dog shit. The small bridge spanning the moat I'd once imagined protecting a castle was as ornately detailed as I recalled, but the creek itself was murky and dark, littered with garbage, and the storybook castle, the structure that completed the fairy tale tableau, a dilapidated two-story structure of grey stone strewn with more rubbish, empty beer cans, broken glass, used condoms, even a moldy mattress. "Is this your castle?" Erin asked, giggling. It all looked so different. "It was a comfort station for the early motorists on the Parkway. You see the *Gentlemen's Room* and *Ladies Cloakroom* signs engraved in the stonework? Very Victorian, and the stonework is lovely. Must've been pretty grand. Way nicer than our apartment! Probably even had bathroom attendants."

"It's wrong. It's all wrong." *I see you.* I turned in a circle. No one. "You hear that?"

"Hear what?"

"Nothing's as I remember it. I told you I didn't want to come here. You were the one who insisted."

"It was so important to you. I just wanted to share it with you."

"But it's not the same place." *Come out, come out, wherever you are.* I jumped. "You must've heard that!"

"No, I don't hear anything, but memory's unreliable. This place existed in the imagination of a small child and you're not him anymore. Don't let it freak you out."

"But I remember it in such detail, Erin. That photo was taken here, I'm sure of it . . . I think. *Come out, come out, wherever you are.* I glanced about again. "Where are you, dammit. Show yourself!"

"I'm right here."

"Not you. The voice. A child's voice. I heard it before. In Mexico. I know it. It's so loud. How can you not hear it?" Discombobulated, I covered my face with my hands. Tears coursed down my cheeks. "What the fuck is happening to me?"

She pulled me tight. "Maybe you're having some kind of acid flashback from that bad trip? I'm here with you. It'll pass, I promise. It'll be okay, honey."

CHAPTER 21

MORE WALL STREET layoffs followed in the wake of Erin's return to school. Several of Kevin's cronies were "retired," those unscathed confident the layoffs signaled a turn for the better. Arthur explained it to me one afternoon at Harry's. "They do the same thing every cycle; the equivalent of buy high and sell low!"

Kevin agreed. "It never ceases to amaze me. They fire a bunch of us just before business turns, then have to scramble to rehire us."

Hopeful wishing, but I didn't care. Many senior guys at Lehman, having raked in the spoils from the long bull run, didn't care to wait out the bear market, and management saw this exodus as an opportunity to drive profitability by moving salespeople from commission to fixed salaries. Risa bitched when Jake trimmed her million-dollar commission payout to a four hundred thousand-dollars salary; he challenged her to match that elsewhere. Art Thierry commiserated with her, but his chatty assistant Gerri confided his salary was one and a half times that for the same level of business. There was a changing of the guard, Ellen and me cheap labor on the receiving end; commissions or fixed salaries, who cared? It was all blue sky to us, and we were picking up our own accounts, Ellen besting me for the primo ones.

In early autumn we underwrote a public offering for a consumer products company and banking hammered on us to get large indications of interest from our clients. Ellen and I shared a cab to the road show luncheon at the Harvard Club, a WASPy hive buzzing with Worthington's, and without provocation she began to cry. It was disconcerting. Seeing her unmasked again, and so publicly. I asked what was wrong. She was doing great. In the catbird seat.

She dabbed the corners of her eyes with a tissue before extracting a compact from her purse to check her makeup. Her mascara was running. "You guys are such clueless assholes. Smugly convinced working hard and being a team player is all it takes . . . you know, rah-rah, go team, pick up yardage, all that male bullshit. For me that's only a dream. I'll never get real respect for what I'm capable of. No one offered me a cigar at the partners lunch. I'm just a pair of tits and a hot ass, another Risa."

"Oh, but what a hot ass!"

She smacked me on the shoulder. "Don't you dare be flippant with me."

"Hey, I'm just trying to lighten you up a little. We're friends. You can talk to me; vent if you need to. I'd never betray your confidence."

"Not even if you could snare my accounts, huh? Wall Street's first sales saint!"

Maybe that hurt so much because she was the only person I'd let peek through my façade. I stared silently out the window while she reapplied makeup, then turned to me, offering both an apology and explanation. I'd no idea what it felt like to be objectified. The pressures placed on women in the business. "Let's say you do something stupid, like get stinking drunk with Kevin and his cronies. You spend a night throwing up and next morning, with the exception of a hangover, all's right with the world and you and the rest of the boys even joke about it."

"That's not true. Jake threatened me."

"You've no idea what it's like to be really threatened. A girl does that, she wakes up in some asshole's bed feeling used, not sure how she even got there! Your future's a straight line, work hard, achieve success; nothing's gonna get in your way, not family, children, much less old-fashioned sexual discrimination. Everyone and everything subsumed to greater ambition. But I act like a guy, I'm labeled a bitch." I thought back to Lucy's comments in UCC class. "I know exactly how Risa feels, the demeaning things we have to do to get through the minefield of this male chauvinist business; it's not right . . . and it's not fair!"

When I shared the conversation with Erin in Boston later that evening she asked me how many women were in the department; did I think there might be a little prejudice? Had anyone demanded I put out for them to advance my career? "It's reality check time, Seth. You're not exactly a paragon of Woman's Lib."

"I know that. I feel bad for her. It's not fair."

"As nice as it is to see you shake off a bit of your own misogyny, does that only apply to Ellen and Wall Street? It's easy for you to be magnanimous with Ellen. You're not in love with her. But what about me? Let me be more specific. If I had to blow my professors to advance my career ambitions, not that I intend to, would you forgive me?" That rattled me. "See, that's the double standard women deal with. We've all been brainwashed. I watched my feminist mother mollycoddle my brothers, place fewer demands on them, treat them like little princes, and to some extent I do that with you, and God knows how I'm going to react with our own sons. But let's be honest Seth, were the situation reversed, what would you forgive for love?" I started to hyperventilate. A bubble of air trapped inside my chest. I needed to burp but couldn't. Was I having a heart attack? Was she going out with other guys at MIT?

"No, Seth, I have higher standards; I prefer Harvard guys. Jesus, why are you so goddam distrustful and insecure? I'm just saying the double standard is applicable everywhere, not just on Wall Street. You get accounts based on your work performance. She's getting accounts based on work performance and blowing her boss. It sucks, it really does, no pun intended, and it's no different here. Do you have any idea how many times I've heard 'Wow, she's pretty smart for a girl' or 'Hey Erin, wanna see what I can do with my slide rule!'" She was silent for a moment. "Ellen's right. You're all a bunch of chauvinist pigs and it frustrates the hell out of me because I was conditioned to treat you like an impulsive child and not demand you act like a grown man, but things are changing."

CHAPTER 22

DESPITE THE LAYOFFS, the Equity division held its annual Christmas bash in a warehouse loft space in SoHo, a seedy but gentrifying area of lower Manhattan attracting urban pioneers, mostly artists and young, childless professional couples. Junkies were shooting up in alleyways and on corners. A sea of used needles littered the street. Derelicts bedded down under dark shadows of awnings or in doorways. The streets smelled of urine and feces. But that night limos and gourmet catering trucks lined Greene Street for simultaneous parties taking place in various loft spaces. Beautiful, well-heeled people alighted, laughing, people oozing confidence that everything they touched would turn to gold. A steady rainfall cast a cleansing sheen over it all. The pavement glistened as if coated with polyurethane. Erin had not been able to accompany me, finishing up finals before heading home to Portland once again alone. I felt her absence like a hollow ache in my gut.

The party was low key, the usual sushi, fried calamari, stuffed mushrooms and other tasty edibles, a fully stocked top shelf bar and a jazz fusion band. I'd heeded Kevin's advice, made vodka my go-to drink and drowned my aloneness in several Stoli martinis. With Ellen preoccupied with her new boyfriend, the only people my age were the pretty sale assistants, also recent college graduates, mostly from local schools, CCNY, Hofstra, Adelphi, Hunter, hoping to work their way into better positions on the Street. Maybe husband hunting. Gerri, Art Thierry's sales assistant, was dancing by herself on the parquet dance floor. I'd failed to notice her remarkable resemblance to Lucy. Maybe it was her dancing. Or the sexy dress. She must have sensed my eyes on her because she came over, took my hand and ushered me out onto the dance floor.

It was already late into the evening when we stopped to catch our breath. We grabbed drinks at the bar and stood by one of the large open casement windows overlooking the lights of lower Manhattan. Enjoying the bite of cold air. I felt indomitable after a few drinks. The scent of rain commingled with the rank odor of garbage, but everything else, the new Twin Towers, the lights of lower Manhattan, the whole electric horizon, was mine for the taking, a twinkling sea of endless possibilities. She drew closer, a moth attracted to my bright light, her eyes glazed, a whiff of maraschino cherry on her breath. I pointed to the twin towers. "Those blinking red lights atop the towers are gigantic sparklers putting on a show just for us. I'm going to make partner someday. You can take that to the bank."

"I believe it. You're the boy wonder." I blushed. Pleased. "It's true; the rest of them are envious." Taut nipples pressed against the sheer black silk of her V-neck dress. The rustle of silk grazed my back as she brushed against me. Leaned into me. Whispered in my ear, hot breath on my neck. "I'll let you in on a secret, but you can't tell a soul . . . and you didn't hear it from me, okay? One of the partner's secretaries told me the Firm's planning a move to the North Tower. Whataya think of that?"

Gazing again at the Towers looming over the Manhattan skyline I responded, "I hope you're wrong. They're awesome from a safe distance. Doesn't mean I want to work in one of them. With all the shit going on with Russia and Israel and the Arabs, those towers are gargantuan middle fingers daring our enemies to fuck with us. Nah, I prefer to gaze on them from afar."

"Wanna get high?"

"Not in those towers. Seriously, I'm already floating. Weed will push me over the edge. Thanks anyway."

She laughed and patted her handbag. "Not pot, silly. Cocaine. My Christmas bonus from Art."

I immediately experienced a too familiar craving. It wasn't a good idea. My problem with amphetamines. My promise to Erin. Gerri pooh-poohed it all. "This is way better than speed and anyway, I don't see any girlfriend here. Come on, it'll be fun." She grabbed my hand and pulled me into one of the bathrooms, locked the door and removed a small vial from her purse. "Have you got a bill?"

I reached into my pocket. Rolled a twenty into a straw like the guys in the office restroom. "You go ahead. I'll watch." She tapped two good sized lines on the marble counter while I salivated, licked my lips; pearls of sweat drizzled down my cheeks. My heart raced. I want it so bad, but that promise.

Her body quivered after she snorted a line, wiped her nose with her thumb and licked it. Her eyes were saucer-like. "Oh my God! This must be pure shit. It's orgasmic! You've got to experience this." I shook my head. "Oh, come on, do it. You know you want it." I looked at the white powder. Erin's admonition. Don't do it. But it's Christmas. It's a party. Just the once. She's not here; she'll never know. Do it. Don't do it. She snorted the other line, tapped out two more. "You're gonna regret it," she intoned coquettishly. Shit! Stop thinking. Just do it.

The rush comes at warp speed. The bathroom lights explode in all the colors of the rainbow. And the reflection of the girl in the mirror next to me is Lucy! Lucy with her heart-shaped face. Long golden tresses. Delectable pert breasts demanding to be fondled and sucked. Lucy tapping out two more lines, and two after that, clasping my hand and leading me back to the garden, to Woodstock, crushing her pelvis against my throbbing erection, her breasts flattening against my chest. Lucy nibbling my earlobes, biting my neck. Pressing my fingers into her wetness. She isn't wearing underwear. Electricity pulses through my veins as I lift her onto the bathroom vanity, her shapely legs spreading impossibly wide, her pussy opening to me like a blossoming chrysanthemum as she draws my engorged penis into her velvety wetness and rocks me, a symphony of movement that rises to a crescendo until I explode and collapse into her, my face nestling into her swanlike neck. Her pussy greedily pumping me for every last drop of my essence.

Gerri stood there, her hand pressed against my groin, waiting for me to do something. My underpants sticky. "Come on, Seth, we both want it. You and me, Seth. You and me. We'll make partner together."

I pulled her hand away from my crotch and gently pushed her away. "I told you; I've got a girlfriend; I've already broken one promise. I'm not going to cheat on her, too." What was I doing here; this couldn't happen. "Look, you're a nice girl, but..."

"YOU FUCKING ASSHOLE," she seethed, angrily readjusting her clothes. "You lead me on," and stormed out of the bathroom, slamming the door so hard faces turned in our direction. My cheeks were on fire. All eyes on me. I quickly grabbed my coat, signaled a waiting limo and hightailed it for home. I wasn't interested in free love, and it wasn't free anyway. There were strings attached, and mine were attached to Erin.

Next morning, I had the hangover of a lifetime. Consumed with guilt though I hadn't done anything. Well, besides snorting cocaine. And I'd relished those few minutes or however long I was cheating in my mind and heart; it was as real as if Lucy had been there in the flesh. I was faithless. I'd breached Erin's trust. I'd make it up to her. Buy her a new dress or maybe a whole closet-full, anything to salve my guilty conscience. If only she'd been with me this wouldn't have happened.

SHE CALLED BEFORE leaving Boston. Sounded off, agitated yet disconnected, like she already knew or had guessed what I had done. I awaited her verbal assault but instead she began to weep. Had something to tell me. Something difficult that couldn't wait. And begged me to listen, just listen; not yell or get angry or judge. What the fuck she was talking about? Angry about what? I was the one who'd broken his promise. "Something happened last night. Something bad." My stomach began to cramp. "I went to a post finals party thrown by a couple of MIT guys in my Building Structural Systems class, a pretty rowdy affair."

I was relieved. A party at Nerd U. "What did you do, get drunk on spiked fruit punch?"

"Fruit punch spiked with MDA."

My heart stopped. "What? You mean you . . . took . . . acid?"

"It's not acid, Seth. It's a completely different chemical compound, more of a hallucinogenic amphetamine. The same stuff you took at that Phi Psi party and it sounded like fun. . . ."

"Fuck the science behind it, It's a fucking love drug, Erin. Why'd you do that? You know you have a problem with drugs and MDA makes you so physically needy, like you'd fuck any . . . oh God, no, not that."

She started to bawl. "It was a frenzy. Everything so electric. Bass pounding from these humongous speakers, everyone gyrating, undulating like a river, like we were mycelium, all connected. Oh Seth, if only you'd been there to hold me, keep me planted on earth. I completely zoned out. Seth, please forgive me."

I bit my lower lip hard, tasted blood. My heart started pounding, my temples throbbed. "You fucked someone, didn't you?"

"I don't know; maybe. I guess I must have. I'm dancing and next I know I'm waking up in some guy's bed. Someone I didn't even know. I don't remember anything." An endless loop's already playing in my head. Some faceless bastard plowing into my perfect girl, her legs wrapped around him, hands on his butt cheeks, driving him deeper and deeper, pure animal lust; drug-induced sex. "I blacked out. I swear to God I don't remember anything."

"Bullshit. You don't want to remember. You're repressing it because you feel guilty. You cheated on me."

"You're the one with repressed memories, not me. I blacked out. It's happened before."

"You fucked someone else, too?"

"No! Please just listen. In high school I got super high with a bunch of kids. Apparently climbed a water tower. I've zero memory of it. Like my brain never recorded it. I only know because Beth told me. She was so scared she climbed with me to keep me safe." Tears cascaded down my cheeks. "I'm so sorry, honey. It's my fault. I placed myself in that position. As soon as I woke up, I grabbed my clothes and left. I swear to God, I wasn't cheating on you, not in my heart. This could have happened to anyone. It could have happened to you. Sheryl warned me not to tell you, said you'd never understand. You'd be none the wiser, but I love you too much to keep secrets from you and I need to feel secure enough, safe enough, to know I can tell you anything, even something so painful. Please believe me. I'd never knowingly hurt you. It just happened. Please tell me you love me."

"Never lied to me, huh? Remember the March on Washington? You didn't go with Reed students. That night in Twin Falls, while you were in the hospital your dad told me you stayed with friends of your parents."

"I was trying to impress you. A harmless white lie." I thought I'd stroke. My mouth filled with blood from lacerating my lip. Black spiders slithered up my brainstem, scrambled all over my head, in and out of my eyes, nose and ears, blinding me with rage. I would've struck her had she been with me. I know it. I saw terrorized Sinead crumpled on the floor. Erin's face distorted with pain in the car. I'd sworn a holy oath that day in a blizzard. I had to keep it. It had always been inevitable. Our dream shattered into a zillion pieces. I would never love again. "Please say something, Seth. I know I've hurt you. I know how jealous you can get; how afraid you are of being vulnerable. I desperately wish I could change things, but they happened and I'm sorry. You've no idea how sorry. It's breaking my heart to think I've broken yours." She started to wail. "I need to feel your arms around me, if only in words. Please tell me you love me; you believe me. You're my partner and I love you . . ."

Her words evaporated into nothingness. That sense of oneness the first moment our fingers intertwined. The first kiss. Her wonderful dream. A world that suddenly made sense. The heartache knowing it would never be my future. End the inevitable. Do it now, goddamit! "WE'RE OVER." I slammed down the phone. Shattered. Reimagining the unimaginable. And me riddled with guilt for having lusted in my mind!

I needed to erase her, block her as she had her infidelity, and I did, in a blizzard of cocaine. The incredible rush. The super-powered sense I could accomplish anything, even shake off shackles of guilt and regret, plug the gaping hole in my heart. And it was so easy to score. Dealers knew where the money was. They hung around the lobbies of the big Wall Street firms like advertising executives dispensing little white baggies that made everything okay. Expensive but so what? I didn't lead a luxurious lifestyle. I had no lifestyle! I could afford it. I keened for it, craved it, would use it as another tool in my arsenal to drive myself toward partnership, show Mitzie what I was made of.

CHAPTER 23

FIRST WEEK IN January 1975 I sat with Jake for my second annual review. 1974 had been a banner year for Kevin who now controlled the highest grossing account package in the equity division, consistently in the top five of the Mclagan broker ratings. I gnashed my teeth, furiously fiddled with my ghost ring while Jake chipped away at my success like a master sculptor. Lehman Brothers fully expected to be number one given our extensive research staff, our capital exposure and investment banking capabilities. With the prestige and power of Lehman behind me I was merely a glorified order-taker; institutional clients had to do business with us. I could be replaced by a trained monkey! I silently simmered as he, having primed the pump, now proceeded to fuck me over, raising my base to $30K, another two-thousand-dollar increment, percentage-wise smaller than the prior year. This time I wasn't going to take it. Fuck the rah-rah crap. "I see numbers on the Firm's scoreboard, Jake, but not on mine, and it's too bad, really. I liked working for Lehman Brothers."

My unexpected assertiveness took him aback and he applied verbal massage. "Wait a minute, Seth. I think you've misunderstood me. You're doing a great job and have a fantastic future here. And you're only twenty-three years old. Why, when I started out, I had a salary of eight thousand dollars!" And trudged five miles through three feet of snow to a one room schoolhouse on the prairie and studied every night by candlelight. "Think of it as paying your dues for the tremendous opportunity in front of you. Focus on the future."

What future? Headhunters were already calling, major bracket firms looking for young bucks like me. I rose from the chair. "I guess we're finished here. Gotta get back to my desk. Have a bunch of important calls to return."

"Whoa, whoa, wait a minute. Sit back down, please." Cogs turned in his mind as he read my reactions and tweaked his approach. "Lehman's put a lot of money and effort into developing you and we deserve a payback, but as a show of faith because you've earned it, we're also giving you a one-fifth cut of Kevin's payout, your accounts commingled with his."

"Kevin's on holiday right now. Has he signed off on this? I'm not going behind his back."

"It's fair. He won't have any problem with it." Fairness wasn't the point. Of course it was fair. I hadn't received a payout on any of the business I did with any accounts, Kevin's or mine, but he'd been good to me, and I'd learned a lot from him. I wasn't going to screw him. "Look kid, you're killing it. Keep grinding out the yardage. I know you have a goal. Trust me, you'll achieve it." Trust him? Was he kidding? I was forcing his hand. I had mental clarity. Things really did go better with coke!

When Kevin returned, we discussed it over lunch at Harry's. If he wasn't okay with it, I'd demand my own account list or leave. Smith Barney already had an offer on the table for a shitload more money, all guaranteed. "I appreciate your sitting down with me. Just between us, strictly confidential, I want to retire within a couple of years and with you my junior partner, with your drive and ambition, I'll make good money even with the split. I've crunched the numbers; they work, and next year we'll go fifty-fifty. After that my account base will be yours. I'll make certain of it. Deal?" He held out his hand. I looked at it for a second. Trust was a black hole, but it would take a decade of hard work and politicking to reproduce his account package, so I clasped his hand and shook on it. Being assigned his sales associate had been the best thing that ever happened to me. I used to think it was Erin. He removed his glasses and polished the lens with his handkerchief. "You seem edgy. Everything okay? It's one thing to be a workaholic, but you have to maintain perspective or you'll burn out."

"I've one goal, Kevin, partnership, and I gotta stay focused. I'll do whatever it takes."

"I appreciate that, Seth, but you're working all the time. Give yourself a break. At the end of the day this is still a job, not your life, and if you haven't figured it out yet no one's gonna love you here. That comes from home, and you're lucky enough to have a wonderful girl like Erin. There's nothing more important than that, so here's the most important bit of advice I'll ever give you." He glanced across the desk at Gerri. "Don't dip your pen in the company ink." He replaced his glasses and patted me on the shoulder.

CHAPTER 24

WITH THE COUNTRY in the midst of an energy crisis manufactured by the Arab members of the Organization of Petroleum Exporting Countries boycotting the USA in retaliation for our support of Israel, gas station lines were blocks long, prices doubling and tripling in days. Tempers flared. People got into fights. Siphoned gas off others. People abandoned their cars and commuted to Manhattan by rail, the trains unbelievably crowded, everyone jostling for inches of personal space.

Every goddam day letters arrived postmarked Portland, letters I let pile up as I had Mitzie's. Women were all the same. You couldn't trust any of them. How stupid to think Erin different, much less perfect. She called the office several times, and so desperate to hear her voice, to feel that special connection, I had to steel myself to not pick up. I was always in a meeting, visiting clients, out of town, whatever lame excuse I had my sales assistant give her. I knew she was attempting reconciliation and I couldn't let my resolve weaken. Better I fade into memory, become the red-headed boy she once knew, the passing fancy, then risk hurting her. Let her share her special dream and make beautiful babies with someone else. Someone worthier. Someone who wouldn't destroy another person's life in a fit of jealousy.

I consoled myself with endless lines of white powder, every line snorted delivering ephemeral moments of positive feedback, fibers in a porous fabric I was weaving to shield myself from the reality of her. I felt ennobled; took perverse pleasure in it. I didn't need her. Everything was great. I was busy, busy, busy spinning gold out of air, a rabid dog, nose red and running, clothes hanging on me, but I traded up a storm, writing ticket after ticket, a one-man Wall Street money machine. Plenty to keep myself occupied, and girls, hell, they'd fawn over me, a Wall Street power broker, because money, sex and cocaine were an alluring combination. *She's gone but I don't worry: I'm sitting on top of the world.* All I needed was a never-ending supply of coke.

One Friday night, after doing a few lines in the men's room at Harry's, I had drinks at the bar and chatted up a cute girl, another Erin doppelganger, a clothing rep or something. We did some blow in the bathroom, made out for a few minutes, but before things got too hot and heavy, she suggested we go back to her place in SoHo, a nice brick walled studio walk up where we snorted several more lines with Stoli chasers. I fucked her with eyes closed, my hands roaming her lithe body, my imagination filling in any blanks while she blathered on about wanting to introduce me to her parents out in some suburb. I couldn't even remember her name! But when I woke next morning hung over, fuzzy and discombobulated, it was Erin's familiar cocooned shape curled against me with her glorious copper curls spread over the pillow. My heart leapt. It had all been a horrible nightmare. "Oh, Erin," I murmured, enfolding her in my arms, my face buried in her abundant frizzy curls.

The girl sat up on one elbow, still foggy with sleep, clutching the blanket to her chest, her good morning sunshine smile turned scowl when she realized I'd no idea who she was, only the crushing certainty of whom she wasn't. Erin's scent, cinnamon and sugar, the aroma of love, missing. She smacked me repeatedly with a pillow. Said I'd sworn my eternal love while we were having sex. "You bastard. You were thinking of someone else, you... you fucking shithead." Yanking me out of bed, she grabbed my clothes and threw them (and me) out her front door into the hallway. "GET OUT! I hate you; I never want to see you again."

I stood there naked, covering my privates with my clothes as several people passed by. "Tough night, eh?"

I had the dream again that evening. *Jonah and I were in our space ship exploring unchartered reaches of outer space, powering past planets and other comets when suddenly a huge meteor heads directly toward us, and we veer our craft to the left, then right, trying to avoid an imminent collision but it's too late, we go careening off course, heading for a black hole, and I reach out to Jonah but he's a jack-in-the-box, grinning and boinging up and down singing "All around the mulberry bush the monkey chased the weasel. The monkey thought 'twas all in fun. Pop! Goes the weasel" and our escape hatch opens, sucking all the air, and me, from our ship, and I tumble alone and powerless into the vast black vacuum of space toward a black hole looming larger and larger and it's going to swallow me and I'm so scared, so scared, so scared.*

I woke trembling, shielding my inner eyes from searing laser-like light seeping through fissures in the barrier that shielded me from the unknown. Horror-struck, I finally understood. The black hole was the gaping maw of the Balrog monster, a revelation that made returning to bed impossible. I wandered aimlessly about an apartment that bespoke of Erin's pervasive imprint: the bookcase, the wallpaper, the soft colors on the walls, the mason jars filled with beans, rice, grains and flour, the stuffed sheep on my bed, everything, everything said Erin, even the scent on the pillow I hadn't laundered for fear it would dissipate. I had destroyed the one good thing in my life, and misery brought me no perverse masochistic pleasure. It merely made me infinitely sad. I suffered a keening ache as if my heart had been ripped asunder by an incompetent surgeon. I saw the monster's image reflected back in every window, every mirror. I swept up vials and baggies of cocaine and flushed them down the toilet, weeping for my godforsaken soul as I snatched her last letter from the unread pile.

January 10, 1975

Dear Seth,

You haven't responded to any of my letters or calls and I can only assume you meant what you said: we were over. It is difficult to find words to express how much you have hurt me. What happened at that party did not change the way I felt about you; you're the only man I've ever loved or wanted. I was drugged that night; not myself. I'm not trying to absolve myself for what happened, but while I'd do anything, give anything, to undo it, it happened. The last thing I'd ever wanted to do is hurt you, but I had to tell you because that secret would have been a wedge between us, and I couldn't live that lie. I needed to talk to you, my partner, the one person in the world I should be able to count on, and you threw it back in my face, demonstrating no faith or trust in someone so loving and trusting she willingly bared her soul to you. That was a rape of my heart.

    I made a mistake, Seth, and I am so, so sorry, but it pales compared to the mistake you are making now. You are throwing away something so precious, so rare, the true love I know you feel for me. I have always been the missing part, that piece that makes you whole, and you know it. I hope and pray you come to your senses, and soon, because my heart is shattered, and I will have to mend it so I can carry on without you. Please don't make me do that.

I love you so much,

Erin

Three long weeks had now passed since that letter, too much time. It fell to the floor. What had I been thinking? I so feared abandonment I'd made it a fait accompli. There was only one truth: a world without Erin, without her dreamy eyes and gentle touch, without sharing whatever happened in our lives, the joys, the struggles, even our human frailties, was not one I could live in. Life without her was meaningless and I had to face her, tell her the sordid truth of what I'd done, even if it threw her into the arms of another man. I could only pray I hadn't already done so. I dialed Erin's number and Sheryl answered. "Jesus Christ! Do you have any idea what time it is?"

"I'm sorry, but I need to speak to her."

"How could you hurt her like that; how could you break her heart? I hope she tells you to go to Hell." There was a long pause, my heartbeat ticking away the seconds. Then a quiet "Hello."

"I need to speak to you in person. I'll be there Friday night." I hung up before she had the chance to say no.

CHAPTER 25

DAVE LOGGIN'S NEW Top 40 song "Please Come to Boston" got lots of airplays on the drive up. Foreshadowing or hopeful wishing? I parked on Lee Street, just off Central Square, walked up to number 16, a somewhat down at the heels three story mid-19th century apartment building occupied by college and grad students. The front door was, as always, unlocked and I climbed the dark stairway to the third-floor apartment and knocked. Sheryl quickly answered, coat in hand, obviously there to run interference for Erin if necessary. She glared at me and silently brushed past, turning just before the steps to tell me how happy she was to see me so wretched, then bounded down and out into the chilly winter night.

Erin was sitting cross-legged in a shabby, oversized chenille chair in their small front parlor framed by large arched bay windows, a velveteen throw across her shoulders, an open book in her lap. Her wild copper penny hair blazed in the soft light of the Art Deco lamp beside the chair but her eyes, those emerald eyes that had dazzled me the moment I met her, were absent their inner flame and I was appalled to be the author of such sorrow. I prostrated myself before her. Begged her forgiveness for not trusting her, not forgiving her, and even were it the death knell of our relationship, I confessed to sleeping with another woman. Relationships foundered on secrets and lies. I'd never deserved her anyway. "Tit for tat, huh? I didn't sleep with another man on purpose."

"I wasn't trying to get even. I was trying to move on, but I can't live without you."

"Why try to destroy us? "

"Every time I closed my eyes all I could see was you making frenzied love with some faceless guy."

"Then open them! You've always had one hundred percent of my love."

"But it's so hard to stop obsessing . . ."

"Then deal with it. I can't help you with that. Only you can. Your silence hurt more than anything. Worse than sleeping with that girl. Worse than using cocaine."

"I don't know what to say. I wouldn't blame you for telling me to fuck off."

"I don't want you to fuck off. I want you to stop obsessing and thinking dark thoughts. They're twisting my insides as well as yours. Don't you realize that? You don't live in a vacuum. I made a mistake. I'm not perfect, but neither are you and I won't tolerate your disrespecting me, breaking promises, sleeping with other women, doing drugs or keeping secrets. Stop expecting the worst in people. Stop wallowing in despair. Stop hurting yourself. God forgives those who forgive themselves. Being happy is a choice only you can make; but I won't remain in your life unless you do."

"I choose you. I choose being happy."

"I'm going to hold you to that. Promise me we'll never talk about what happened at that party ever again. Break that oath and I'll leave you ... after I eviscerate you."

I promised, but I knew I'd never erase the erotic image of Erin with another man. Painful though it was, it perversely fed my masochism. This secret I did not share.

CHAPTER 26

I MARKED THE days until the end of her school term refusing to believe my good fortune until she was actually physically present in the apartment. Erin anchored me to the Earth. She was everything good in my life and I wanted to be the same in hers.

We were tentative at first, having hurt each other, and I worked on being more open and trusting, more sensitive to her moods and feelings, and remarkably, our interwoven lives flowed more seamlessly. She returned to the NYC Department of the Environment as a paid intern, and changes were afoot at Lehman as well. Kevin took more personal time, leaving me to play lead with our accounts. I made most of the personal appearances, alone or with an analyst in tow, scheduling lunches with analysts and dinners with the PM's, always armed with ten fresh ideas I could rattle off to demonstrate the breadth and diversity of Lehman's research product and my unique focus on clients' individual interests. Kevin, the man of many maxims, told me good salesmen were circus ringmasters setting the stage, shining the spotlight on each analyst and bringing everything to a transactional conclusion. Always in control. And his advice worked. Lehman's analysts vied for my attention, pissing off other salesmen. With the exception of Kevin, I was friendless, Ellen having departed for a guaranteed two-year contract at Bear Stearns, but as he had noted, if I was looking for love, Wall Street was not the place to find it. Surrounded by vultures circling Kevin's accounts, waiting for me to stumble, I redoubled my efforts to become Jake's most valuable player without the benefit of mother's little helper to get me through my busy day.

Having already built the wall unit, several bookcases and retiling the apartment's bathroom, Erin now spent evenings entranced in *The Upholstery Bible*, reupholstering a dilapidated old suede couch with frayed arms and missing buttons, a cast off from Joel and Marsha. Another Ms. Fixit like her mother who called one night asking Erin to come home for a visit, the McGuire's refusing to come East, claiming Portland's summers were too lovely, though I think they wanted to avoid me. They despised me for the psychic pain I'd inflicted on her, stupefied she was still talking to me much less living with me. But Erin, every bit as stubborn as her mother, demurred; her internship ran through August, and I was always working. They pressed her; that still left a week before classes started. Even her brothers missed her. "Really pulling out the big guns, huh? Hold on a sec. Let me ask Seth. He hasn't taken a single day off since starting at Lehman."

"HE DOESN'T HAVE TO COME" boomed through the phone. I'd turned her wonderful family against me. I understood their anger. I'd feel the same way.

"I'm not coming without him."

THE THOUGHT OF asking Jake for any time off terrified me. I steeled myself before walking into his office. This was a test of my priorities. I'd been in the game long enough to know Wall Street was a lifestyle, a commitment to an inflexible mistress demanding all your time and attention. You don't get something for nothing. There were always strings attached, ours spun of gold. He put down the sales report he was perusing. "Just looked at your numbers, Seth. Really racking up the yardage! You're making the other guys nervous."

"They all hate me."

"If you're looking for love you're in the wrong game."

"Kevin says that all the time. That's what I need to talk to you about. I've been here two years without a single day off and believe me, I wouldn't ask now, but my girlfriend wants me to fly to Portland to spend Labor Day week with her family."

"Meeting the parents, huh? Must be serious. How'd you find time for a social life? Ha ha." He came from behind his desk and leaned against it. "Portland, Maine. Love it up there. Did I ever show you the photo Cindi took of Johnny and me fly fishing on the Kennebec River?" He picked up a framed photo, Jake and a smaller copy of himself standing waist deep in a river, waders held up by suspenders, fishing lures dangling from floppy hats, and sighed. "Johnny caught his first rainbow trout up there. Wish I had more time for stuff like that." He repositioned it on his desk amidst other photos of his family engaged in various activities, none including him. "Sometimes I wonder if this is worth it," he muttered but caught himself. "So, how long you guys been together?"

"Erin's from Portland, Oregon. We met in college, but she transferred to MIT when I graduated."

"Portland OR E GONE ... I hear there's some pretty good fly fishing out there."

"Wouldn't doubt it. Beautiful country."

"MIT, huh? Smart girl. Anyway, Firm policy entitles you to two weeks paid vacation."

"I know the policy. Will I still have my desk if I take any of it?"

"Kid, you just keep putting those numbers on the board. Clear it with Kevin; it's fine with me. This serious? You guys planning to get married?"

"I hope so, if she'll have me."

He lightly patted his upper lip. "Say, I've got an idea. Help you move that process along a bit. Why don't you take her to La Grenouille for dinner Saturday night?" La Grenouille, a sanctuary for the rich and famous, not guys scraping by. "As my guests, of course. The maître d' will take care of the rest. You couldn't find a more romantic place. Consider it a promotion present. I've been meaning to send a memo to HR. Taking your base to sixty thousand, in line with the other senior guys. Long overdue, and with you seriously involved, believe me, you're gonna need more cash flow. A limo will pick you up at your place in Douglaston at 7:30 Saturday night. Have a great time and keep me up on your plans. You know, kid, I've watched you develop into one helluva salesman. You've got a great future here, and I want you and Erin to be part of the Lehman Brothers family."

ERIN'S MOUTH DROPPED open. "SIXTY THOUSAND DOLLARS! I swear, my head is spinning. WE'RE RICH! We can buy a bedframe for our mattress. No more sleeping on the floor! I can't wait to tell my parents."

"And we have dinner reservations at La Grenouille Saturday night."

"Even the name sounds expensive. And I don't have anything appropriate to wear."

"It's a promotion gift from Jake. He's sending a limo for us. Buy a new dress; something black."

She called Mitzie for advice, and I could hear her through the phone. "La Grenouille! Jerry took me there for our twenty-fifth wedding anniversary. The place is drop dead gorgeous."

"Seth thinks I need a black dress, Mitzie."

"Every woman needs one. How are you going to accessorize it?"

"Well, I have the silver heart, or the emerald necklace you gave me."

Within the hour she and Dad were at our door with a black satin dress and a strand of cultured pearls, the same ones Mitzie wore the night they met at Beloit. Erin was blown away. "I saw the dress at Saks Fifth Avenue and bought it for your birthday, but now's as good a time as any. Let's go try it on." Mitzie and Erin disappeared into our bedroom. Always drawing Erin deeper into her web.

"I know those pearls were expensive, Dad; I promise we won't lose them."

"I hope not; they're Erin's now."

The satin dress fit perfectly, hugging every curve of Erin's lithe body, the scoop neck just low enough for the pearls to rest in the subtle valley of her cleavage. Mitzie embraced Erin. "I'd hoped for a daughter to give my jewelry to, and now I have you, Erin. I'm so lucky." I couldn't help but be suspicious of Mitzie's motives, but Erin had demanded I focus on the positive. So I tried. I really tried. And at exactly 7:30 Saturday night a black stretch limo pulled up in front of the building. A well-dressed driver came around and opened the door for us, curious neighbors peering down from windows. "Mr. Matthews, Mrs. Matthews, please . . ." He ushered us into the vehicle. Erin gave me a flitting smile. She'd never been in a limousine. It was cavernous, and I recalled happy early childhood memories of Dad's new Cadillacs before their elegance morphed into cringeworthy symbols of bourgeois excess. A working-class hero was something to be but sinking back into the plush butter-soft leather I realized I no longer fit that category.

A bottle of Moet Chandon Brut Imperial was chilling in a small, built-in fridge, crystal stemware in the side door. "Jake says enjoy!" the driver said. I popped the cork, careful to hold it away from us as an enthusiastic burst of bubbly showered the plush carpet. We drank it all, kissed our way through the Midtown Tunnel and across town, only coming up for air when the driver, Tony, came around and opened the door for us. Erin reapplied her lipstick before we alighted. "Have a fabulous time," he said. "I'll be out here when you're ready to leave."

LA GRENOUILLE, ON Fifty-Second Street just off Fifth Avenue, was sheer elegance. Massive crystal vases dispersed throughout the large dining room were artfully arrayed with tall flowers and tree branches; smaller, similar centerpieces adorned each table. Erin took it all in and gushed, "That's Baccarat crystal, Seth."

Expensive art lined the walls, including works by Monet and Renoir. Soft peach lighting cast a delicate sheen on snow white tablecloths, and mirrored walls reflected it all as we were ushered across a room full of skeletal women awash in diamonds and pearls, all in basic black, and well-groomed men in power suits. It sure beat the Gun Club. We were led to the chef's table where the maître d set a silver wine bucket on the marble tabletop, extracted a chilled, glistening bottle of Billecart-Salmon Brut Rose, and displayed it. "With Lehman Brothers compliments. May I?" He recounted the famous people who had dined at this table as he poured the rust hued bubbly into the fluted crystal. President and Mrs. Kennedy, Sir Lawrence Olivier, the Burtons, Dali, Jagger and now two kids playacting adults. "Only the few get to experience this, and I am sure you noticed everyone looking at you, wondering who these beautiful young people are." He beamed at Erin. "Your young gentleman must be quite important at Lehman Brothers. Bon Appetit, Monsieur, Madam!" He inclined his head to us and left.

Erin, bathed in the soft peach light, leaned across the table, a mischievous glint in her eyes. "He forgot to check my ID!" She looked so stunning I wanted to sweep my arm across the table, scatter the crystal and flowers and silver and porcelain and ravish her on the spot. "What are you thinking, Seth? You've the sweetest expression on your face." She reached out and squeezed my hand. "Thank you for asking for the week off. I know that was a big deal and it means a lot to me."

She ordered lobster in a curried sauce for her main, lobster bisque for appetizer. "We can't get lobster in Portland," she confided to our waiter, who responded, "Very good Madam. Excellent choices." After ordering the Dover sole served table side, with bass tartare and carpaccio as an appetizer, I apologized for the lack of a lobster dessert, but she said not to worry. Dessert would come later.

Tony put up the privacy glass on the trip home. "Bon Appetit!"

CHAPTER 27

EVERY SATURDAY AFTERNOON she'd drag me away from my interminable pile of research to spend a few hours surfing at Robert Moses State Park. We'd share a couple of beers, watch the best surfers for pointers. One afternoon, she zoned in on this one dude riding inside the curve like a pro. He could've been one of her Outward-Bound buddies. "Check him out, Seth. He's totally choka." Choka? "Get with the lingo. That means he's dynamite, Seth." And he was. Unbelievably graceful. Reminded me of an older, buffer version of John from Haven Hall. His surfboard was unlike any I'd ever seen. Radically different than ours. "I've got to get a closer look at that board," Erin said, rising and brushing sand off a tight little ass barely concealed by her string bikini.

The guy gave her an appreciative once over, drinking her in. "It's a Ben Aipa Split Rail Stinger, shorter than your boards; more maneuverable. Wanna check 'er out?"

"Really? I mean, I don't want to be a beach leech or anything."

"No worries, Betty. But don't blame me if you can't go back to your old ride." Was he talking about me? She duck-dived through the breakers, caught a perfect wave, cutting in and out like a pro, shrieking with delight while the guy hooted and clapped. He looked my way. "Check her out, brah. She's just goin' off." Afterwards, they chatted animatedly for several minutes.

"Nice ride?" I asked when she returned.

"Dynamite," she beamed.

"What were you guys talking about?"

"He asked me out. Figured you for my brother."

"What'd you tell him?"

"Yup, he's my brother all right. Just tell me when and where, brah!" She started to laugh. "Oh my God, you should see the look on your face. Priceless!"

"You've every right to do as you please. Like you said, I don't own you."

"So, you don't care?"

"Of course I care, it's just after . . . after . . ."

"Seth, sweetheart, I'm kidding. I was flattered but told him we were a couple. Probably broke his heart." She stretched out in the sand. "He'll just have to get over it."

"If you ever leave me, I'll convert to Catholicism and enter a monastery."

"Hah! Another Jewish priest. Don't most Jewish mothers think their sons are the second coming?" I wouldn't know. She lay across me, her head on my chest. "Remember when we were kids, how interminable summers seemed; this one's going by way too fast, but you know what?" She sat up. A glint in her eyes. "We can surf our way around the world, toss everything else to the winds, an endless summer, you and me. What do you think?"

"If you want one of those Ben Aipa surfboards I'd better get back to that pile of research."

We stopped at the lobster pound on the way home. Erin went off to shower and wash her hair while I boiled the two pounder, let it cool for a few minutes, cracked the shell and extracted meat I mixed with mayonnaise and celery. I was cleaning the green goop off my hands when I felt warm, damp breasts press into my back. Her nipples tickled me. She kissed the nape of my neck. Hands slid down my torso and deftly untied my surf shorts, which slipped to the ground. She turned me around. "My lobsterman. I can't get you in Portland." But she could, and after making love, she asked if everything was okay at Lehman. She noted how much I loved my job, how suited I was to it. How much I craved the adrenalin rush.

"Everything's fine at Lehman, but I want you to be happy. I'd give it up for you."

She grabbed my hands across the table. "That's so sweet."

"They have good coffee out there, right? And I can get away from Mitzie."

"Your mother's not as bad as you make her out."

"How can you defend her? She treated you like shit. And she's never loved me."

"She was wrong, and she's admitted it. Trying to protect her turf. Afraid you'd move three thousand miles away and she'd lose you, too. You're all she's got, honey. Hasn't it ever occurred to you she's as insecure as you and just as desperate for your love?"

"No. When the private detectives told them they couldn't find Jonah and presumed him dead she wished I'd died instead. I was at the top of the stair landing. Heard every word."

"Are you sure you didn't misinterpret them? You're prone to that, you know, jumping to pre-ordained conclusions. Maybe she wished she'd died instead.

Under stress we don't always say exactly what we mean, and you've conditioned yourself to assume the worst, to obsessively analyze every word, search for innuendo, catch someone in a lie because you're afraid to trust them. You promised you'd stop doing that."

"I'm trying. I'm doing better, aren't I?"

She took my hands. Pressed them to her lips. "I'm not a psychologist like Bart but I play one on the Seth Matthews Show. I know what I'm talking about. I've no doubt she hurt you, but it cuts both ways, and if you're going to find true peace with yourself you have to find it in your heart to forgive others, and that starts with your mother. I know you want her in your life. And just so you know, east or west coast, I'm happy so long as I'm with you."

CHAPTER 28

BEFORE FLYING OUT to Portland Erin presented the findings of her Lead Paint Poisoning Project to the NYC City Council. Mayor Beame took a photo with her, gave her a letter of commendation for her work and the department offered her a fulltime job upon graduation, but she seemed reticent to commit. Was she reconsidering my offer to move? Finding employment in Portland that matched my personality would be like pissing up a rope!

The flight was exhausting. We arrived late afternoon, the temperature hovering above ninety. I'd anticipated cool, misty weather, but the reception I received from the McGuire's was chilly enough. Famished, Erin told her mom she could eat a horse, and Mrs. McGuire freaked. "Oh my God! You're pregnant!" The only rationale she could imagine for Erin staying with me.

"No Mom, just hungry. We tried the special Hindu meal; got two dry rice cakes! Never thought I'd be envious of people eating airplane food." She looked about. "Where are the brothers who missed me so much?"

"Home playing that stupid board game; I swear it's more addictive than TV."

Dr. McGuire gently put his arm around his wife. "Mom made her specialty, Dungeness crab cakes!" Bet Erin can't get those in New York! In fact, they were delicious, way better than lobster, and I would've enjoyed dinner had tension at the table not been so palpable. Mrs. McGuire glared at me. El diablo! Grateful when Dr. McGuire uncorked a bottle of wine. A Pinot Noir. Swirling the inky liquid in his glass, he let the first sip roll around his tongue. "This is from Erath Vineyards, a present from one of my students. It's pretty good."

I mimicked him and nodded in agreement. "Dark and brooding. A liquid version of film noir." No one laughed but it seemed a safe enough topic. I mentioned trying lots of different wines at work. Big mistake. Mrs. McGuire looked aghast. Now I'm an alcoholic, too! I fumbled for words. "I mean, not every day; it's served at road show luncheons and client dinners."

Dr. McGuire tried to help. "Do your parents serve wine with dinner?"

"Actually, my father drinks Pernod. It smells like anise."

"Eww!" Liam interjected. "Smells like an anus? I'm gonna form a band, call it Searching for Uranus, get it? Ur-anus." Even Mrs. McGuire laughed.

AFTER DINNER I offered to help with the dishes, but Mrs. McGuire pushed me into the adjoining family room. "Go play that stupid baseball game with the boys." She wanted time alone with her daughter.

I chose the 1961 New York Yankees, as I had on my prior visit, but really wasn't into it. I wanted to eavesdrop on Erin and her mom, could just make out their conversation in the kitchen. I wanted her approval, to be accepted into the family.

Liam complained it wasn't fair; he wanted the 1961 world champs, so I took the 1927 Yankees, the original Murderer's Row. Ryan took the World Series champion 1967 St. Louis Cardinals. "I've got Steve Carlton and Bob Gibson in my starting rotation. I'm gonna crush you guys." I appreciated how they simply accepted me as a given.

Erin and her mom were at the sink. Mrs. McGuire washing, Erin drying. "The brothers like Seth. Can't you be nicer to him? He's sorry for what happened; he knows you're angry. He said you should be."

"Of course, we are. He hurt you..."

"Mom! Speak lower. He can hear you!"

"So what? Let him hear. I don't care. Why him, Erin? There are so many nice young men right here. I thought you loved Portland."

"I do, Mom, but I love him more. He makes me feel beautiful. He believes in me; encourages me to follow my dreams. I'd never have considered MIT without his push."

"All I know is one day you're leaving for college and next we know you're living with that boy! You never gave yourself a chance to date anyone else. You gushed over that boy Randy when you came back from that Outward Bound trip. Beth says he's right here in Portland and still available."

Ryan poked me in the ribs. They were awaiting my turn.

"He's passionate and intense and..."

"Exasperating?"

"He blames himself for his older brother's disappearance."

"I didn't know he had an older brother. Children often blame themselves when incomprehensible things happen to their parents or siblings."

Ryan knocked on my forehead. He held out the dice with a look of exasperation.

"Has he talked to you about it?"

"A bit, but there's more behind it. He was adopted. His parents won't tell him anything and it haunts him. I'm trying to help him."

"Listen Erin, I feel for him but why saddle yourself with a renovation project?"

"Because I see all the beauty inside him."

Dice bounced off my head, jolting me. Ouch! I'm going, I'm going.

"Mom, something's been troubling me. About his brother. What if you're right, what if . . . wait, hold on a second." The door shut.

Ryan threw his cards down in disgust. "Geez, Seth. Your head's not in the game. You're making stupid moves, not even trying to win."

Minutes later Erin walked in, sat next to me. Put her arm around my shoulder. I looked up questioningly. "Girl talk," she said with a peck on my cheek before making strategic moves for my team. Liam and Ryan protested. Erin always won.

CHAPTER 29

WE SET OUT early next morning for Maupin, Oregon, in brilliant sunlight that blasted through the deep gorge demarcating the states of Washington and Oregon. Dr. McGuire had booked a white-water rafting excursion on the Deschutes river two hours east of Portland. Absent snow-blinding blizzard conditions and a speed-crazed mind, I could now view the majestic cliffs that loomed a thousand feet on both sides of the Columbia River. Wind-rippled evergreens dotted the reddish-brown rock face, gradually giving way to dusty pastel browns of the high desert plain.

Upon arrival, I left the airconditioned car for hot, sauna-like herbal scented air, and once outfitted with life jackets and paddles climbed into a rubberized craft manned by a guide, another Outward-Bound type. He instructed us on the do's and don'ts of the eighteen-mile rapid run down the turbulent Deschutes, whose churning water whipped up a froth as it rushed through an obstacle course of jutting rocks and boulders before squeezing through a narrow canyon of low hanging cliffs tickled pale yellow by the sun. I looked at the McGuires, all gung-ho, Erin now engaged in a heated debate with her siblings over who got to ride the bull first that ended with a round of Rock/Paper/Scissors.

The boys groaned when Erin gleefully thrust her arms in the air, turned to me with a triumphant high five. We'd won, whatever the fuck that meant. "We get the class four rapids!" Oh joy. "It's like riding a bucking bronco. Hang your legs over the front end of the boat and hold fast to the ropes. Just do what I do." Erin wasn't the only danger junkie in the family. They were all nuts.

I mimicked her moves and held on with a vice-like grip for dear life as we launched, scared shitless but resolutely determined to play the part of Outward-Bound man, if a white-knuckled one. If I fell in, I'd swim for the side, boulders never more than a few meters from the craft. Or drown. It was that simple.

Entering a deep pool, the guide instructed us to "Lean in, lean in" and

"Dig, dig, hard forward" and the McGuire's paddled furiously. At one point, the raft fast approaching a huge boulder, our guide shouted "High side, high side" and the McGuire's shifted to the downstream side of the raft to avoid a collision but Erin and I had no control over anything riding the bull. Maybe I'd been overly disparaging of Dad's halcyon boating jaunts with ham sandwiches, martinis and itsy-bitsy teeny bikinis.

We cartwheeled around another rock, the raft turning sideways as it continued to plunge downriver toward a deep drop between two large boulders, the water churning, the current upwelling into a convex mound. With our bird's eye view of what lay ahead all I could think was FUCK ME as Erin grinned and looked at me with a wild glint in her eyes. "ARE YOU READY? THIS IS A CLASS FOUR RAPID. LEAN BACK!"

Prepared for certain death, we approached a roiling whirlpool and plunged below the surface, a huge wall of water engulfing the craft before bottoming and springing up like a rocket, almost airborne. Erin shrieked with delight as we hit the surface again with a resounding smack, drenching us all. I was still in the raft. Exhilarating in retrospect, an adrenalin kick like speed or cocaine or doing a monster trade. Erin needed it as much as me.

The McGuire's whooped it up as we navigated a series of drops that resembled a staircase, a brief respite before the guide screamed "BACK PEDAL, BACK PEDAL" as we approached a flat, foamy surface backflow. It didn't look dangerous, not like that class four, but Erin pointed to a large boulder looming just below the surface of the water as we cartwheeled around it. "WOULDN'T WANT TO GET CAUGHT ON THAT."

I happily relinquished the bull when Ryan and Liam demanded a turn, and we all exchanged high fives as we brought the raft ashore just shy of an impossible plunge into a deep chasm where native fishermen with gigantic poles and nets lined both sides of the cliff face angling for huge, iridescent salmon.

I was ready to picnic and swim in a placid pool formed by a column of rocks diverted away from the rapids with the rest of the McGuire's, but Erin insisted we hike along the cliffs overlooking the river to some favorite spot. I immediately flashed on Lena and Umo disappearing into the mystical forest of raining leaves at Devil's Lake. Fifteen minutes later Erin stopped and pointed. "This is it; where we jump."

Jump? I looked down, the water so sparkling clear I could see the bottom maybe fifty feet below. She couldn't be serious. "Don't be such a wuss. I've been doing this since I was a kid. Piece of cake." Without further ado she jumped off the edge shouting, "YIPPEE," entering the water feet first, disappearing below the surface for an instant before bobbing back up. Sunlight sparkled off the sheen of water on her face. "Your turn. Come on." She flapped her elbows as I backed away from the edge and made chicken noises. "Come on, scaredy-cat. Guess I know who'll never be an Outward-Bound man."

I'd once played a trust game at a Lehman corporate event. You'd let yourself relax and fall backwards into waiting arms, and now, preternaturally calm, I simply jumped. And it was so curious. This body below me gasped for breath, crushed under a weight as suffocating as those leaded X-ray shields they place over you at the dentist's office. I reached out toward a distant bright, reddish aura at the end of a long corridor. The beyond; the unknown. And I was still hovering over myself when, with a resounding whack, I fell back into myself. My lungs greedily sucked air like an accordion and the reddish aura morphed into Erin on her haunches pumping my chest, blowing air in my mouth pleading, "BREATHE. BREATHE. BREATHE."

I gagged. Vomited up river water. "STOP, YOU'RE KILLING ME." The pressure on my chest so excruciating.

She sat back, sobbing, "I thought you were dead. I've never been so scared. I'm sorry I teased you. Please be okay."

"I'll . . . be . . . fine," I rasped through grit teeth. Anything to stop her resuscitation efforts. "Wha . . . what happened?"

"You belly flopped, hit the water with a huge SPLAT, out cold, floating face down. I was so scared. I dove back in and brought you to shore. I'm so sorry. Please forgive me. I don't know what I'd do if anything happened to you."

My yelps echoed through the canyon as she helped me up and supported me as we made our way back to the swimming hole. The boys were having a water fight. The senior McGuire's sunning themselves on the narrow strip of beach. Hearing our approach, Mrs. McGuire took one look and gasped, "My God, Erin. What did you do to him?"

"He belly-flopped."

"Not that cliff?" Erin nodded sheepishly.

Dr. McGuire placed his hands on the sides of my head. My blurry eyes were going in and out of focus. A kaleidoscope of images circled about me. I was wheezing, struggling for air. "Carol, we have to get him to an emergency room. I think he's punctured a lung."

Erin started to cry. "Oh Daddy! He's going to be okay, isn't he?"

"Why'd you let him jump?" Mrs. McGuire scolded. "He's from New York!"

Liam took it all in, clearly impressed. "That was sooo stupid. Mommy and Daddy said you were a fucking idiot, but I . . ."

"LIAM!"

X-rays at the Hood River Memorial Hospital revealed two broken ribs, a broken collar bone, dislocated shoulder and my second broken nose. My right arm was taped to my chest, swaddled in bandages. The McGuire's so distraught

I tried to make light of it all when I reappeared in the waiting room, dragging one foot and making grumbling noises. Liam smiled. "I know. You're Boris Karloff as *The Mummy*."

In tears, Erin carefully embraced me. I assured her I'd be fine. Just needed to keep bandaged for several weeks; time and extra strength aspirin will do the rest. "I don't want to live without you, Seth, not ever. Will you marry me?" The happiest moment of my life.

PART FIVE
THE POWER BROKER

CHAPTER 1

THE INSTITUTIONAL EQUITY division was subdivided into equity sales, trading and research. Atop each desk sat a squawk box; anything said in one department could be heard on every desk, assuming anyone cared to listen. Sales and research personnel seldom interfaced with the traders; each department deemed sacrosanct by its denizens. Class distinctions had a lot to do with it, sales and research manned chiefly by sons of privilege, private schools and Ivy League colleges, trading more egalitarian, personnel often advancing from the floor of the NYSE or Amex, educated in public schools and the SUNY system. Mistrust was palpable. The lack of cross fertilization cost the firm opportunity, hence money, and marshalling so many large egos was near impossible. But it was my responsibility to try. I now ran the morning equity research call. "Okay, people, listen up." The sound of my voice reverberating through the hoot and holler system thrilled me. "We've got five analyst calls this morning so let's get started."

There was an audible groan from the institutional sales desk. "Jesus, Seth. Five calls?"

"It's a new day, guys! The clock's reset to zero. Let's get started."

Art Thierry tapped the end of his Mont Blanc pen on his desktop. "I preferred Jake running the call." Gerri shot me a venomous look. "Yeah, this is fuckin' bullshit."

Risa merely shook her head. "Who put the Boy Wonder in charge?"

Jake approached the sales desk. "I guess that would be me. Tell you what, folks, you start putting up Seth's numbers you'll run the call; until then shut the fuck up and let him get on with it."

"If I'd been handed Kevin Egan's entire account package, I'd be pulling some pretty sweet numbers, too!" Risa harrumphed.

Art leaned back in his chair, still tapping away. "But Risa, think how sore you'd be."

I stifled a laugh, but Jake wasn't amused. His lower lip quivered, a sure sign he was getting pissed off. "Seth represents your interests on the firm's stock selection committee and works harder than all of you combined. Furthermore, whom I assign accounts to is none of your fucking business. That's the firm's business, and I do what's in the best interests of the partners. Are we clear on that or would any of you prefer a private conversation in my office?" He retreated.

I waited for his door to slam, cleared my throat. "Okay! We've got a new telecom recommendation this morning." I motioned for the analyst to come up to the podium and walk us through the key points and when all the analysts had finished their presentations, I succinctly recapped them, noting with satisfaction Art, Risa, and others furiously taking notes. It was my call they'd make. "Okay, everybody, hit the phones, and remember, be careful out there!"

Back at my desk, my assistant Irene rolled her eyes. Feigned exasperation. Another college theatre major. "Your wife's holding; she really needs to talk to you... again."

"I'll take it." Erin didn't call to chat; she knew better. "What's up, honey? Everything okay?"

"I'm sorry to bother you at work but I've been puking all morning. Do you think something's wrong? I worked around all that lead paint and asbestos the last two summers..." And now she was stripping wood, sanding walls, using paints and finishes with God knows what's in them. I'd begged her to hire a contractor but having decided to forego, at least for the time being, an internship in architecture while she raised little children, found renovating our brownstone a satisfying use of her skills and passion. Her one concession was hiring a long-haired hippie, Jeff Weaver, who'd just taken over his father's appliance repair business, to refurbish the ridiculously outmoded kitchen appliances she adamantly refused to replace and refinish the kitchen cabinet fronts.

"Don't some women get morning sickness?"

"I'm just worried is all. Think it's all the olives I'm eating? I can't help it. I crave them."

"At least you're not sending me out in the middle of the night for ice cream and pickles. Did you call your mom?"

"Do New Yorkers ever remember there's life outside the Eastern Standard Time zone?"

"Oh yeah, sorry. Call Mitzie. She's been through this... once, anyway. I'm sure everything's fine... oh, and honey, I'm going to be home late tonight. I've got a stock selection committee meeting after the close, and dinner with one of my Boston PMs in town."

"Again? You're never home, Seth!"

"This weekend we'll go look for that thingamajig you wanted, okay? Look,

I gotta run. Got a zillion calls to make. See you tonight, and make sure you eat enough, okay? You're eating for two now! I love you!"

I looked across the desk and asked Irene to grab me another cup of black coffee. "Anutha one? Is that your third or fourth . . . I lost count." With a dramatic sigh, she trudged off to get it.

CHAPTER 2

EARLY SATURDAY MORNING Erin held a mug of black coffee under my nose. "Your morning amphetamine, sir." She placed it on the nightstand and climbed atop me. "Good morning, sleepy head! You said we'd go shopping." I looked at the alarm clock and groaned. It was only eight a.m., my one chance to sleep in, although the pressure of her body atop me kindled other thoughts.

"You smell like Greek salad. I'm going to eat you all up."

"Ho-ho-hope you like olive breath!" she giggled, breathing on me while caressing her rounded tummy. "And you did sleep in. We've been up for hours."

"What do you think?" I whispered into her belly bump. "Should Mommy and Daddy go shopping or make love?" I listened a moment. "Yup, okay, I hear you." I looked up at Erin. "He says make love."

"And SHE wants us to find that missing knob for the stove, so get up, Daddy, brush your teeth, wash your face and get dressed because you're not at Lehman Brothers. Today you're mine!" I tossed off the covers. "Jeff gave me a list of places to go. Apparently, your mother and I aren't the only kooks who treasure these old appliances. We'll find it."

I pulled on a pair of sweats, went downstairs and topped off my cup while perusing the kitchen, a work in progress dominated by the large butcher block center isle ringed with old oak cabinets, beefy wood mouldings, leaded glass windows, and an entire wall of oak shelving housing Erin's Ball jars of bulk grains and beans, flours, dried fruits and vegetables. Picking up the Saturday *Newsday*, I noticed one of the Douglaston apartments listed for one-hundred and twenty thousand. I sighed and dropped the paper on the counter. "Damn. We should have held onto that apartment as an investment. I told you we sold too soon!" This one didn't even have a porch.

"We got ninety-six thousand dollars for that hole in the wall, double what we paid."

"But if we'd just waited a year we could've done better. We virtually gave it away."

"I don't care. I love this house. I'm still pinching myself!"

I HADN'T TOLD Erin I'd purchased the brownstone on Carroll Street two weeks before we married for seventy-five thousand dollars. The house needed major renovations but was only two blocks from Carroll Park, Court Street, and the best Italian specialty stores. I wanted it to be a surprise and let her assume we'd live in the Douglaston apartment while house-hunting.

It was a late Thursday afternoon, the last day of our post-wedding cross country schlep from Portland, when we pulled up to the derelict three story building. She'd been napping. I roused her. "What are we doing here, Seth? This isn't Douglaston."

"We're in Brooklyn. Carroll Gardens. I wanted to show you this place."

"Oh Seth, really? Can't you make an appointment for another time? I mean, don't get me wrong, I really like these Romanesque and Renaissance Revival brownstones and I'd love to see it, but right now I want to get home and run a hot bath."

I hopped out of the U-Haul truck. "Aw, come on, honey, humor me."

"All right, all right. I'll look, but just for a minute." Alighting the truck, she immediately perked up. "The red brownstone façade is lovely. Very typical of turn of the century, and ooh, those stained-glass panels framing the bay windows remind me of my aunt and uncle's in Chicago. Those were probably Povey and I'm guessing these..."

"Definitely Tiffany," I said as we approached the steps. "Be careful." The front garden was a mass of overgrown weeds, paint peeling off the low wrought iron fence, the front stoop cracked and separating from the main structure. "Watch the gap."

We walked up the nine steps to the front door. She turned to me. "Yup, you're right. classic Tiffany. I'm impressed."

"I learned from an expert." I reached into my jeans pocket for a key and opened the massive oak front door.

"Wait! What are you doing, Seth? How'd you get a key to this place?"

In the entry hanging from the parlor room door was a small envelope wrapped in pink ribbon. "Go ahead, open it." Inside a card was inscribed "Welcome Home Erin Matthews."

She turned to me, now fully awake. "Are you serious; this is ours?" and proceeded to run through the rooms turning in circles with arms spread wide, green eyes glistening, her expression sheer joy, like Snoopy doing his happiness dance in the *Peanuts* comic strip. "Look at this fireplace, these doors, the herringbone mahogany inlay in the parquet flooring, and the mouldings, the columns!" She ran from room to room, reciting its virtues far better than the realtor who sold me the house. "Oh my God! Look at this library, the built-in bookcases, the leaded glass French dining room doors!" She pushed open the swinging door into the kitchen, quivering with excitement. "And these appliances. To die for. I can't wait to show Mitzie."

The refrigerator was a large white box on Queen Anne legs, the stove a queer combination of electric burners on one end and a boxy oven on the other, also on legs. Erin saw inherent beauty and infinite possibilities; I saw a complete mess, but the moment I'd never forget was when she rested her head on my shoulder, looked at the card again and noted, "It should read Welcome Home Matthews Family." I was stunned. We'd only gotten married the prior week. How could she possibly know? "I just do, and it's going to be a girl."

The very next night, a Friday, I returned from work to a card table set for Shabbos dinner with Grandma Matthews' candlesticks, a bottle of wine and a challah, Erin standing beside the table with her head covered and eyes shielded, soft candlelight flickering on her face as she said the Sabbath blessings. It brought tears to my eyes.

I gazed in wonderment at her now, my Madonna with child. How could this be my life, my wife, pregnant with our child, our home? What had I done to deserve such a happy fate? There was a surreal quality to it all. I opened the refrigerator door and turned to my girls. "If we're going shopping for some thingamajig this morning, let's at least have breakfast first. What would you two ladies like?"

CHAPTER 3

I STOOD AT the head of the birthing bed, brilliant white overhead light casting an almost unearthly glow on Erin's sweaty face, crimson from exertion, the vibrant focal point in the otherwise antiseptic hospital delivery room. Legs spread wide in metal stirrups, ready to deliver new life, the beginning of a family. The obstetrician and nurse at the foot of the bed offered a steady flow of encouragement.

"Huh, huh, huh. Whoo, hoo, hoo." She took a deep breath and pushed hard. "HAAAAAAAAH." I applied a cool compress to her forehead. Dr. Wyatt told her she was doing great. She grabbed my hand, squeezed with a vice-like grip, and continued panting. I squeezed back, helpless to do more. Nothing in the Lamaze class prepared me for this (though I'd been comforted to see the other first-time dads also in uncomfortably tight blue jeans). I focused on the monitor measuring the peaks and valleys of Erin's contractions, awaiting a dip in the indicator so I could helpfully reassure her the contraction was almost over and she could relax.

"RELAX? ARE YOU FUCKING KIDDING? How'd you like to deliver a football through your penis!!! HAH, HAH, HAH, HU HU HU." The nurse and doctor suggested I focus on applying cool compresses to her sweaty face. Apparently, many first-time fathers were equally helpful.

Erin redoubled her efforts to bear down, crushing my hand. The doctor said he could see the crown. "She's almost here, Erin. You're doing great."

She took another deep breath, her flushed face puffing up like a blowfish. She pushed hard and grunted "IS . . . SHE . . . COMING?" panting in staccato-like bursts of breath. "CAN . . . YOU . . . SEE . . . HER?" Excitement in her voice blasted through the pain.

"One more push, Erin. One more and she's here!" and from my vantage point I could see a little baby girl emerge, all pink and slippery and gooey, so perfect in every detail I gaped in awe, tears flowing down my cheeks. She was the essence of purity, a tabula rasa, a bundle of infinite possibilities. With her first breath a connection was forged between us that would never dissolve; I was hardwired to her for life, would do anything for her, would lay down my life for her. No God could be bad Who could create this.

Erin, exhausted, deliriously happy, cradled our baby in her protective arms and immediately guided the little mouth to one of her nipples. I cut the umbilical cord with a shaking hand. "I told you we were having a girl, Seth. She told me her name was Meara."

"Meara is a beautiful name, Erin. She's like a delicate pink rose."

Meara Rose Matthews, born March 21, 1977, nine months to the day we got married, at University Hospital in Cobble Hill, 8 pounds, 6 ounces. She was mostly bald, little wisps of reddish hair sprouting like fresh spring grass, blue eyes open, staring in vacant wonder at this strange new world. A chubby little bundle of pink. Erin attached her to her other breast and Meara nursed; tiny hands balled into fists as she suckled life with intensity. I put my arms around them, astounded. "Thank you, Erin, thank you, thank you, thank you" I repeated over and over as I kissed her forehead, her eyes, her cheeks and chin, her lovely swan-like neck.

She pressed my arm with fervor. "You and me, Seth. We're immortal, part of the cycle of life."

WE WERE NEW life on the old block, Meara everyone's grandchild by proxy, the Italian grandmothers always ready to lend a helping hand should Erin need to run an errand, delighted to have Meara to themselves, bounce her on their knees and feed her homemade goodies, their own children having absconded to the suburbs in New Jersey or Long Island while they'd remained resolutely attached to their brownstones, gardens, parishes and social clubs. We'd had a small dumpster outside our brownstone since we moved in. Erin, pregnant with our second child, would fill it, call the waste company, and fill it again. On weekends, the only time I was ever home given my workaholic schedule, I regularly carted out construction debris, my presence duly noted by Mr. Manzoni next door. He'd gently scold me from his front stoop, where he regularly held court. "How can you leave your beautiful young wife alone so much?"

"Someone's gotta make the money; Erin's renovations are never-ending!"

"A woman like this should not be taken for granted. Someone is keeping her pregnant. That's the only way we know you live here."

"Let me know If you start seeing the mailman hanging around!" Or Jeff Weaver for that matter, always there with one excuse or another.

I'd met Jeff shortly after we moved in. He'd come to our house with his dad, a craggy-faced, gruff old guy in overalls who took one look at our ancient appliances and laughed aloud. "I haven't seen a Westinghouse Dual Automatic refrigerator in twenty years, and that stove... that's a Hotpoint Hi-Speed range! I've no idea when they stopped making that unit, but I still remember the advertising campaign—*Release the magic speed of electricity*!"

He asked if I knew our fridge was the first to have an electric light. Like I gave a shit, still annoyed Erin insisted we keep old junk that reminded me of that detestable stove back in Huntington, but when Jeff asked if they could fix the stuff his father's response was priceless. "We can fix anything; the only question is why?" My sentiments exactly.

CHAPTER 4

ONE WEEKDAY EVENING, arriving home early, a rare event, I flung open the French doors to our cozy parlor, about to shout "SURPRISE" when I saw Erin atop a step ladder eight feet off the ground, stripping old wallpaper. Startled, she almost slipping off the rung of the ladder. "You're pregnant. Get down right now and be careful."

"What are you doing here? Did something happen at the office?"

"No meetings for a change. Figured I'd surprise you. Guess I did."

Meara, happily jumping up and down in a bouncy toddler seat blasting *Three Blind Mice*, chortled with delight when she saw me. "Dada, Dada," she babbled as I lifted her out of the seat and circled the room like an airplane. "It's Meara, superbaby! VROOM. VROOM. Able to leap tall cribs with a single bound! When'd we get that bouncy seat? I don't remember it."

Erin held her arms out for Meara. "Mitzie came over this morning. Said it was essential for Meara's motor coordination. I think she needed a grandchild fix and that was as good an excuse as any. We took several steps today, didn't we, Meara?"

"Mitzie, huh? What else did she want?"

"Geez, Seth. Must you always assume she has devious intentions?" That's who she was. "Look, I didn't grow up in your household. I know what you've told me, but I see a mother desperate to have a relationship with her son. I can't count the times she's tried to talk with you, ask about work, compliment you, only to be shunned. When are you going to cut her a break? Did it ever occur to you she's trying to reach you through me? I appreciate her visits. It's nice having someone mother me when mine's so far away. I'm here all by my lonesome with a little baby."

"She's not my real mother. Stop guilt-tripping me."

"Jesus Christ! I'm so sick of you saying that. And I'm not trying to guilt-trip you, dammit; I'm just trying to help you see outside yourself. She's sweet. She cares about us. She even brought me an assortment of olives. We went to Toys 'R' Us and bought the bouncy seat."

I tossed my coat over the banister, walked over to the bouncy seat, turned the sound off. "Saw one of those damned Douglaston coops listed for 155 thousand dollars!"

"Seth, how many times do I have to tell you to use the Stickley coat rack in the front entry?"

"You used to complain when I hung up my coat. Call this progress."

"And you're still obsessing over an apartment we sold three years ago. So much for progress." She held out her free arm. "Come here, sweetie." Her little belly pressed into me as she kissed me, and I wrapped my arms around the three of them. "Mm, that's so nice. Since you're home, would you take all this old paper out to the dumpster?"

"Lemme get out of this suit first." I picked my coat off the banister and hung it on the rack. "We sold too soon, that's all I'm saying."

I scampered up the two-story open stairway, my hand gliding over the smooth refinished mahogany railing curling its way upstairs, Erin yelling after me, "Jeff was here today. Heat compressor on the fridge went on the blink again. Apparently, when it was introduced in the Thirties something called a 'Watchman' feature was supposed prevent that; even came with a lifetime guarantee."

I returned wearing my favorite ragged Guatemalan shorts and Lehman Brothers Power Brokers T-shirt. "A lifetime guarantee, huh? Whose lifetime? Replace the goddam thing; it's costing us a fortune. The oven too while you're at it."

"Oh no, Seth, I love them. They're part of the romance of this house!"

"So is Jeff, apparently. That long red hair, the ponytail and earring, definitely your type."

"He reminds me of you in your hippie period . . . physically, anyway."

"I'm still a hippie at heart."

"Hippies wear Armani?"

"That's the costume that comes with the role."

"Play a role long enough, it starts to become your life."

"See these shorts? This is the real me. A working-class hero."

"Mm, I can see all of you in those holey shorts. It's kind of chilly. Why don't you start a fire in the parlor room while I put Meara to bed."

I WAS ADDING fresh logs when Erin came up behind me and kissed the back of my neck. "It's nice having you home for a change." She placed a tumbler of Glenfiddich on the coffee table. "I think you may need this. Something happened today . . . something important." I startled. My heart skipped a beat. "Don't worry. We're fine."

I sunk back into the old couch, relieved, and watched the firelight dance in her emerald eyes as she snuggled into me, said she had something to show me, and handed me an old timey photograph of a little girl with soft red curls and freckles. I looked at it, then at her. "Aw, your grandmother was so cute; you look so much like her."

She shook her head. "Guess again." It was too old-fashioned to be a contemporary family member, too modern to be one of those dour-looking great-grandparent portraits hanging on the living room walls of her parents' house. I gave up. "Mitzie insisted on paying and when she opened her wallet—I was standing right next to her holding Meara—I saw what I assumed was a photo of you and asked to see it. She abruptly snapped her purse shut, refused to show it to me, real defensive-like, and you know me, once my curiosity gets piqued . . ." Our first morning together. "Like mother, like son, if you ask me. Anyway, I hounded her until she relented. Apparently, only Jerry's seen that photo. It wasn't you. It was her mother, Seth, redheaded with blue eyes, like you. Your grandmother."

I almost dropped the tumbler, spilling scotch in my lap. I didn't want to believe it. I couldn't. "No, no way. That photo's been doctored. They used to paint them."

"It's true, Seth."

"How come she never showed it to me? Why don't I know anything about her family?"

"Did you ever ask?" My silence spoke volumes. "I thought not."

"No! She's lying. This is bullshit. Jonah told me the truth when I was ten. It's like yesterday to me."

She placed my glass on the coffee table and took me by the shoulders. "Stop being so goddam stubborn and listen. Yesterday's over; there's only now and the future. I don't know how it was diagnosed back then but your grandmother was a manic depressive. She committed suicide when Mitzie was twelve. She'd just returned home from school, smelled gas, ran into the kitchen and found her mother dead with her head in the oven. Can you imagine anything so awful?"

I clenched my eyes tight. Mitzie rushing into the kitchen. Me half dazed against the wall, blood pooling under me, burnt match still clutched in my chubby little hand. The open oven. The smell of gas. Jonah laughing. And something else, something new. Mitzie rocking me in her arms weeping, my head pressed against her breast, screaming at Jonah, not me. I cradled my face in my hands. "Oh my God. Oh my God."

"Jonah lied to you, honey, and God knows what else he did, but don't you see, you're a Matthews. If you hadn't looked so different, I would've questioned your adoption years ago, but this," she exclaimed, holding the photo in front of my face, "this is irrefutable. Let all that emptiness, all that aloneness, go. Let yourself be happy. Like you promised."

"How do I do that, Erin? It's not that I want to be unhappy. But all those tortured years. They had to have meaning. Had to stand for something."

"No. You embraced all that darkness and let it define you."

"But after Grandma Matthews died, Jonah was all I had. Mitzie didn't love me. Only he did. He was the best big brother ever."

"That's a crock and you know it. What about that incident before your Bar Mitzvah? His cruel lies? If he was so goddam great why'd you want to hurt him? You've been using that false image of Jonah; worse, you've been using Mitzie, to block whatever you've repressed."

I was bombarded with images: the stove; the demon; kids beaten up. Spiders. I tried to push back at them, deny them. Picked up my whiskey and downed it in one gulp. She didn't understand. I saw the way she was with Meara; all the love, the way she held her and hugged her and made her feel secure. We were both hardwired to love Meara the moment we saw her. It was instinctive. But not for Mitzie, and now it was too late. "All you're doing is opening a Pandora's box."

"It's time to let it all out."

"I can't. It scares me. There's something else. Something worse. I don't want to know."

"I swear, you're like this blind boy I knew in high school. When he was fifteen, he was offered an operation that would give him sight, but he refused; he'd learned to see the world his way. You're doing the same thing." I understood that blind boy's fear of the unknown. He'd found his comfort zone. I'd found mine. "You're making yourself miserable and unhappy, hurting everyone who loves you."

I closed my eyes and saw a set of bright eyes emanating from the depths of a deep, dark forest. They drew nearer and nearer, grew more and more brilliant, until they filled my head with unbearable light. *I SEE YOU*. Shaking, I poured myself another drink. No. No. Close the lid, reseal the box, deflect all that amorphous dread onto Mitzie. Someone tangible. Someone you abhor. "Please, honey, let's not waste the evening arguing. I just want to hold you and enjoy the fire."

"Open your eyes, Seth. This has been going on for too long. You need to call your mother. And that's who she is, honey. Your mother."

"Okay, okay. I'll call her from the library, but I'm closing the pocket doors. No prying eyes and ears!"

CHAPTER 5

MITZIE SOUNDED RESIGNED. Had been expecting my call. "It's true."

"Why didn't you tell me about your mother? Why'd I have to hear this from my wife?"

"No one knew except your father. I didn't want pity. I'd had enough, passing through a series of foster homes from the time I was twelve. All well-meaning people who felt sorry for me and saw to my physical needs, but never loved me. I told Erin because she's been my only conduit to you and . . . and because I know she loves me."

"You hated her at first."

"I thought she'd take you away, thwart any chance to bring you back into my life, but I was wrong, Seth; I realized that when she came to New York that first time. She was going to bring you closer to me. I've always had difficulty expressing my feelings, and when you were born the spitting image of my mother I was completely traumatized. Everything, the horror, pain, guilt, it all came back. I couldn't deal with it. The doctors called it post-partum depression, but I knew it was God's punishment for what I'd done to my mother." She started to cry. "The morning she committed suicide, before I left for school, we had a big fight. I told her I wanted to leave her like my father had. She was crazy. She embarrassed me. I wanted a normal life, like everyone else. I wished she was dead." I thought back to what Erin had told me about her mother and the blue jeans. "Your father shared the conversation you had before Mexico. I was appalled, but I couldn't talk to you. Our relationship had become so toxic."

"You should have tried. Something so critical. I needed your assurances. All I had were my own experiences. You never hugged or kissed me or comforted me when I was scared or upset or overwhelmed by the world, things that make a real mom. Even when you threw me a crumb and watched me lap it up, thinking finally you loved me, you stomped on it. You passed your pain forward. You were never there for me. Not when I was little. Not when Jonah lied to me."

"He was jealous of you. Knew he was different. Exploited your insecurities and used you as a punching bag out of frustration. Said what he knew would hurt you most." And she let him. "I needed everything to be normal. I walked on needles. Watched for signs. Feared my mother's mental instability would pass to you and your brother. And then, when things happened, undeniable things, I refused to see. Your brother was manic depressive, like my mother." She rambled on, but I couldn't make out all her words. Something about letting me out of her sight, being so tired. Needing to close her eyes for a minute. Grandpa and Grandma reassuring her they'd make everything okay. It was gibberish, and finally, out of frustration, I interrupted her. "What's normal?" I asked. "I'm an obsessive-compulsive control freak. I have trust issues. I'm narcissistic. I keep secrets, abused drugs, hurt people I cared about. I've become just like you."

"I know it sounds like I'm making excuses, but whenever I took my eyes off Jonah something terrible happened. And you, so needy, demanding and hyperkinetic, I couldn't handle it all. I became embittered when you transferred your love to Grandma. I should have known I'd never be a good mother, not after a childhood like mine."

Her words sent a chill through me. What terrible things? I flashed on the old stove, the hiss of gas, the flaming match. The deep, impenetrable darkness. The forest. The Balrog. The spiders. The disembodied voice. I shook it off. She'd fostered the environment he'd taken advantage of, armed him with the ammunition he needed to shoot me. And if she got in the way of the blood splatter, that was poetic justice. "The day Jonah told me I was adopted I swore you'd never be my mommy, and the sad, pathetic thing is I wouldn't even have cared if I was adopted," I cried, "if only I'd known you loved me."

Erin, eavesdropping on the other side of the door, heard Mitzie's wails. Asked if everything was okay, but nothing was or ever would be between me and Mitzie, no matter how sorry she was. And she was still holding something back. Yet I empathized with her guilt and struggled with an impulse to reach through the phone. She was a doting grandmother. A loving mother to Erin. I had to do something. She was my mother. I had to make room for her in my life, if not in my heart.

CHAPTER 6

IN THE WAKE of my mother's revelations, the murky images gained more clarity. White eyes peered from the darkness of the dense forest. The chilling, disembodied voice an endless loop playing in my head. I attempted to obliterate them by taking on additional responsibilities at the office. Became Jake's go-to guy, but Erin felt the additional toll on our family life. Demanded I spend more time with Meara; give her a moment for herself, to catch her breath, maybe get some exercise. Husband and father were the most important roles I'd ever play. "Is it too much to ask for you to take care of your own daughter on a Saturday morning?"

I held up a sheath of research reports. "See what I bring home every day? I'm building a business for us. Things may look good but don't kid yourself. My job's only as secure as the business I bring the firm tomorrow and..."

"Blah, blah, blah, I've heard it all before. You're racking up yardage, keeping your sight on the goal line, you're gonna make partner." She sneered "You should hear yourself sometime."

"I'm serious Erin. Look around you. None of this would be possible if..."

"If there weren't two of us working hard as partners! Think everything here gets done by magic? Your suits and dress shirts automatically dry clean themselves? The fridge miraculously fills with healthy food, meals cook themselves. I balance the check book, do the taxes, make the pediatrician appointments; I'm finishing the renovations, taking care of a toddler, checking out preschools—ad nauseum!"

That stopped me cold. I hadn't given it a moment's thought. It simply got done, like at the office with Irene handling all the mundane yet essential tasks that kept my business life running smoothly. I suggested hiring additional contractors to take over more of the renovation work, free up more of her time; like Kevin said, that's what money was for. But she thought I was being purposely obtuse. The renovation work kept her sane, her opportunity to utilize her education and skills outside of motherhood. "I'm not complaining; I wanted children more than anything. But the only partnership that matters is ours. You already make a great living. I need you here with us! Lehman's a job, not life and death. You've nothing to prove to anyone. Be honest with yourself. Wall Street's Mexico redux. You're hiding, honey, that's what you're doing. You're really skilled at it. It's a lifelong habit."

Frustrated, I tossed the reports on the desk. "Fine, I'll watch Meara. You obviously need some exercise," then immediately wished I could recall those insensitive words. "I mean you love to run. Just do it. Find a running partner."

CHAPTER 7

RETURNING HOME FROM a hectic a two-day trip to Boston, I found Erin curled up in bed reading. She looked exhausted. I leaned over and kissed her. "Meara's finally asleep. Kept me on my toes all day. So excited about the baby. Collected a bunch of toys in her room to give to her little sister. I hadn't the heart to tell her she was getting a brother. Quinn talks to me. Thought we'd name him after Dad's father. That okay with you?"

"Heck, if he already knows his name, what's for me to say? I had a good road trip with my computer analyst. He thinks within a decade everyone's gonna have a personal computer in their home. Why is anyone's guess. Recommended clients participate in a late round financing we're managing for a company expected to go public next year, Apple Computer. Interesting fact. The founder attended Reed College for a while. Wonder if he had your father?"

"Everyone's going to want a computer, Seth. They're already in wide use on college campuses. MIT has a whole floor dedicated to them, and Mom's learning computer language as head librarian at Reed. Now you know what to get me for my next birthday. Computers are the future. Know that dumb quote machine on your desk? The Quotron? Someday you're going to be able to do everything on it."

"Duly noted. Anything exciting happen while I was gone?"

"I replanted the front garden with Mr. Manzoni's help. Tomatoes, peppers, eggplant, all kinds of greens, a separate section for herbs like oregano, thyme, marjoram, savory and basil."

"The aromas of Italy. What happened to my Japanese Garden idea?"

"Maybe I'll do something like that in the back yard. Oh, and Jeff was here today. The oven wouldn't start again."

"Has it ever occurred to you he half fixes stuff so he has an excuse to hang around here?"

"Don't be silly. Why would he do that?"

Such an innocent. The guy was crazy about her. Ever-present, rehabbing the ancient appliances; refinishing wood cabinets and counters in the kitchen and scullery; putting antiqued fronts on Erin's only concessions to modernity, the dishwasher, washer and dryer; inserting stained glass panels in the cabinet fronts. "Maybe because he's madly in love with you?"

"Maybe I can turn water into wine, too!" she chortled. "Did you know he has a degree in philosophy from the University of Chicago, like my father? Didn't know what he wanted to do with his degree so when his dad offered to apprentice him, he figured why not? Weaver Appliances is pretty successful and he's a runner, too. Maybe he'd be interested in running with me."

In Erin's eyes Jeff had remained a free spirit, hadn't succumbed to enlightened self-interest or cut his hair. One of those sensitive male types, hanging on her every word. And so chatty. Heck, he even sported a small diamond stud in his right ear. Erin wanted me to get one. Talk about career suicide! And the way he was always hanging around! He needed his own wife; not mine. "He's a repairman, Erin, not a friend."

"He's become my friend. I love it here, and I'd assumed people our age would flock to Brooklyn but I'm still waiting, and with Ellen moving to Greenwich and our friends scattered across the country . . ." She closed her book with an emphatic snap. "You know, I'm gonna ask him. Wouldn't you rather I run with someone?"

"Sure, but I was thinking a women's running group. Anyway, that guy makes a fortune off us."

"So what? You make a fortune."

"Chump change; nothing compared to Joel."

"Do you find spouting that crap motivational?" She jutted out her jaw and affected a husky voice, a lion with a severe head cold. "I'm only as good as my next trade. If I don't kill it now someone else will have my desk tomorrow." Terrible acting, but I couldn't help laughing. "Your whole perspective is warped. Get real. We made over three hundred thousand dollars last year!"

"It's not about the money, Erin. Never has been. I don't know how much we have and don't care. Success or failure is measured in commission dollars. That's what defines me."

"That one of Kevin's famous maxims? Well, here's another one: 'There's nothing more important than your family.'"

"For a girl who buys fancy William Morris wallpaper, Povey stained glass and renovates absurdly old appliances . . . hell, you spend our money as fast as I make it . . ."

"It's Tiffany, remember? Povey was based in Portland, Oregon. Just say the word, Seth, and we're outta here. Your offer to move to Portland had no expiration date, remember? Maybe it's time I took you up on it, go west and lead a more balanced life." She swept her arms in a circle around the room. "I'm not married to all this . . . stuff. I'm no different than you. You're driven to be the best. Me too. We just work with different palettes. You want to climb to the top rung of the Wall Street ladder. I wanna return this house to its original glory! At least my motivations are straightforward and anyway, these are just things, ways I express myself as something more than wife and mother." She put her book on the nightstand and reached out to me. I pressed against her; felt the baby kick. Erin was right. This was what life was all about.

CHAPTER 8

I ALWAYS STAYED at the Lenox Hotel in Boston's Back Bay, a turn of the century hotel that exuded old world warmth and charm, from the massive fireplace in its marble floored lobby to the gold filigreed columns and mouldings, so unlike the nondescript hotels starting to populate every city. Yet another Kevin aphorism: always frequent the same hotel once you find the one you like. They'll greet you by name, know your favorite room, what you order from room service. Become chummy with the barman! My business in Boston was burgeoning. I'd held daylong meetings at Superior Management, the biggest account in the country, scoring my first face to face dinner meeting with the industry's number one portfolio manager. A solid relationship with him would render me untouchable. I was so pumped! I wanted to call home, tell Erin about it, but it was late and between Meara and pregnancy she was exhausted by early evening. Probably asleep. I went instead into the City Bar off the lobby for a night cap and Mike the bartender, jerking of his head in the direction of a lady at the far end of the bar, placed my usual, a Stoli martini, in front of me. I raised it in her direction, a gesture she took as a signal to maneuver onto the bar stool next to me. Everything about her screamed Long Island, the expensive jewelry, the gravity defying breasts, stiletto heels and French-manicured nails that had never seen the inside of a sink. She was a glimpse twenty years forward of that girl Mara from Mitzie's parade of flesh. I hoisted my glass again. "Thanks for the drink."

"My pleashuh. You seem awfully young to be hanging around here."

No one would have to card her. I pulled out my wallet. "Had to show my ID to Mike first time I came in here. Here, you can verify I'm legal."

"Ooh, not necessary. I like my men young." She gave me a dazzling smile and extended her hand. "I'm Sarah. I'm in pharmaceutical sales." She twitched her nose like Samantha on the TV show *Bewitched*. "The best kinds." I suspected she wasn't talking Bayer aspirin and my heart beat a tad faster.

"I'm Seth. I'm in investment banking. Nice to meet you."

She edged so close I could inhale her Cosmopolitan. "This is a spendy hotel. You must be one of those power brokers."

"I do all right, I guess. I always stay here."

"And so modest." She placed her hand over mine. She was coming on to me! Had to be over forty. Apparently, this was new territory for her, and she peppered me for recommendations of places to go. I started to rattle off several of my favorite Boston haunts, but she cut me short. "Actually, Seth, I was thinking of places we might go. I see you're married. So am I. How perfect is that?" Opening her purse, I followed her eyes down to a large vial of white powder. "Pharmaceuticals, right?" She winked and twitched her nose again. "*I used to be Snow White, but I drifted.*"

My mouth went dry at the sight of that powder. I started thinking lemons. "That's a Mae West quote, right? From *It Ain't No Sin*, 1934." No way she'd seen *The President's Analyst*.

"Hmmm. A young man who knows his movies. I like that." She placed a key on the bar top and straightened my tie. "*Why don't you come up sometime and see me.* That's from *She Done Him Wrong*. 1933. I'm in room 417. Join me for a different kind of nightcap . . . and whatever."

As she sashays into the lobby my hands begin to shake. I taste metal. Tiny needles prickle my nose. I twirl my wedding ring. Lick my lips. Take a sip of my martini. Avoid staring at the key. Such a long time ago. I'm older, in control. I can handle it. Just a snort, nothing more; an exchange of movie quotes with a friendly fellow traveler. The key inches closer. Oh God, my temples are throbbing. I chew the cuticle on my thumb. Take another gulp of vodka. It's right in front of me, calling to me, and I glance at the mirrored bar back. It's the grinning monster! He's nodding. That's right, Seth, you've been so good, you deserve this, no one the wiser, just a couple of lines. That's what I'm talking about. Hit the pause button; restart your promise tomorrow. I reach toward the key, then hesitate. Risk everything for this? I push that radioactive key as far away from me as possible. Glance at the bar back. It's my own reflection staring back. I sit back with a sigh. I've passed the test.

Mike came over and glanced at the key. "Another martini, Mr. Matthews? On the house."

"I'm Seth, Mike. My dad's Mr. Matthews."

"You got any kids, Seth?" I nodded. "I've got four. The treasures of my life." He pulled out his wallet. "Got some photos here. Lemme show you. This is Mike, Junior. Goalie on the BU Hockey team. Full scholarship. Damn proud of that boy. And this is Jenny and Janine, both go to St. Mary's, Jenny's a junior,

Janine a freshman, and this little one, Megan, boy, does she love her daddy. How about you?"

"Just one, Meara, but another on the way. Hold on, got a photo here." I pulled out my wallet. "This is her with my wife."

"Gorgeous! Both of them. Bet you love them more than anything in the world." I took a sip. "And you'd do anything for them, right?" I nodded, trying to calm my heart. "Nothing more important than family, right?" My eyes followed his down to the room key. I told him the lady had left it by mistake. He'd make sure the concierge returned it to her. Placing a fresh martini in front of me, he poured himself a glass of sparkling water, held it up to the light and saluted, a gesture that spoke volumes. "To family, Seth. To knowing what really matters."

Next morning, still a bit fuzzy headed from the martinis, I called Erin. She sounded hurt and pissed off, wanted to know why I hadn't called, where I'd been. I explained the dinner meeting ran late. Assumed she'd be asleep. Didn't want to wake her. I could hear Meara in the background screaming "Mommy, Mommy, I wan' milk, I wan' milk!" and Erin's "No, Meara, put that down. Mommy will get that for you," followed by a groan. "Oh, Meara, it's all over the floor now." Meara now wailing.

"Hold on a sec, Seth. I've got to clean up a spill. It's okay, sweetie. Don't cry. Mommy knows you didn't mean to do that." A minute later she was back on the line, her tone scolding. "You've always called me, Seth, every night we've been apart since the day we married, and I look forward to it."

"It sounds like I caught you at a bad time."

"This is my all the time. I don't get to leave for days on end and stay in fancy hotels, eat in fancy restaurants and whatever else you do for entertainment, and I don't mind because I love my family and the chaos and my husband, whom I'm thinking about all the time." A long silence was broken up by Meara's demands. "I wan' more milk. I wan' Ses'me Street. I wanna go to the park...."

"Erin, I didn't mean to upset you."

"Jeff was here all day. The removable burner element went out on the Hotpoint; he had to rebuild it." Again? Doesn't that guy have anyplace else to go? Her intonation was flat. She was erecting an emotional barrier. Our bond fraying fiber by fiber.

"Please honey, whatever you've imagining, you're wrong. Listen, I've got a great idea. Call Mitzie. See if she'll babysit Meara Saturday morning. We can go surfing at Rockaway, close to home."

"I'm exhausted and pregnant and you want to surf?"

"I want to do something nice for you."

"Be here for me. That's what I'd like. I swear I've become a single mom. If it weren't for Jeff, I'd go out of my mind." Can't that rooster find his own hen house? But excitement slowly crept into her voice. "Do you really think I could surf, I mean, I'm the size of a blimp!"

"Why not. You're an Outward-Bound woman, remember? There's nothing you can't do. We'll pick up lobsters on the way home."

CHAPTER 9

ERIN WATCHED ME unload our Aipa boards from the top of my old sturdy Lancer, nervously cradling her large basketball shaped belly, wondering if this was a good idea. Her belly button protruded so far out it seemed the baby was attempting a breakout by poking a stick through it. "It's just, I mean, look at me. I should be wearing a tent, not a bikini."

"You look dynamite. Sexy as hell," I said, carrying her board down to the water. I held my breath as she duck-dived out and managed to cut through a wave without wiping out, her large belly leading the way. She shrieked with delight, her frizzy red hair afire in the sunlight. After several runs, we sat at the water's edge watching other surfers dart in and out, listening to the sound of rollers breaking on the shore, to squawking seagulls and laughing children.

She crossed her legs. Buddha in a bikini. "Are you going to tell me why you didn't call me from Boston? No secrets, remember?"

I explained about the woman at the bar. Her pro-offer of cocaine. My refusal to go to her room. "I didn't do anything bad." But she wasn't worried about me cheating. She felt disrespected. I hadn't looked at it from her perspective.

"Those nightly calls are our connection when you're on the road. I want to hear about your day, tell you about mine, no matter how mundane. When you didn't call it hurt, like my day wasn't as important as yours. I tolerated your self-absorption when we were kids but we're grownups now, partners raising a family. I count on you, honey!"

I took her hand. "I'm so sorry. Please don't stop loving me, honey."

"How can you worry about that after all these years?"

MY MOTHER WAS reading in the parlor when we entered. Erin sat down on the couch next to her. Asked if Meara had given her any trouble. "She was a doll.

I fed her and gave her a bath. She sang "Rubber Duckie, You're the One." The sweetest voice, sounds and looks just like Seth as a toddler . . . and my mother."

I bristled, and Erin, sensing an impasse, hugged her. Mitzie placed her hand on Erin's abdomen. "Girl or boy, Erin? What do your maternal instincts say?"

"Oh, a boy, definitely."

"How are you feeling, sweetheart?"

"Fine. I actually managed to surf for a while."

"Amazing. I could barely move when I was that pregnant with Seth."

"Give me a fucking break," I shot back. "I know you're my mother. So what?"

"You hate me," she cried.

"It's not hate, Mitzie. It's pity."

Erin frantically rubbed the sides of her head. "My God, Seth. You're not a child. Don't talk to your mother like that."

I glared at Mitzie, head throbbing, pressure building like too much carbonation in a shaken bottle. A sea of spiders swarmed over me. I pointed a quivering finger at her. "Why should I love you? Yours was always conditional. Only Jonah loved me and protected me . . . from you. I lived in fear you'd get rid of me. After Grandma died who comforted me when I was scared? Let me sleep in his bed and . . . and . . ." Spiders clambered up the parlor room walls. Eviscerating words. Rejection. Cruelty and laughter. No. No. He loved me. He did. He did. I picked up the photo of Jonah and me. Tangible proof. I shoved it in her face. "This is what love is. This is what you never gave me."

Mitzie went ghostly pale. "You can't possibly remember . . ."

I didn't have to remember. That photo was so precious. My hands began to shake. I squeezed my eyes tight. Searing light radiating through fissures in my cordoned-off chamber of secrets. *I SEE YOU. I SEE YOU. I SEE YOU.* I shut my eyes, pressed my hands to my ears and screamed, "GET OUT. GET OUT OF MY HOUSE NOW!" and she ran for the front door bawling, Erin on her tail, begging her to stay, assuring her I didn't mean it, but too late, the door slammed shut and Erin turned the full force of her ire on me.

"I'm so ashamed of you. You're breaking her heart!"

"You're being a Pollyanna. She doesn't have a heart."

Trembling, she shrieked, "GO AFTER HER; STOP HER," then gasped as water puddled on the floor. "Oh my God, Seth. The baby!"

I bolted out the door. What had I done? How could I lose control like that? Please don't have left, Mitzie. Please don't have left. And she hadn't. She was sitting in her car, engine running, crying. I rapped on her window. Begged her to open it. "Erin's water ruptured. I don't know what to do," I cried. "I've hurt her and our baby. Please come back. I need you, Mitzie!"

Erin appeared to be in shock, rooted to the spot, and Mitzie took immediate charge. Guided Erin to the sofa. Asked if she'd packed a hospital bag. Sent me upstairs to retrieve it. Was on the phone with Dr. Wyatt at the hospital when I returned, Erin still sitting there dazed, murmuring, "He's coming, he's coming" over and over. I begged her to keep her thighs clamped shut. Mitzie ushered us to the door. "Drive safely and don't worry about Meara. Everything is going to be okay, Seth. Everything will be okay. Go."

    I drove through pedestrian and car-choked streets like a madman, blinkers flashing, arriving at University Hospital in the nick of time for Dr. Wyatt to deliver a healthy 5 pound, 15-ounce boy with no hair, no eyelashes, eyebrows, any of those little finishing touches. I hadn't seen anything so beautiful since Meara was born, and on his eight day, August 17th, 1979, surrounded by family, thinking about Grandpa Matthews, about how I was carrying on the Matthews line, a ritual circumcision was performed for Quinn McGuire Matthews. I closed my eyes so I wouldn't pass out watching the mohel snip off the end of my son's penis and tentatively reached out to Mitzie. I clasped her hand and gently squeezed it. The mohel quipped he worked for tips, and Joel noted that's why Jews were such optimists. Snipping off a piece without knowing how big it would get. "There's confidence for you."

CHAPTER 10

EVERYTHING ON WALL Street was changing by the time Elisha Ariel was born on July 7, 1982. President Reagan's Economic Recovery Tax Act of 1981 popularized the Individual Retirement Account, lightning bolt legislation resulting in massive inflows of fresh capital, a jolt of energy to the moribund market, and a boon to Wall Street investment banking firms. New technologies were evolving, Wall Street rapidly automating, market timing increasingly critical, and a fresh breed of institutional investor emerged: hedge fund managers, sons (and daughters) of immigrants, second generation Americans breaking through once sacrosanct barriers erected by old school, preppy WASPs vainly protecting their turf. These were aggressive type A personalities seeking an edge, faster and smarter than traditional "Old-Money" managers. Like me, they were obsessive multi-taskers with OCD, insecure and nouveau riche, in need of constant reaffirmation of their brilliance. I knew I'd make a killing covering them. Things were about to pick up. The smell of fresh money in the air. I asked Jake for a meeting, and over lunch at Harry's he joked about my burgeoning brood. "Three kids! You and Erin are doing your part to prevent zero population growth!"

"And we're only at the halfway mark."

"That's a lot of college educations to pay for but at least you're in the right business. I like the name Elisha. It's pretty."

"Thanks. It's the first time Erin let me pick one of our children's names. It's in honor of my mother's mother, also named Elisha. In Hebrew it's Elisheva, which means My God is My Oath."

"I'd always assumed you were Irish."

So had I. "Jake, I've been wanting to talk to you for a while. The business is morphing. Hedge funds are going to dominate trading activity, and with information discounted so fast now the era of working an idea for weeks or even months is over, which means the role of the institutional salesperson has to change as well." I paused to make sure he was following me. "Most senior salespeople won't go near these guys; they're too fast and smart, aren't interested in being wined and dined. You always have to be looking for an edge and that means staying glued to your desk during market hours."

Jake sipped his chardonnay. "You're exactly right. That's why we're here to discuss your new role as national sales manager. I've made partner, heading up the entire equity division. I want you to quarterback the institutional sales department."

"Wow! Congratulations, that's dynamite. But I like being a salesman, I'm good at it, and I'll make Lehman a fortune covering the hedge fund guys. I'm telling you, there's huge money to be made."

Jake tossed back the rest of his glass. "Don't bullshit a bullshitter, kid. You know more about what's going on in the Equity division than anyone ... except me. You understand my game plan and how to execute it. You're a take charge guy, and with offices all over the country now, and our booming banking business ..."

"Can I have some time to mull it over?"

"I'm not asking. I'm telling. You're the new national sales manager. You'll be well-compensated and," he leaned across the table conspiratorially, "it's the path to partnership, Seth."

Those hedgies were so ripe for the picking, but partnership, the ultimate goal, was too tantalizing. I wanted it all. "Let me be a producing sales manager, cover the hedge funds with a commission payout on top of my guarantee. That way I'll lead by example."

He was dubious but agreed so long as my sales role didn't interfere with running the department. "In two weeks, I'm bringing all the salespeople and traders in from all over the country. I want you to make a presentation about how we leverage our sales, trading and research capabilities in this new trading-oriented environment you've so aptly described."

We finished lunch and returned to our new world headquarter at One World Trade Center. My stuff already in Jake's office, Irene ensconced at her new desk looking like the cat that ate the canary, queen bee of all the sales assistants. All eyes on the institutional sales desk followed me in, animosity now tempered with fear.

FOR A GUY who spoke in football metaphors Jake had class, taking over the Odeon in Tribeca for the all-hands institutional equity division meeting. I spent two weeks preparing a speech. Like opening night of a new show, I'd only get one shot at wowing this audience, and Erin was such a trooper, my sounding board for each iteration as I sought to nail my message. I asked if she saw the causal connections I was trying to make while she breastfed Elisha, her eyes half closed. "I'm trying, honey. I'm so tired. I can barely keep her attached to me!"

"We don't leverage our sales and trading capabilities, Erin. It's all about communication. I'm talking basic blocking and tackling!"

"Sweetie, how about going deep to the kitchen and making me a cup of tea? I'm parched!"

"Sure. And I've got this idea of getting the trading desk to make the abbreviated research call to their trading counterparts, and..."

"I can't wait to hear it, honey, but the tea?"

She was sound asleep when I returned. I covered her with a blanket, put Elisha in the bassinet, checked on Meara and Quinn. When I returned, she was curled into a cocoon.

TOO NERVOUS TO eat before the meeting I downed a couple of glasses of Jordan Cabernet Sauvignon to steady myself. Jake formally introduced me as the new national sales manager and I looked out at the huge audience, the biggest room I'd ever played, all eyes on me. This was the role of a lifetime, an actor's dream. "Equity sales, trading and research are equal parts of a three-legged stool," I said, and proceeded to outline the way forward for Lehman's institutional equity division in an era of ever-increasing volatility and renewed interest in equities as an inflation hedge. I talked for half an hour, power surging as I made them buy into my vision of the equity division's future. I was a thirty-year-old power broker. I was King Kong atop the Empire State Building.

Later, I pigeonholed the head of trading and suggested sales and trading do joint client dinners to demonstrate teamwork and send the message to our institutional clientele that at Lehman Brothers the whole was greater than the sum of its parts. I even cajoled the head of research into employing a more uniform approach to research reports. This was my moment; I wouldn't let it slip through my fingers. Several partners congratulated me. Jake clapped me on the back. "You're making me look good."

"That's my job."

I could hear Kevin in my head saying "Smart, son, very smart."

CHAPTER 11

STAID OLD LEHMAN Brothers became a trading and banking powerhouse driven by obsessed money-making machines whose spouses needed periodic assuaging, so the partners, awash in money, booked Broadway theatres or concert halls, threw lavish cocktail parties and fine dinners at glamorous places like Four Seasons and Lutece, everyone mixing and mingling with rock or movie stars. One night Erin sat at dinner with Christopher Reeve, basking in his attentiveness, lost in his blue eyes. On another, Paul McCartney at the piano dedicated *"Maybe I'm Amazed"* to the ginger-haired Irish lass in the second row. And every winter a stretch limo would pull curbside at our brownstone, whisk us away to some fancy tropical resort and fawn over Erin, acknowledging her forbearance of my Type A work schedule, a diamond trifle from Tiffany's always awaiting her. For that week she was not just mommy to four demanding young children, our newest red head, Aiden Benjamin, arriving on September 17, 1984. For that one week, the world of Lehman Brothers was hers.

ONE NIGHT, ARRIVING home late after a long flight from San Francisco, I found Erin relaxing in our parlor, the kids already asleep. She was toking on a joint, reading the feature article *Business Week* had just published: "Lehman Brothers-Pirates in Pinstripes." Tossing the magazine on the table laden with architectural magazines and books, sketches and blueprints, she said, "I like that! Lehman's not one of those conservative, white shoe investment banking firms. You're swashbucklers laying waste to the competition!"

Speaking of wasted! "Did you see I was mentioned in the article? Aggressive, visionary young national sales manager. Pretty cool, huh?" I took a couple of tokes.

"Big deal! Where's your peg leg and eye patch?"

"Jesus, you are so stoned!"

"And you once accused me of fake toking! Carry me off to my boudoir and ravage me."

I lay her across our big brass bed, Botticelli's *Venus*, her flaming red hair spread over the coverlet, her fuller breasts and the subtle roundness to her belly testament to four children. Her beauty never ceased to astonish me. When we made love, it was as if for the first time, every time, and it was only when Aiden woke crying in the bassinet, I remembered she wasn't eighteen.

While Erin nursed, I described a visit to a new hedge fund client whose super deluxe office suite in Pacific Heights overlooked the bay. "I cooled my heels for 15 minutes before he finally deigned to see me. Guy had to be 350, 400 pounds, legs like turkey drumsticks in jogging pants, huffing and puffing, gliding back and forth on one of those Nordic Track machines, sweat literally pouring off him as he watched a humongous TV screen with stock quotes flashing by. Would make a helluva infomercial: Nordic Track—takes a lickin' and keeps on tickin'. Swear to God, I could hear the machine groaning."

"Thanks a lot. That image is a real mood killer. Well, I've got something funny to tell you, too. When Meara came home from school today, she stood up on a chair and proudly shouted 'Mommy, I learned to say no to drugs!' I had to bite my tongue. Thank you, Nancy Reagan!"

"That's cute! So anyway, the guy gives me the usual 'You've got 30 seconds to tell me why I should do business with you' blah blah blah and I of course assured him he'll be my first call . . ."

"As you tell them all."

"Yup. Then he cuts our meeting short 'cause his personal trainer is waiting, and I'd just flown 3000 miles to see this asshole."

"Why are you covering accounts in San Francisco? You've got a sales office there."

"He insists on New York coverage. Figures my branch guys get sloppy seconds, not in the flow of what's happening at the firm, and he's totally right."

"So, assign it to one of your New York salespeople."

"Erin, I'm the only person who can handle this guy and it could be a million-dollar account. It'll make me untouchable!"

"But you're the national sales manager. You're already untouchable . . ."

"Don't kid yourself. I'm only as good as . . ."

"Spare me that old trope! Didn't you say you'd be home more? I thought managers delegated. You missed another parent night at school. Everyone thinks I'm a single mom with a secret sugar daddy."

"Parent Teacher conferences for first grade and preschool? Come on, Erin, it's not like I'm really missing anything."

"Tell that to Meara, Seth. She was pretty disappointed." She burped Aiden, placed him back in his bassinet, climbed back in bed and was asleep in seconds.

CHAPTER 12

THE NEIGHBORHOOD WAS transitioning, many of our dear friends passing on or forced by adult children to move closer to them, and Erin became a one-woman welcome wagon greeting the young urban professionals finally flocking to Carroll Gardens, attracted to the unique atmosphere and magnificent old brownstones. She was a parent teacher room rep in Meara's classroom at the Berkeley Carroll School, active in social justice committees at the Brooklyn Heights Synagogue, the temple she insisted we join so our growing brood would have a religious foundation, made large charitable contributions to the Sierra Club, Greenpeace, the ACLU and other worthy causes, and endlessly renovated our brownstone already worth three to four times what we paid for it, not that it mattered as Erin and our house were a single entity, as psychically and physically attached to our neighborhood as she'd once been to her childhood home in the Pacific Northwest. But then again, Erin found or created happiness wherever she was.

And she'd transformed our backyard into an Eden, a blue-slated terrace lush with vegetation, bamboo and climbing vines, melodious wind chimes, even a small cascading waterfall in the corner of our property that meandered through a stone garden path into a pool of colorful Koi fish. A place I'd find peace away from the hubbub of my Wall Street life, and it was there I found her the next evening, sitting on the outdoor sofa listening to the trickle of the water feature and the rustle of our bamboo border swaying in the light summer breeze, the smell of honeysuckle wafting through the air, sipping a glass of wine as she sketched out plans for renovating our attic space. The children, as usual, already asleep. I kissed her and started to crow about the huge order the new San Francisco client had placed on our desk when she interrupted me. "What do you think of these plans for the attic?"

"Do we really need the additional living space?"

"It's not a question of need, Seth. The very first time I went upstairs, I had a vision of the attic as it should be. Not really an attic. More a natural extension of our living space. I'm simply executing that vision."

"Well, I guess it's a good thing I'm covering that new account in San Francisco. A half million share order placed on the desk this morning, Erin. I told you I was the only person who could cover this account."

"That's nice honey. Oh, I met the new couple moving into Mr. Manzoni's house today. They seem really nice. She's pregnant with their first child, still working at a downtown law firm. He works in advertising..."

"That was just an opening order to get my attention. I'll do a lot of business with this guy. This account could be huge."

"... and we walked through the house, then went upstairs to their bedroom where they tore my clothes off and ravished me, a ménage a trois..." My mouth fell open. "As usual, you're not listening, Seth. Your body's here but your mind's at work. I'm talking about our new neighbors the Fosters!"

"I am listening. Sad to see Mr. Manzoni pass. Such a character. Crazy about you and the kids."

"I was actually talking about our new neighbors, honey, not Mr. Manzoni, but I'll miss him, too. I think of him every time I use the garden implements he left me. He was like a grandfather to the kids. But finally having people our own age next door will be nice. I invited them over to see our renovation and I'm having lunch with Peggy tomorrow. The Manzoni house is still in original condition, like our house was. It'll be fun to renovate."

"You planning to be involved?"

"Can't see why not. Meara's in school all day, and Quinn a half day. Mrs. Castellano is always begging me to let her watch the little ones. It's an opportunity to utilize my talents and play with other people's money for a change. After the attic there won't be much left to do here, and between Jeff and me we've got a lot of experience now."

"Wait a sec. What's Jeff got to do with this?"

"He's joining us for lunch. He's got great ideas."

As our home renovation neared completion, piles of architectural magazines, sketches of kitchens and landscapes littered the parlor room table, evidence of Erin's mounting restiveness, of new ideas and architectural projects she discussed with Jeff, who shared her interests in design and construction. They spoke a common tongue, like her Outward-Bound friends. It was disquieting. Carol McGuire had once suggested I was Erin's first renovation project, but renovators moved from project to project. Was this wonderful Japanese garden, this Eden she'd so lovingly designed for me, a swansong?

CHAPTER 13

HENRY STEIN, OUR consumer products analyst, rushed into my office with breaking news and demanded I put him on the system immediately. Proctor and Gamble was going to introduce a potato chip with no calories. He said it was a huge deal, but to me a potato chip with no calories sounded like an oxymoron.

"I don't have time to explain the chemistry to you. You wouldn't understand it anyway."

"Maybe not, but I do control access to the system, so try."

"It involves a fat substitute. Think Teflon. It simply goes right through you!"

"That sounds truly disgusting. Can't wait to see that ad campaign. Hope PG owns Depends. They'll get the business coming and going."

"Seth, Kimberly-Clark owns Depends, not PG. Look, we really don't have time for this right now. This is BIG NEWS. Only we've got it, but it's a short window."

I stood up, shrugged and pointed to all the empty sales desks. All at lunch with clients. His was a voice in the wilderness. I clicked on the hoot and holler system, told everyone to listen up, we had breaking news on PG, and Henry went through his story. Afterwards, frustrated by the inattention, he muttered, "Goddamn salesforce," and handed the phone back. I assured him they'd hear it when they returned and I would reiterate it with the trading desk immediately. "Thanks. Great job, Henry."

It was a hot story, whether an increment to PG's bottom line or ultimately a complete disaster impossible to predict, but by the time that mattered we'd be long gone, hawking another idea. I called my fast money clients, breaching trading desk protocol by extracting orders through the phone—100,000 shares from San Fran, 50,000 from Dallas, 250,000 from LA, then ran the orders over to the trading desk. "Listen up guys! You all heard Henry over the system, right?" Dumb stares. I reiterated the story, told them to call their trading counterparts and yelled to the head of the position desk "Start accumulating PG. I've size to buy and more behind it." Everyone hit the phones and I was conducting an orchestra, barking orders to traders on all sides of the U-shaped desk, them responding immediately. The noise level ratcheted up, sales traders screaming to the position desk: "I need 100,000 PG"; "I need 250,000 PG," the position traders scrambling to accumulate more shares. "Find me stock, people," the trading manager barked. "I need every share you can find!"

PG, flat on the day when Henry first approached me, is now up a half dollar, then a dollar, and I'm getting more orders, another 250,000 shares from Texas, 100,000 more from LA, and the stock's up two dollars now and climbing, the entire trading desk in a feeding frenzy, a school of piranhas with the taste of blood working the phones, grousing about absent salespeople, putting me on with their trading counterparts, lights blinking on their consoles like it's Christmas on Wall Street, and the stock's up three dollars, my hedgies already making huge profits by the time the sales force slowly drifted in. Pissed at missing the easy money call but desperate to get in on the action, they hit the phones, and the stock's now up four dollars and still climbing with new buy orders flooding in, and I'm selling into their buyers to create liquidity and locking in millions for my clients in minutes. I was so fucking pumped; what a rush. I owned this moment, controlled the entire desk, an entire market. Step aside He-Man, I was the fucking Master of the Universe! No drug ever provided such exhilaration, sense of power or control. Joel said doing big trades was better than sex. He was right. It was better than anything!

After a celebratory evening at Harry's, I limo'd home cresting a wave of indomitable power, then fell flat on my face tripping over a wooden block toy on the parlor room floor. So much for superpowers! Rising, I found myself staring directly at the Alley Pond Park photo and had a flash of insight, something about Grandma and Grandpa, but it vaporized before I reached the second-floor landing.

Erin was reading the latest issue of the *Old House Journal* in bed, propped up with fluffy pillows.

"I just did the biggest equity trade in Lehman's history!"

"That's nice. Check this out, honey." She turned the magazine toward me. "This is a Brooklyn-based publication. I'd like to get them to do a feature on our house."

"That all you have to say? I made the firm millions. The biggest trade ever."

"I had a big day, too. We got the Foster remodel, a total renovation of their brownstone, but you know what else? Aiden took his first steps today. How's that for news?" She slammed the magazine on her nightstand. "Leave your power broker skin at the office. You walk into this house a husband and father, and if you wanna don a cape and be faster than a speeding bullet, play Superman with your sons; they're superheroes too! Uncle Jeff was here to see his first steps."

"Uncle Jeff? What the hell was he doing here, and since when is he a member of the family?"

"Your children see a lot more of Uncle Jeff than of you, and we were signing the contract for the Foster job. He also fixed the fridge. The condenser went out again." She removed her reading glasses. "You know, when you're here, when you're actually focusing your attention on me and our children, there's no place better, but you rarely are. I watch you talk about things like this trade with such excitement and intensity. That's the way you described *Shane*. How you used to look at me. That was my Seth, the boy who took my breath away. I want him back!"

"Erin, you are my world."

"THEN SHOW IT, GODDAM IT! I have four children under the age of nine. Our dinner conversations revolve around hysterical body functions like farts and poop. Finally, I have something special for me, something that utilizes my skills and passions, things you once encouraged but now barely acknowledge." I reached out to her, but she pushed me off. "No, just listen. I'm not complaining. I love my children. I wouldn't change a thing except I need you here, present in our lives. I want our memories to merge the way my parents can finish each other's sentences, the way they look at each other and smile and know exactly what the other is thinking. I want that, Seth, I need that. Don't you?"

It was a conundrum, work and home life as irreconcilable as my need to know what was hidden and my fear of its revelation. "Let's get away, all of us. It's February. Mitzie and Dad are in Florida. Let's go down there for winter break. I'll clear my calendar. I promise. Okay?"

"But we just got this job! Am I always supposed to be at your beck and call those rare moments your sun shines on us?"

"It's Jeff's company. Surely he can handle it for a week without you."

"That's not the point. I expect you to be as supportive of me as I am of you. You're trying to buy me off the same way the partners mollify me with Tiffany trinkets. Where's the boy I fell in love with, the man I committed my life to?" She looked at me imploringly. "I miss him! Where's my partner?" Was she becoming Jeff's partner? "I'm the one who made this happen, Seth, and the Foster's and Jeff are counting on me. But okay. I'll work it out. I'll let Jeff know he'll be flying solo for a week. I'll ask him to bring in our mail." She pursed her lips. "Hmm. You know, there actually is something you can do for me."

"Anything. Just name it."

"Sell Girl Scout cookies at the office for Meara's Brownie troop. It's like a competition. All the dads get involved. There's 12 boxes to a case and I committed to two cases, just to kick things off. Katie McCleary's dad sold 400 boxes last year. Blew everyone else away. He's a salesman with Merrill Lynch. Obviously, I don't expect you to come even close to that..."

"That's like 33 cases. Yeah, no worries. I've got you stopped." She looked at me quizzically. "Just consider it done." I can outsell Katie McCleary's dad with one arm tied around my back.

I CORRALLED IRENE as soon as she arrived at the office next morning. "Anutha cup of black coffee, right?"

"Not right now, thanks. Could you grab a pen and pad and come out to the trading floor with me? I have to sell some Girl Scout cookies for Meara." She followed me out, grumbling. This was not part of her job description. Guys were on the phone, others kibitzing, bemoaning another abysmal Knicks defeat. "Listen up, guys. I'm selling Girl Scout cookies, looking for indications of interest."

My Texas trader was interested in a box, but when I said cases only he indicated for one. The guy next to him gave me an indication for two; Texas countered with three. The head trader indicated five, matched by the fixed income manager. Then the OTC Desk started bidding, as did several research analysts and Irene was yelling for everyone to slow down, she couldn't write that fast. Within ten minutes I had firm indications for six hundred boxes, fifty cases, returned to my office and called Erin. "Let's see Katie McCleary's dad top that."

"Wow, Meara will be thrilled. You are so competitive. Thank you, honey."

CHAPTER 14

THE DOORMAN AT Mom and Dad's Palm Beach condo handed me a thick envelope as we entered the lobby after a day on the beach. The kids, sunburned despite constant lathering's of SPF 50 lotion, coated with sand like cornmeal-crusted catfish, were exhausted, ready for baths, dinner and bed, Erin and I excited about having a night on the town. The envelope contained a travel voucher. I read Jake's attached note: "*Sorry about this Seth, but we just got the Telecom deal and meet with banking at 8 a.m. tomorrow morning. A limo will pick you up at 7:30 p.m. for your 9 o'clock flight. Go directly to the Vista Hotel. We wouldn't have gotten the lead on this deal without our distribution capability, so kudos to you and the equity team! Tell Erin we'll make this up to her. See you tomorrow morning at 8.*" Oh fuck.

I sheepishly handed it to Erin, who became apoplectic. "This better be Jake's idea of a joke, Seth. We just got here yesterday!" She crushed it in her fist and Meara started to bawl. "Daddy, you're leaving? You promised to teach me how to body surf and take me to the ice cream shop and . . . YOU'RE NEVER HERE!" And that set off the others while poor John, the doorman, looked on in dismay. It had been such a nice day. Dad had played with the little ones while Erin and I surfed up at Lake Worth beach. Meara and Quinn had their first body surfing lessons. Dinner reservations were at Charley's Crab. Erin had purchased a slinky Dolce and Gabbana dress for the occasion.

The limo pulled up in front of the building two hours later. I hugged her as the driver opened the passenger door. "Honestly, Erin, I'd no idea. I'll make it up to you, I promise."

"This trip was already an attempt to make up for your constant absence from our lives! Some vacation. The kids are so disappointed. They thought they had their daddy to themselves for a change, as did I. Just call me when you get to New York so I know you arrived safely, okay?" She walked back into the lobby.

IRENE GROUSED OVER her job description's burgeoning elasticity when I asked her to limo to our house Monday morning and pack me a week's worth of business clothes. I'd barely a moment to breathe, responsible for developing a viable marketing plan, prepping the issuing company for a road show, holding informational meetings with the domestic sales force and coordinating the entire process with the lead investment bankers over a night cap at the Windows of the World bar atop the North Tower of the WTC, one hundred floors above the hotel, 50 floors above Lehman's world headquarters.

The view out the floor to ceiling glass windows atop the North Tower, the world I'd vowed to conquer, was astonishing. I could see Brooklyn, Queens, Staten Island, the Statue of Liberty, Ellis Island, the Empire State Building, Central Park, even as far north as the lights of Yankee Stadium in the Bronx. Yet, my heart was in Florida with Erin and my kids. I'd checked in with her earlier in the evening to see if they were having a good time, hoping she wasn't too pissed at me. "Everything's just honky dory here in Carroll Gardens South."

"Erin, I'm really..."

"Yada, yada, yada! Meara is boogie boarding. Took to it like a duck to water!" Just like her mom. "Quinn's frustrated; needs his daddy to show him how. Elisha and Aiden are having a blast with Dad, playing on the beach and in the pool. Only time we see Mitzie is when she comes down with lunch. Doesn't swim, complains about us tracking sand into the condo. Some old biddy complained Aiden was too young to be in the pool, but Dad got right in her face. I love him! And I almost forgot, your great aunt Tilly showed up..."

"Oh no, not a restaurant recommendation."

"Yup. The old battle ax drove over after getting her blue hair shellacked. Can you believe she's ninety-five and still driving? How scary is that! And she insisted we go to her favorite Chinese buffet."

"The only thing worse than Tilly's cooking is her taste in restaurants."

"You got it. Here I am in Florida, land of southern cooking, catfish, ribs, bacon smothered in bacon, and we wind up in a greasy, cheap Chinese restaurant specializing in ptomaine poisoning, for their early bird special no less. Meara called it the 'Chinese barffet'!"

"Are you having a good time?"

"As good a time as can be expected for a single mom, but I'm used to that. You're the one missing out. My green bikini is so tiny when I removed it my luscious breasts were creamy white against the sunburn, my nipples all rosy, and my freckles are freckling all over my hot, sexy body..."

"Stop, honey, you're giving me a hard on."

"Not just you. I wore that sexy Dolce and Gabbana dress out to dinner tonight, or should I say afternoon since we ate at five p.m.. Gave a few geezers' heart arrhythmias to go along with their early bird specials. One guy, I swear he must've been in his seventies, hit on me. How's that for action?"

"Tonight I'll go to sleep imagining I'm kissing every one of those freckles. It'll beat counting sheep. We should have this whole thing wrapped up by the end of the week; it'll be an incredible pay day for the firm . . . and us."

"Seth, do you love me like you did when we were kids?"

"I love you more than anything in the world!"

"I know this week's not your fault but sometimes I feel we're living parallel lives, like you're still not really seeing me. Good night!"

IT WAS PAST eleven when I got back to my room. Erin's tone nagged at me. I needed to talk to her again. Hoped I wouldn't wake the house. She picked up, alarmed. "Everything okay, honey? Two calls in one day. I think that's a record. Everyone's asleep here. I'm in the living room reading with the sliders open, listening to the waves lapping on the shore. There's a cool salty breeze. It's so lovely, but lonely. The beach lights are all off to protect the sea turtles; they're laying their eggs in the sand. Led to a lively discussion with Meara about the birds and the bees. A first. And it's so dark out. The water looks phosphorescent and I can see the entire Milky Way. I saw several shooting stars . . ."

"Really? Did you make a wish?"

"Uh huh. I hoped there wouldn't be any hitches on the Foster job while I was gone, but Jeff called and assured me everything is going fine."

"Geez, won't that guy ever leave you alone?"

"Come on, honey, be a bit more understanding. He's lonely and I'm his best friend. Maybe one of the few people in his life he can be himself with. It's tough for him. I wish the world was free of discrimination but it's not. You grew up with Jonah, so you know what I mean." I didn't know what she was talking about. What did Jonah have to do with this? "Do your sensitivity receptors only work on Wall Street? Seriously, I can't decide whether you're naïve, oblivious or both. He's gay, Seth. Surely you knew that."

OH! Thank God. "Did . . . ah . . . you wish for anything else?"

"I saw multiple shooting stars, right? I also wished you'd miss me so much you'd call again. And you have."

"Erin, please come back Friday. I'll pick you up at JFK. I don't want to spend the weekend without you. I haven't even been back to the house. No work! I swear. Just you and me and the kids. Just fun."

CHAPTER 15

IRENE ALMOST BLEW a gasket when I asked her to call all the metro Volvo dealerships to check available stock for immediate purchase. Not quibbling over price, I drove to JFK in a shiny new metallic silver seven seat Volvo 760 turbo station wagon, the Young Upwardly Mobile Mommy must-have car, and parked in an outside lot. Meeting them at the arrivals gate the kids jumped all over me shouting "Daddy, Daddy," all talking at once about the manta ray they saw with Papa, the birds and alligators in the wildlife sanctuary, and especially the ice cream cones at the Ice Cream Club in Manalapan. Meara proudly announced she finished an entire two scoop cone! "Me, too. I got banana ice cream," Quinn added.

"No, Quinn," Meara immediately corrected. "That was only one scoop."

I lifted Quinn in the air before he had a chance to pout. Told him that was my favorite, too. He squealed with delight. I couldn't believe how much I'd missed them; how much I'd taken their presence for granted. I handed Erin the itinerary for a week's vacation at the famous Rock Resort in Virgin Gorda. "I had Irene book us a luxury waterfront suite. It's Lehman's way of thanking you for being a team player. And I've got something else for you."

She looked at the itinerary, all smiles when she saw the destination, then furrowed her brow and handed it back to me. Fool's gold. "This is a couples only resort. What about our four kids?"

"Already covered. Irene got your parents round-trip first-class tickets to New York. They're excited about having the kids to themselves. This trip is just for you and me."

"But my project? I can't just up and leave whenever you get the rare urge to get away."

"But this is special for you. I . . . I really thought you'd be excited."

"Oh damn, I hate you looking so disappointed. I'll see what I can do."

Once outside, Erin's eyes widened when I tossed her the keys to the new

Volvo station wagon gleaming in the late afternoon sun. "Remember when you told me to imagine we were in a covered wagon? Well, here's one for my urban pioneer, minus the canvas top, with black leather interior, a turbo engine and seating for seven. My way of saying thanks for putting up with me."

"Don't tell me you had Irene shop for this as well."

"Uh, well, actually, she did kinda call around for me, but I picked it up myself early this morning and parked it in the underground garage. First and last time I'll do that. That garage is a labyrinth; must have four or five sublevels. Reminded me of the spring break I went spelunking with Umo in Kentucky, crawling through miniscule crevasses two hundred feet below ground, hoping the earth didn't shift an inch and crush me to death. I told you about that."

"When the two of you got so high on Thai sticks you couldn't remember where you were going and had to pull over to the side of the highway until you could remember who you were?

"Yeah, that stuff was dynamite."

"I can't see you driving your old beater to work anyway, Mr. Working Class Hero."

"Not planning to, but now we have a car all shiny and new."

"Not we, me, and I'm not sure I'll even let you drive it. And by the way, don't think for one second I don't know what you're doing. Kids, look what Daddy got us. Hmmm. Seats seven." She counted us all up and grinned. "Looks like there's room for one more."

I unlocked our front door and entered, our front parlor filled, floor to ceiling, with cases of Girl Scout cookies. I turned to Erin. Asked her what was going on. What were these doing here? She reminded me. Fifty cases, six hundred boxes and asked what I thought I'd been selling. These weren't shares of PG. These were cookies. Made with flour, eggs and sugar. You eat them. And now I had to deliver them. "Welcome to the real world, sweetie!" She gave me a high five. "Our Brownie troop is going to trounce everyone!"

CHAPTER 16

HALF A LIFETIME ago I'd journeyed down the Yucatan coast with Terry struggling to escape myself, desperate for a new identity, a skin I could settle into. Now, two decades later, I was married to the most wonderful woman, blessed with children I adored, and feted at a posh resort catering to the rich and famous. I'd always strived like a horse with blinders reaching for that carrot, but wondered if that unhappy boy would again overtake me once I ran out of goals to distance myself from him.

The resort could have been the setting for *South Pacific* in all its Technicolor splendor, anything and everything we could possibly desire at our beck and call. Every morning, after breakfast served on our private terrace, we'd be whisked onboard a catamaran and shipwrecked on uninhabited islands with catered lunch and chilled champagne. We snorkeled at the Baths, a labyrinth of huge boulders the size of our brownstone half-buried in the clear blue water and dove through tunnels and arches. We made love in secluded grottos, sailboarded or biked to Spanish Town, partook of sumptuous lunches and dinners served on a veranda overlooking the aquamarine Caribbean. Huge silver bowls overflowed with lobster meat, propelling Erin to shellfish heaven. Evenings we'd stroll down the beach until the lights of civilization had dimmed, lay back in the sand and gazed through gauzy curtains of stars into the past, the future, into infinity. But I was no longer a meaningless speck in the vast universe. I reached for Erin's hand and pressed it to my heart. I was tethered to the Earth. Erin my gravity.

I wanted to freeze-frame this moment, make it forever, and almost nine months to the day, on November 22nd, 1988, my wish came true with the arrival of our fifth child, an adorable boy whose shock of black, curly hair resembled baby photos of Jonah, as unlike our brood of redheads as I was to my brother and parents; beautiful, yet different. Tears cascaded down my cheeks. I had found Jonah in the Caribbean after all. "Did you know we were having a boy?" I sniffled. "Did he tell you his name?"

She smiled and handed him to me. "Terry and I have been talking for months..." I must have looked surprised. "Hey, maybe he wanted you to name a child after him, too." I'd often wondered whether he and Kate had found true love. I sure hoped so.

I leaned over the birthing bed, kissed Erin and cradled Terry in my arms. "Terry, you'll never be the ugly duckling in a pond of redheads. You're unique."

Erin reached up and wiped away my tears. "I just gave you another son. Now I need you to do something for me. Open your heart to your mother. I know you love her. You know you love her. Let that love shine through."

My parents arrived at the hospital a few hours later. Erin, exhausted, had dosed off, Terry asleep in her arms. I put a finger to my lips as they entered the room. Quietly approaching the birthing bed, Mitzie gasped when she saw Terry and collapsed in a chair I pushed under her just in the nick of time. Tears of joy streamed down her face, and I opened myself to my mother for the first time without fear, without expectation, and allowed unspent love and empathy flow through me. She looked up at me, eyes shining. "He's beautiful, isn't he?"

I leaned over her chair and embraced her. "I love you, Mom."

Erin woke, her bright eyes welling at the sight of us, mother and son.

CHAPTER 17

AFTER A WEEK-LONG business trip to my sales offices in Chicago, L.A., and San Francisco I arrived early evening at The Mansion on Turtle Creek in Dallas, Texas, my favorite hotel. The doorman always welcomed me back by name, the front desk handed me the key to my preferred room, lobster tacos and a half bottle of Sonoma Cutrer Chardonnay already on the way.

Exhausted, I looked forward to a quiet respite before morning meetings with my Dallas sales force and lunch with a hedge fund client, an insecure, foul-mouthed Jewish guy fond of screaming I was the stupidest person on the face of the earth and he'd no idea why he bothered taking my calls. He'd regularly slam the phone on me. I'd count off 30 seconds, call him back and extract a large order.

Swathed in a plush bathrobe emblazoned with the Mansion logo, sipping chilled wine and munching on a lobster taco, I called Erin. Terry had been accepted into the pre-school program at Berkeley Carroll, the private school attended by our other four children. "With all five kids there in September, Terry there half days, it frees up more of my time. Hey, are you eating something?"

"Yeah, lobster tacos. The chef's preparation is outstanding. Thick chunks of fresh lobster in a piquant lemon butter sauce wrapped in warm, hand rolled tortillas, with cabbage slaw and salsa fresca."

"You're making me jealous. We dined on Annie's Mac and Cheese and fish sticks, a Matthews household favorite."

"I thought that was your go-to meal when we were going out for the evening."

"Still is. Jeff and I met with the couple moving into a brownstone on Clinton Street. They could only meet at dinnertime, so Mrs. Castellano came over to watch the kids. Meara complained it was unnecessary but Mrs. Castellano's like a grandmother to her, so she doesn't make too much of a fuss . . . not yet anyway."

"She's not old enough to babysit."

"I was watching my brothers at thirteen, and Meara is pretty responsible. Anyway, like I was saying, with all the kids now in school I've been doing a lot of thinking. Ever since Bob Foster got us featured in that *New York Times* Home section article about yuppie urban pioneers Jeff's business has boomed; it's outgrown one person, and you know he's been after me to come on board full time for years. He's filed reincorporation papers as Weaver Construction Company and wants me to be his business partner."

Consulting was one thing, but a full-time commitment? "You realize you don't have to do that. We don't need the money."

"I know. That's what's so nice, and I really appreciate it, honey. I don't have to; I want to. I'll finally be able to utilize my education and even make money! You won't need to work as hard."

I dropped my half-eaten lobster taco on the plate. Took a moment to digest her news. I was compelled to work hard. Rapprochement with my mother had not diminished my persistent sense of disquiet. It seemed to draw me closer to the source of it. I knew Erin would be fantastic at this new job, but I'd been hoping we'd buy a piece of land in Amagansett and she could design and build a vacation home for us. She loved the Hamptons. Maybe we'd have another child. We were still young. Stupid me, buying a car that only sat seven. Whatever. She'd set her heart on this, evidently. "I think it's great, honey," I finally offered. "I'm proud of you. I really am."

"Do you really mean it, Seth? It sounds a bit like you're trying to convince yourself."

"No. You'll be great. Look what you did with our house and the Foster job, the writeup in *The Times*. I just hope between our two busy schedules, we'll still have time to do stuff together as a family and a couple."

I glumly downed the rest of my chardonnay.

CHAPTER 18

IT WAS A fait accompli, and I was awed by her ability to seamlessly juggle home and business responsibilities, something I'd never mastered, and she proved a brilliant designer and salesperson, inveigling me into investing in the fast growing yet undercapitalized business, even insisting I become the chief financial officer. I agreed. It would give Erin and me another point of connection.

Demand for Weaver Construction services grew exponentially and our home phone rang so incessantly I bought her one of those new cellphones. Damn thing so large she wore it in a holster like a cowboy's six-guns. When it rang, she'd pull the trigger and go off to talk privately, usually to Jeff.

I tried to make it home for the occasional dinner or worked late in my study to free up more weekend time, but as I had feared, our schedules now often conflicted, even on weekends. One Saturday morning I suggested surfing at the Rockaways but she demurred. Swamped. Had an appointment; meant to tell me. I protested this was family time and she agreed. "Your kids will be thrilled to have special family time with you." Even attempted to placate me. "I'll be home by dinner. Pick up lobsters and we'll have a romantic dinner on the back terrace. I'll even shell yours. How's that for a deal?" Her cell rang for the umpteenth time. "Yeah, Jeff, I know . . . I'm on my way. Listen, Seth, make the kids pancakes, pack a lunch and plenty of sunscreen. We're meeting at the McCain's. They just bought the Mongeluzzi's old place. Should be a huge job. See you later, okay? Love you."

I watched her head toward the front door. "Don't think I don't know what you're doing."

"Cats in the cradle, Seth; I learned from the master." She blew me a kiss and was gone.

Handling five kids alone was beyond terrifying (even with Meara's assistance), so I loaded them into the Volvo and drove out to Winona beach. Dad joined us; Mom arrived later with lunch. Meara, blossoming into a facsimile of her mother when we first met and fell in love, ensured I basted everyone, including myself, with sunscreen, then swam with me out to the third float where we watched boats cruise in and out of Huntington Harbor. My little baby was growing up, and my heart ached as I watched her eyes follow a flotilla of Sunfish sail across the water to Sand City. Where had the time gone? "Bet you'd rather be with those other teenagers than your old man, huh?"

She sat at the edge of the raft, her feet dangling in the water making little figure eights with her toes. "I'm happy being here with you, Daddy. Are you and Mommy okay? You know, a lot of my classmates' parents are getting divorced. Katie McCleary's dad just moved out." So much for Girl Scout cookies. "I'm not a child; you can tell me."

"Everything is fine, really. It's nice to spend some time with you. Mommy had appointments today and I've the whole weekend free." I reached out to hug her and felt self-conscious resistance. Where was the exuberant little girl who used to fly into my arms?

CHAPTER 19

RETURNING FROM THE partners dining room after celebrating Jake's retirement and my promotion, the trading room was empty save for janitors cleaning up from the day's frenzied activity. Green and red lights still pulsed on the desktop monitors, their electronic hum echoing through the cavernous chamber, a constant reminder money never sleeps. I entered my office, picked up the phone and called home to share my big news, but Erin sounded harried. Had no time to talk. The winter storm had wreaked havoc at the McCain job. The roof was leaking. They'd probably have to replace parts of the wood flooring. "Did you hear me? I just made partner. Can't you spare a couple of minutes, at least congratulate me?"

"I heard you. It's great. But you're not hearing me. I've got a disaster on my hands. Jeff and I have to run over there right now and tarp the roof. Make the kids dinner and I'll see you later, okay?"

So much for celebrating. "What'd you plan for dinner?"

"Nothing. You're an actor, right? Improvise. Look, I'm sorry but I gotta go."

I slumped back in my soft leather armchair. I'd worked zealously for that brass ring on the Wall Street merry-go-round, the Academy Award for best actor in Investment Banking, the pinnacle of my profession. I could count myself amongst the elite of the industry. An office on Partners Row. Instant access to anything and everything I could ever want. More money than I could ever imagine, much less spend. A legend, but only in my mind. So much for being the straw that stirred the drink!

I gazed at the family photos arrayed on my desk, a photographic essay of life lived vicariously. I had indeed become Jake. Meara on toe at a ballet recital; Quinn, arms thrust victoriously in the air, scoring the winning goal for his soccer team; Aiden, Elisha and Terry in Erin's home sewn Halloween costumes hugging Dad at the Pumpkin Patch on Old Northern Boulevard; beaming Erin, clad in bib overalls, gloves and sun hat, surrounded by Mr. Manzoni's gardening implements, proudly displaying the results of her green thumb; Erin on the podium at the Berkeley Carroll school accepting the Volunteer Parent of the Year award. Tears dropped onto the prospectus of the IPO we were lead managing. I hadn't been physically or emotionally there for any of it, too immersed in my own ongoing drama. Striving for something that ultimately didn't matter in order to obscure things I didn't want to see, I'd made no accommodation for anyone else's life story and now it was coming home to roost.

I picked up a photo of Erin and me at a Lehman Brothers function honoring me as institutional salesman of the year. Erin Matthews, hair coiffed, eyes lined with mascara, wearing the same poufy dress Melanie Griffith had worn to the Academy Awards, teetering in unaccustomed high heels; Seth Matthews, tuxedoed, salt and pepper red hair tamed, exuding the confident aura of power broker. Both of us role-playing. Truth was, the most thrilling moments of my life were those in which I had participated, not controlled—the births of my children; Meara and Quinn standing on the Bima reciting from the Torah at their Bat and Bar Mitzvahs, knowing they would continue an unbroken line; the heart-stopping sight of Erin standing on the prow of a catamaran in the blazing Caribbean sun, copper hair aflame, her sparkling eyes capturing the mysteries of the universe and my soul. I'd summited the peak of Wall Street achievement while everything that really mattered, the moments of bliss that connected me to the world, remained below, in base camp. Like King Midas, everything I touched had indeed turned to gold, but success left a bitter residue; you can't eat gold.

Ignoring the typical late-February weather, I cancelled the limo awaiting me downstairs and trudged the three and one-half miles to Carroll Gardens to afford me time to sort out my emotions. The raw, wet wind whipped my face and drenched my wingtips. My overcoat a sodden mess within minutes. I had indeed become the man in Harry Chapin's song, "The Cat's in the Cradle." There'd always been planes to catch and bills to pay; my children had learned to walk while I was away, and now, when all I desired was to celebrate with the one person in the world who completed me, she was becoming like me. I was a chocolate Easter bunny, all shell, hollow on the inside.

CHAPTER 20

"DADDY'S HOME!" AIDEN shrieked with unabashed delight, bounding upstairs to tell the others while I removed my drenched overcoat and threw it over the banister. They all joined me in the warm parlor room where Erin had lit a fire to chase the winter chill that blanketed the city and seeped through our single-pane leaded glass picture windows. I hugged them all in turn, grateful they were there to validate an accomplishment that seemed pyrrhic, but Meara stood apart, stone-faced, eyes filled with recrimination. "You got fired, didn't you? That's why we've been seeing more of you. That's why Mommy is out all the time now. She has to work."

"Many people whose houses she's renovating work outside the home and can only meet at night."

"Katie McCleary's dad had his excuses, too," she fumed, stomping up the stairs as the others looked on with concern. Meara, the big sister, the leader of the pack.

I planted a big smile on my face. "Daddy just made partner. We should celebrate. What should we have for dinner?"

"PIZZA! Mommy said we could have pizza."

Meara scowled at me throughout dinner, then quietly loaded the dishwasher while I refrigerated the leftover Caesar salad the little ones refused to touch. They asked if they could watch TV and I turned it on, immediately upbraided by Meara. "Mommy has a no TV rule in this house during the week."

"But it's a special occasion," I asserted feebly.

Quinn entered the kitchen holding out a sheet of paper and asked for my help with a math problem. It was hieroglyphics to me. I suggested he ask Erin in the morning but Meara, with a sigh affirming my utter cluelessness, snatched it from my hand. "It's simple algebra. I'll help him."

Everything at home seemed beyond my control and I vainly attempted to assert some authority with the others, demanding they turn off the TV and get ready for bed, but even they dissed me. "Come on Daddy," Elisha protested, hiding the remote behind her back. "*Fraggle Rock*'s not over yet and you're not the boss of me."

"You're not even supposed to be watching; let's go, turn it off. Elisha and Aiden, into the shower."

"Oh Daddy," they collectively groaned. Meara looked on, sniggering, and when I asked her if she could help with bedtime said she'd too much homework and wished me luck. She disappeared upstairs with Quinn, leaving me to deal with three obstreperous children who wouldn't budge.

"I mean now," I commanded. "I'm gonna count to five, and if you guys aren't upstairs... ONE, TWO..."

Aiden crossed his arms; stared at me defiantly. "Whatareyougonnadoaboutit?" And when adorable little Terry piped in he was sick of this fucking bullshit, I knew all was lost. Any authority I had at the office evaporated on the home front. How did Erin deal with this crap?

"I'm going to tell your mother, that's what!" Magic words. They scrambled upstairs.

I bathed Terry, made sure Aiden used soap in the shower, both brushed their teeth. I read them stories in their shared room and tucked them into adjoining twin beds. When they asked much I loved them, I spread my arms wide. "This much," I said, but when I hugged them goodnight and started for the door Terry began to cry. I returned to his bedside. I'd forgotten to add, "With all my heart and soul." Apparently, Erin always said that and the boys wouldn't be able to sleep without those magic words. Elisha was reading in bed, entranced in a book. I kissed her and told her I loved her with all my heart and soul. "Lights out, sweetheart."

"I'm just finishing this chapter."

"What are you reading?"

"*Little Women* by Louisa May Alcott. Daddy, why is Meara mad at you?"

"Because I haven't been paying enough attention to you guys, but that's going to change, I promise."

"The house feels happier when you're home. Good night, Daddy. I love you."

I blinked back tears. "I love you too, sweetheart."

CHAPTER 21

PAST ELEVEN I got into bed and stared blankly into an open book whose title I couldn't even recall. I was thinking about my children asleep in their beds. Thinking about the empty space next to me. Thinking how we were all connected, like the mycelium Erin had once described, mutual support and stability in an ever-changing world, a microcosm of the family circles I attended as a small child. I'd taken Erin's superpowers for granted, her calm, her innate ability to be productive amidst chaos. I'd pursued that partnership with single-minded focus, convinced I was doing it all for them, giving them everything, when all they ever really wanted was me.

When Erin entered our bedroom past midnight and started undressing as if nothing was amiss, my relief turned anger. "Where the hell have you been? It's late. Not a call. Nothing!"

"Sorry, didn't mean to worry you," she said, nonchalantly stripping off wet clothes and hanging them to dry in our bathroom. Wet socks slapped against the bottom of the tub. "Had to tarp the entire living room floor. Couldn't get on the roof. It's still sleeting. The ceiling will have to be replaced. What a mess."

"Worry me? You were out to all hours. You should've called; that's what the damned cellphone's for. Better yet, you should be here, at home with your children . . . and me!"

"Oh, I see. I'm supposed to be the good little wifeypoo always at your beck and call, living through your Wall Street exploits, my self-worth and identity defined by yours. Consider this is a little taste of the last 20 years of my life. I know all about no calls, late nights . . ."

"Erin, are you working to get even with me?"

She rushed over to our bed, facial muscles twitching, grabbed my wrists and squeezed so hard my hands went numb. "Jesus Christ! I can't believe you'd actually think that, much less say it! How dare you project your own insecurities on me, be so distrustful, disrespect my hard work. I remember when you gave me those architecture books, encouraged me to apply to MIT, be my best, and I loved you for it, more than you know. But that was all in the abstract, wasn't it?" She started to cry. "You should be proud of me, as I've always been of you, but this narcissistic small-mindedness is too much. It really hurts and I'm so exhausted and frustrated and angry. I can't think straight right now." She pulled the covers off me, yanked me out of bed, grabbed my pillow and a blanket, shoved everything in my arms and pushed me toward the door. "It's high time you grew up! Go sleep in the guest room."

"But we need to talk. I'm having breakfast with Pete Masters tomorrow morning."

"Like you really care what I think! I hope you and Lehman Brothers will be very happy together! Good night." Slam.

CHAPTER 22

I TOSSED ABOUT in the darkness, alone, abandoned, aching for the comforting impression of Erin's body against mine. My worst fears come true. Stripped of ego, I comprehended the injury my insensitivity caused her. I'd rent the taut fabric of her love; had failed to heed the clarion call of her own heart, cede space for her own personal growth. She'd remained the innocent girl I'd fallen in love with and still adored. I played power broker, but she was the master of my universe, creating our home, raising our children, organizing every critical aspect of my life save one, I was the bread winner, and now she even had the means to do that. She was my Eve, and our Eden existed because she'd taken my hand and stumbled through life's vicissitudes with me. Now I faced loss beyond reckoning. Exhausted, I set the alarm clock; I had to be up in four hours.

Jonah and I are in our space ship exploring unchartered reaches of outer space, powering past planets and other comets when suddenly a huge meteor heads directly toward us, and we veer our craft to the left, then right, trying to avoid an imminent collision but it's too late, we're careening off course, heading for a black hole, and I reach out to Jonah but he's a jack-in-the-box, grinning and boinging up and down singing "All around the mulberry bush the monkey chased the weasel. The monkey thought 'twas all in fun. Pop! Goes the weasel" and our escape hatch opens, sucking all the air, and me, from our cabin, and I'm a toddler, tumbling alone and powerless into the vast black vacuum of space screaming JONAH, DON'T LEAVE ME, I'M SO SCARED, DON'T LEAVE ME ALL ALONE.

Good Morning, New York! This is Jim Kerr with the Morning Rock and Roll Show on Q104.3 on your FM dial. It's five a.m., Friday, February 26, 1993, twenty-seven degrees and sleeting, going to a high of thirty-two. Brrr, it certainly looks like time to get those plane tickets to Margaritaville, Shelli.

I bolt upright, damp with night sweat, slam the alarm button and reflexively reach out for Erin, my hand grazing over cold sheets. I stumble toward the bathroom, internal light pouring through the crumbling walls of my secret chamber, bend over the toilet and retch. The image now clear: It's me! I'm the small child and I'm being abandoned in a dense, dark and impenetrable forest, listening to the snarls of invisible wild beasts, to the rustling limbs of child-eating trees, and I'm crying out: "Where are you, Jonah? What's happening? Are we still playing hide and seek? Where are you? Come out come out wherever you are," expecting him to spring from behind a tree and say, "Peekaboo, I see you." And I'm scared. I wanna go home. I want Gramma! I want milk. I wanna lie on the couch, wanna watch Tom and Jerry. "Okay Jonah, you win. Come out come out wherever you are. Please, I don't want to play anymore. Please take me home. Jonah? Jonah? Where are you?" Sobs of anguish and terror absorbed by the impenetrable forest. Alone. So scared. So scared. I retch again. Stumble back into the bedroom. Throw open the curtains and press my face against the cold leaded glass. Sleet splatters against the pane like the rat a tat tat of buckshot. I beat my head against the glass and wail. He'd shattered me, robbed me of innocence, stolen my ability to trust. Jonah had abandoned me in Alley Pond Park.

I watched breathlessly at the open doors of my children's rooms for the subtle rise and fall of their little chests, their existence my connection to the dream I shared with Erin, to everything that mattered. Our Woodstock. I tiptoed into the master bedroom, the sight of Erin's glorious copper curls spread across her pillow, the lissome curve of her hip under the comforter, overwhelming. I wanted to rush over. Embrace her. Be embraced and comforted by her. I'd erected a barrier of cold barbed wire between us. It serrated my soul.

Stealthily entering our closet, I quickly dressed in sweats and sneakers, tread lightly down the stairs into the parlor and froze in front of the decades-old, framed photo of Jonah and me. Me astride his strong shoulders. Ensconced in the safety and security of his love. In the unquestioned faith and trust in my little world. The photo I'd cherished. The photo that had for so long defined the burden of guilt I bore. Toxic.

Trembling, I pick it up, immediately assaulted by another rush of memories. Mommy, Daddy and Grandma and Grandpa Matthews in the forest with us, Grandma crushing me to her ample breast as I sob hysterically, rocking me back and forth cooing, "Meyn kleyn mlakh, meyn kleyn mlakh," her comforting scent calming my ragged breath. Daddy screaming, "How could you do that to him" while Grandpa pleads, "Calm down, everyone calm down," telling Jonah to lift me onto his shoulders. Mommy shrieking, "SMILE GODDAMIT" through grit teeth. The click of her Brownie camera.

I smashed the picture frame against the sideboard, shattering the glass, and tossed it in the waste basket. Staged, all staged. False memories implanted to safeguard me from the awful truth, a delusion that had brought nothing but sadness and pain. I scribbled Erin a short note: *I've peered into the darkness. I remember everything; I'm not afraid anymore. I love you more than life itself*, then grabbed my winter coat, the keys to my old beater, stepped outside the front door and wept in the freezing rain. I'd blinded myself to what really mattered, my wife, children, even my parents.

CHAPTER 23

I DROVE OVER the Gowanus Canal onto Ocean Parkway toward Coney Island. Parked in the empty lot abutting the boardwalk that had thrilled millions for decades, now a buckled and warped wasteland awaiting either urban renewal or continued blight and ultimate demolition. I stood by the ruins of a pier, wooden pilings like so many Pickup Sticks scattered on the sandy beach adjacent to an abandoned steeple chase, now a rusted monolith. An old carousel stood directly across the boardwalk, its rusty hinges shrieking. The hand-carved animals faded and chipped. I heard ghostly echoes of children on the wind. I shuddered, rubbed my freezing hands together, then glanced at my watch. I had missed my partnership breakfast with Pete Masters, the most important person in the firm, but I no longer cared. Wall Street merely a performance stage, another addictive drug. If I had to quit cold turkey, so be it. Real life resided in my home. In Erin and our children.

An old couple strolled the boardwalk arm in arm in the weak, early light, the man in long overcoat and fedora, his neck bound by a scarf, the woman diminutive in an old, mangy fur coat. She stopped; wound his scarf tighter. Caressed his face. He leaned down and gently kissed her. Took her hand. Life partners: lovers facing the elements together, decrepit yet so beautiful. They could finish each other's sentences, share unspoken thoughts, and I ached for the feel of Erin's hand, for the tie that bound me to this Earth.

My eyes swept west over empty lots interrupted by concrete monoliths heaving out of the flat vista, boxes filled with people living out their personal dramas, one atop the other. And beyond that, lower Manhattan, the World Trade Center's Twin Towers barely perceptible through the heavy mist, toothpicks flashing red as they had those many years before. Before I knew what really mattered.

I stood at the shoreline watching a solitary garbage scow drift lazily toward the grey Staten Island coastline rising from the flat leaden sea. Frozen rain pelted me. Sand shifted in the wind, but no longer beneath my feet. I stood on solid ground of self-awareness. I had encased my core self in darkness. Taken masochistic pleasure in misery. Allowed corrosive thoughts to obliterate my potential for joy and the love of others. I'd flayed myself for every mistake, every transgression, real or imagined, refused to open my eyes to a world of nuance. I'd tried to control my world by arranging the socks in my drawers, alphabetizing LPs and books, hanging clothes neatly in the closet, making perfect hospital corners, developing perfect stock scripts, but I was so, so wrong. Life was messy and chaotic but the only one I'd get. And every skin I'd inhabited, everything that had happened for good or bad, was part of me and there wasn't a goddam thing I could do about it except not waste another moment wallowing in it. The past was quicksand; the more I'd struggled to escape it, the more mired I'd become. As Bart and I had discussed so long ago, it was all about choices, and I chose to let go the child abandoned long ago and experienced the lightness of being me.

I glanced at my watch again. Already past eleven. Impossible to tell from the leaden sky. I'd been here hours, a sodden, sandy mess, a fool to think I'd extinguished her love over a fight! And one missed breakfast wasn't going to undo two decades of hard work. I wiped my eyes. Blew my nose on my sleeve. The day wasn't over. Pete Masters would meet the real me, not the costumed actor, and that felt right. I'd drive downtown and accept that partnership offer, with one caveat—nothing came before my family.

Traversing the Belt Parkway along the shoreline approaching the Brooklyn-Battery tunnel, I visualized the fabulous platter of olives I'd bring home to Erin after the meeting. Exiting the tunnel I found myself staring up at the architectural marvels that were the Twin Towers, their top floors shrouded in mist.

Turning onto West Street I approached the entrance to the North Tower public parking garage and started to turn in, but the entry was blocked. The lot full. I glanced at my watch again. Dammit. 12:15. I'd have to find another parking lot. I backed out into the street, almost halfway down the block when the ground began to rumble. An earsplitting explosion ricocheted through the canyon of skyscrapers, the sky suddenly raining debris. I slammed the brakes, turned around. A hellish maelstrom of flame and dense black smoke expelled from the mouth of the parking garage. I gasped for breath, heart pounding in my chest. Tears trickled down my cheeks.

It's going to be okay. It's going to be okay.

THE END

ACKNOWLEDGMENTS

THE GENESIS OF this novel was a journal I kept of my adventure in Mexico when I was eighteen. For decades, that journal sat in a desk drawer waiting to be turned into a memoir, but with the passage of time that journey became but a small piece of a larger, more intricate mosaic that morphed into this novel. A special thank you to my writing critique group of Wendy Gordon and Nancy Johnson, who took this journey with me offering encouragement and critique. As Francis Bacon said: "It's very pleasant to be praised, but it doesn't actually help you," so I am especially grateful to Bobby Gordon; Mike Fell; Sara Proctor; Rhianna Walton; Marsha Maser; Russ Ratto; Lukas Gordon; Ethan Seltzer; and Melanie Plaut for their constructive criticism. I would also like to thank my wonderful publishing team of Ann Weinstock, Kristen Weber, and Mary Bisbee-Beek who guided me from manuscript to print. But most of all, a very special thank you to my life partner, Wendy Gordon, my sounding board for each iteration of this novel over the past six years, for her patience and good humor, even when woken in the middle of the night for some new revelation, and to my children: Rhianna, Tom, Jessica, Alex, Emily and Lukas, and my grandchildren Halle, Leda, River, Lilianna, Maisie and Leo, the joys of my life who keep everything in perspective. This book is dedicated to anyone who has ever suffered despair, loss or abandonment. Ultimately, you are the arbiter of your own fate.

DISCUSSION QUESTIONS

1. How does the theme of abandonment play into this novel?
2. What do you think of Seth's self-perception as always acting, searching for a skin that fits?
3. How does Woodstock serve as a metaphor in the novel?
4. How does Seth's desire for control find its expression on Wall Street?
5. Does the novel's description of Wall Street defy stereotype?
6. What do you think are the major turning points in the novel?
7. Why is Seth initially drawn to Sinead? Can a relationship between two damaged people be successful?
8. How does Jonah's disappearance affect Matthews family dynamics?
9. What are the dynamics that make the long term relationship between Seth and Erin work? In what ways are they alike, despite their different upbringings?
10. Do you find Seth and Mitzie empathetic characters? If so, why? If not, why not?
11. What is Seth's perception of fate, and how does it play into the novel?
12. How do you interpret the ending?